Chasing Mercury

"A lyrical, erotic and embodied prose of resistance and resilience, *Chasing Mercury* has the audacity to make us love."
>—Sarah E. Kornfeld , Author of What Stella Sees

"*Chasing Mercury* is a cinematic journey on the page! "Brimming with African American and First Nation culture and history, this romance-suspense-saga teaches as it entertains and pirouetting in the center of it, a passionate love affair that keeps the pages turning and without a doubt will keep eyeballs glued to the movie screen."
>— Monice Mitchell Simms, Author of Address House of Detention and Nana' Fridge

"The best of the romance genre, wrapped in an introduction to human and environmental rights."
>— Eric P. Carlson

GOOD READS AND AMAZON REVIEWERS

"What makes it stand apart is a tinkling, sweet quality... in the midst of tragedy the special something remains that gives glitter and shine to the story."—SX

"I've been unable to finish a book since my daughter was born ('cause sleep superseded anything other than her needs) but I found myself staying up past 1 AM to read this amazing book" —AH

"A transcendent novel that takes a moral stance..." —RS

"A fascinating and eye-opening read..above all it is a love story on so many levels..." —BA

"This is truly a lovely book, very enjoyable novel that combines romance and mystery and does it through a bond of relatable and well developed characters." —S

"I loved how it kept me connected to the story..." —PA

"Engrossing story bringing attention to environmental and social justice..." —MLGMDJD

"A story of protest, lineage, family, historical relationships, personal determination, and growth...." —WJP

"I didn't even know what I didn't even know!" —BJF

"Intelligent, strong, mind-pecking." —B.O.

"Crossing barriers, risks, and danger too..." — DU

"Legitimately, top notch stuff..." —DLB.

"September Williams has done a great job of making us think with 'Chasing Mercury'. She has made us think of how we, as a human race, are sometimes so caught up in the small things and that we really ought to wake up and look at the bigger picture. "—PA

In a world of danger that lurks in every corner, a story of love and adventure rises through —SA

September Williams is a heck of a wordsmith. Language is as an identifying factor among writers as jersey numbers are on the shirts of basketball players, and she has got a wonderful gift of sentence-crafting. --DLB

CHASING MERCURY

Gaines-Jones Education Foundation
PO Box 3016 Novato, CA 94948

CHASING
MERCURY

SEPTEMBER WILLIAMS

COVE INTERNATIONAL PUBLISHERS
MILL VALLEY, CALIFORNIA

Copyright © 2016 September Williams
Cove International Publishers, Mill Valley, CA, USA
http://www.septemberwilliams.com/cove-international-publishers/
First Edition ebook 2017, audiobook 2017, paperback 2018
Developmental Editing by Susan Dalsimer
Copy editing by Eric P. Carlson
Proofreading by Pamela Rex
Beta Reading by Abagail Hansen (as reader #1)

Williams/September
Chasing Mercury/September Williams
ISBN 978-0-692-05966-1
1. Romance/Fiction 2. Suspense/Fiction 3. Memoir/Fiction 4. African America/ Fiction 5. First Nation/Fiction 6. Mercury/Roman mythology 7. Virgil/Classics 8. Ballet/Arts 9. Powwow Dancing/Arts 10. mercury/physics 11. mercury/gold mining 12. Aboriginal Rights/ politics 13. Minamata disease/medicine 14. epilepsy/ medicine 15. Environmental Justice/Bioethics 16. Cold War/politics 17. Hollywood Black List/politics 18. Anti-apartheid/politics 19. Canada/ internationalism 20. Human Rights/psychology

Book and Cover Design by Marta Elise Johansen
Typefaces: Archer, Alegreya and Libre Baskerville
Printed in the United States of America

To

Curd, Autumn, Tre, Joi, Robert, Marta, Anna,

their parents, grandparents, and Bill

— for our times on the waterfront.

Mercury Sent to Admonish Aeneas

Joseph Mallord William Turner

Exhibited 1850

"The first of four pictures telling Virgil's story of Aeneas's stay at Carthage, delayed from his destiny in Italy by his love for Dido. Mercury is not discernible...having perhaps melted into thin air as Virgil's story describes."

Tate Gallery, London
Exhibition Plaque

1

ST. LAWRENCE SEAWAY

JULY 1973

LEAPING OVER LUGGAGE IN her path, she races through the Montreal Airport, looking for other travelers in her party. They are not there. Taking eyeglasses from the leather bag slung over her shoulder, she props them on the bridge of her nose. The slight angle of her neck shows a practiced elegance even in the reading of her boarding pass, "Sicily Marshall, July 28, 1973, Montreal, Zürich, Berlin, 7 AM..." Sucking an ear guard on the glasses, her gaze expands, scouring the Swiss Air departure lounge. Then she sees Him—

His legs stretch out in a mile of blue jeans and cowboy boots. On his neck is a bone choker with twinkling clear glass beads, and a suede medicine bag partly obscures a silver cross without a Christ. Smooth dark braids, bound with beaded ties, rest on either side of his heart. There is a perfect patina to his bronze skin.

Gravitating within an arm's length of his boots, the spectacles still dangling from her lips, her mouth gapes open in awe. The eyewear tumbles toward the floor. His single swift motion catches and returns the lenses to her hand, a breath before he resumes his repose.

"Th-Thank you," she says.

"You're lost," he says.

"The people I'm looking for are the ones lost."

In the seat next to him feathers flow to the floor like a fountain or a flock, red, yellow, orange, gold. Moving the feathers to make room, he says,

"Come talk to me until they find themselves."

'It would be too obnoxious to pull out my camera,' she thinks, never having seen anyone look this damned good. He seems older, probably in his mid twenties. 'Everyone says I'm mature for my age,' she rationalizes her growing attraction.

He watches her also. How could he not? A thick black elastic band thwarts dark curls from escaping the fountain of spirals at the top of her head. Her travel attire is a soft yellow wide legged pant of T-shirt fabric with a matching boat necked shirt, displaying her sculpted clavicles while the pastel illuminates her Manzanita skin. Ankle-tied flat sandals, worn vainly to camouflage her height, match the beige pashmina wrapped around her waist. An understated elegance sets her apart from other travelers. Her eyes glance between his and those feathers.

"Can I touch?" she asks.

"Depends on what..." he says.

"I mean the feathers."

"Dancing gear, a headdress." He nods once.

"Pretty." She pets the plumes as if they are a more exotic relative of the peacock.

"They're a pain in the butt to carry across the ocean."

"Where are you going?"

"Berlin, dancing, the World Youth Festival..."

"I'm going to Berlin and dancing too."

Spare with words, he has a jazz to him which is the essence of 'cool'. Lacing fingers in her lap, a technique inherited from her childhood dance classes, almost masks that he makes her nervous. Standing, he positions himself directly in front of her chair. She wilts. Holding her shoulders, he shifts her torso this way and that, looking behind her.

"What exactly are you doing?" she asks.

"Looking for your feathers."

"Do I look like Josephine Baker?"

"More like Maria Tallchief."

"Maria? The Firebird? In my dreams—but I do dance ballet—leotards travel better."

"I might need me some of those."

Normally disinclined toward being manhandled, somehow she is neither frightened nor offended, more puzzled. Resisting the desire to rest her cheek against the thigh of his jeans, she breathes him in. He's spicy like smoke from a campfire built of pine needles, sage, and lavender. "I'm imagining you in leotards. Don't get me wrong, your body is perfect for them."

Still holding her kissing distance from his groin, he releases his grip as if dropping a hot potato.

"I do Powwow, Men's Fancy Dance. Leotards aren't an option." He bounces to his chair.

"Isn't that the most athletic traditional Indigenous American dance form?"

"Yeah, agility, stamina, jumps, leaps, twirls." He is impressed that she knows what Powwow dancing is. "I never saw a Black chick, or anyone else your size, do ballet," he squints.

"Then you've never seen Maria Tallchief. We are exactly the same height." She meets his gaze. "Honestly, at five foot nine, I haven't seen five foot since I was nine."

"How old are you now?"

"Old enough," she says.

"Not old enough to be runnin' around the world unescorted lookin' like you do."

"I can take care of myself. At least, if you are going to Berlin, I'm in the right place to meet the rest of the American delegation."

"You mean, The United States. America is more than the USA. That flight took off. The Canadians will be here soon. I hang with the Quebecois."

She looks confused.

"French Canadians—One on one, they're more fun than the English. We have our tussles since they, like us, also seek sovereignty."

His explanation soars over her head.

"Are you all right?" he asks, seeing her dazed.

"No, I flew to Montreal from San Francisco on short notice. I'm exhausted and don't handle details well when I'm tired."

"Not many of us do," he says.

Biting her lip she contemplates whether he would think her an imbecile if she admits what is on her mind. She blurts out, "Fatigue contributes to my delayed recollection of being on the Canadian delegation. I'm from the US but my new Canadian stepfather and my mother arranged this trip. They're in Winnipeg, where I'll go to study for the first time after the festival. In my family, we do most things on a 'need to know' basis. That's part of why I never have a clue what I'm doing."

"Umm—that almost makes sense," he says. Tilting his head to see her from a slightly different angle he continues, "Okay, you said that's part of the reason. What's the other part?"

"I'm not as smart as I look. Anyway, what's your nationality?"

"First Nation..."

"I expected you to say US or Canadian."

"I'm what you'd probably call 'Indian'—"

"Actually, I say Native American... more accurate and politically astute."

"'Native American' is an ethnicity or a race. First Nation is a nationality usually delineated by a specific affiliation."

"And what is your 'affiliation'?"

"Mum is Dené. My father was Potawatomi and Ojibwa."

"Ojibwa?"

"Long story. Pop's folks used to hang out around Lake Superior and built damned good birch boats."

Rarely does she feel informationally outmatched. This is clearly one of those times, a situation she intends to rectify.

"Dené?" she asks.

"Like most First Nation names it means The People." He surmises beneath the surface of this smart, romantically awkward, gorgeous ballerina exists a detail-oriented obsessive-compulsive. "The Dené come from the edge of the tundra, in the boreal forest. It circumnavigates the Arctic above the 50th parallel but below the 60th at Hudson Bay. Mum lived near Tadoule Lake—another long story."

Delighted to find he knows things she does not, hopefully he will tolerate her barrage of questions coming next.

"What passport do you carry?" she asks.

"Don't usually," he says.

"Doesn't that make it hard to cross borders?"

"I try not to go where they don't recognize the legitimacy of my nations or my people."

'Talk about your limited audience...' she thinks.

He is blessed with the gift of intuition, and she cursed with transparency.

"It limits me as much as being a giant Black ballerina does you," he says.

"Yet, I have the advantage of a passport. How do you cross borders?"

"United Nations aboriginal papers and sometimes my Canadian Indian Card."

Until now their banter is fast paced. Unexpected silence causes a noticeable gap. "Are you doin' all right?" he asks, several times. Too many beats later, she registers his question.

"Few people notice when I space out," she says.

"'Space out'? Is that what you call what just happened?"

"Sometimes I have out of body experiences."

"That's a good thing in my cultures. And of course in the twilight zone."

"In mine, it's a seizure, the partial complex, absence type."

"Should I do something if I see you having one of those moments?" he asks.

"Make sure I don't fall, burn myself on a stove, or stab my hand with a fork."

"Umm—your parents must be concerned about you."

"They know I'm hard to cage and almost legal."

"Legal, meaning...?"

"Age of majority, voting, can be a felon in my own right, won't need anyone's consent to make love or donate blood."

"Good to know," he says.

Sure she has given him too much intimate information, she returns to the clinical. "It never happens while performing."

"Muscles can run on auto-pilot, like sleep walking. How does it feel?"

"The seizures? Who knows? They are blank spots. Like reading sentences without consonants, I've no comprehension. A dead skunk in a chimney smell, or noise turning to flashes of light warns me, without prevention. Strobe lights, missing meds, shock, exhaustion—all the kiss of death." She unfolds her legs, stretching. "How did you notice?"

"Safe to say, I pay attention to all kinds of things others don't." He slips off his chair to the floor, crossing his boots at the ankle, sharing her eye level. "Where are you from?" he asks, checking one more fact, hoping he hasn't fallen off a precipice into a disaster—

"You mean like what planet, since I'm spacey?"

"Let's stick to terra firma."

"Los Angeles, well, I lived in Marin County, in Northern California and—"

"I mean your people."

"Ahh... Oklahoma... I even have some Seminole going on in me... I was born in St. Louis... but my stepfather is actually exiled from apartheid South Africa..." She babbles like the Mississippi breaching a levee. Taking a breath, she says, "Now you know all about me and I don't even know your name."

"Forest, Forest Odjig—what do they call you again?"

"Sicily Marshall..." Realizing his inquiry was peculiarly worded, she asks, "Why did you say, again?"

Forest puts his palms over his eyes, hoping not seeing her might help. Sicily catches her bottom lip between her teeth.

"Your parents..." he says.

"Vern and Ellie?"

"They thought I might run into you."

"You made a fool of me..."

"It took a bit to realize who you were. I expected to see you in Berlin, with the Americans."

"You mean the US delegation."

Forest masks his smile with a hand. He shakes his head at how quick she is.

"I think you were playing me, a cat with a ball of yarn," she says.

"More like a dog chasing a kite."

"Say you're not supremely evil and duplicitous—how do you know my parents?"

"Mostly through struggle," he says.

"And what are you struggling for?"

"For better. I wasn't trying to hurt you. Never doubt that my wanting to know you has nothing to do with your parents. Sicily, I exist in one tense at a time, mostly the present."

"Be quiet. Are they acquaintances or are we extended family?"

"Do you want me to 'be quiet' or speak?"

She glares at him.

"From what I know of your folks, you're a sister."

"I was hoping for a different relationship than that." She had not meant to say that aloud.

"Careful what you ask for," he says. Unearthing the silver cross from beneath his other neckwear, he unclasps the chain, handing the bobble to her. It dangles at the level of her eyes. Each of the four post are divided in two, making eight.

"Damn. I should have noticed. This is one of Ellie's favorite protocols. You are my guardian angel," she says.

"Maybe a guardian, but I'm no angel."

"If someone has this cross, I know that Ellie means for me to trust them. It carries her weight. The way it works, you give it to me only if I won't follow your instructions. Otherwise, you return it to Ellie."

"She told me."

"You can hold onto this." Sicily places the cross in his palm, certain she would follow this man anywhere. The public address system squawks in French.

"Our flight is boarding," Forest says. Standing, he reaches out a hand to help her. She ignores him, floating up from the ground, seemingly without use of a single muscle. Pulling a well worn leather bag from under his chair, Forest hoists it over his shoulder. Grabbing the headdress at its crown, the train flows to the floor at his back. Walking to the gate, others passing gawk at them, quills garnering most of the admiration.

Sicily looks around asking, "Where's the rest of the Canadian delegation?"

"The English Canadians and Quebecois were to meet at Terminus Centre-Ville then come here on a bus."

"Why didn't you travel with them?" Sicily asks.

"Quebecois and English rarely cooperate. I didn't expect they'd manage to catch a plane together."

Swapping seats with other passengers enables Sicily and Forest to sit together during the transatlantic crossing. The flight attendant wants the headdress crushed into the overhead compartment. Forest protests, sliding into the window seat without stowing his dance bonnet. Wrapping his arm around Sicily's waist, he pulls her closer to him. Draping the feathers over them coyly, as if hiding illicit activity, Forest says, "It's not luggage. It's a blanket." The attendant rolls her eyes and moves on, reminding them to fasten their seat belts.

The jumbo jet roars. The two dancers are perched between possible death and the birth of something new. They reach escape velocity.

"See that little ribbon of water...?" Forest asks, looking out the window, "That's the St. Lawrence Seaway. It connects the Arctic Ocean and North Atlantic to the Great Lakes, including Lake Superior..." He looks at her intently. "Tell me the rest of it," he says.

"The rest of what?" Sicily asks.

"Your whole story, it's a long trip."

Sicily sees his flickering smile and suspects she will be his inflight entertainment.

"Are you with me?" he asks because she is silent.

"Sometimes, I'm quiet because I'm thinking."

"Are you with me?" He is more emphatic.

"You're asking a lot for a guy who couldn't remember my name. Besides, I don't know my whole story," she says.

"But, you know what you've been told."

2

LAKE DECATUR

SUMMER 1955

I WAS BORN AT the Florence Home for Unwed Colored Women, as was my mother before me. The persistence of such a venue, in 1955 St. Louis, challenged both of our legitimacies. My mother, being born in 1937, was named Ellie, for First Lady Anna Eleanor Roosevelt. My grandmother, Vanessa, had hit the oppression trifecta: Black father, Seminole mother, and raised poor in Oklahoma. Vanessa was more damaged by racism, sexism, and classism than any of us who came after. Yet, Grandmother had the good sense to admire Mrs. Roosevelt.

The first bit of fortune in my grandmother's entire life, though she did not know it at the time, was giving birth to Ellie. The Florence Home had referred Vanessa and baby to Lucille Smith's 'Boarding House'. Lucille Smith, aka Big Momma, five foot in heels, was the fanciest woman in St Louis. Blessed with good taste, fine looks, and rich dead husbands, Lucille had it all—except her own children. Big Momma's House on Page Street was an impressive four story Romanesque Revival limestone place with gargoyles. When my mother and Grandmother arrived, a naked god with wings on his hat sat on each of the four roof corners, mouth open, draining torrential summer rain.

Big Momma loved Vanessa and Ellie as though they were her own. The relationship between the three of them was sealed by Lucille becoming Ellie's godmother. In the two hundred year old French tradition of St. Louis, women of the night and upstanding citizens—Lucille was both—kept close ties with the Catholic Church. On Saturday mornings Big Momma said confession. Early on Sundays, back to church for Mass, Communion, and a donation. Afterwards, a big dinner was laid in the formal dining room. Anyone welcome during the week could partake. Lucille had only one rule: "No shenanigans, never on Sundays."

The furnishings and drapery were burgundy velvet, accentuated by polished wood floors and wainscoting. On the first floor of the House on Page Street was the kitchen, dining room, and parlor. The second floor held the suite of Mrs. Lucille Smith, as all the gentlemen visitors were required to call her. The third floor was a brothel, the fourth for 'respectable boarders,' including Ellie and Grandmother Vanessa. The back stair was the path of renters, enjoying smells of the family kitchen while going to and from their rooms. The gents and their hostesses used the broad front staircase, as if to lend respectability to their pastime.

When Ellie was two, Franklin Grant arrived at the house's front stairway. Long and tall with dark skin and a well trimmed mustache, he cut a fine figure in his meticulously tailored, broad legged Zoot Suit. Franklin knew it was time he switched paths when he first saw Vanessa, a Lena Horne look-alike. But he also fell in love with Ellie. On my mother's third birthday, Franklin proposed to my grandmother. The day after the marriage, the groom loaded his new wife and daughter into his car, driving them to his home in Springfield, Illinois.

Before Ellie reached adolescence two things were clear. The first was that she was uncommonly smart for her age and on track to finish high school by sixteen. Vanessa was proud, she herself not having had the advantage of completing her upper school education. The second truth was that Ellie had a mind of her own. My grandmother and mother often clashed, as Vanessa aspired to be a middle class 'colored' wife. My mother's inclinations led elsewhere. Ellie was a true Bohemian, kicking off her shoes at the front door—if she had bothered to wear them at all.

Considering Vanessa named my mother after Mrs. Roosevelt, she should have expected the daughter she got—a feminist and a progressive, before such words were common. Admitted to Langston University at age sixteen, Ellie left home for Oklahoma. Langston, a landgrant, historically Black college, was named after civil rights pioneer John Mercer Langston, the first African American member of the US Congress from Virginia and founder of Howard University Law School. Ellie's natural inclinations toward social change were reinforced by education, putting her increasingly in opposition to Vanessa's thinking.

Vanessa's protective activities on behalf of her daughter sometimes demonstrated pure ignorance. During her first summer vacation from Langston, in 1954, Ellie brought her fall philosophy reading assignments home to Springfield. The books included The Nichomachean Ethics of Aristotle, An Introduction to Zen Buddhism, The Communist Manifesto, The Souls of Black Folks, Mein Kampf, and The Bible. Black universities and colleges took seriously their obligation to properly educate 'the talented tenth'. My mother had carefully tucked the books under her own bed, instinctively hiding them from Vanessa. While Ellie was out carousing with friends, Vanessa cleaned under her daughter's bed and discovered the reading material.

Other than The Bible, Grandmother didn't know what most of the titles meant. It seemed to her that the Rosenbergs had been convicted and sentenced to death because of a word on one of those books. My Grandmother was not about to have her daughter going to jail, being executed, or, worst of all, getting pregnant out of wedlock. When Ellie returned to the house, despite the hot muggy midwestern summer day, a fire had been lit. The Bible was on the coffee table next to the hearth. The rest of her books were a pile of ashes in the fireplace. Only one charred red book binding was recognizable.

During the fall of Ellie's second year of college, 1954, she stumbled on the library steps, dropping her notebooks and purse. A gentleman, John Marshall, gathered her belongings and dusted her off. Their spark was immediate. He took her home to meet his parents, who lived locally in Oklahoma. John's mother being Seminole and father Black, like Vanessa, Ellie was immediately considered kin.

When John was younger, a man who lived up the road a piece from his parents taught him to fly a crop duster. John took Ellie up in that plane. Her eyes were widened with terror and exhilaration. In January of 1955, John Marshall was off to Frankfurt, paying back his college tuition in the recently formed, and desegregated, United States Air Force. Ellie, an aspiring premed student, was left behind. "You promised to marry me on my first furlough, don't forget," John Marshall had joked. Ellie had many reasons she wanted to keep that promise.

Ellie's second summer of college was the first since John had left. She arrived home to Springfield, more subdued than on other holidays. Reluctantly, she joined a few of her high school girlfriends at the beach. When she was reticent about swimming, one of the friends said,

"You've put on weight, but it's only us girls."

"You're right about the weight. But that's not why I'm avoiding swimming... It's things I learned in biology class," Ellie said. "People in the town of Decatur only drink bottled water because this lake has high levels of a chemical called nitrate."

"Good grief, we're swimming in it, not drinking it," the friend said.

"Nitrates come from fertilizer used on nearby corn fields. They cause something called blue baby syndrome."

"What exactly is this 'colored baby' thing?" another girl asked.

"Oxygen attaches to hemoglobin, that's the thing that makes blood red. When nitrogen connects instead, no oxygen can be carried around the body."

"One more time?" the girl asked.

"The important part is that nitrates stop oxygen from being used. Babies' fingertips and lips turn blue and they can die, suffocating," Ellie said.

"This is what happens when you go to college too young. You learn to be scared of things," the friend joked.

"Those 'things' still exist whether or not you're afraid," Ellie said. Pressing her lips together, she sighed and added, "You're right about me growing up fast at college. If my dates are right, I'm eight months pregnant. I should deliver next month, near my birthday." The sympathetic beachgoers stood eyes wide, calculating. Ellie would be eighteen.

Unable to contain her excitement about her daughter's birthday, Vanessa gave Ellie the department store-wrapped box, weeks ahead of time. Wearing a poodle skirt with an oversized sweater, despite the muggy summer, my mother's weight gain had not been noticed by Vanessa. Nor did Grandmother see the dread on my mother's face when ordered into the bathroom to try on the gifts. When Ellie failed to emerge with a fanfare, Vanessa tapped the bathroom door then pushed it open. The dress gaped at Ellie's back. That zipper could not have been lifted with a crane. Vanessa recognized the evidence she saw and was enraged.

Before the second blow crossed her face, Ellie stopped Vanessa's hand midair. In college psychology my mother had learned that beating one's offspring was the highest level of self-hate. Now, Ellie's pregnancy torpedoed Vanessa's carefully groomed new bourgeois self-image. It didn't take much to push Grandmother back to her old abusive habits, which had ceased under Grandfather Franklin's guidance.

Storming out of the bathroom Vanessa screeched, "Get your things, you are leaving—now." Lillie, Ellie's four-year old sister born in wedlock, was dragged to a neighbor's home. Ellie was hustled into the car with luggage and (secretly) her books. After five hours, she and Vanessa arrived at the Florence Home for Unwed Colored Women in St. Louis. Ellie was escorted to a room shared with two other expectant mothers to get settled while my grandmother checked us in.

"The baby will be put up for adoption," Vanessa explained to the nursing nun at the desk, using the highclass voice she learnt as a child, working as a maid. Ellie was a minor. Vanessa signed adoption papers knowing this would not be her daughter's own choice. "You'll see. It's all for the best," Vanessa said, kissing Ellie on the cheek. Without sharing the adoption arrangements, she left.

A few weeks later, while doing the Funky Chicken at her birthday party, Ellie's water broke. I was reluctant to be born. My breech position was obfuscated by lack of prenatal care. The midwife did a sophisticated maneuver. I was delivered, breathing though quiet and alert. The silence suggested neurological injury.

Vanessa had refused to divulge Ellie's and my whereabouts to Franklin. On Ellie's birthday, Big Momma phoned Springfield to speak with her goddaughter. Lucille's powers of coercion were greater than Grandfather's, as was her deductive reasoning. She knew Ellie could only be at the Florence Home. Lucille rearranged the House on Page Street. Ellie and I would have a two-room suite of our own. Big Momma considered telling Grandmother about rescuing Ellie and me. Then she decided not to extend 'the fool' the courtesy. Vanessa would eventually figure it out.

Having participated in desegregating the lunch counter at the St. Louis Stix, Baer & Fuller Department Store, in the spirit of equipoise, Lucille frequently ate there. Wearing the furs and hat worn when previously arrested at civil rights demonstrations, fortified with a tuna salad sandwich, her shopping spree began. The baby merchandise was wrapped in an enormous pink and blue box, with tasseled white ribbons, addressed to 'Ellie Grant c/o The Florence Home'. Babies being angels in the godmother's eyes, everything she sent was white.

When Lucille arrived, Ellie's booming voice reverberated through the Florence Home's linoleum halls. Ellie was holding me, the now half-filled gift box next to her. "You're out of your God damned minds. I'm not putting my baby up for adoption. At eighteen, my mother does not have the legal right to decide what I do with my child," Ellie said. The attendant attempted to wrestle me away.

Big Momma intervened with the clarity of a mouth in which butter would not have melted. "Now son, you don't want to put your hands on her or that child. You'll leave Ellie with only one option. It would be an option you wouldn't like," Big Momma said, knowing she had personally taught her goddaughter to throw a punch.

With me in her arms, Ellie was escorted by the previously overly exuberant staff member to a gleaming new 1955 white fishfinned Cadillac. Others put the box and bags in the trunk. Doors were opened for the ladies. We were wished well by the staff, who each received a dollar tip from Mrs. Lucille Smith.

While Big Momma drove Ellie and me home, the car radio played September Song. The singer was Sarah Vaughn, and this was her most recent hit.

"I first heard this song in a movie I saw with my daddy in 1950," Ellie told Big Momma. "It was filmed on location in Italy. He was able to show me all the places he'd been during the war—Rome, Naples, and Sicily."

"I know that movie," Big Momma said, keeping her hands steady on the steering wheel. "It was sad, wasn't it?"

"It's a story about lovers at odds with responsibility and destiny."

"I would rewrite that ending."

"I would too," Ellie said. "Daddy and I sang September Song all the way home from the theater—like we are doing now."

As the car pulled to the curb in front of the House on Page Street, Big Momma asked Ellie, "What do you think you want to call your baby?"

"Sicily."

"Good, 'Sicily Grant'—it's got a nice ring to it."

"She's not 'Grant'. If her father were here, she would never have been born at the Florence Home," Ellie countered her godmother.

Big Momma was skeptical. That was not how those things went in her experience. She suggested, "It might be confusing with you two having different last names."

The day I was named Sicily, Ellie and I both claimed my father's surname, Marshall.

3

LAKE ZURICH & LIMMAT RIVER

JULY 1973

GETTING TRANSIT VISAS AT the airport, Sicily and Forest plan to spend most of the twelve hour layover in Zürich. They take a bus to the city. The Swiss landscape is so proper it could have been trimmed by garden sheers. "These are the 'alive hills and mountains' of the Sound of Music," Sicily says. Once in town Forest hails a taxi. He tells the driver, in French, their destination and the best route to travel.

"Where are we going?" Sicily asks.

"To a restaurant I've been told is good," he says.

"Did you study French in school?"

"Mostly, I learned from Metis family and traveling."

"What's 'Metis'?"

"'Metis' used to refer to French and Indian. Now, it means pretty much Indian and anybody else, crossover people. Some Metis speak a combination of French and their Indian language."

"You mean 'First Nation,' not Indian."

"Jesus, I've created a monster. Metis are often disenfranchised from treaty rights by their crossover heritage—but also are denied the privileges of the majority population."

"What a waste of life, dividing people by supposed purity. Ellie always says, 'Nobody and nothing in the universe is just one thing, not even gods.'"

"Ellie doesn't strike me as a woman who puts much stake in deities. Though, I agree, the gods can be especially duplicitous, some more than others."

"Ellie is an atheist. Yet, she'll fight for anyone to be able to honor their god, as long as it doesn't block her own agenda. She started my political education with Greek and Roman founding religious myths."

"Like Homer and Virgil?"

"Yep—she even had me read the history of the Peloponnesian War. That's how I learned about the damage of dividing and conquering, never mind the meddling of gods in human affairs. I'm good with ancient history though not great with this century."

"Must have been interesting growing up with her as a mother," he says.

"Then and now... What about your mother? I doubt she represents the norm."

Forest laughs without addressing her question, hustling her from the taxi.

⌣

The Restaurant Lindenhofkeller, established in 1860, is above the Limmat River. Waiting to be seated, Forest points out the river's course. "It begins at the outfall of Lake Zürich," he says, extending a long bronze index finger into the magnificent view beyond the city. "From Zürich, it flows northwesterly..."

Sicily aims her camera toward the snaking stream. CLICK, CLICK. She captures six shots, surreptitiously including Forest in the foreground.

"In the 1950s, toxic algae grew in the lake. It was almost spread around the world through the river," he says.

"How do you know all of this?" Sicily asks.

"I have a Bachelor of Science degree in Biology."

"Ahh—and here I thought you were a dancer."

He pauses briefly, gauging her reaction. Then he continues, "Eugene Thomas, a scientist, realized phosphorous in newly developed sewage treatment plants caused the algae overgrowth."

This is more detail than Sicily can bear. He is no longer in the moment with her. Laughing at her own jealousy, directed at a river for consuming Forest's attention, she sublimates her foul emotion by looking through her camera lens. Forest's First Nation singularity is accentuated by his still carrying the headdress. People notice. The feathers look as if they have been stolen from the prop room of Balanchine's *Firebird*. She is relieved when they are called to be seated.

Walking into the restaurant, Forest is hailed by a loud whistle. He jogs toward a wild, short, dark haired, bearded man in a combat fatigue jacket. In this tidy Swiss cafe, the man is more out of place than his First Nation comrade. The headdress inadvertently slips from Forest's hand as the two men hug. Sicily catches up in time to prevent the feathers splashing to the floor.

"Jorge, this is Sicily," Forest says, freeing her from the burden of plumes. With his French Canadian mother and Chilean father, Jorge kisses Sicily on both cheeks reflexively. This untamed man is also headed to the festival.

"Which passport do you carry?" Sicily asks.

"Passports, plural, Canadian and Chilean" Jorge says.

"Which delegation is yours?"

"Lucky for me, I don't have to decide."

"Why?"

"The Canadian and Chilean delegations share billets. It's done by alphabet." Jorge already has a table, and they walk toward it. "My problem is after the festival," Jorge says, "I've passed the bar in both Quebec and Ontario." Forest gives his friend a congratulatory hug.

"Why is that a problem?" Sicily asks.

"I have to decide to either go home to Canada to be an associate at a law firm or..." He pauses, pursing his lips as if choosing his next words carefully.

"Or...?" she asks.

"Or, I return to Chile to fight the military junta that will try to take the government."

Not fully following Jorge's dilemma, she makes a note to read up on Chile.

Sicily is introduced to Camille and Pascal, both Francophone Canadians, who sit at Jorge's table. They had previously travelled with him in South America and are also separated from their own delegation. Camille's hair is a light blonde cloud drifting over her wise angelic face. By contrast Pascal, though already a medical student, is boyish with dark romanesque features. Camille is likely older than Sicily, Pascal younger. Pascal's eyes demonstrate an appreciation of Camille which increases the boy's sophistication by the minute. Forest already knows the couple. They all exchange hugs and kisses. Extra chairs being brought to the table create a disorder not familiar to this particular restaurant. Eventually, the majority of the patrons stop staring.

"How are you two related?" Sicily asks.

"We were friends in college. Now we're brothers," Forest says. He pulls out her chair.

"Not you and Jorge, you two..." Sicily lifts her chin toward Camille and Pascal.

"We are lovers." Camille is matter of fact.

"Lovers," Sicily repeats the term. It is an unused word in her teenage parlance.

Forest watches Sicily. Even her mouthing the word excites his desire. His eyes trace the curves of her lips, over her chin, down her swanlike neck toward her cleavage.

The waiter slides a menu in front of Sicily. It serves as a poor beard for her blush caused by her travel companion. She hesitates to order. "I can barely read it," she says. The multitude of selections are in microscopic print.

"You might want to take out your glasses," Forest says, implying that she is vain.

Even with her glasses, the annotations are in a language unintelligible to her. The three digit prices, in an unfamiliar currency, look expensive. Only having twenty American dollars she asks, "What's the Swiss exchange on the dollar?" In her pocket is also a fifty dollar check, sent with her Canadian documents by her stepfather. She knows it will bounce if cashed before the end of the month. Extra money for decadences is a rare thing in Sicily's family. Her experience with restaurants is limited. Funds beyond necessities are donated to some aspect of social change. Once, Ellie had decided to buy a brand new car that had never been owned by anyone else. Someone was arrested during a demonstration and needed bail money. After that, they needed a defense. Needless to say, Ellie never did get the new car.

At the festival, all of Sicily's accommodations will be free. The long layover in Zürich adds a hunger factor. 'Luckily, dancers don't eat much. However, we do need to eat something,' Sicily thinks. Eyeing the equally confusing wine menu, she shares, "I've never had alcohol past my lips." Her comment causes the Quebecois at the table to riot. They chose the restaurant because of the 600 wines on the menu.

"The Swiss have no food of their own, only that of their neighbors. However, they have the good taste to adopt wisely. The wines follow their siblings," Forest says.

"The house specialty is prime veal." The multilingual waiter graphically explains the preparation. While in an alternative high school on a California sea ranch, Sicily had shown calves at fairs. Despite her non-violent mostly American Friends Society teachers, her prize winning animals had been slaughtered. A vegetarian since age thirteen, Sicily feels it rude to raise the point in this congenial company.

"I hear they make a mean grilled cheese," Forest says.

"Then that's what I will be having," she says.

"Elle prendra également une Feldschlösschen," Jorge adds, ordering Sicily a beer.

Beer in Switzerland, at least in this restaurant, comes in 24 ounce bottles as elegant as crystal from Galway. Sicily takes a sip, narrows her eyes, puckers her lips, and gulps.

"I see no reason to acquire a taste for this," she says.

"I wouldn't have taken you for a Puritan. You having your grilled cheese without beer makes me reconsider," Jorge says. Then he adds, "Vous n'êtes pas son type."

"Sorry, I only speak English," Sicily says.

"You're not Forest's type," Jorge says.

"He's not drinking either."

"That's because his friends mostly drink enough for him and themselves."

Sicily presses the shapely beer bottle into Jorge's hand. He takes it happily.

"Hey, Jorge we just met," Forest says, softly.

"I would have never guessed. You seem like old friends," Jorge says.

"Not yet," Sicily says, exuding confidence.

After they finish eating, Forest leans over, speaking seductively in Sicily's ear. The heat of his breath is distracting. "Well, yes, I have lipstick," Sicily answers.

She doesn't wear makeup when offstage. Her brown leather carry-on bag has everything needed for a performance or a formal affair. The propensity to quickly switch to the correct attire comes from dance, but it also reflects her parent's political necessities and her own genetics. Forest hovers near her ear. She hopes he is entranced by the scented oil dabbed behind it the morning before. He whispers, "Put some on and come with me. I have one more stop to make." Applying the lipstick slowly, her mirror is the affirmation reflected in Forest's eyes.

The group of friends doublekiss goodbyes. Forest drops a large random amount of Canadian money on the table, seemingly disinterested in making conversions or receiving correct change. Sicily is prevented from leaving her twenty dollars.

"Make sure they don't take off without us," Forest begs Jorge.

"I will lay under the wheels of the aircraft on the tarmac," Jorge flamboyantly assures.

Forest scrutinizes Sicily's look one last time. Nodding once, he takes her hand, leading her out the door. Hopping into a taxi, Sicily does not bother to ask where they are going, thinking she would not understand if he told her. He chooses to tell her anyway.

"The Swiss Bank Corporation, SBC, recently acquired Banque Commerciale de Sion, consolidating their international financial power base. We are going to visit them," Forest says.

"Ellie shielded me from most things capitalist. I was in high school before I even dropped a coin in a vending machine. I've no clue what you're talking about."

"Your parents aren't into making money. Instead, they make social change."

She giggles at his silly joke. Climbing from the taxi, Forest takes a caramel-colored corduroy blazer out of his shoulder bag. Slipping it on, he says, "Walk like a dancer and follow my lead."

"I haven't got much choice in either," she says.

Sweeping into the front door of the bank, Forest leads Sicily to a desk. He drapes the headdress on the back of 'the lady's' chair. In character, she fondles its train as if it were her boa. He refers to the gentleman behind the desk by name.

"Good afternoon Monsieur Baise—"

"How are you Mr. Odjig?" Baise extends his hand.

"Quite well, thank you. I would like to make a deposit," Forest says.

"Of course, sir," Baise says, beckoning Forest to sit. The banker takes a form and a pen from his desk drawer, placing them on the blank desktop. "May I have your passport?" Baise asks. Forest removes a Canadian passport from the breast pocket of his jacket and passes it to the banker. Hidden from Baise's view by the desk, Sicily kicks Forest's calf with the foot of her crossed leg.

"Are you all right, darling?" Forest asks, placing his hand on her thigh above her knee.

'Hell no, I'm not all right,' Sicily thinks, sucking her teeth, and keeping her mouth shut. 'After all the discussion we had about crossing borders, you handed a Canadian passport to a banker.' Forest tosses Sicily a wink. She pulls her thigh from beneath his hand, coming as close to a scowl as her luscious red lipstick allows.

"May I have your account and routing numbers?" Baise asks.

Forest recites the inordinately long numbers by heart.

"The amount, sir?"

"Seven hundred and fifty Canadian," Forest opens his shoulder bag, handing Baise seven hundred and fifty-thousand Canadian dollars. "What are the gold reserves today?" Forest asks.

"Still forty percent." Baise is proud as if having mined the ore himself.

"This is Mlle. Marshall." Forest turns to Sicily whispering loudly enough for Baise to hear, "Your passport, darling..."

Confused, Sicily gives him her travel papers. Forest hands the documents to the man behind the desk, then speaks in French. Baise responds. All Sicily understands is, "Oui, tres bien." The banker writes Sicily's passport number and name on a form, handing it to her for a signature. She looks at Forest, who nods once. Taking the pen from Baise, she signs, scowling.

"May I assist you with anything else, M. Odjig?" Baise asks.

"Please change three thousand Canadian dollars, splitting them between West German Deutsche marks, American dollars and Swiss francs." Forest hands Baise the additional currency.

Awkwardly enthralled by the amount of money in the finished transaction, Sicily wants to escape the bank quickly and question Forest. She wonders if she has become an accomplice. Forest receives the cash and a receipt, tucking both into his jacket pocket with his passport, bidding the banker goodbye. Sicily nods her farewell, without speaking, playing Matahari. The two exit the bank, leaving the lingering erotic scent of Sicily's patchouli oil, floating over the occasional feather falling from the headdress.

In the taxi, plumes stuffed safely between them, Sicily demands to know,

"What was that I just did?"

"I wanted to see how easy it is for someone else to get access to my Swiss bank account. Swiss banks are the most secure in the world," Forest says.

"I've heard, probably in a movie."

"Their money, in large percent, is backed by real gold. Today that percentage is forty."

She squints.

"I see we need to start at the beginning. Did you know the element mercury is used to extract gold from its ore?" Forest asks.

"No," she says.

"For centuries, mercury has been mixed with gold ore and water. The two elements make an amalgam. The amalgam sinks to the bottom, some free mercury and rocks floating above. The process is repeated multiple times until pure gold is freed from the amalgam mechanically by shaking—"

"Why are you telling me this?" Sicily asks.

"Because mercury is a proxy for capitalism and capital itself. That's why some of the namesakes of the god Mercury are commerce and mercenary. The element mercury, like the god and his progeny, reflect the essence of duplicity."

"Did I ask for an economics or chemistry lesson?"

"It changes from liquid to solid, then gas, within only a few degrees—mercurial and dangerous. It's embedded in most of what is called 'development'— white paper, coal burning power, fertilizer—but can be equally evil as helpful."

"I want to know how you got that money," Sicily persists, rolling down the taxi window, turning her face to the air.

"I stole it, legally."

"What does that mean?" She jerks her head back facing him.

Forest's gaze is directed above her eyes. He is momentarily seduced by backlit tendrils of her hair fountain shimmying in the breeze. "Stealing? It means ill-gotten gains. Taking something that doesn't belong to you," he says.

"I know what 'stealing' is. By definition, it's illegal," she says.

"Stealing can also be simply immoral. It's an occupational hazard, that dancing on the edge of legality and morality."

"I'm not familiar with dance or biology as morally compromising."

"I'm also a journalist," he says.

"And now I'm more confused."

"Can't I be more than one thing?"

"... Apparently you are many more."

"I dance Powwow because it's my culture. My first degree is in biology, and my master's in journalism and broadcasting."

"Journalist? Like Johnny Truedell?"

"What do you know about Johnny Truedell?" Forest asks.

'Is that condescension in his tone?' Sicily wonders to herself. Deciding the answer is 'yes,' she takes a deep breath then has at it, machine gunfire rate—"John Trudell, Native American activist and leader, tribal affiliation Santee Dakota, Nebraska, political allegiance, American Indian Movement."

"We all read newspapers," Forest says.

"Johnny was also the voice of Radio Free Alcatraz, before the Feds forcibly shut down the occupation. He has a strong understanding of the struggle of all people against racism, oppression, and poverty, and he is a poet. For your information, three days a week, after dance class I was on a picket line supporting the occupation, if not the Campaign to Free Angela. I lived on a ranch in Northern California. I wasn't buried under it." She is annoyed that he has rattled her composure.

"How did you end up in the San Francisco Bay area?" he asks.

"When Professor Angela Davis was falsely accused of murder, before being moved to Santa Clara and acquitted, she was held and tried in Marin County, California. One of her lawyers, Alex, is an old friend of our family. He and Joanna, his wife, moved up from Los Angeles while he helped work on the case. Joanna was my dance instructor in Los Angeles. It was safest for me to stay with them. They had a ranch near Point Reyes National Seashore. I took dance where Joanna taught, the School of the San Francisco Ballet, and attended a nearby alternative high school. That way, Ellie worried less about me while she traveled for Angela's campaign."

"Do you know Angela?" Forest asks.

"I sent her Snickers bars when she was in jail in Marin County."

"She's supposed to speak at the festival on closing day."

"I know."

"Will you see her?"

"With millions of star struck people in Berlin? I doubt it. I'm not on the US delegation."

Leaning his shoulder against the taxi door window, Forest turns to see Sicily more squarely. Though he had known her mother worked on Angela's campaign, he hadn't thought about her daughter in that context. The young woman before him is neither naïve nor as delicate as he had once thought. She is a working class princess—a veritable poster girl for the Declaration of Human Rights. Giving a delayed answer to her question, he says,

"Well, yeah, I try to be a journalist as honest as Johnny Trudell." Then he asks, "Why are you upset?"

"My relationship to human consciousness shouldn't need me to signify. It should be evident by who I am, not by who I say I am."

"I apologize for my narrow assumptions. Though I'd like to understand what made you think you had to tell me who you are," he says.

"Rain check. But you still have to answer my question. What was that we did at the bank?"

"You may be as smart as you look after all." Forest stares at her intently.

"Don't try distracting me by flirting," she says.

"This is not me flirting. When I flirt, you'll know the difference."

Sicily's incredulity gives way to a sniff of insult.

"I only mean, I wouldn't mix the two—seduction and business," he says.

"It would be of no interest to me one way or the other." She tells a thinly veiled lie.

"The gold economy became important because of my mining pollution research in Northern Manitoba and Ontario. That's when I first met Mercury."

Sicily rubs her temples with the heels of her hands and says, "I'm simpler than that. I only want to know about the bank."

"God's honest truth, no one is going to arrest you. Well, not for this caper," he says.

"What's with you? Why couldn't you have told me what we were doing?"

"I heard somewhere you were a girl who could function 'on a need to know basis.'"

"That applies to my family."

"Ouch—I also got the impression you would follow me anywhere."

"Did you?"

"You were magnificent at the bank. Thank you." He hands her roughly fifteen hundred dollars worth of mixed money.

"What's this?" She waves the handful of currency back at him.

"Money," he says.

"No need to pay me." She attempts to return the bills. He refuses them. She drops the currency. The breeze from the window blows the cash into dust devils. Her rolling up the window restores gravity. The feathers, car seat, and floor are littered with dollars, marks, and francs.

"If we should get separated, I think you ought to have plenty of cash with you," he says.

"Where did you get this money?"

"Come on, let me be a good guardian angel. Having different currencies to swap can be handy in Berlin, or anywhere..." he says.

"It's too much, especially under such mysterious circumstances."

"I'm not paying for your performance at the bank. You've got something else for which I'm willing to pay."

"What the hell would that be?" She speaks with the venom of one who's been called a whore.

"Trust, your trust," he says.

"It's not for sale..." she says. He cannot buy that of which she has already freely made him the beneficiary, even though she does not know why she has done so. "If you believe you have my trust, you could reciprocate by respectfully telling me where you got the money," she says.

"It's a long story, for another time."

Responding to the driver's fare request, Forest selects the appropriate amount from the loose bills. Bundling up the feathers, getting out of the vehicle, the rest of the money tumbles onto the taxi floor. Defiantly, Sicily climbs over the cash, leaving the cab. Using his knee, Forest slams the door closed behind her, then walks toward the terminal, feathers flowing.

Sicily takes a few steps, following Forest. The cab driver calls out, "Mademoiselle." Turning back, she sees the cabbie holds out a wad of money. She sighs, walks to the taxi, takes the money, and shoves it into her bag.

The rest of the Canadian delegation has finally arrived in Zürich. They lounge on the floor at the departure gate, singing. Jorge reaches from behind, covering Sicily's eyes. "It's a famous Quebecois folk song. We are trying to build unity between our two sides, the Quebecois and English. Repeat after me, 'Au chant de l'alouette...'"

"Jorge, I can't repeat the song when I can't see your mouth move," Sicily says.

He uncovers her eyes, turning her around to face him. "Au chant de l'alouette..." he enunciates. "The story is about a magic lark whose song is only understood by little girls," he says.

"Also, I can't sing before going to the restroom," she says.

"I'm right behind you," Forest says as he hands the headdress to Jorge.

The couple walks toward the signs designating two genders. Quebecois women see the long line at the ladies room. Chatting in Joual, the French dialect of working class Quebecois, les femmes march into the less congested men's room. "There you have it, the difference between French and English Canadians," Forest says.

A man collides with Sicily, without excusing himself. He is the type everyone calls only by his last name. Wearing a seersucker plaid shirt with a collar and tie, along with black dress socks and sandals, he stands out. Most of the delegation is clad in bell bottoms and T-shirts.

"You must be Sicily Marshall." The man checks her name off a list on a clipboard.

"Sicily, this clumsy, discourteous oaf, lacking any semblance of fashion sense, is the coordinator of the Canadian delegation to the festival. He won the job in a lottery, which he most likely 'fixed'. His name is Roxley." Forest holds his hand out in presentation.

"After I go to the restroom, I'll be happy to meet you," Sicily says.

"Give me your passport," Roxley says.

Ellie's daughter knows better than to surrender any of her documents to a random stranger who is not wearing a uniform. She hands her passport to Roxley but waits.

"Good thing for you we had this layover. Alone, you might have had problems at the German border," Roxley says.

"How come?" Sicily asks.

"Sometimes things get tight at Checkpoint Charlie with Americans."

Quebecois women saunter past on their way into the men's toilet. Sicily looks at them, longingly. She envies them. Roxley languidly flips pages of her nearly virgin passport. "USA, with a Canadian landed immigrant visa. This shouldn't be a problem. When you are asked your occupation at the checkpoint in Berlin, tell them you are a student," he says.

"Roxley, she is a student. Let the woman pee," Forest says.

"Where do you study?" Roxley asks Sicily.

"I'll be at the School of the Queen's Ballet," Sicily says.

"That's not good, dancers are likely to do almost anything. Tell them—where is your Canadian address?" Roxley asks.

"Winnipeg," she says.

"Winnipeg? Tell them the University of Manitoba, studying English. No, say science, better still, premed."

"But I don't."

"Tell them that anyway."

'Roxley is clearly not beyond lying,' Sicily thinks, then says, "I have to go ..." She snatches her passport from the functionary's hand and dashes toward the men's restroom.

"The 'Ladies' is to your right," Roxley yells after her.

Looking back at the self-designated potty police, she is still able to hear Roxley say, "Odd, Forest, you're not traveling with the rest of the Native American delegation. Have a tiff with your brothers?"

"Piss off, Roxley," Forest says. The Powwow dancer takes two steps toward the coordinator, who scurries away.

Sicily walks under the sign reading 'men' in six languages.

If it weren't for the other women also in the men's room, Sicily might have been uncomfortable. Forest, having relieved himself, joins her at the sink.

"He wants me to lie. I was never good at it and am likely to flub this one," she says.

"Ignore him. He makes up reasons to be important. He's not, and he won't be a problem by commission of any acts, though maybe by omission," Forest says.

Their flight is late, then cancelled. The nearly 100 member Canadian delegation is stuck in Zürich. Roxley ineffectually gnaws on the Swiss Air agent like a rat on fake cheese. Finally, it is resolved. With two days left before the beginning of the World Youth Festival in Berlin, the only option is to take a bus.

"Why are we taking the bus?" Forest asks Roxley.

"There was a fire aboard one of the Swiss Air flights. They had to land at Orly. Fatalities occurred because of carbon monoxide, a cigarette discarded in the aft toilet," Roxley says.

His blasé attitude suggests that he fancies himself one with superior knowledge.

"Swiss Air said all that?" Sicily asks.

"My brother-in-law was an airline pilot. I called him to check that Swiss Air wasn't giving me the runaround," Roxley says, attempting to gain credibility from his aviator relative.

"Incidents like this ought to be enough to keep him out of the commercial airline business," Forest says.

"Some people have to work for a living," Roxley says, herding the delegation to the bus.

Sicily and Forest lag behind the others.

"How do you know him?" Sicily asks Forest.

"Roxley? I know him as an obsequious bastard."

"You are not good at this whole answering questions thing," she says.

"True, I mostly demand answers. His brother-in-law is a friend of mine."

"That guy is in a family with someone you call a friend?" Sicily asks.

"They're only related by marriage, and that's a bit tenuous," Forest says.

⌢ ‿

On the bus, sitting side by side, Sicily divulges to Forest that all her world geography and history is from Hollywood movies, most of which she watched at the end of the elementary school day. Having skipped several grades in primary school, she missed the social studies curriculum that entailed drawing the map of Europe and singing cute songs about states or countries. By grade eight, her alternative high school filled her days with riding horses, hiking, dancing, and shooting photos.

Her parents think this trip will improve her geo-historical perspective better than the US school system would have. Her stepfather, Vern, had said, "Get to the San Francisco Airport, take Air Canada to Montreal, then Swiss Air to Berlin after a stop in Zürich. Tickets will be waiting." However, it had never occurred to her, until now, that she would be crossing the Iron Curtain.

Forest explains,

"The Canadian relationship with the Soviet Union and its allies is different from that of the USA."

"Which Soviet 'allies' will my US passport be seeing?"

"Through the Alps, besides the German Democratic Republic, Czechoslovakia is the only other country without diplomatic relations with the States."

"I barely know there are two Germanys."

"I can help you with that." Forest begins with the real story of the Von Trap family from the Sound of Music, ending with the establishment of the Berlin Wall, the worldwide players in the Cold War and its pawns. "The Cold War is a boondoggle, diverting attention from the real point."

"What's the real point?" she asks.

"It's the gap between rich and poor—on all sides of the Cold War."

"How do you know all of this?"

"Not through the Founding Myths of Rome—ignoring history, and how people are led to slaughter, is not a luxury indigenous peoples have ever afforded."

"I think I'm going to start calling you Aeneas," she says.

"Aeneas? The Trojan warrior?"

"Yeah, you seem prone to extraordinary, if not impossible tasks."

"If I'm Aeneas, can you be Dido, the Tunisian queen loving me to distraction?"

"Only if you are prepared to have the god Mercury rip us apart."

"How the hell can you know volumes about some things and zip about others?"

"Ellie's been talking to me for eighteen years—I listen, albeit selectively."

"Eighteen? You are only eighteen?" He puts the back of his hand to his forehead.

"Actually, not for a week if you use the Gregorian calendar, but yes in the Chinese."

Forest pulls back to catch his breath, looks at her, then squints.

"Is this where we stop talking?" she asks.

Shaking his head he says, "No. But, we are going to have to only talk... at least for the next week." Running his index finger from her nearest elbow, over satin skin to the large bone on the outside of her wrist, he taps it. A wave of lust passes between them.

"Ok," Sicily murmurs. She watches him lift his arms over his head, lacing his fingers, twisting his wrists. His palms face upward while his lean muscles stretch and relax. Myriad blue veins run beneath his copper skin, a map of rivers coursing to the lake of his heart. He gathers her in those arms. Her head rests against his chest. Comfortable, she asks, "Would you like to know why that Maltese Cross is given to my guardian angel?"

4

MEDITERRANEAN SEA

FALL 1942

BY 1942, THE ALLIED Forces were being defeated by the Axis powers. At thirty-three, married with a child, Grandfather Franklin was not conscripted into the army but volunteered. The induction center had a photo booth where a famous family photograph was shot. Grandmother Vanessa sat in a straight back chair, long legs crossed at the ankles, cream colored skin, with hair in an upsweep—oh so Lena Horne. Ellie stood next to her, with her dark black skin, accentuated by white bobby-socks and a knee-high dress. When the photographer asked her to smile, she wore the scowl of a devil child, forcing him to capture her true mood.

When Grandfather's first letter to Ellie arrived from North Africa, it began, "On a clear day, looking across the Mediterranean, I can see the island of Sicily. Peace will be close when we get there." His monthly letters prompted Ellie's full scale review of all things Sicilian, Italian, and North African. Only five years old, Ellie was the youngest, smartest, and most opinionated child to ever grace a Springfield public library. Catching the librarian's interest, she was given a special book. It was a children's version of Virgil's epic poem about the founding of the Roman Empire, the Aeneid. Writing a detailed review with the help of the librarian, Ellie sent it to her father by United States Military Post. She wrote,

"Mercury is the god of messages. He flies around the world, and the underworld, telling others what Jupiter, the head god, wants. The messenger was ordered to tell a defeated Trojan warrior, named Aeneas, to go to Italy and build Rome. On Aeneas' way, his ship gets lost in a storm. He ends up on the island of Sicily, happy to be safe. When he leaves there, he goes the wrong way. This time he winds up in Africa where he falls in love with a beautiful queen from Tunisia. Her name is Dido. Then, Jupiter orders Mercury, the messenger, to go back to Aeneas. The warrior has to leave Dido for Italy. The queen is sad and she kills herself. Poor Aeneas has to see the smoke from her funeral fire while he sails away."

My mother's conclusion was that, "Mercury was wrong to separate people in love." Long before the Nuremberg Trials, Ellie had already identified and rejected the doctrine of superior orders—or doing immoral things because your commander said.

My Grandfather Franklin returned from war different from when he left. "Fascism," he said, "is the final result of racism." There was another problem. Shell shock, they called it back then. The blue satin-lined boxes with medals had not dispelled the heinous effects of even a justifiable war on Grandfather's psyche. Corporal F. Grant had been a member of the 92nd Infantry. It was the only combat unit of entirely 'Colored' troops in Europe. From August of 1944 through the end of WWII in May 1945, they covered 3,000 square miles, capturing and killing more than 20,000 German soldiers, particularly in Italy. Twenty-five percent of Franklin's fellow combatants were wounded or killed in action. "They planned to use us only as cannon fodder. But we could fight, having done it all our lives," Franklin said. His two medals were among the twelve thousand given to the 92nd Infantry.

If Ellie and Vanessa touched him while he slept, Grandfather jumped up with the look of a person capable of murder.

As an apology, following one such sleepless horror, he extracted from the bottom of his army footlocker an object wrapped in a square of foreign newspaper. It was twice the size of his thumbnail. When he unwrapped it, a handpounded silver cross toppled out. Franklin scooped it up quickly.

"This came from a friend in the British Forces wounded in a battle called The Siege of Malta," Franklin explained. "I lifted the stretcher off the boat that brought him to North Africa."

"But where's the Jesus?" Ellie asked.

"This is different from a crucifix. A Maltese Cross is a symbol for a group of people who provide service to those in need."

Franklin held the bobble up by the chain. It shifted, catching sunlight from the window. The reflection helped Ellie believe the cross was magical.

"When my unit shipped out for the island of Sicily, he gave it to me for protection," Franklin said. "My friend was certain the cross kept him alive. I believe it looked after me in Italy. See how the four corners are divided in two?"

"Um huh," Ellie said.

"Each point on the cross stands for a virtue."

"What are virtues?" she asked.

"They're characteristics that make people excellent." Pointing to the cross tips he recited, "Loyalty, respect, generosity, bravery, honor, fighting against death, helping the sick and poor, and respect for people's religions." Then, he fastened the bobble on Ellie's neck.

"Don't you want it?" she asked.

"It helped me feel safer during the hardest time of my life, reminding me why we were fighting. Now I want you to have it."

The ability to pay the rent on the Grant house during the war was covered because Vanessa worked at a recreation center. On Franklin's return, Grandmother continued teaching school kids to play baseball, stretch, do cartwheels, tumble, and walk on narrow beams. While their mothers worked, the recreation center caught latchkey children. Even though Franklin was home, Ellie still joined Vanessa after school. My mother was a hero of the softball and baseball teams. If sports had not been segregated by gender, as well as by race, all the boys' teams would have drafted Ellie. She hit harder than most of them, whether with a bat, fist, or her mouth.

Vanessa had promised to continue taking Ellie to the 'good school' near the State Capital while Franklin was overseas. On his return, he did not get his job back. Instead, he worked as a garage mechanic, frequently picking up Ellie after school. When Ellie had been five it was obvious that she was beyond kindergarten academically. Now nine years old, Ellie's teacher assigned my mother seventh grade work. Before Franklin left for war she often did arithmetic and handwriting assignments in the legislative gallery. Then she would peak over the rail and watch her daddy finish his day as an assistant page on the floor below. When he was home again, Ellie begged her father to visit the State House. Franklin finally agreed.

The Speaker of the Legislature looked up, seeing Ellie sneak through the gallery door. He gave her a little wave as he had done years before. A king on his throne, the Speaker ordered, "All stand, we are in the presence of a 'War Hero'. Mr. Franklin Grant is in the gallery." Clapping, the assembly looked up at Ellie and her Daddy. Down on the legislative floor, members shook hands with Franklin, asking what he was doing for work. He explained he was a mechanic but wanted to study refrigeration and air conditioning. One assemblyman inquired about why he was not using his GI Bill to fund taking a course. Franklin reminded all of them, "Only White trade schools have those classes." Articulating his case, no stone was left unturned.

From then on, much activity happened at the Grant house. My grandparents were determined to integrate the Illinois technical and trade schools. Skilled in the struggle for equality, members of the National Association for the Advancement of Colored People came weekly. They drank gallons of coffee. Vanessa made sandwiches with soft white cheese, cut into squares, sometimes using special puffed bread. In the living room, Ellie served appetizers to parents of kids with whom she had played ball.

Charlene came from Chicago with her father for a meeting. Though only a girl she was already famous for participating in desegregating the Windsor Theater in her hometown.

"How old were you when you did that?" Ellie asked.

"Thirteen..."

"How old are you now?"

"Seventeen."

"You are only seven years older than me," Ellie said.

"And you are only three years younger than I was when we did it."

"How did you do it?"

"The Black kids sat in the White section, and the White kids in the Colored section."

"Only that?"

"Sweet and simple... The ruckus of the cops moving us, every Saturday, was losing the theater more money than if they desegregated."

"What do you call a person who thinks up things like what you did?" Ellie asked.

"An 'organizer'..." Charlene said, spelling the word aloud.

"O-R-G-A-N-I-Z-E-R," Ellie said, "that's what I'm going to be."

5

BOHEMIAN FOREST WATERSHED

JULY 1973

THE FEATHERS MAKE A colorful canopy hanging from the luggage rack, a curtain over Forest and Sicily. The two sleep, her head nestled on his shoulder. The bus jerks. Sicily wakes.

"It smells like Christmas," she says.

"Spruce. It's the dominant tree in the Bohemian Forest, which is not actually a woods."

"I'll bite. Why not?" She yawns.

"It's a mountain range, dividing watersheds of rivers feeding the Black and North Seas."

"I only know the Bohemian Forest, opus 68/5 by Dvorak." Will she never stop amazing him?

The hot breaths of all the delegates fog the windows. Round balls of light bounce off the driver's windshield, flashing light beams. The officer boarding carries a side arm. "Everyone please to take out your papers to show the authorities when you leave the bus," he says in rehearsed English.

"What's going on?" Sicily asks.

"We're likely about to meet the Czechoslovakian border patrol, then the German. Let me go first. I'll make a ruckus, you escape into the trees," Forest jokes. Sicily recalls every Cold War spy flick she has ever seen.

Passengers reluctantly file off the coach. This would have been a good time for Forest to use the Canadian passport instead of the 'Indian Card'. He doesn't. The officer shines a light back and forth between Forest and the tribal identification. Relieved, Sicily sees the glint of two Czechoslovakian crystal wine flutes even before the soldier's smile. A third officer pours white wine. Heavily armed uniformed guards lift their own goblets, some of them German, the others Czechoslovakian. The officer with the pen light makes a toast in English, "To Freedom, Friendship, and Solidarity."

⌒‿

As the sun rises, the bus crosses the River Spree, pulling through the gates of Berlin's Humboldt University. Hundreds of young adults perch in the stone courtyard, some hanging from the balcony, guarded by marble pillars and neoclassical Roman roof sculptures. Guitars in hand, a chorus of 'C's' serenade them—Cape Verdeans, Cambodians, Cameroonians, Czechs, Chileans, Colombians, Costa Ricans and Cubans. They greet the tardy Canadians, voices filling the sweltering damp dawn with Cat Stevens's song Baby, Baby It's a Wild World.

A few hours later, marching in the 10th World Festival of Youth and Students opening ceremonies, the cheering of thirty-thousand people in the grandstands overwhelms Sicily. Confetti falls, lights flash near strobe frequency. Instinctively, she closes her eyes to avoid a seizure. Jorge puts his dark sunglasses on her.

"We've done nothing but get on a couple of planes and buses," she says.

"But we had the nerve to cross the Iron Curtain," Jorge says, marching to her left.

Sicily stumbles. Preventing her collapse, Forest and Jorge wrap their arms around her shoulders and waist, Like Sherpas they carry her for a multitude of laps around the stadium, her feet barely touch ground. "Am I dreaming?" she asks. "Or are people throwing gardens of flowers?" Indeed they are.

Jorge yells over the crowd, "In 1947 the first World Youth Festival was held in Prague."

"Why Prague?" She shouts.

"To rebuild a town leveled by the Nazis," Forest yells.

"What town?" she asks, her voice cracking.

"Lidice."

"Why?"

"—Nazi governor was murdered—the fascists wiped out 500 people—gassed children with car exhaust."

"500?" she asks, over a volley of the crowds cheers. He nods.

Women dancing with scarfs of blue swirling like the sea divert Sicily's attention. Awe struck, she realizes they are the most beautiful dancers she has ever seen.

"Vietnamese," Forest says, close to her ear.

'Their beauty is obscenely omitted on TV news in the States,' she thinks.

"See that woman, passing us to get to the podium?" Forest asks as the crowd is reverently silent. They are near enough to see horrific burn scars, partly covered by a scarf on her neck. Under other circumstances she would be considered a girl, but not after what she had been through.

"Yes," Sicily says.

"Look closely—recognize her?"

"Wait—Life Magazine, My Lai?" 'A trench filled with dead bodies and a girl wandering through them,' Sicily remembers. In 1968, though the photos were not made public for a year, United States military troops raped women and children and killed near 500 people in the Massacre of My Lai. It was the dancing girl's village. Sicily shudders thinking, 'Five hundred, the magic number for exterminating whole towns.'

The opening ceremonies end with thousands singing the World Federation of Democratic Youth anthem, Everywhere the Youth are Singing Freedom Songs. Berlin's streets are

SEPTEMBER WILLIAMS

packed with the indomitable spirit of young people challenging
the world as it exists. There are 30,000 international delegates
and millions of German nationals walking, talking, translating, and interpreting. Sicily now understands that the USA is
not the center of the universe, despite behaving as though it is.
In 1973 the world's youth surf a wave of both revolutionary and
evolutionary proportions.

Heading back to the dorms, Sicily, Forest, and Jorge notice
that even the passing out of Gay Rights leaflets, to notoriously
homophobic old line communists is beyond the host city's attempted control.

At night the rows of bunk beds, in dorms vacated for festival delegates' use, are a school unto themselves. Tales told are
vivid. The summer before, the massacre at the Munich Olym-
pics had occurred. One of the delegates had been there, a girl
younger than Sicily, a Canadian swimmer. "How could you
bear to step foot on German soil again?" Sicily asks.

"Ignoring suffering does not make it go away," the swimmer says. "I wanted to understand how evil works and what I
can do about it. That's why I came."

Confused by the world's geography, Sicily gets other delegates to draw her maps on everything, including bed sheets.
These cartoons illustrate South America being on the verge of
losing its oldest democracy, Chile, to fascism. Other graphics
show German families separated by the Berlin Wall, marking
the geography of the Cold War. Poorer nations are pieces on a
game board represented by the crude cartography of the planet—it is as Forest had said. "How could I have not known what
is going on in the world?" Sicily asks herself aloud, only to be
answered by Pascal,

"You are oppressed at home by racism and class. But The
Star Spangled Banner spares you other countries' realities." He
speaks with a deafening sweetness.

"While the world around crashes, I've been in relative heav-
en by the sea," she says.

"Your period of ignorance is over. We are not two generations from the Holocaust perpetuated by the land on which we are standing. The world is always crashing and going forward. But don't feel guilty. You and I are stronger for not being beaten down early. With strength comes obligations," Pascal says.

Camille enters the room, kissing Sicily on both cheeks, then melting into her lover's lap. He nestles her golden hair, unabashed. The ballerina envies this couple's courageous passion, which spits in human desperation's face. On the other side of the dorm room, a violent rhetorical polemic erupts between Forest and Jorge. Forest jumps off a top bunk to the floor. He is directly in front of his louder but much shorter friend.

"The best guidance for the world lays in arts and letters," Jorge screams. The opening ceremonies only five days gone, Sicily is surprised he still has a voice while hers remains hoarse.

"The check on philosophy is science," Forest says.

"Next you'll pull out that cheap rhetorical trick, the Null Hypothesis."

French, English, Chinese, Portuguese, Spanish, Russian, and German translations of the argument swirl about the room. Thanks to colonialism, everyone speaks at least one of these languages.

"What's the 'Null Hypothesis'?" Sicily asks. The room falls silent. 'I suppose everyone else here knows already,' she thinks.

Jorge nudges Forest into answering.

"The 'Null Hypothesis' is a logical way of eliminating considerations in complex systems, by assuming they are not true and searching for evidence you are correct. If you don't find that evidence, the assumption is false, and the opposite likely valid," Forest says.

Sicily's mind swirls, until she gets to the root of Forest's logic and the argument between her two friends. "If philosophy comes from arts and letters, and the structure of science comes from the arguments of philosophy, aren't they each sides of one coin? Both essential?" Sicily asks.

"Yes," Forest says.

"Yes," Jorge says.

Both men look at Sicily. She only flicks her eyebrows up. Forest and Jorge cock their heads to opposite sides, trying to understand how the ballerina undid, and supported, both their arguments. Multiple translations create a low hum in the room.

"What's going on?" Sicily asks. It is her most frequent question.

"Roughly, they are saying, 'Her breeze rattles the tree of knowledge,'" Forest says.

Grateful for the resolved polemic, at least for this night, students hug and disband with no hard feelings. Forest walks Sicily across the Great Hall toward the corridor to her room.

"You have a good head for science," he says.

"How can you say that? I've never studied it, unless animal husbandry and natural history at my weird alternative high school count," she says.

"Science is a way of thinking."

They walk past the oil paintings hanging on the walls.

"These guys were all educated here," he says.

"Engles, Plank, Marx, Dubois, and Einstein—" Sicily reads aloud, touching the name tags.

"They are scientists and philosophers driven to hazard models explaining how things work—men, women, life, death, the infinite universe and it's machines."

"Are quoting Dr. Zorba from Ben Casey to me?"

"Drs. Zorba and Casey are the most important philosophers and scientists in recent history." Forest laughs.

"Too bad they only existed on TV."

"Hey, you better rest up," he says.

"Why?"

"We're rehearsing together for the first time tomorrow, remember?"

"I'll be fine. But you may have trouble keeping up with me."

"Not likely," he says, stopping at her dorm room door.

Sicily slides an arm around Forest's waist. Kicking one of his legs from beneath him, she catches him in a dance pivot, pushing him against the door. Raising his arms above his head, her hands acting as handcuffs. Giving him a full open mouth kiss, he melts under her weight. Well, not all of him. Coming up for air, Forest is happily confused.

"Didn't I tell you?" she asks.

"Tell me what?"

"I took martial arts from Lee Jun Fan in San Francisco when he was studying ballet." She twirls Forest back to his original position. "'Lee Jun Fan' is the recently late, great, Bruce Lee's Chinese name." Her clarification is tinged with sadness. She slips through her door, closing it behind her. Abandoned in her wake, Forest tries to comprehend the compassion, and lust, she evokes.

⌒

Mirrors line three walls of the rehearsal room. The familiarity of the multiple reflections washes Sicily with emotion. She plops to the floor, the business of pulling demi-pointe shoes from her bag prevents her from crying. Unsure about the dance surface, she applies extra chalk to the toes. "Thank you for the rehearsal space. This is the first time I've felt at home since leaving the States," she says to Forest.

His dance gear sits on the floor at the furthest corner of the room—headdress, matching feathered leggings, and drum. During their performance an orchestra will play Stravinsky's Firebird score, while a tech crew amplifies Forest's drum and song. For today, he brought a borrowed portable reel to reel tape recorder.

"Why are the other Canadian First Nation people traveling in the American Indian delegation?" Sicily asks.

"Because we don't recognize colonial borders. 'American' means all of it."

"Why aren't you traveling with them?" A fair question—from November 1969 to June 1973, everyone Sicily knew supported the American Indian Movement in some way or another, occupations, marches, lawyers, bail. How could Forest not travel to the festival with the large Native delegation?

"Mostly because of Jorge—I needed to see him. These are hard times in Chile, his father's homeland. Also, he thought I could gather some international data for my research."

"This 'research' is more important than a movement?" Sicily asks.

"People respect my work enough to excuse me from other duties."

Sicily does a few demi pliés, checking her posture in the mirror. Closing her eyes, she feels her position. Annoying, like an itch on her nose during a dance performance, she senses Forest's refusal to share. Now is not the time to raise this question. Still she says, "Sometime you should tell me exactly what that work is." She repeats her moves grande then adds, "Roxley might be right, maybe we've bitten off more than we can chew."

"Roxley is never right," Forest says.

"'Even a broken clock is right twice a day.'"

Hearing the sound of Forest rustling in his corner, she flutters her eyelids to slits, sneaking a peek as he strips to the waist. The chain of the Maltese Cross and the medicine bag on his neck dangle on the insides of his nipples, between his braids. Trying to avert her eyes is useless. His reflection is everywhere. Placing the Firebird bonnet reverently on his head he utters a prayer.

Sicily peels out of her sundress, exposing a beige sleeveless tank leotard and leggings. Forest watches her as she had him.

At first dancing separately, they each work on their solos. Forest's opening movement unfurls a turn choreographed in the depths of history, honoring the four seasons. His sinew and muscle defy the command that human beings should not fly. He hurls her into a new dance reality, one where she has to up her game. After two hours, each satisfied with their solos, eyes riveted to one another, they begin work on their 'dance for two'. She enters this physically and emotionally dangerous territory en pointe. Her planned escape is fast twirling sequential pirouettes. Their dance shares every element of a Tango. He says,

"Close to the end, you should leap into my arms."

"It would be the final performance of the festival. Could we pull off two separate forms and now flying?" she says, sharing her doubts.

"You were doing that when I first saw you," Forest says.

"What?"

"You were leaping over luggage in the Montreal Airport."

"Are you admitting you noticed me before I dropped my glasses?"

"Do I have to?"

Not answering, she escapes to the far corner of the studio. Catching her breath, she gives Forest a few instructions for lifting while protecting his back, and hers. "You are more than physically fit, but balancing another person in motion is not easy," she says. Running, she flies into a jeté grande, her legs open like giant scissors. He catches her at the waist, lifting, twirling in three circles, kissing her navel. She pikes forward from her abdomen as he scoops her up. She is to swing her leg over his right shoulder, the momentum allowing him to raise her to his highest reach. But her lower limbs become a helicopter propeller gone awry.

They both suppress panic, realizing the need to combine their centers of gravity. Forest slides her down toward his chest. She wraps her legs around his waist, beneath the train of his headdress. Arching into a back bend, she rests her hands on the floor, averting a disaster. They breathe, relieved.

Her pelvis is locked into his, an ideal match. Over her leotard she feels him harden between her legs. The recorded powwow drum is intertwined with Stravinsky's Firebird.

"I'm sorry," she says.

"Quiet, the Great Spirit is talking."

"Yes, and she's telling me I have to go to the restroom."

"Lucky there's a toilet here." He points to one of the mirrors and its tiny latch. "You'd better hurry. It will take you a while to get out of those tights."

Unwrapping her legs, walking away cautiously avoids her bladder jiggling. Tossing him an over the shoulder glance she says,

"Sweetie, dancers don't take off their tights to pee."

"Then how...?"

"You should be able to sort that one out."

"No, seriously—"

"I don't have time to tell you."

"Can I see for myself?" He raises an eyebrow, knowing the boldness of his request.

"I'm not in a position to stop you," Sicily says, flipping the lock on the WC.

Laying his feathers on the floor, he follows her. Fascinated, he watches. She reaches her right hand through the opposite leg of her leotard, grabs the waist band of the tights, pulling them down to the middle of her thigh. Her left hand yanks the leotard's leg hole up toward her belly button. She squats over the commode, relieving herself. Forest looks as if a meteorite touched earth.

"The technique is standard," Sicily says, washing her hands at the adjacent sink. While the water runs, Forest pulls her by the hips until her buttocks press against his groin.

"If you can get things out of you that way, it stands to reason, I can get in," he says. Turning her to face him, he slides one of his hands up the inside of the leotard, demonstrating the procedure he has learned. "I've always been attracted to ballet." He pulls down her tights on one side. "Do I have this right?"

"Time will tell," she says.

Their eyes see from the same retina. Forest whispers, "Exactly when is your birthday?"

"Let me see, what's the date?"

"August 2, 1973," he says.

"Then—it must be today."

"Happy Birthday..." He slips deep inside her. His hands are free to drop her shoulder straps. Frustrated, he rips the stretchy cloth bodice, cupping her breast. She arches against the porcelain faucet. The still running warm water splashes her back. He lays her farther into the liquid. It squirts her shoulders, dripping over her breasts while he squeezes them forming a cup. Lowering his head he drinks from her.

The second time is on the cool hardwood floor of the dance studio. Forest drapes the feather train of the headdress over their naked bodies.

"Is using the feathers this way sacrilegious?" she asks.

"Love—how could it be?"

6

SAN PEDRO BAY

WINTER 1956 TO 1958

WORD FROM MY FATHER finally came when I was seven months old. Ellie would be raising me alone. The thick paper stock, which the military reserved for solemn occasions, referred to Ellie as John's wife and me as his child. John's belongings were bequeathed to his widow, including his death benefits.

Ellie had enough college credits to enter nursing school. John's funds payed the cost. Good money bet the first time my mother was called a 'mackerel snapping nigger' at St. John's hospital, in Springfield, her nursing career would be over. Somehow, disinterested in deranged helpless racists, her main concern was with those patients truly suffering.

Grandfather Franklin finished his refrigeration and air conditioning training in 1957. The modern industrial complex of California called out to him. He was recruited by three shipyards and four aircraft companies—every one of them an asbestos lung disease factory. At age 47, even if Franklin had known the health dangers of these industries, he still would have been lured. He accepted a job at Todd Shipyard, located on the San Pedro Bay, south of Los Angeles. Second to being in the military during the throws of desegregation, membership in a labor union was the best chance to ensure his family's future. Todd was unionized, and Black workers were paid parity with White. Though the Grants and Marshals were geographically separated for many months while Ellie finished hospital practicums in Illinois, that was a watershed period for our family.

When I was two, Ellie and I reunited with my grandparents and my six year old aunt Lillie in Los Angeles. We all lived on 55th Street, a few blocks off Western Avenue. The street was lined with top-heavy palm trees. Our house was owned by Vanessa's great aunt on her dead mother's side, Hazel. Born in Oklahoma, Hazel was the matriarch who had herded most of her ten siblings to California in 1930. Hazel was also the nasty piece of work who had taught orphaned Vanessa to hit by beating her. Believing the Grant-Marshalls were at her mercy for want of living accommodations, she took liberties with our dignity. An ugly drunk, her disposition was attributed to her 'lousy liver'. Hazel was always located in the house by the tinkle of ice in her highball glass.

Our first Christmas without snow was cataclysmic because of Hazel. I was three. Perhaps I had spilled orange juice on Hazel's red velvet, claw foot, antelope horned chair, while reaching for an ornament on the tree, daring to suggest it was an accident. Scolding, Hazel added disparaging remarks about Ellie raising me to 'talk back'. Children expressing themselves at all was contrary to the remnants to of the oppression from which the old aunt had not escaped.

Grandfather Franklin, a gentleman, was rarely angry. Abuse of his children released him from reason, creating a whirlwind. That joyless Noel, a flurry of words and curses exchanged between Franklin and Hazel, who squawked from her bedroom perch. Franklin pulled me onto his hip, took Lillie's hand, and signaled to Ellie to open the front door. The Grant-Marshalls walked through onto the porch. Franklin spat his words back inside, "You may speak about your own children in that way, but don't ever again presume to do the that with mine."

A few days later, Lillie and I wrestled on the floor of our room, as we often did. Lillie called time-out. I ignored her. Lillie got up. I chased. Lillie laid on the floor. I tripped over her. My scream was a long single sound, like an air raid siren in a small tiled space. The arm hurt too much to breathe when Grandfather lifted me into the Pontiac. I held my breath until close to blacking out. When forced to gasp, the shriek began again. Coming from the bus stop after her hospital shift, Ellie heard my pain as she walked up the street. Swooping like an angel, in all that nursing uniform white, Nurse Ellie stabilized my arm. Momma Ellie struggled not to collapse with fear.

The closest hospital was at the intersection of Manchester and Western. The corner was typical Los Angeles—a gas station, grocery market, bank, liquor outlet, Chinese restaurant, and sporting goods shop. The neighborhood was called Morning Side Park, as was the one story hospital built of redwood, washed grey and trimmed in green.

Ellie, still in her white nurse's uniform, looked like the other nurses in the room except their skin was also white. Recognizing my mother's thinly veiled terror, her colleagues bantered about Cedars of Lebanon combining with Mount Sinai, resulting in more jobs. Chatter is a nursing protocol that mutes the gravity of emergencies. The doctor arrived, looked at my arm, and pronounced it broken. After saying the limb needed a cast, a few things were taken from a cabinet and passed to a nurse, including a carpenter's saw. The tool seemed as large as the doctor himself to me, just before I lost consciousness.

Opening my eyes, I found myself alone on the back seat of the Pontiac. The car was parked on a half circle of curb, a cul-de-sac. Looking out the windshield, I saw the gray and green hospital. Ellie, Lillie, and my grandparents walked on a lawn belonging to a ranch style house. The picture window at the front of the house was the size of a movie theater screen. A sign was planted in the middle of the large square of grass. I recognized the number '4' on the placard. Not yet having learned to read, I didn't know it actually said, '4 Sale'. The cul-de-sac separated the hospital from the house's wall. One of the White nurses peered around the corner, waving a thumbs up to Ellie. Ellie returned the gesture. Before my fourth birthday, Franklin bought that ranch style house.

7

RIVER SPREE

AUGUST 1973

IN THE UNIVERSITY COURTYARD, grabbing Sicily at the waist, Forest prevents her from boarding a bus for yet another factory tour.

"I thought you had something else to do today and couldn't spend time with me," she says.

"It was to visit an 'Indian Club,'" he says.

"East Indian?"

"American..."

"What do they do?"

"Germans dress in what they think is traditional Native American clothing, listen to powwow music, burn and eat as they think we do, chant, that sort of thing. I'm begging off this particular homage."

Sicily's laugh is gut splitting. "Sorry, I'm busy, and I like the factories. The Germans are rightly proud of them," she says.

"We only have four days before the end of the festival. But if you don't like me as much..." He releases her shoulders.

"Well, maybe I shouldn't miss time with you to see books bound, again."

"Good," he says pulling her camera strap, dragging her toward him, twirling her in a hug.

Other delegates watch, shaking their heads, knowing the two are a lost cause for the day.

A hidden exit at the rear of the university's Great Hall empties into a garden. A quarter mile beyond is a grove of trees which they traverse to reach a street. Catching the type of bus normal residents of the city use, they travel an hour. Of no surprise to the driver, they debark at a thick ring of heavily florescent leaf laden forest. Trekking through this magic thicket they emerge into a wide space of carefully planted rows of bright yellow sunflowers and corn.

"Where are we?" Sicily asks.

"I thought you might like a break from the city. It's called Grunwald."

The grayness and age of Berlin, even with the wildness of the festival, wrenches Sicily's Northern California ranch girl soul. Forest recognizing her need for country makes her love him all the more. A farmhouse and barn are at the furthest edge of the corn. Headed toward it, they trample between the rows of ten foot flowers, coming to a break in the plantings because of a pile of stones. "What's this? Why don't they move it?" Sicily wonders aloud. CLICK, CLICK, she snaps photos.

"Rubble from the war is sacred in these parts, a reminder." Forest says.

"What war?"

"World War II"

"Like from...?"

"—Land mine blast."

Realizing that someone may have died where she stepped, her tears wet the view finder. She lowers the Leica from her eye, saying, "I hate war, fighting, practicing and justifying them, all of it."

"I'd be surprised if you liked it." He takes the camera from around her neck, placing it on the ground. Holding her in his arms, first he kisses her tears away, then her mouth. Clearing a few stones, pulling off his shirt, he lays it on the ground. "Let's plant love here," he says. Gently lowering her, he wishes it were to a bed of roses. Covering her body with his, Forest applies enough pressure to fuse their molecules with the earth below. Sleepless for nights, up arguing politics, among other more intimate things, the sun is high when the two wake after making love.

"See that in the sky... straight up and to right of the sun?" Forest asks, pointing.

"Um huh."

"That's Mercury, it's the fastest planet in the solar system. By dusk we'll see it on the opposite side of the heavens."

Until the farmer and his son laugh, the lovers are oblivious to their presence. The adolescent's hair is blonde, while his father's white. Except for age and hair the two Germans are identical, average height, sunburned round faces accentuating green eyes. Their coveralls are the type Sicily's grandfather wears. Forest drapes Sicily in his shirt then slips into his jeans. The Germans respectfully turn their backs as Sicily dresses. Studying English, the boy wants to practice his skills. Initially, the lovers only explain that they are Canadians and accept an invitation for a drink at the farmhouse.

Reaching the front door of their home, the men hang their coveralls on hooks outside. "That's where my grandfather leaves them," Sicily says. The house is spare except for plenty of books. The unlit lamps run on kerosene. Windows without glass have shutters open to the fields. The farmer's son, whose name Sicily would never remember, wants to know about Canada. With difficulty, she explains moving from the United States. The son's eyes light up.

"You know the Supremes? Hollywood Street?" the boy asks.

"Yes," she says, both being true if 'street' means boulevard.

The boy gets up from the table. He goes to an ancient record player, popping on a stack of 45s, all Motown. The first song is "Stop in the Name of Love". They dance, the farmer, his son, Forest, and Sicily. She sings the verses, moving seductively, inciting Forest to approach. His dance response shows an inability to resist her allure. Whenever he comes within kissing distance, her hand flies up in the universal open palm signal for 'Stop'. Then he stumbles like a man shot in the gut. All present sing the refrain. Each time Sicily shows him her palm, Forest becomes just a touch sadder. He is aware that he is fully capable of breaking her heart. The ruckus causes the farmer's wife to come from outdoors, bringing along a couple of workers. They too join the party.

Four horses are in the barn. Two of them still pull the plow. The other two are Arabians, who by their apparent closeness are a mare and her grown colt, now a young stallion. Sicily runs her hand along the stallion's side, pats his left flank, then lifts his leg, checking the hoof. The barn falls silent. Forest's mouth hangs open. Sicily looks around, seeing him and the astounded Germans. "I lived on a ranch in California for a while," she says. The animal stamps when his foot returns to the ground. The audience exhales. In halting English, the farmer's son asks if she would like to ride. "Yes," her excitement is, well, unbridled. She hands Forest her camera. Slipping the bit into the horses mouth, she coos to him. Sticking her knee into his belly, forcing him to breathe out, she tightens the saddle cinch.

"You know how to ride this thing?" Forest asks.

"Remind me again, exactly what kind of Indian are you?" She jokes.

"The type whose boarding school didn't have an equestrian hour and I couldn't speak my native language or see my parents."

"Poor you," she says. Sticking her tongue out at Forest, she almost misses the transient darkening of his mood. "Where should I go?" she asks. The boy signs, directing her between the corn rows, planted far enough apart to accommodate the horse. She starts the ride in a trot. When all watching are certain she can handle herself, they turn their interest elsewhere. The horse flies into a canter, without a whisper of provocation. Tapping his flank with her heels, wearing sandals not boots, she doesn't expect he'll much notice. Surprise—the steed is exquisitely responsive. Within a breath, they are in full gallop.

The corn opens into a field. 'We should turn around,' she thinks. The stallion gives no hint of slowing his pace when Sicily tugs on the reins. The horse is out of her control. 'Thirty-five miles per hour' wind on her cheek tells her. Sicily panics. They head straight for the river. Feeling she is about to tumble, she chooses to guide the fall. Slipping one foot out of the stirrup, she swings a leg over the saddle while holding tight to the reins, stealing herself for a hell of a tumble. Luckily, the horse stops when her foot grazes the ground.

Her legs are scratched instead of broken. She stands and dusts off, burrs littering her hair. Then, she sees it— miles of concrete, barbed wire, and electrical fences, lining the River Spree. This is the Berlin Wall up close, separating east from west, sisters from brothers. The view weeps with humidity, and she with the gravity of what she feels. The horse drinks from the river. She chances mounting him again.

The farmers and Forest see her galloping approach. Not sure how she will stop the stallion, Sicily hopes the onlookers share her distress. They don't, despite her flying past them at full speed. Unable to control the animal beneath her, an idea slits her fear. She yells, "How do I stop a horse in German?" Forest doubles over laughing.

When she circles the spectators again, the Germans all together make the sound 'BRRRRRRRR!'

She is doubtful but has nothing to lose. "BRRR!" The Arabian jerks to a halt within two strides. Sliding off the saddle, feigning composure, she removes the frothy saliva covered bit. Handing the bridle to Forest, he receives it as though it bears the plague. Holding the lead rope, she walks the animal to cool him down. Forest and the farmer's inquisitive son join her.

Declining a supper invitation, Forest says in German, "Our comrades and mates will worry if we are gone too long." Previously unaware of her lover's Deutsch, Sicily raises her eyebrows. At the edge of the sunflowers, Forest grabs a long piece of oat hay, putting it in his mouth. The farmer's son smacks the straw out of Forest's hand.

"Poison," the boy says.

"What do you know about poison?" Forest asks.

"Everywhere, pesticide, old metals," the son says in English.

"Mercury?" Forest asks.

"Yes," the boy says, without a doubt.

"Are people sick from it?"

"—When use the river water to cook, drink, wash. And... the ones swim the river many times to get over the wall..."

Sicily recalls what she saw when the horse led her to the water.

Forest nods his understanding, "Who is fixing it?"

Carefully crafting his sentence the boy says, "People die here for truth."

"In North America too," Forest says. He sticks out his hand in a solidarity shake.

"Good luck, friend," the boy says.

Sicily gives the horse a gentle pat. Handing over the lead rope, she kisses the adolescent's cheek. He blushes. Forest places Sicily's Leica around her neck. The lovers tramp through the yellow and black sunflowers, which seem taller than earlier. Their young host waives until they are out of sight.

Finally reaching the hidden garden door to the Great Hall, Sicily asks,

"What was all that about?"

"What?" Forest is irritable.

"The pesticides stuff."

"What it's always about, but that's a long story for another time."

"What if there is no other time?" Sicily stops, putting her hands on her hips. "I'm showing you mine, my whole story, you show me yours."

"I need to figure out how to get samples of that river."

"Why?"

"Because all life is connected by water." He is angry, as if absorbing the planet's suffering. Picking up his pace, he walks ahead of her. She stops. He looks back. Grabbing her by the elbow, he hustles her down the hall, whispering, "I need to escape the garden door's proximity." As they approach the dining hall Roxley appears.

"Where were you two all day? You are supposed to let me know if you make plans that are not on the schedule."

"Piss off, Roxley," Forest says, pushing the Coordinator out of the way.

At supper the lovers regale friends with tales of Sicily on the German horse and dancing to Motown.

"You did all that in a sundress?" Jorge asks Sicily.

"And sandals, without wearing—well, anyway, I'm exhausted," Sicily says. Instinctively, she follows Forest's example, commenting on neither the River Spree nor the pollution, the truly important parts of their adventure. Yawning, she stands, stretches, and takes her camera from the table. "I'm going to bed. Good night," she says. She moves quickly. Forest sprints to catch up with her in the corridor.

"Let me walk you," he says.

"Not unless you talk to me."

"Not in the dorm—can we do it tomorrow?"

"It's now or never. I always live with lots of secrets around me. In your case, I have to know where you've been, to know where I am going."

"Some of what I know could end up hurting you," he says, grabbing her upper arm for the second time this evening.

"More than you are hurting me now?" she asks, looking at his hand cooly. He lets her go, sure to never display that particular gesture again.

"Is this about that money?" she asks.

"Sort of—"

"Tell me about the damned money. We can do one secret at a time."

He silently leads her up a grand staircase to the second floor. The doors to the balcony are locked. The latches which could open the lower half of the high arched windows are fifteen feet above their heads. Forest scales the pane's moldings. Stretching, he pops a lock and jumps back to the floor. Pushing the window up, climbing through, he reaches back for Sicily's hand. Rejecting his assistance she moves on her own steam. Separated by six feet, they sit on the cool granite floor between the balcony's pillars.

"I negotiated a deal with the Hydroelectric Power Company in the Province of Manitoba. It left twenty acres, my mother's land, for family use. I sold my father's twenty-two hundred acres for which I was paid twenty-million," Forest says, abandoning the burden of his secret.

"Twenty-million what?" Sicily asks.

"Canadian Dollars…"

"Is it a gold mine?"

"Of sorts, it's key to completing the province's hydroelectric power river diversion."

"When did you sell it?"

"It will be five years this coming spring. I was twenty-one—1968—and the man of the family after dad died. The deed to the land was willed only to me. He wanted me to sell it, and I did."

"Why didn't he sell it himself?"

"My mum wouldn't let him. It's rare anyone goes against my mum. Her twenty acres are in the center of what was his."

"Why would you hide money that made your family millionaires?"

"Native people are guardians. Our job is protecting the land, not abusing it. Because I didn't protect it, Mum not only never touched that money, she won't stay on the remaining acres."

"I see," Sicily says.

"It's worse," his voice quivers. "Mum no longer speaks to me."

"I can't imagine how hard that must be."

"It gets more horrible and complicated."

"Try me," she says, pulling her knees up, wrapping her arms around them.

"When the snow pack melts in the spring, after the hydro-electric power diversion finishes three years from now, our land won't be an intermittent flood plain. It will be permanently underwater, a reservoir."

"Obliterating your mother's land too?" she asks.

"Worse, there's pollution in the flood waters. More than one type—but my interest is mercury."

"How do you know?"

"I've tested the rivers leading to the dams."

"You, yourself, tested it?" she asks.

"Yes, and I've found mercury travels with other pollutants in waterways feeding Hudson Bay. Before the flow gets there, some rivers go through Lake Winnipeg, one of the largest inland fisheries in Canada."

"People are eating mercury contaminated fish?" Sicily asks.

"Especially people who have nothing else to eat, subsistence fishers, like on most reserves up north."

"What's a reserve?"

"It's a Canadian euphemism for 'reservation'. Think apartheid South Africa's 'Bantustans.'"

"Did you know about the mercury when you sold the land?" Sicily asks.

"Not then, it was Vern who hipped me to the hydroelectric diversion connection."

"How did you meet Vern?"

"It was in 1969. The Arctic is large but sparse in people. I knew the pilot who flew Vern to Churchill. He told me about this guy who was studying engineering. We were both twenty-two, and he had been in exile from South Africa since he was seventeen. Gypsy's Coffee Shop is the only place a stranger can find breakfast in that town. Even under the arctic winter cloak of daytime darkness, I recognized Vern through the haze of water trickles and frost. His skin was universal brown, like mine. He was six three and too overly bundled for an Indian—east or Native American. When a table opened near the back, I invited him to join me. He explained that he was an engineering student at the Provincial University and his thesis was on water resources."

"When was that?" Sicily asks.

"Three years ago..."

"When the pleasantries were over and the coffee poured, Vern asked me about my work. I explained investigating mercury pollution from the gold mining industry in Canada's far north as a freelance journalist. Vern wanted to know what I had found out."

"And what was that?" Sicily asks.

"In Ontario, a bunch of abandoned deep gravel pit mining quarries used mercury to shake out every ounce of gold from the dregs. Now those open holes masquerade as wilderness lakes. Developers purchase the land around those ponds and build lake houses. They look real pretty. I didn't know the sort of contamination, but I knew there had to be some.

"The lab didn't want to release my first water sample results. When they finally did, mercury levels were high enough their scale could not accurately measure them. With those findings, Vern wasn't surprised the construction company security guards shot at me. They were not trying to kill me but shut me up. Now I'm matching levels of mercury in water with methyl mercury in blood. The higher the mercury levels, the worse the nervous system symptoms of mercury toxicity. I'm doing it in a lot of different environments where mercury is emitted or used industrially."

"Can you do that?" she asks.

"I know how, and I have the money. Vern explained the master's thesis he would write. It has to do with dams. Only a minor part of mercury in water comes from rocks—that's called elemental mercury. Industrial, coal burning, and agricultural contamination making up the bulk of the rest. Plankton use the elemental mercury to create methyl mercury which causes end organ damage in higher animals—like us. But hydroelectric diversion projects are culpable no matter what the mercury source."

"Why's that?" Sicily asks.

"That's what Vern's thesis is about. The way electricity is created through hydroelectric turbines increases acid in reservoir waters. Acidification triggers plankton to methylate more mercury. Fish eat plankton, we eat fish, methyl mercury gets incorporated into our cells. Vern's hypothesis is that fish behind dams will have more methyl mercury than those spending time in the wild. Am I going too fast? It's a lot of detail."

"Nope, I got it," Sicily says. "The mercury cycle is one of the few bits of science I know something about."

"What do you know?" Forest asks.

"I know the worst cases of methyl mercury toxicity are called Minamata disease, named for the Japanese fishing village where it was first identified... When did you meet Ellie?"

"That's where the protocols came from. They invited me to their house in Winnipeg about a year and a half ago."

"Around when Angela was out on bail and my Mom was in Canada part time?"

"That sounds about right."

"Ellie has had an interest in environmental pollution because of the danger to agricultural workers—one in particular. Also, among my favorite photojournalists is a Concerned Photographer—Eugene Smith. Somehow, security guards of Chisso—a Japanese industrial company which makes plastics that polluted Minamata Bay with mercury— ended up attacking this world famous photographer last year." Sicily could not be more facetious. "He and his wife were documenting the movement that emerged against Minamata disease."

"And now you're worried about me," Forest says.

"Mostly I'm worried about Smith's photographs—at least his wife, Aileen Mioko Smith, will finish the work, no matter how long it takes. She's like a redwood," Sicily says.

"Wow. How could you hide that you knew about mercury poisoning?"

"Well, first off, you never asked me. I learned about Minamata disease from a friend, Henry Akira, who spent the summer before college working in Japan because his father was..."

Forest interrupts, "Would Henry's name actually be Haruki?"

"Yes," she says, "but he prefers to be called Henry."

8

PACIFIC OCEAN

FALL 1959 TO 1960

ATTRACTING AN EXULTATION OF butterflies, wild flowers grew at the vacant curve of the cul-de-sac, where it seemed another home should have been. I learned to catch the delicate winged creatures then release them. The ranch house was at 8726 South Bethune Street. The neighborhood was good. You could tell because streets were named after colleges. The cul-de-sac kept Bethune from being used as a route to places other than the street. People living on our dead end were connected by it.

The neighbors called us the Grant-Marshalls. The Andrews lived across the street from our house. Theirs was a pink Spanish Mission styled place with a red terracotta tiled roof. Mr. Andrew would have been a physics professor in a different reality for a Black man. Mrs. Andrew was a busty black woman with white skin and blonde hair. They had three kids. Marian was bookish at age ten. I liked her best. Wonder Wilbur was a year older than me and a genius like his dad. Louie was elastic as a rubber band, dancing while playing and trading 45s with Lillie, who was also age eight.

Harvard Elementary School was the venue of all the cul-de-sac kids' education. Though the school was behind our house, we couldn't use that route because our backyard abutted neighbors with a none-too-friendly dog. Sunday nights everyone on the cul-de-sac would watch Ed Sullivan. On Mondays, walking to the temporary bungalow classrooms, Louie demonstrated the choreography of the Black entertainers who had been Sullivan's guest. To and from school, we practiced twisting and shouting up and down our street.

Houses on Bethune had plants cut into shapes, mostly animals, by Mr. Akira, a gardener. The Akira home was furthest from the cul-de-sac. This meant they had more access to the rest of the world. They never seemed to value that.

Mrs. Akira dressed differently at home than when she was out. Around her house, the gardener's wife wore silk gowns embroidered with flowers and mythical animals. Mr. Akira must have gained inspiration from those clothes. The Mrs. Akira out shopping wore a regular boring wardrobe. I had thought, 'If I could wear flower garden robes, I wouldn't be caught in Bermuda shorts.'

Haruki and I were in kindergarten. I was only four, having started school early, and Haruki five. Try as they might to remember his name, all his teachers and every kid on the block, except me, called him by anything starting with an 'H'—Harold, Harry, Harvey.

"If I'm going to be called something I'm not, I want to be called Henry. That's Hank Aaron's real first name," he said, showing me his baseball cards.

"Why do you wear your hair cut that short?" I asked.

"Didn't you see the cards? Baseball players always wear flat top crew cuts or a Quo Vadis haircut," he said.

In the beginning, when we tried to get Henry to walk to school with us he always said, "I have to go with my mother." This was the single rule Henry followed, otherwise he ran his own agenda.

"Then we will walk with your mother too," I said.

From then on, all the kids waited for Mrs. Akira and Henry's newborn baby brother, Tony. This is how the Grant-Marshalls began to know the whole Akira family, except for the father, Mike, who we only came to know later. By dawn, Mr. Akira's truck was always long gone, hauling hedge carving tools to the Hollywood Hills.

Henry and I were matched in wit and intellect. Before long, we were as close as a boy and girl of that age could be. More than anything, I asked questions—where Henry always listened, like a fly on the wall, absorbing. He was more philosophical than me. Ellie and Mrs. Akira, Linda, also found a natural affinity. They were the same age and spent time having tea in Linda's kitchen, imagining what their children would become. Ellie had practically written Henry's reference letter to college before he was six. Linda wanted him to go to UCLA and study science. Ultimately, Ellie and Linda were bound by the vagaries of racism and fantasies of their children's escape.

In 1940, Mike Akira and Linda had met on a San Joaquin Valley farm. They were each six years old. Their parents were crop pickers. Linda and Mike were separated when her father got a job in a shipyard. Poor working conditions resulted in this older Japanese man joining the movement for a union work place. The union organizing caused friction with the management. The 1941 bombing of Pearl Harbor was used to the company's advantage. They charged Linda's father with sedition. Proof wasn't necessary during that era because he was Japanese. He was arrested. Becoming ill in prison, he was denied expedited medical care and died.

Linda and her mother were sent to a camp called Manzanar, near Lone Pine, California.

"Summer camp for adults?" I asked Henry.

"No, it was a concentration camp," he said.

"That can't be. I'm going to ask my mother."

Henry was right and I was wrong. Linda and her mother were both citizens of the USA. Like 100,000 other interned American Japanese, ethnic origin and bigotry caused them to be held at Manzanar. There, fatherless Linda met Mike again. After Manzanar closed, the families still shared housing. Orphaned by their parents' deaths, Linda and Mike married and began a family. They found their house on Bethune Street, in the burgeoning Black tradesmen community of 1950s Los Angeles. Secure in the knowledge that citizenship alone did not confer civil or human rights in the land of their birth, the American Japanese couple had not considered themselves crossing the color line, instead acknowledging where on it they stood.

"What shipyard did your father work at?" Ellie asked Linda.

"Todd, in San Pedro," Linda said.

"My father works there now. He chose Todd because it had been unionized."

The rhythm of life on the cul-de-sac was at the mercy of the adults' work. Franklin got home from the day shift at the shipyard before Lillie and I came from school. Changed from coveralls to polyester leisure suit, he was a gentleman reading his newspaper, sipping coffee, and smoking filterless Camel cigarettes when we arrived. He supervised our homework. Before dinner I routinely planted myself on the floor next to Franklin's swivel space age recliner. We watched Walter Cronkite on the evening news, then the 'Shoot 'em ups,' which others called Westerns.

Grandmother Vanessa now worked with senior citizens. They took trips to theaters and concerts. On Saturdays, I would go with them. Unlike Lillie, who had her own set of coveralls and tools for working with Franklin, I was a prissy girl. My gloves matched my hats. The skirts of my petticoats entered rooms ahead of me. Mother's dedication to her uniform also won my notice. It was starched and white with matching nurse's cap, shoes, and stockings. Each day, she rode the bus in that costume. How she kept it clean all the way to Beverly Hills and back, I never knew.

Plenty of hand wringing happened over those white stockings. Nylon had replaced silk. Panty hose weren't yet invented.

The little clips on the garter belts fell off and got lost. Periodically, the whole family hunted all over the house for them. If you had white skin, a 'run' in a stocking might go without notice—a Black nurse was dead in the water. After the stockings were washed and draped over the bathroom towel rack, someone would invariably see a streak from the top to the toe. Stockings were expensive. Frequently, money was scraped together for the late night purchase of new white hosiery, in time for Ellie's 5AM bus to work.

Sometimes Ellie worked at Cedars Lebanon Hospital, others she worked at 'the Registry'.

"What's 'the Registry'?" I asked, while Ellie handwashed her whites in the utility room sink.

"It's part-time work," she said.

"Is that bad? I like it when you're home."

"We need to buy groceries all the time, not just sometimes," she said.

The adults on the street focused on improving their lives. They went to night school or had second jobs. The women on the cul-de-sac, including Ellie and Linda, formed a catering service. On Friday nights, they would gather in Calliope Richards's kitchen, in the house next to ours. It had the most counter space.

Theodore and Calliope had no children. Mr. Richards worked at Douglas Aircraft. During peacetime more planes were built than boats. His income was larger than that of others on the cul-de-sac. Childlessness kept the Richards's cash outflow low, leaving money for a more elaborate house. In 1960 nothing more evidenced the Richards's relative affluence than the possession of a color television. On that TV, we cul-de-sac kids first saw a toothpaste company sponsored broadcast of the Wizard of Oz.

My fear of Calliope's poor fitting glass eye, the real one having been shot out by a racist attacker in Mississippi, was compensated by her ebullient cooking. While we kids soared over the rainbow, Calliope and our mothers made a different magic in the kitchen. Satisfying catering clients required expansion of our pediatric palates. We were the taste testers, checking on the chefs' progress during commercials.

Dough pressed flat was cut in circles by the open end of a water glass. The circles were folded in rolled triangles, painted with butter and placed in the oven. Fifteen minutes later, out popped crescent rolls. Chicken livers and water chestnuts were rolled in strips of bacon, held together with toothpicks. Placed on a cookie sheet, they cooked at 450 degrees, not a degree less. Ellie had read that poorly cooked chicken carried a dangerous bacteria, overcooked was better than under. In 30 minutes, out came Rumaki.

Mrs. Akira charged Franklin with bringing home fresh tuna and hamachi fish from commercial fishers near the shipyard. She taught the other caterers to make sticky rice with vinegar and sugar, and to slice the raw fish and avocados thin. It was all rolled into dark green parchments of roasted seaweed, then cut into sliced bite-sized flowers. Mrs. Akira wore flowers. Mr. Akira grew flowers. It wasn't surprising the family Akira also ate flowers.

Ellie read measurements and instructions aloud for things like beef bourguignon, "Julia says, 'It should be served in a chafing dish.'" I wondered, 'Who is this Julia, and how is a chafing dish different from any other?' For Christmas and birthdays, the women would give one another chafing dishes, bone china, and elegant flatware. Combined, they had cutlery and plates to serve two hundred people, the size of a good Beverly Hills' Bar Mitzvah.

The caterers wore black dresses with Ellie's white nursing stockings and starched white aprons. Ellie always looked a bit different from the other women. Her hair was close cut, not pressed or pinned up. In the early 1960s the hairstyle was called a 'Makeba,' named for the famed exiled South African singer. Ellie also presented plenty of boob in her choice of black dresses, having well more than the average bust to show. She was in a starched white buttoned up uniform all week and refused to be in a black one all weekend.

During one of the catering jobs, Ellie met Milton and Dorothy. Milton struck up a conversation with her. Ellie leaned against the counter, looking at a painting of a mermaid. It turned out to be an original Marc Chagall.

"Do you know anything about art?" Milton asked. As it happened, Ellie did. Her college in Oklahoma taught her about Renaissance art. She learned about Impressionism, Modern, and Abstract on her own. Figuring he was another pandering old white man, she kept her butt out of his reach.

"Do you make art yourself, paint... sculpt?" Milton asked.

Ellie looked askance. No one had ever asked her such a thing. "No, but I enjoy it," she said. Milton invited her to come back at another time and see his work. 'Yeah, right,' she thought, 'here it comes, he's going to ask me to model nude for him.' Ellie was worried about being too flippant. Odd as he was, this catering job was surely in this man's home.

"If you make art, you appreciate it more. Also, if you make art you surrender a part of your soul to the universe, where it belongs," Milton said. "Yes, you should visit my studio, we'll start you out on water colors."

'This is a new one...' Ellie thought, while politely saying, "I have one day off a week and I spend that with my daughter."

"How old is your daughter?" he asked.

"She's four."

"Bring her with you." He waived to his wife, Dorothy, who joined them from across the room.

Dorothy's full name was Dorothy Parker. She wasn't actually Milton's wife but on a break from her real marriage. The lady was quite a famous poet and satirist who also wrote movies. Milton was both wealthy and chivalrous. Despite Dorothy not being the typical damsel in distress, he was compelled to protect her, during what was an emotionally tough time, because she was a great artist in her medium—as well as lots of fun. Dorothy was also a humanitarian wrapped in wolf's clothing. Seeing the exploitation of children on film sets for thirty years, she had developed an interest in studio tutoring. She found techniques to help kid actors learn to read quickly—in case they never got back to school. Dorothy told Ellie, "I'm sure if my reading approach works for actors, it will work even better for bona fide children."

The day after meeting Milton, Vanessa was annoyed by Ellie's chatter about the new friends. "Those people might get Ellie in trouble. I'm not saying I agree with the Hollywood Blacklist. But if famous people get persecuted, imagine what could happen to a young Negro husbandless nurse with a child," Vanessa said.

"What's a 'blacklist'? We're Black. Are we on it?" I asked at the Sunday dinner of leftovers from the previous night's catered party. My question tickled Grandfather Franklin.

"I don't think we are, though one never knows. A 'blacklist' is a list or a register of things or people who are being denied privileges, service, or recognition of their work," he said.

"Is that like Mr. Andrews not being a college teacher when he should be?" I had heard adults say that.

"In a way—around the time your Mommy was born, a group now called the House Un-American Committee has been trying to keep different actors, writers, film people—along with many academics like Mr. Andrews—from enjoying the rights most American citizens have."

"Like right from wrong, or like left from right?"

Grandfather laughed because all applied. "A right is also an idea. It is something that you are born with, even if someone tries to stop you from using it, it's still your 'right.'"

"Like what?" I asked.

Grandfather could see by my expression that his watered down version was not going to satisfy me. He launched into a summary of the structure of the constitution. Grandmother Vanessa groaned as he moved into the First Amendment. Lillie asked to be excused, but she had to help clear up first. Ellie put her elbows on the table and cradled her chin in her palms to listen. I mimicked her.

"It prohibits the making of any law limiting a person from choosing or not choosing a religion, blocking freedom of speech, freedom of the press, interfering with the right to peaceably assemble or to gather in protest, like the ones about Black people having the right to vote," Grandfather said.

"Are Mommy's new friends on a blacklist, like grandmother says?"

"I don't know and neither does your Grandmother. The 'blacklist' she is talking about has a lot of Hollywood workers on it, because ideas shared in stories have so much power," he said.

"Are the ideas of the people on the list bad?" I asked.

"Some people on the Hollywood Blacklist have ideas that might even help."

Vanessa interrupted her husband, reaching in front of him to take his plate, she said, "If you all want dessert, discuss this later." She meant years later. Vanessa had come a long way since burning my mother's books. Yet, her lifelong task was still protecting Ellie from trouble, while Ellie's penchant was to seek it out.

Contrary to Vanessa's wishes, Franklin capitulated to church only on Easter and Christmas. He called it his biannual 'just-in-case' visit. Ellie worked on Saturdays catering and on weekdays or nights as a nurse. That was her excuse for not going to church. She and Grandfather had their own gathering—coffee, politics, news, and analyzing a variety of racist and classist things endured on their jobs.

Lillie and I attended Sunday School because Vanessa insisted. Kids' classes were in the McCarthy Memorial Christian Church annex. Adults 'worshiped' in the main sandcastle, a Gothic Revival sanctuary. The ceiling was cathedral high. I was seduced by the beauty of the stained glass window depicting a pensive Christ on Mount Olive. My wish to examine that work of art closer was empowered the Sunday all of us children were herded from the annex into the main building. Climbing into a pew behind Lillie, Franklin and Ellie slid in next to us. I couldn't imagine what was going on.

The pastor, Reverend Kring Allen, had seemed a white man to me before. Now I had doubts. He was yelling from the pulpit, "We are angry and will stand for no more." He continued on, talking about 'Negro' and other college students who had put their lives on the line to peacefully desegregate a lunch counter in Greensboro, North Carolina. It was February 1960.

Instead of heading to the cul-de-sac after Pastor Allen's speech, Ellie drove me north on Western. One of the catering clients offered to sell Ellie a 1956 Chrysler Imperial for cheap. Grandfather checked it out. That morning Ellie made the purchase with the money from catering. The car's upholstery was covered with embossed crowns. The Imperial had room for lots of people and food trays. Gone would be Ellie's bus rides to the hospital for work. Nursing, Ellie had seen enough vehicular disasters involving children that I always had to sit in the back seat. When we crossed Wilshire Blvd everyone was White and, by their cars, peculiarly wealthy. I wondered how they would respond to demonstrations at lunch counters in their neighborhoods.

"Where are we going?" I asked.

"If you don't want to go I can take you back to the cul-de-sac," Ellie said, glancing at me through the rearview mirror.

Ellie was my favorite person. I never wanted to go home.

The Imperial climbed the vertical driveway. The house at the end of the road seemed even larger than the sandcastle church. Ellie rang the bell. A Black woman wearing dark slacks and a pink cashmere sweater came to the door. Casually, she said, "Hi, I'm Carla." Carla led us into a large room. It was filled with leather sofas and armchairs. A White lady sat on the sofa barefoot, reading a book and smoking a cigarette. The cigarette was stubbed out immediately on seeing me. She introduced herself as 'Dorothy,' holding her hand out to shake mine.

"It is a pleasure to meet you Miss—do you have a last name that I should call you?" I asked.

"Darling, I've been called a lot of names. You would get confused—best if you just use 'Dorothy.'" Stacks of books were piled on a nearby coffee table. They had bright colored covers with drawings. Dorothy patted the seat next to her suggesting I should sit.

"Do you like books?" Dorothy asked.

"My mother and grandfather are teaching me to read because my kindergarten teacher moves too slowly."

"I can help with that," Dorothy said. She turned to Ellie adding, "Milton is in the studio. He's been painting all morning."

"I'll check to be sure he hasn't fallen off the ladder again," Ellie said.

"Please. We will entertain ourselves here fine," Dorothy said.

Ellie winked at me, then headed toward another building through the garden. Carla brought cookies and placed them near the books.

It was dark when Dorothy and I were eventually interrupted by Ellie and Milton. Milton was covered in different colors of paint, toes to nose, as was my mother. My laugh infected everyone.

"You look like the people in the books I learned to read," I said.

"You learned to read?" Ellie asked. She wiped her forehead with the back of her hand, spreading yellow paint over her brow.

"Dorothy taught me."

"Well, let's hear," Ellie said.

I opened a book and began, "One fish, two fish, red fish, blue fish..."

After that, Ellie and I visited Dorothy and Milton following Sunday School. I read more Dr. Seuss, Stuart Little, and about Charlotte the spider and her pig friend Wilbur. We would eat, do crossword puzzles, and play Scrabble. Dorothy and I were always a team.

9

MINIMATA BAY

AUGUST 1973

SLIGHTLY SHIVERING, SICILY SAYS, "Henry is as close to a brother as I have ever had." Forest senses more to this story. Illuminated by distant stars, the hard floor of Humboldt University's balcony, where they still sit, is colder now. He removes his jean shirt, slipping her arms into its sleeves.

"I fell in love with your mother the day I met her."

"You can't be faulted for that. Ellie is a superhero. I've always known it."

"I know what you're talking about. The first time I arrived at Vern and Ellie's house by the river, guests were leaving. It was the end of a fundraising social for the Defense and Aid Fund for South Africa. Yeah, it was '72. The head of the fund in London got word from Dulce September. Dulce was still under a banning order from the South African apartheid government and couldn't leave for the UK. But she still managed to get word out. A married couple was arrested by the apartheid government. Provisions had to be made for their children and defense.

"Ellie had to double book herself that night. I was late. Surprised by the number of people pouring from the house, I knocked on the front door only when it seemed all the guests

SEPTEMBER WILLIAMS

were gone. She opened the door, gave me a hug, and told me how much she had looked forward to meeting me.

"Vern was driving people home. She took me to the kitchen where she was cleaning. I asked if she needed help. She said eating leftovers was all the help she needed and made me a plate at lightning speed. The event was a cocktail party with appetizers, supper of curry, and desserts—cream puffs and Baklava. It had been years since I had seen such good food. Clearing a space on the counter, she wanted me near her in the kitchen while she worked. Then she got straight to business, explaining that the history of colonialism links all aboriginal peoples, including those in apartheid South Africa. Now I was in heaven, always having held a similar belief.

"When she launched into the thick of mercury issues, for a moment I was a deer in the headlights. She trusted I would catch up and didn't bother to slow down. Ellie went deeper into the science of mercury than I had expected. She raised the specter of Koch's Postulates."

"Whose postulates?" Sicily asks.

"Koch's... They are the four criteria needed to prove any specific thing has caused a disease. I remembered and recited them as I learned while studying biology in college. That's when Ellie lowered the boom. The postulates, she explained, are the path to proving or disproving Minamata disease exists outside of Japan. According to Ellie, all I had to do was saddle up my horse and get on the road. If I did, everyone from South African miners trapped in dangerous jobs by apartheid to First Nation people of the White Dog and Grassy Narrows Nations in northwest Ontario would be grateful.

"I was thirsty. A glass of water appeared before me without my having asked. Then Ellie continued. She made it all sound easy. Get blood and water levels of people with and without symptoms over time and in different locations. I would need a reliable lab and a way to get them transported. Then of course there were the research protocols. 'Me?' I asked Ellie. You know what she said?"

"Ellie's my mother—she said, 'If not you, then who?'"

"Exactly—I took a minute and looked around the kitchen. Ellie's way is to use what she has, and to reuse what other's would waste. I saw pickled water melons and cucumber rinds in mason jars on shelves. Dandelions made wine, tea, and greens. Sage, mint, and lavender hung from the ceiling between the pots and pans for use later in the winter. Asking for a napkin, Ellie handed me a cloth serviette, neatly folded in a triangle, instead of a paper one. Winking she told me we shouldn't be making garbage, and if we do, we should have to go out in the cold to throw it away. There was no trash can in the kitchen— such a radical idea. That's when I decided to trust your mother completely.

"She wrote the names and numbers of the Japanese Minamata disease scientists and put a star next to 'Haruki' followed by Henry in parentheses. Ellie interviewed, recruited, and assigned me while she cleaned the kitchen until it gleamed, all before I ate dessert."

⌢ ⌣

Forest shifts his place against the stone pillar of the balcony. Sicily climbs on his lap, her thighs tight against the sides of his chest. Sensing she isn't intentionally being comely but wanting to be warmer, he wraps his arms around her, resisting stealing a kiss before he continues,

"At that time I was a producer on a show about Indigenous issues for the CBC, out of Winnipeg," Forest continues.

"What's the CBC?" Sicily asks.

"The Canadian Broadcasting Company—as I got closer to exposing the developers at the gravel pit mines, I started drawing more heat," he says.

"Heat?"

"I was rocking the boat. My executive producers decided I was a liability to them, or they to me. They let me go. It's okay because the guy they hired is a close friend. His position has been helpful. Sometimes they still carry my freelance stories."

Sicily squints quietly, absorbing.

"You've run out of questions," Forest says.

"Don't you wish. Why is your money in a Swiss bank?" Sicily asks.

"Jorge—"

"Jorge?" Sicily is surprised.

"While at Carlton University I met Jorge. His first degree is in finance. Then I got my master in journalism and he his law degree. We had been wild and crazy together during school and remained close. Jorge advised me, 'Save some money for your family. They will eventually come around. Invest half and put some in a Swiss Bank.'

"I lived in Europe as an exchange student for a year, France and Switzerland. After my master's degree I returned to Europe for a year to hone my language and journalistic skills. And yes, that's why I speak both French and German, and a few others. I'm good at languages."

"Why didn't you tell me that when I asked you about your French?"

"It's not my way to share personal details," he says. Sicily stares, refusing to take that bone, forcing him to continue, "My first deposit with M. Baise was about five years ago, right after the sale of the land, before I knew about mercury. As investments paid off, I periodically transferred profits to the Swiss account. Expecting a layover in Zürich, our flight was delayed longer than I imagined. Needing to run the errand at the bank, by then I already knew I wanted to spend every minute possible with you."

Shifting her position on Forest's lap, Sicily feels him harden between her legs. But she manages to stay on topic, asking, "What will you do with the research results?"

"If they are what we think they are, I'll publish in the science journals, then springboard from those to blow the whistle."

"Who will you expose?"

"Governments, contractors, the paper industry, mining, hydroelectric power companies, coal burners—I have to get finished. I can't take the isolation much longer."

"Isolation?"

"From community and family—also, lots of folks think I'm nuts or worse," Forest says.

"What's 'worse'?" she asks.

"Either I'm the devil incarnate, or I am right. Proving mercury pollution will take away people's livelihoods, working in mines, fishing, tourism, hydroelectric plants, farming, fish canneries, and paper factories. These are jobs people exist on in the far north, if they can get 'em."

"Isn't it better than having your children sick or dead?" she asks.

"Some don't agree. They gotta have a way to live before they die."

"I see."

"I'm most worried for babies in-utero, concentrating mercury when mums eat contaminated fish and drink polluted water." Forest sobs. Seeing his tears overflow, Sicily presses her cheek against his to share them.

"Someone will always be trying to stop me until I go public. Stuff is gonna get uglier. Folks I care about are not safe around me, including you."

Adjusting her position on his lap, Sicily's hands are on his shoulders. She pushes his back against the wall, as if banging some sense into him. "Don't beat around the bush. You think someone will try to kill you," she says.

"Only the story, I would be collateral damage. Listen, if anything happens to me, Jorge's your man. He's going to ask you to go with a group to Czechoslovakia after the festival. I think you should. Prague is full of bridges, water, and gypsies."

"Are you coming?" she asks.

"No, I have to get back to work. I'll let Ellie and Vern know. They won't be surprised," he says.

"Where?"

"Everywhere—I need you to promise me something."

"Depends on what it is," she says.

"Promise no matter what, you won't hate me."

"I will always be yours. I will always love you. You should know, it is my considered opinion that loving someone enough to let them go is for cowards."

Sicily sleeps on the bottom bunk in her dorm. Hyper-erotic dreams about Forest have become her norm. He's the gift that keeps on giving. The current dream touch, caressing her breast, feels heavy handed. She opens her eyes to find a ruddy-faced hulking white man groping her. She is not dreaming. Her screaming alerts her bunk mate, who subsequently wails like a ship's whistle. The man covers her mouth. She bites him hard. He recoils, allowing her to hit him square in the jaw. Diving over him, out of the bed, she pulls him by his legs backward. Her assailant bangs his chin as he hits the bed rail and then again the floor. Blood squirts from his balloon tight face. Then her rage kicks him everywhere. Sicily is an errant pacifist.

Wearing only their underwear, Jorge and Forest burst through the door. Forest pulls Sicily off the man, who is now curled into a ball on the floor. Jorge restrains the perpetrator in a police hold with a knee in the back. Sicily is determined to finish her mission of murdering the pararapist. Forest hugs her from behind, her legs and arms flailing.

"I can't let you kill him, sweetheart. The prisons are not nice here," Forest says.

"Good, because that's where he is going," Sicily says, still struggling to break free. "The government here needs to stop worrying about gay people and focus on real criminals like this bastard!"

The girl from Vancouver still blows. Camille comes in from the hall, surveys the mess, and assists the whistler on the top bunk to inhale. Roxley follows too late for any substantive help, true to his character. Wearing a bow tie and carrying his clipboard, it is clear he has bothered to dress for a middle of the night emergency. "This is what happens when you don't lock your door," he says.

Without warning, Forest releases Sicily and pins Roxley to the wall by the neck, saying, "Go get the fucking police." His volume rattles the light fixtures. Roxley can't move because Forest won't bring himself to let the man's neck go. Jorge still holds the criminal on the floor. Camille is busy with the whistler, and Sicily has no desire to intervene. Luckily, Pascal arrives in time to pry Forest's hands from the rat's neck. Roxley runs out, presumably to seek the authorities.

This is the fourth assault by a gang of German men invading the dorms for the purpose of molesting women. Swearing previous victims to secrecy by inventing his fictitious involvement in laying a dragnet, Roxley hopes to prevent sullying his dubious reputation.

Jorge is decisive while others wallow in emotion. The men in the delegation will share rooms with the women. Camille and Pascal knock on doors, rousing people to switch beds.

When things calm down and Sicily is showered, dried, and covered with lotion and oils by Forest, they crawl into the lower bunk together. Forest asks,

"How the hell did you learn to street fight like that?"

"The hard way," Sicily says, turning to the wall.

"I am supposed to protect you."

"You couldn't have known." She yawns.

"But there are some things I can anticipate," he says, watching her sleep.

⁀ ‿

Forest and Sicily's pas de deux is selected as one of the performances closing the festival at Alexander Platz. Stealing every minute together, the two miss the Canadian delegates' bus to the performance square. They run out of the Humboldt

University gate and flag down a passing bus. The driver waves them aboard. Settling in the last two open seats, Sicily says, "... Must be millions of extra people in Berlin today."

"Yes," Forest says, oddly distant. He looks out at the crowds on the sidewalks. Someone taps Sicily on the shoulder from behind, then bends down to whisper in her ear,

"Are you Sici?"

"Yes," Sicily turns to see a Chicana with a broad smile. Without noticing, they have jumped on a bus transporting American delegates.

"I'm Vicki, and there is someone who would like to say, 'Hi' at the back of the bus."

"Do you think you could look after these for a minute?" she asks Vicki, pointing her chin toward the feathers. Vicki nods. Sicily and Forest protect their balance while they weave toward the rear of the moving bus. Sliding into Vicki's empty seat, Sicily throws her arms around Angela Davis. The two talk quickly, covering everything from earrings to parents, stuffing chapters into a minute.

"This is Forest—he's my dance partner," Sicily says.

"Good to meet you, Forest," Angela says, giving him a hug as well.

The bus grinds to a stop. "I think this is where we get off," Sicily says, kissing Angela on both cheeks.

"Break a leg," Angela says, "—sorry, that's for actors, not dancers."

"You too," Sicily says. The lovers zip up the aisle, bundling portions of the headdress between them. They leap off the bus. The feathers swirling around them, the two dancers appear to fly. They shift into a full run toward the stage.

As they take their places, Forest rips a piece from the feathered train of his headdress. Sicily gasps. "My sister made it, and she will fix it. Don't worry, our love can only honor the Great Spirit," he says, tying the strand around her waist. He steps onto the stage and into his solo. She is mesmerized by him, nearly missing her cue. When the spotlight captures the two, their eyes lock on one another instead of the thousands watching them. In her final move, Sicily improvises. The Firebird offers her Prince the feathers from her waist. Her spotlight fades, while his expands to the beat of his drum. He sings in Ojibwa. The sun drops to the horizon. Catching her breath, still on bowed knee, Sicily sees the twinkling glass beads and the virtue of the Maltese Cross reflecting from Forest's neck.

The crowd of thirty-thousand claps—not the random clap of a concert audience but in unison, as a sign of solidarity. Violins rise, then come the brass horns as the applause subsides. Multiple search lights circle the massive audience of youths to find an International Youth Orchestra at its center. The musicians play the opening measures of *Beethoven's Ninth Symphony*, the symphony of revolutionary form, personal struggle, and celebrating the joy of friendship. The cast of the final performance grab hands, bowing as one.

Under the cloak of the first movement's score, Forest and Sicily are the last of the performers to melt off the stage. Carrying their shoulder bags and feathers, they almost forget they have given the performance of their lives before thousands. They are reminded when mobbed by autograph hounds. Forest shouts, "Not tonight. It's our last night." He grabs Sicily with one hand, using his other to hold the feathers high above his head as the two run. The crowd of well-wishers reluctantly parts to let them pass. Little German kids in Pioneer Scout blue shirts, waving autograph books, eventually block their escape.

"How can we reject these tiny hosts who count on us to tear down the Berlin Wall?" Sicily says. The children share small round buttons from their shirts. The fans want their guests to take a piece of East Germany back to North America with them, while the lovers want their last moments together.

Later that night, Sicily will be leaving to spend four weeks in Czechoslovakia. Camille and Pascal, like Forest, also have obligations back in Canada. "I know what to do," Forest says, frozen in the horde of well-wishing kinder. Whispering a thankful prayer in Annishinaabe, he throws the dance bonnet high into the air. It arches away, the feathers taking wing, soaring over the crowd, evoking awe. The fans follow the floating feathers.

The last movement of the Symphony, the "Ode to Joy", begins. The delegates sing the choral, each in their native language, as they practiced in the dorms. Learnt from Ellie, Sicily has known the piece since childhood. The sky lights with electricity, heralding an impending storm and saluting the symphony born of like energy. Rain falls hard. The mass of youths stand singing in praise of the moment,

> "All Thy works with joy surround Thee, earth and heaven reflect thy rays, ..."

Sicily lets go of Forest's hand and reaches into her shoulder bag, finding her camera. She raises it to her eye, photographing wet compatriots, dancing for the rain. CLICK, CLICK, CLICK.

> "Stars and angels sing around Thee, center of unbroken praise..."

Sicily pulls the camera from her eye to find she is separated from her lover.

> "Field and forest, vale and mountain, flowery meadow, flashing sea, Singing bird and flowing fountain call us to rejoice in Thee..."

Only a moment passes before that intimacy of friend, lover, and brother is swept by the crowd onto a train. The doors close. Forest and Sicily, separated, touch the glass from opposite sides. "Forest, Forest!" Sicily screams. The engine pulls away. He's gone. The music stops. Sicily's profound sorrow is swallowed by the thunder and the rain.

1 0

RED RIVER WATERSHED

SEPTEMBER 1973

ENTHRALLED IN THEIR LOVE affair, the ballerina and powwow dancer have neglected exchanging contact
information earlier on, as common sense might have dictated.
On Sicily's return to Humboldt University, Forest is nowhere to
be found. Jorge insists she and he still must board the Prague
train that night. Making light of Forest's absence, Jorge assures
Sicily, "He will find you in Canada."

The American and the Chilean-Quebecois duo spend weeks
together in Czechoslovakia. Sicily logs more hours with Jorge
than she had with Forest. She mostly pumps her travel companion for information about her lover. At the end of the journey, she and Jorge wait in the Prague Airport. He returns to
Chile, while she begins a life in Canada. Regarding Forest's
whereabouts, Jorge laughs,

"I can't even give you my own address," he says then promises to look for Forest's sister's contacts in his belongings on
arriving in Santiago.

"Of course—how could I have forgotten. Forest has a sister," Sicily says.

"He always moves around, but she is stable," Jorge says.

"What's her name? Where does she live?"

"Laura, and she lives—honestly, I can't say—in Canada, the middle, far up north."

"Is her last name Odjig too?" Sicily asks.

"Different fathers... She has some type of license, nursing maybe. No, Forest told me because sometimes lawyers need one. She's a private detective."

"Also an artist..." Sicily recalls the beading on Forest's thrown away dance headdress.

"Right, a bead working detective," Jorge says.

Jorge's flight is called for boarding. While hugging, Sicily suddenly lets go of him.

"Take this," she says, gleefully shoving a wad of bills into the breast pocket of Jorge's fatigue jacket. "Turn it to dollars when you change planes in Zürich."

"Where did you get this?" Jorge asks.

"Good North American money saves lives in certain circumstances. That's something I learned from comrades this summer. It should be close to twelve hundred."

"And...?"

"It came from Forest. He wants you to have it," she says. Struggling to button Jorge's cashstuffed pocket she thinks, 'I'm becoming Forest's money launderer.' Patting Jorge's chest, after kissing him on both cheeks, she turns him around, pushing him to march toward his plane. She yells, "Thank you for getting me drunk in that wine hall. Without you, I'll never do that again."

"And you for dancing to Motown with gypsies and me, then breaking me out of the thirteenth castle tour," he says, looking back at her over his shoulder.

Sicily watches Jorge disappear on the gangway. She finishes, whispering, "I wouldn't have been able to endure the sorrow of the memorial at Lidice without you..." Wiping her eyes with the back of her hand, looking up, she sees Jorge appear again next to her.

"And without you, I never would have seen the crown jewels that killed that Nazi bastard with a curse. Though I may not believe in God, now I believe in curses," he says, shoving something into her hand. "Sicily Marshall, I expect things of you." Off he runs, down the ramp to the plane, blowing a kiss to the flight attendant holding the door.

Opening her hand, Sicily stares at the contents, trying to make sense of what she sees. It is Ellie's Maltese Cross. Jorge has accepted the responsibility of her security. This is a logical way for the talisman to be returned. But it means the two men had to have met that night after she lost Forest at the train. Jorge got the cross from Forest. In no combination could the details of Forest's disappearance make her comfortable. Herded to the Czechoslovakian Soviet-made plane, prepared for the long haul back to Montreal, she mulls the pieces in her mind.

On September 11, 1973, Sicily arrives in Montreal from Prague at 6AM, melancholy and alone. It is the place were she had first found Forest. Changing planes she flies the Canadian Pacific Airline to Winnipeg, the capital of the Province of Manitoba. Winnipeg sits at the confluence of the Assiniboine, Manitoba Seine and Red rivers. On descent, Sicily notices the three branches merge, leaving the city to the North as one single waterway, the Red. In the distance, the integrated flow sweeps through the prairie emptying into Lake Winnipeg. The watershed, she has learned from Forest, eventually meets Hudson Bay and the Arctic Ocean. Now directly below is Manitoba's romanesque, Golden Boy sculpture adorned, domed provincial legislature building. Nearby tree lined streets already slip into autumn colors.

Ellie and Vern wait at the door when Sicily clears customs. The three hug. Her mother will not let Sicily go. Whispering into her daughter's cheek, Ellie asks, "Did you meet any Chileans?"

"Yes," Sicily says with exuberance, "we were close at the festival and I traveled to Prague with one in particular, Jorge."

Ellie, barely audible says, "My Darling Baby, the reports are that most of the Chilean students, returning home from the festival, were killed this morning..." She continues, explaining that the Chilean coup is occurring right now. The military junta of conservative Augusto Pinochet is overthrowing the democratically elected Chilean government of President Salvador Allende. Ellie's mouth continues moving. Sicily hears nothing else. She shutters and screams. Her mother absorbs her daughter's wail into her own chest and heart. Sicily abruptly becomes silent, eyes blinking, lips smacking, then she falls, seizing.

Laying on the car's back seat, her typical post-seizure sequelae yields a heightened environmental sensibility. All colors are saturated to the point of florescence. She sees through the car window her new house, #1 Creighton. The sloping front yard, is filled with wild ferns and untamed yellow petalled black-eyed susan, extending to the river's shore. Tiger lilies and pink peonies line the walkway to the combined mudroom and sun porch. She glances at the neighboring house on her left where an old boat, a cabin cruiser, sits in the driveway. Raining wetness confers a luminance on the dry-docked vessel and all else.

"Pretty here," Sicily says, flatly.

"It's a common working class prairie house," Vern explains, ushering her into the living room. A large picture window covering half the wall is reminiscent of the family home on the cul-de-sac, in Los Angeles. House plants everywhere make the living room an extension of the outside tree canopy. Washed turnip greens drain in the kitchen sink. The place smells of ginger, cardamon, cinnamon, pepper, turmeric, and garam masala—curry.

"Darling Baby, did you remember to take all of your medications?" her mother asks.

"I may have forgotten a few doses over the past weeks," Sicily says, ashamed.

"Take an extra dose now. I will check in with one of the doctors we know from the Defense and Aid Fund. He'll know if other adjustments should be made before you are enrolled in the National Health System. With regular sleep and medicines you'll be okay."

"May I be excused?" Sicily asks, groggy.

"Let's get you to your room, you must be suffering terribly," Ellie says.

"I did well at the festival."

⁀ ‿

"It's not surprising that you should have a seizure, exhausted from the flight and shocked by the tragedy," Her stepfather comments, climbing the steep stairs to the second floor ahead of her. Sicily thinks Vern is kind, but she cannot find the words to say it. She sits on the bed next to her bag. Digging deep in the satchel she pauses on finding handfuls of buttons from well-wishing German children. She fondles one button, then drops it back in the sack. Unearthing the medicine bottle, shaking a tablet into her hand, she puts it in her mouth. It sticks to her parched tongue until rinsed down with a shot of water, brought by Vern. She lies down and closes her eyes. Vern covers her with a blanket, shutting the door as he leaves.

Her little bed is in a small rectangular room. A similarly shaped window is draped by the red foliage of a large maple tree. Wading the jumble of her sorrows with her disadvantaged brain, she dozes again. Nurse Ellie prevents seizure recurrence by rousing her daughter to take her medication at twelve hour intervals, for two days.

On the third day, Sicily flies out of bed. Her sense returns. She finds her parents in the dining space off the kitchen—a breakfast room. The only window comprises the entire wall facing the river.

"Would you like some coffee, Sici?" Vern asks, pulling out a chair for her.

"Please," she says.

Ellie, sitting at the table, is dressed for work in a white nursing uniform. She takes one of her daughter's hands in her own and kisses it.

"I need help," Sicily says.

"What sort?" Ellie asks.

"Do you know how I can find Forest? Jorge, his friend, our friend, is dead."

Vern shrugs his shoulders. Carefully constructing her response, Ellie speaks,

"It is not as easy to say as I wish it were."

"Why? He must live somewhere. You do know him, he told me. Has something happened?" Sicily's eyes fill with tears.

"Forest is likely fine. He is, well, nomadic, having no known address... not to us anyway."

"Momma, what does that mean? Is he homeless?"

"No, he is not homeless. It's the opposite, he lives everywhere. Pinning him down requires catching him in his irregular orbit."

"How do you expect me to believe you don't know where he is?" Sicily says. Opening her hand, she shows Ellie the Maltese Cross. "My safety depended on a man you can't locate? He could have been an axe murderer."

Ellie takes the cross from her daughter and fastens it to her own neck. "How did you come to know he had this?"

"He told me about it because he didn't want to be lying by omission."

"Perhaps when he returned it to you, you should have asked where he could be located." Ellie's tone suggests her daughter's inquiry is now tedious. It's almost certain to Ellie that Forest would not have given Sicily such information.

"I gave it back to Forest, so he could return it to you."

"Yet, you have it," Ellie says.

"Forest gave it to Jorge when he left. Jorge gave it to me when he boarded the plane for..." Sicily chokes.

"Still, I am not able to tell that which I do not know. That is perhaps also why you don't know it either," Ellie says, placing her hand over her daughter's resting on the table.

"He will show up, he always does," Vern says.

"He did send us a card," Ellie says, riffling a stack of mail on an armoire behind her. She produces a postcard with a photo of the only part of the River Spree with no barbed wire from the Berlin Wall.

"He did?" Sicily asks, her expression a mixture of glee and disturbance.

"'Dear Folks, S is well, headed to P. In good hands...'" Ellie finishes reading and passes the postcard to Sicily.

"Where's the postmark?" Sicily asks, flipping the card over.

"He didn't mail it," Ellie says.

"He drops them in our post box or has someone do it for him," Vern clarifies.

"Why?"

"It's important to his work that he is not easily located," Vern says.

"I know where he will be next month," Ellie says, unsure how much Forest had confided to Sicily.

"Next month? That won't help now. This is absurd," Sicily says.

"No, Darling Baby, this is Forest." Ellie scrutinizes her daughter, intuiting Forest's and Sicily's relationship is deeper than that of protector and his charge. As a mother, she is not sure she likes the idea. As a political activist, she knows she does not. "First, let's take care of other business, over which we have some control," Ellie says.

Sicily has pressing problems. Her acceptance to the School of the Queen's Ballet is contingent on two things, a successful audition and having completed 'Upper School'. News to Sicily, in most of Canada finishing grade 13, not grade 12, means you have finished Upper School. Joanna, Sicily's dance teacher in San Francisco, had omitted this detail.

"The audition is scheduled for Friday," Vern says.

"Friday? What is today?" Sicily asks.

"Wednesday, that gives you two days."

"It's not enough."

"It has to be, because that is when it is," Vern says.

Sicily is quiet, a full minute. Her parents assess her consciousness closely.

"Is there a performance of the Queen's between now and then?" Sicily asks. The young woman realizes that watching others dance might be the only thing she can control at this moment.

"We got you the last seat. The curtain is at 8PM tonight," Ellie says, shuffling the stack of mail. Locating the single ticket, she passes it to her daughter.

"Gisselle," Sicily reads. She knows this story. It's about a woman who dies of despair, after losing the man she loves.

1 1

ASSINBOINE RIVER

OCTOBER 1973

A WIRY THIN WHITE woman, aging gracefully, wears a simple black dress with long sleeves and matching pumps. She sits at a table. Next to her is Victor Benson, principal male dancer of the Queen's Ballet, 'The Black Nureyev'. Up close he is a giant among dancers in stature and talent. Recalling Benson's performance two nights before, Sicily wants to vomit. Her skill set is completely mismatched for this dance company. Worse, the audition setting is too formal for the barefoot modern dance piece she had planned. The music, Miles Davis's Sketches of Spain, will not match if she changes her dance from Modern to Ballet.

The damned mirrors lining the walls magnify her ineptitude as she ties her ankle ribbons. Inopportunely, the glass also recalls making love with Forest. There is an 1836 upright Ivors and Pond piano in the far corner of the room. The pianist looks as old. She walks reverently toward the musician. "Please, sir, can you play Erik Satie's first Gymnopedie?" she asks. He nods his head without smirking, though he should have given her unimaginative choice of audition score.

The woman wearing the pumps says, "Sicily Marshall." It is not a question, a welcome, or an introduction, only a statement. Never having had a seizure while dancing, under such pressure Sicily thinks, 'This might be the first time.' She starts with Center Moves, Pliés—first through fifth—demi then grande. Pas de chat—another, another, followed by a full Jeté, an arabesque, and lots of ballet improvisation. The music ends twelve whole minutes short of the audition requirements.

Launching into a ragtime version of the second Gymnopedie, the pianist surprises Sicily. He expects her to follow. She does, breaking into the Cake Walk, then a Turkey Trot, finishing with the Grizzly Bear. Forest is her playful imaginary partner. The musician drags her back to formal ballet with an atmospheric third Gymnopedie, filling the mandatory fifteen minutes. She rests.

"We have your information," the woman with the pumps says. Neither she nor Victor bother to dismiss Sicily. They make no eye contact with the dancer or, for that matter, with one another. Breathless, the ballerina picks up her bag. The pianist refuses to catch her glance of appreciation. She walks out of the audition hall, certain the need to complete grade 13 is now moot.

Two weeks later the phone rings at the Creighton house. Leaning against the wall, looking out the living room window, Sicily answers.

"Is this Sicily Marshall?" a man's voice asks.

"May I ask who's calling?" Sicily asks, still looking through the glass at the river.

"I apologize that it has taken this long to reach you."

"May I ask with whom I am speaking?"

"This is Victor, from the Queen's Ballet. We delayed making you an offer because there is a limit on the number of foreign students we can accept."

"I understand." She is disappointed.

"We were delighted when your teacher in San Francisco told us your stepfather is Canadian. It makes a world of difference."

"Yes, I am a landed immigrant," she says.

"Joanna also reminded us that high school only goes to grade 12 in the USA."

"I realize that's another problem."

"If you're willing to complete your upper school requirements simultaneous with your first year of scholarship, we can work something out. It will be difficult. You will still be required to understudy or dance in the Corps de Ballet several times per season," Victor says.

⁓ ‿

The walls of the University Collegiate are constructed of sandstone blocks extracted from local quarries in the 1800s, near the end of the British Regency Period. On her first day, Sicily looks at those walls closely. Seeing trilobite fossils, she hopes that archaism is not reflected in the school's educational approach. The Collegiate program will give her simultaneous credits for grade 13 and the first year of a college degree. She must maintain at least a B average. "Blow this year, I blow everything," she mutters as the class bell rings, tossing her into the throngs of rushing students.

The Collegiate is a mile from the ballet school. Both are on Portage Avenue. Several times a week Sicily traverses the distance between the venues. Halfway between the two locations is Broadway Street, an artery running to the Manitoba Legislature—a 1920s neoclassical design, set on manicured grounds. Despite having no time for a detour, Sicily walks toward the building, which overlooks the Assiniboine River. Various conservative bronze monuments adorn the lawns. Different from those, there is a three-story modernist sculpture of Louis Riel. "'He was the Metis commander of two rebellions in Western Canada against The Crown—convicted and hanged in 1885,'" She hears Forest's voice say, so vivid in her memory, it is as if he stands beside her.

"I know, you told me already," Sicily says. She adds, "He was posthumously pardoned in the 1960s and named the true founder of the Province of Manitoba." Realizing she is having an imaginary conversation with the memory of someone who obviously doesn't care about her, she screams long and loud. No one else is present to hear.

Three months have passed since Forest's disappearance. Looking him up in the reverse directory, she finds no listing. Yet, she sits twice a week in the library trying over and again. A woman artist named 'Odjig' is traveling in Europe. Laura's Private Investigator's license is a dead end. Sicily searches for Forest, around corners, as doors open, and under every jean jacket with a turned-up collar. Resolved to get a grip on her emotions, Sicily says, "Bonne Soiree, Louis..." She waves to the sculpture. "— And for you, dear Forest, this is goodbye." Sicily walks aways, toward Portage Avenue.

"Hey, you dropped something," a voice calls out. Sicily turns. In the middle of the sidewalk is a tall willowy figure wearing sun glasses, blue jeans, a jean jacket, and an Ojibwa choker. Sicily freezes, overcome with deja-vu. But it is a woman who holds out her hand. In that hand is Sicily's leotard, which has bounced out of her book bag.

"Looks like you might be needing this," the voice speaks again.

"Thank you..." Sicily says drifting back to reality.

"No problem—Are you doin' all right? You're lookin' a bit spaced. Be sure to cross at the light, eh?" the woman says, failing to release the cloth until certain Sicily heeds her warning.

"Yeah, I'm okay," Sicily says. The stranger lets go of the garment. Sicily walks away, then turns back asking, "What's your name?" Maybe by miracle this is Forest's sister, Laura.

"Rainy—" the woman answers.

"Nice to meet you," Sicily says. Disappointment shows on her face. Again she turns her back to Rainy, then stops, looking over her shoulder. "I'm Sicily," she says. Rainy has vanished, perhaps through the door of a nearby pub.

Though only early October, snow is falling. The head of Sicily's bed is against the window. Opening her eyes to the stark moonlight, on the other side of the glass, an eyelash length away, she sees her first pile of perfectly shaped snow crystals accumulate. They are large. It's a view you would expect under a microscope or painted on Christmas wrapping paper. Vern doesn't have to work driving a milk truck before his classes this day. A slave to his internal clock, he is still up early making morning coffee and corn meal porridge. Sicily dances down the stairs singing, "It's snowing, it's snowing..."

"Let's see if you are still celebrating by spring," Vern says, pouring her coffee, then dialing the radio to the CBC news. The reporter speaks authoritatively in the background.

"Did you know Forest when he was a journalist?" Sicily asks.

"Yes, and he still freelances."

"Where did you meet?"

"I was on a field trip for my engineering program, up in the Arctic."

"How did you meet?" Sicily secretly hopes to confirm the veracity of Forest's account.

"In a way, your mother and I are together because of Forest," Vern says. "In 1970, Ellie was on a speaking tour in Canada on behalf of the Campaign to Free Angela Davis. After her talk at the University of Manitoba, she handed me her business card, having written her address on its back. She told me to look her up if I was ever to be in Los Angeles.

"In those days, Ellie still kept that apartment on the rental property your grandfather owned. You were already stowed safely away with Alex and Joanna up north in Marin County. The rare Southern California summer rain had left Ellie's louvered windows spotty. The cleaning of windows is still a piece of housekeeping your mother can't abide being left undone. From the sidewalk in front of her flat, I watched her remove the glass from their moldings, wash them with vinegar, then buff them dry with cloth towels. She reinserted them lovingly, one by one. Looking up, she saw me on the pavement. Her head tilted curiously. I was vaguely familiar to her.

"Most people staffing Angela's campaign knew when to 'duck and cover'. A variety of fringe lunatics, besides various cops and paid informants, looked to make a name for themselves, some violently. Mine wasn't the usual approach of a hit man. She unlocked the screen, ushering me in. Having showed up without notice, I explained trying to call but not reaching her. She had arrived home that morning from a campaign organizing trip in London. Having walked to her house, apparently I'd strolled through a twelve mile stretch of LA called the 'Jungle'. I tried to joke about it."

"Oh—that couldn't have gone well," Sicily says, "Let me guess—something about Africans not being afraid of jungles?"

"Your mother was not amused either. She wanted to know why I had braved my life to find her. Being a bit dense, I explained that I hadn't seen a bus. Ellie laughed, but I was certain she thought I was mentally delayed. Yet, she invited me for coffee anyway. Between sips I reminded her of something she had said when I first met her at her speaking engagement. For me her comment was a guiding light. For her it was a throwaway line."

"She has a lot of those. What was this one?" Sicily asks.

"'There has never been a social change in the United States that was not facilitated by the combined efforts of the Black church, workers' unions, and rich white progressives.'"

Sicily rolls her eyes and says, "Sounds like my mother."

"I explained being a member of the African National Congress of South Africa in exile, doing an engineering thesis on hydroelectric power plants in Canada's Arctic. This is where Forest came in. He had told me about his mercury pollution concerns. We in South Africa would also have to identify mercury poisoning from mines and industry. Our observer delegation at the United Nations barely gets out for lunch, never mind talking to the rest of the people on this continent. Forest made me know that had to change. We were missing opportunities to form connections around common concerns. I made Ellie a proposition."

"Do you realize the word proposition has several meanings in standard North American English?" Sicily asks.

"Actually, I hadn't known. But, Ellie being taken aback was clarifying," Vern chuckles. "Then I explained to her that we of the ANC could help get Angela's case into the hearts of people around the world in exchange for assistance with ending apartheid. I'd seen your mother in action—and I'd never seen anyone quite like her before. She was at once sarcastic and idealistic, not to mention beautiful. Almost immediately she translated my vague proposal into a plan—linking Angela Davis's case to freeing Nelson Mandela and all political prisoners as a means to sensitize people to apartheid. In fact the campaign had already thought of it before I showed up. That was the precise moment when I fell in love with your mother. A revelation facilitated by Forest brought our family together, in this God forsaken frozen wonderland," Vern says.

Sicily's eyes glisten as she stares out the dining room window. Snow falls steadily in straight lines onto the shore of the sluggish river.

"You know, it will freeze solid," Vern says, handing Sicily a cloth serviette.

"What will?" Sicily asks, using the napkin to catch her tears.

"The river... One morning you will wake to leafless trees, believing that verdant life is over. Gradually that changes. The leaves come back, and the water moves again," he says. Sicily's heart ache is nearly tangible. "Forest will turn up, and if you are thinking your mother is intentionally withholding his whereabouts, I am fairly certain she is not."

"That never occurred to me. Fairly you say? It would be out of character for her to lie to me, wouldn't it?" Sicily asks. The mother and daughter have lived separately for the better part of three years because of the campaign and Sicily's desire to complete high school where she had started. Does she know her parent as well as she used to do?

"Come, I'll give you a ride to school," Vern says.

"It's early, I can catch the bus," Sicily says.

"With the first snow today, the buses will be slower than usual, as will you."

It takes ten full minutes for Sicily to put on the winter regalia. Blue jeans and a turtle-necked woolen jumper covering her Long Johns underwear. The circa 1930s ankle length beaver fur coat is from the Salvation Army. Knee high, double fleece-lined leather Mukluks with Cree beadwork, the footwear, are a gift from Ellie. A mock Russian army hat, with ear flaps, squishes Sicily's hair. The polyester mittens make it difficult to hold her book bag. The dancers' petrification of breaking limbs by falling on the ice is essential to every step she makes.

Traffic prevents Vern from pulling up in front of the Collegiate. He drives a block to a part of Portage Avenue where Sicily has never walked, the opposite direction of the dance school. Letting her out of the car, Vern pulls away. Sicily realizes that one of the nearby buildings is a branch of the Canadian Broadcasting Corporation, where Forest had worked. Standing at the door, she looks at the directory hanging near it. Checking her watch, she walks into the building.

On the second floor a man ahead of her speaks with the receptionist. Sporting dirty blonde long hair pulled back with a beaded tie, he wears a leather bomber jacket, the type worn by pilots. Handing a legal sized envelope to the receptionist he says, "This is copy for Ben Wolf."

"He will be finished in a few minutes, you can wait," the receptionist says, flirting.

"I need to get back up north. Make sure Ben gets it." The man walks toward the elevator.

Sicily approaches the desk asking, "Do you know a reporter named Forest Odjig?" The messenger turns facing the receptionist, who looks past Sicily, gauging his reaction.

"I'm sorry, Mr. Odjig no longer works here," the receptionist says.

"Have you a forwarding address for him or a phone number?" Sicily asks, feeling the weight of her fur coat.

"I'm wouldn't be allowed to share that without his permission. I'm sorry," the receptionist says.

Sicily decides to leave while she is still able to choke back her tears. She joins the messenger in the bomber jacket at the elevator. He looks at her intently saying,

"Maybe if you left your name and number and asked her to reach him..."

"That's a good idea, thanks," Sicily says, walking back to the receptionist.

"Unfortunately, I do not actually have a phone number for Forest. Write your information. If someone comes by who knows him, can I give them your number?" the receptionist asks, pushing a pad and pen toward Sicily.

"Please," Sicily says, scribbling. The secretary, answering a phone call, gives Sicily a reassuring nod. Sicily returns to the elevator. The messenger, apparently having changed his mind, passes her, heading back toward the desk and taking a seat.

Leaving the CBC, Sicily feels hopeful, until realizing she is missing her entire first period class. The cold blisters her lips as she slips awkwardly up the icy pavement.

1 2

MANITOBA SEINE

NOVEMBER 1973

SURROUNDING THE UNIVERSITY COLLE-GIATE campus, the downtown residential neighborhood is abysmally dilapidated. Scads of inner city residents are disenfranchised by race, class, and culture. Some are migrant workers in the far north, others aged or injured out of jobs in fish canneries, mines, and construction. First Nation peoples without resources are forced off their treaty lands by development projects, like dams, which primarily benefit non-Native city people. The poor of the city are frequently relegated to badly kept, single room occupancy tenements. Kids also live in those too cramped quarters, from which they often escape into the night.

This November of 1973 an arctic ridge of high pressure begins sprawling across Manitoba, bringing the coldest winter temperatures in forty years. At minus 39, the difference between Celsius and Fahrenheit dissolves. These circumstances prompt Collegiate students, among them Sicily, welcoming street kids in from the cold on Wednesday nights. It's the only weekday Sicily has no dance obligations.

The Rotunda is a large round room with a marble floor. By day it's the crossroads between classrooms. Finding the doors open and the rotunda warm at night, the kids just come. No permission is required from parents. Surnames are never requested or given.

A girl, Sophie, arrives each Wednesday night with an old lady. From the first night, seeing Sophie walk across the marble floor, Sicily had realized the girl's gait is slightly off. The barely perceptible limp is the sort of thing immediately catching a dancer's eye, though Sicily mostly pushes the observation to the back of her mind. Sophie is also the only child accompanied by an adult. Weekly, the girl announces she is six years old. No one wants to know. Cursed with a voice sounding like nails scraping a chalk board, she never talks as much as the other kids, self-conscious about her screech. Fortunately, Sophie's face so sweet it makes her voice tolerable.

By clothing, jewelry, and style, the old lady escorting her is First Nation. She only speaks with, or through, the young one, whose nationality is less discernible. Their language is beyond Sicily's understanding. The youngster only stays about an hour and never wants to leave. At first protesting, Sophie eventually becomes accepting, waving goodbye until she is out the door.

Dancing is the least of Sicily's interests on Wednesdays, but she is often stiff and stretches at every opportunity. Leaning against the wall of the rotunda, as if it were a ballet bar, Sicily does a few pliés. Most of the Wednesday night kids run around her with an abundance of chaos. An outdated radio sits in the corner unused. One night Sicily turns the contraption on and finds the Jackson Five singing. The children's energy is organized into a dance party. Sophie's response is to mirror Sicily's movements, from the sidelines, tucked behind the old lady's skirt. Sicily's hand floats up like a feather, Sophie's too, a beat behind. 'This kid loses her limp when mimicking me to music,' Sicily tells herself.

Thermos tea, hard candy, and board games are initially available for the Wednesday Night Kids. Dance is added because of Sophie. Then a third grader shows up who wants homework tutoring. The few Collegiate students proctoring are able in language and the arts. None of them are proficient in maths or sciences. Science types study at night rather than play with children. Sicily is charged with finding, elsewhere in the Collegiate population, a colleague to help with hard homework.

As usual, at the end of this Wednesday night, Sicily is responsible for locking up the Rotunda. It takes two hours of cleaning to prepare the space for school the next morning. Some of the Wednesday night kids linger to help. Sicily holds the door open for the street waifs. "Please go home," she begs them, not knowing if they have one, or where they really go.

Around midnight, wrapped in her Sally Anne beaver fur coat, Sicily locks the heavy wooden door of the Collegiate, heading to the bus stop. She keeps her back to the stretch of dive bars littering the frozen block behind her, pretending to erase them from her mind. A woman flies through a nearby pub door under the force of a gigantic, extremely drunk First Nation brother. Using her body mass for leverage, she tips the giant forward, dodging while he swings. Her innate beauty and grace, engaged in these incongruous moves, make Sicily stare. The man's blow misses the woman. Still falling, he drags her to the ground. The woman yells in Michif, a combination of Cree and French.

Sicily looks down, seeing the woman's startling blue eyes, and says,

"Rainy... I remember you."

"Wonderful," Rainy says, her voice strangled by the weight of the man on top of her.

"Are you okay?"

"Eh... What the fuck, do I look okay? Help me." Her English has that end of a sentence up-lilt common in First Nation language speakers.

"Do what?"

"Get this son of a bitch outta here before the cops come and beat the shit out of him. Merde, he's out cold."

The SOB is sprawled over Rainy, who lies on her back against the icy sidewalk. Rolling him into the street, she frees herself. Standing, she places a hand under one of his armpits, telling Sicily to put hers beneath the other.

"He's much lighter than I expected," Sicily says.

"You're not lookin' close enough," Rainy says.

'How could I be so unobservant?' Sicily asks herself. The SOB's leg on her side is hollow, while his arm near Rainy is amputated above the elbow.

An empty bus pulls up. The door flaps open, heat wafting to the outside. "Encore, Rainy?" the driver asks from behind the wheel. Rainy shrugs her shoulders. He gets out of his seat and helps the two women lift the SOB onto the bus. Rainy and Sicily prop the drunk man between them on the long front seat. In French, Rainy begs the driver to take them over the Seine River. Not the one in France but the Manitoba Seine, in St. Boniface, the French quarter of Winnipeg.

"It's not the route," the driver says.

"Ma fille a l'école le matin, et je ne peux pas rester dans la rue toute la nuit." Rainy wipes her nose with the sleeve of her jean jacket. Sicily does not understand the ensuing long French negotiation.

"D'accord," the driver says, getting off the bus.

"Where's he going?" Sicily asks.

"Drivers don't get regular bathroom breaks. We watch the bus, he goes piss in the pub and takes us where we want."

"C'est la dernière fois," the driver says, climbing back behind the wheel.

"It was the 'last time' the time before this one too." Rainy laughs.

Passing the sculpture of Louis Riel, the bus crosses the bridge over the Assiniboine, where it merges with the Seine, near the confluence with the Red. Here the driver stops, helping the two women haul their semi-conscious companion onto the street. "Bonne chance..." he wishes the trio much needed luck.

The house is dark except for the kitchen, where a bare light bulb burns overhead. Sicily helps Rainy lay the inebriated man on the floor. Two mugs of cold tea sit on the table. Next to the cups a cutting board holds a large white flat biscuit. "Bannock," Rainy says, "... a First Nation staple made of snow white flour, water, baking powder, salt, and whatever oil you can afford."

Tiptoeing into another room, Rainy returns carrying a red woolen Hudson Bay blanket with a black stripe down its middle. She shoves the SOB. He rolls to his side. The blanket floats over him, a flag over a coffin. Making a bowl from tin foil, placing it near his mouth, she says, "For when he pukes." After washing her hands, she flips on the stove's burners, heating the room. The tea, with the bags, gets poured into an aluminum pot and set on a flame, brewing again. The refrigerator contains only eggs, milk, and a rectangular carton from which the host removes a white waxy block.

"What's that?" Sicily asks.

"Pig fat—lard," Rainy says, slicing it like butter.

"I'm not sure that's good for you."

"I think you mean 'you,' yourself."

"I mean anyone."

"Feel free to not eat," Rainy says, splitting the bannock, wedging lard between its layers.

"I'm hungry too," Sicily says. If she had a tail, it would have been between her legs.

The bannock sits near the burners while the tea comes to a boil. Poured back into the cups, it's liquid and solid simultaneously. Looking around the barren kitchen, the novice nervously ponders her first bite of pig fat.

"Thanks," Rainy says.

"For what?" Sicily asks.

"Jeez, for helping me..."

"It's nothing."

"You know, it isn't good to lie. It's something to you, and to me."

"You are welcome," Sicily says, biting the bannock, preventing something else stupid slipping from her mouth.

"What's a sweet Black chick like you doing in a place like this?" Rainy asks.

"Good question—guess going to school, living with my parents, sorting it out."

"What are you studying?"

"Dance, at the Queen's Ballet, and for my upper school matriculation."

"Wow, must be hard to do both."

"Especially since this summer in Europe I fell in love with—let's say science." Sicily longs to share her real dilemma. She has not banished the distraction of constantly imagining Forest in the periphery of her vision.

Rainy squints and cocks her head, questioning Sicily's honesty.

"There's this guy..." Sicily says.

"No shit," Rainy giggles.

"We got separated at the end of my trip in Europe. He's someplace here in Canada."

"Does he want you to find him?" Rainy ask.

Damn, another question daily plaguing Sicily since she lost Forest.

Rainy continues, "Getting dumped isn't all that odd. Know the definition of torture?"

"When someone hurts you beyond what you can tolerate," Sicily says.

"Nope, it's when someone makes you hurt yourself. If you breathe, you drown. If you drop your arms, you get beaten. If you love, you get hurt." Soothing is not Rainy's forte.

"I'm afraid something has happened to him."

"Something has happened, or something is gonna happen? Which one is better?"

"What?" Sicily asks, confused.

"Would ya rather he died in a ditch and that's why he's not with you? Is that better than if he just rejects you?"

"I wouldn't wish him death even if he didn't want me." Sicily's voice cracks with conviction. "Besides, I know he loves me."

"Then there's nothing to worry about. Any of his friends you could check with?"

"None I can reach anymore, except my parents. They don't have a contact for him."

"Your parents? I guess this is more 'odd' than usual."

"If I'm smart, I'll focus on my two schools, not him."

"Education—that's what I want for my daughter."

"You have a daughter?" Sicily asks. Rainy seems ageless, possessing a beauty that would be as resilient at sixty as at thirty. She could certainly have her pick of men.

"She's four. I would show her to you but I don't want to wake her, or him," Rainy lifts her chin in the direction of the man on the floor. He snores, exhaling foul alcohol.

"Where are you coming from tonight?" Rainy asks.

"Some of us students do this thing on Wednesday nights to keep kids off the streets. We bring them into the Rotunda at the Collegiate. Mostly we play with them."

"Mum takes Sophie there," Rainy says.

"Sophie? She's only four? Isn't she six?"

"She told you that, right?" Rainy asks, shaking her head.

"The old lady didn't correct her."

"You mean Grandmother, not 'old lady'. At the least you mean 'woman'. Don't say 'old lady' like that. It's not good. Mum, she knows English, but won't speak it."

"I didn't mean to be disrespectful," Sicily says.

"Most people don't. Sophie can't wait until she's six. Then she'll go to 'real school'. She's not even interested in kindergarten. She wants grades with numbers. It's gonna be a long couple of years."

"Why does she come on Wednesday nights? You don't live downtown?"

"Mum brings her. Gives us more time if they ride the bus with me when I go to the bars."

"Isn't it too early for the bars?"

"In reality, it's years too late. I never manage to get anyone not to go in, but I can tell who's gonna need rescuing by closing time."

There isn't an ounce of pity or sympathy in the voice of this woman. Rainy states the facts as if talking about a dinner party. Only about Sophie and Mum is she warmer.

"Mum is always trying to give the kid more."

"More than what?" Sicily asks.

"More than this..." Rainy looks around the kitchen. Her eyes piercing the walls. "Livin' in the city sucks the life out of me."

"Can you move to the countryside?"

"Got no land to go home to. My mum lost her rights when she married a non-treaty man."

"I'm sorry. Where are they?" Sicily says.

"They died. But I got declared non-Indian at birth cause of my blue-eyed daddy."

"Mum isn't your mother?"

"She is. Even if it's not legal, kinship by adoption is strong as by blood."

"Could you marry a Native man and get your rights back?" Sicily assumes Sophie's father is off the table.

"The price is too high for me to pay."

"Women lose land because of who they marry? How can that be going on?"

"Add this to the long list of indigenous people's rights violations. Besides, I need to be in the city because of Sophie," Rainy says, getting up from the table, wiping down the stove with a cloth. She wraps a hunk of bannock in tin foil before continuing, "Sophie has problems with coordination. She's a lot better than they expected by this age."

Not bothering to tell Rainy she has noticed Sophie's gait issues, Sicily says, "You can train the body and mind to overcome things. I was a total 'spaz' when I was younger, scoliosis and seizures. Look at me now, I owe it all to dance." Sicily twists her body, jerking. Delighted, Rainy laughs then pokes the SOB with her toes. About barely making reference to him all night, she says, "I don't talk about other people, especially if they're comatose in the corner." The two women pull the man to his feet. In the bathroom, Rainy props him in front of the toilet. Placing a clean towel on the sink, she says, "Brother, this is far as I go." In the hall she listens at the door. Hearing the tinkle of urine she adds, "Good, he hit the toilet. It's always a mess when they don't."

"They who?" Sicily asks.

"People I drag out of the bars."

"Why do you do that?"

"I told you, so they don't freeze to death passed out in the street, get the shit beat out of them, arrested, or plain get killed."

"Killed?"

"Winnipeg's murder rate is the highest in Canada. First Nation people make up at least half of it. A lot of them are sisters. Cops hardly look for the murderers. If you wanna kill an Indian, somewhere near Winnipeg is definitely the place to do it." Rainy knocks on the bathroom door, saying, "Hey brother, you all right in there?" They hear the SOB running water. Rainy continues, "Suicides are high too—you lose your land, family, get moved like cattle from one reserve to another. If alcohol doesn't work, drugs are expensive, death by your own hand is a form of resistance."

"You know this guy?"

"Something like that. He used to be a cameraman," Rainy says.

"You mean like a job?"

"You're thinking to be a drunk Indian you have to be worthless. There are too many reasons to be a drunk Indian. A job alone is never gonna erase 'em."

"He's a stranger?"

"Are you a stranger?"

"Doesn't feel like it since we've been talking."

"Everyone is a stranger until they speak."

"But he isn't speaking."

"He'll say something," Rainy says. The toilet flushes behind the bathroom door.

"Aren't you scared doing this?" Sicily asks.

"Bar rescue work? Do I look scared?"

"Not really..."

"The morning edition of the Winnipeg Free Press, with the overnight body count—that scares me."

The SOB comes out of the bathroom smelling like Dial soap, having used it to wash his face, hands, and even his mouth. His wet hair is pulled back into a long neat braid. The grungy towel, also used to polish the porcelain sink, is neatly folded. No mean feat with one hand.

It's still dark out except for stars and the occasional street light. In the mudroom, Rainy shoves the foil wrapped bannock under the SOB's arm stump. Limping down the stairs, he says, "Thanks."

"You're truly welcome," Rainy says. Turning to Sicily she adds, "I told you he'd say something."

Closing the door, Rainy realizes she does not know her new pal's name. "What do they call you?" she asks.

The familiar phrase catches Sicily off guard.

"Sicily... like Italy," she says.

"Yeah, I got that," Rainy's piercing blue eyes can't hide that she is recognizing this giant Black ballerina for the first time. "Sophie and Mum—" she says.

Sicily knows she is being dismissed and interrupts Rainy saying, "No problem, I need to get to school on time too."

Ellie and Vern's home is on Creighton Avenue in the North end of town. Their house was bought from ancient Bolsheviks who moved to assisted living.

"It only takes ten minutes to walk," Rainy coaxes Sicily to cross the frozen river.

"I'll catch the bus," Sicily says, apprehensive about walking on ice.

"You have to know how to traverse water, it covers seventy percent of the earth. You can't be scared of it, liquid or frozen."

Sicily armors up in her cold weather gear. Rainy's dress is frighteningly sparse—cowboy boots with no socks, no hat, no gloves. At least she buttons her jean jacket. A third of the way across the river, their feet crunch the snow loudly. They yell to hear one another. There are dog tracks.

"Dogs always know what they are doing. Can't go wrong following them," Rainy says. Her voice echoing against the ice covered banks, she adds, "Come back sometime in the daylight."

"I'm in school during the daylight, all six hours of it. I dance evenings, except Wednesdays."

They get to the middle of the river where Rainy intends to turn around. "See those lights right by that big house on the outer bank?—it's on Creighton Avenue." Rainy points to #1 Creighton, Sicily's house.

"Shit, you're rich," Rainy says.

"We are not rich. My dad drives a milk truck for the Co-op dairy starting at 4AM, then goes to the university for classes in engineering. My Mother works twelve hour shifts as a nurse. That leaves enough time for them to try to change the world."

"You can be affluent without money and poor with it," Rainy says.

In one night, Sicily has learned more from this woman than from Forest and Jorge combined.

"Wednesday night, outside the bar, same time..." It's Rainy's command, not a request.

Awed by this lithe sister's strength, the ballerina wonders how this woman functions with unique grace in such a tough life. Rainy's different, and Sicily knows different when she sees it.

1 3

SANTA MONICA BAY

SUMMER 1960 TO 1962

THE BRUNCH BUNCH WAS the name I took to calling the group. It stuck. Dorothy and Milton's beach cottage was north of the Santa Monica pier, halfway between the wharf and the Jonathan Club. An icon of the beachfront, the Jonathan Club probably would not admit its first woman, Jewish person, or Black person for another twenty-five years. Beside disdain for that restrictive private institution, Dorothy's brunch guests had other things in common. Conversation was replete with fascination for the Sunday New York Times Crossword Puzzle. They used grand words to argue about everything. Whether or not the exchanges finished in consensus, all agreed to end up laughing.

How the New York Times got from the East Coast to Los Angeles by brunch was my weekly preoccupation. The meal always included round plain bread donuts, soft white cheese, and pink fish. While I drank orange juice and seltzer, the adults downed a gallon of Mimosa by the time Knobby arrived. "'Knobby' was named for the state of his adolescent knees," Ellie said. He was her old friend from elementary school, found again at the brunch table. They had lost track when he moved from Springfield, to study for the priesthood, and she to Oklahoma for college. Now he lived in the cabana apartment, behind the beach house, which is how he knew Dorothy. It made no sense that he was always tardy given he lived close. "I'm a priest and go to church on Sundays," Knobby explained to me.

"Are you like Rev. Kring Allen at McCarthy or Rev. Dr. Martin Luther King?"

"I hope to be like them. I'm a Liberation Priest."

"What's that?" I asked.

"It's a priest, in my case in the Catholic Church, who supports the social movement that tries to make sure all people live equally well. But, neither the 'priest' nor the 'liberation' part are as easy as it sounds."

I liked this guy. He took me seriously.

"Not only that, the head of the Catholic Church is in Rome, and Knobby says mass in Latin," Dorothy said, knowing I had inherited Ellie's interest in all things Roman.

Knobby was a lightning rod, adding diversity to the table— having religion and all. What followed was a round robin of comments from the Brunch Bunch about religious mumble-jumble expressed in old dead languages. Ellie sheepishly divulged that both she and I were technically Catholic. Big Momma had arranged my baptism as a baby, as she had my mother's. Pouring himself a large Mimosa, Knobby explained how he hadn't 'seen that coming.' Neither had I, nor did I know why it mattered.

Alex, a lawyer, was as funny as Dorothy. He had once said to a brunch guest, "Before Ellie started coming to brunch with us, she was a skinny little White girl..." It wasn't true. Ellie was a five foot eight, 180 pound Black woman. But out of Alex's mouth the absurdity seemed plausible.

Another member of the Brunch Bunch was Guy. Writing his new novel, Voltaire! Voltaire! Guy asked for my opinion on one of its points. It was a high honor for a girl only four. "My best book is the Werewolf of Paris. But, you'll have to wait until you are older to read it," he said.

"I have already seen movies about werewolves on TV. Why can't I read the book?" I asked.

"Because, dear girl, you might understand too much of it, too soon," Dorothy said, nipping the bud of a conversation on first amendment rights which would surely ensue. The un-expurgated English version of the Marquis de Sade's Justine, translated by Austryn Wainhouse, would make a cameo. Dorothy knew my inquisitiveness would defy resistance to the erotic book's content.

One of the brunches we celebrated my fifth birthday. It was my third party that week. Guy also drew doodles, one of which he would give me to take home each week. But for my birthday he gave me a copy of his soon to be published, Voltaire!

Voltaire! It was a manuscript in a form called 'galleys'. I was honored to be given such a gift. Few people had seen this book, which he inscribed to me in French. He refused to translate his note, making me promise to learn the language someday and read it myself. Because Guy was an artist who also wrote movies and gave me excellent answers, I chose to ask him, "Are you on the Hollywood Blacklist?" Everyone else at the brunch table stopped to listen. They wondered how Guy would explain this to me.

First he talked about selling movie scripts. His name was Guy Endore, but he also had written as Harry Relis, which was his brother-in-law's name. He explained that he and others were denied the right to work for a living because they believed in Communism, though not necessarily how different countries applied that philosophy. Going on he clarified, "People on the Hollywood Blacklist have gone to jail not for a belief in Communism, but for believing in the United States Constitution." This was that long story for which Grandmother had threatened to withhold dessert. As he went on talking about Marx, and the poor working for the rich, I sensed, like 'Liberation Priests,' Communists also dealt with the devil in the details.

Though Guy ranked high in my heart, Edie was higher. She made costumes for films. On the weeks she managed to come for brunch she brought me hats. Placing high fashion masterpieces on my head, pulling my chin up to see me through her big round glasses, she always said, "Bubeleh, hats are for you."

Various 'guest stars' arrived at Dorothy's table en route to and from elsewhere. Paul Robeson, with his deep voice, visited on a layover between London and Australia. It turned out that Paul and Dorothy were also on the Hollywood Blacklist, as were other frequent brunch guests. At some point, Alex had been the lawyer for all of them.

A man named Abe was the most long awaited brunch guest who eventually came. He captured Ellie's full attention. Abe was building a spa close to San Francisco for those who wanted to self-actualize. Apparently, he was an expert in this human phenomenon. Twice weekly Ellie had an evening psychology class at the University of California, Los Angeles. We often spent our time together reading her assignments aloud. Summarizing Abe's books for me, Ellie had said, "A person is self-actualized when they are the best of themselves." With whole classes of people, races, and nations at risk for losing this human potential, Ellie was determined I wouldn't be among them.

While Abe delivered long stanzas of talk, Dorothy was comedic. Her elegant humor confirmed she was listening carefully, only pretending to deride. Dorothy filtered all things through laughter or maybe champagne. "If you don't laugh, you cry, and I hate when my eyeliner runs," she said while building an impossibly long word on the Scrabble board.

After I finished my dessert of finger-sized cinnamon and sugar filled Rugelach, the languid paced Sunday brunches were half over. Crossword puzzle and Scrabble game completed, the adult conversation became more like a meeting. Milton was an 'ethereal seeker,' not a political handmaiden. Recognizing my boredom, he tasked me to take Aphrodite for a weekly romp. "Aphrodite is named for the goddess of love," Milton said, introducing me to the seventy pound grey Husky.

The dog and I usually began our weekly journey running straight toward the ocean. A quarter-mile of sand crunched under our feet. Reaching the life guard station, receding waves left crabs digging between our toes. Whole sand dollars were carefully collected. When my pockets were full, we ran south along the shore. Near the pier, we watched surfers ride the waves.

Some Sundays, instead of going straight to the water, I walked the promenade where there was a large red brick armory. During WWII the building stored munitions, anticipating a Pacific attack. In front of the armory was a volleyball net. I would watch games sitting on the cinder block wall separating the boardwalk from the sand. The people who played volleyball were men. They were more interesting than the game itself. Sometimes they wore shorts. Often, they overdressed. Compared with other beachgoers, the Players were incongruously stylish. Shirts were invariably dark colored with classy stripes. The fabric wasn't cotton and didn't wrinkle. Pants had creases. I even saw one of them playing while wearing a long skinny neck tie.

The men at the net were of all races, Black, White, Brown, Yellow, Red. Some spoke with accents, Spanish, Italian, New York. To a man, their hair shined, slicked back with VO5. Every one of them wore sunglasses. Half of them had cigarettes hanging from their mouths—based on the packaging, their brand was always Kools. It seemed some of their feet had barely ever touched sand. A mélange of flip-flops lined up outside the area of play, stepped into immediately at game's end.

Even with abundant peculiarities, the people in front of the armory played volleyball like Greek or Roman gods. It was as if lives depended on the game. Otherwise, the Players were as cool as their cigarettes. Unlike the surfers, they showed not a shred of interest in me. They were not unfriendly, only disinterested.

The last Sunday before Labor Day, I sat on the wall in front of the armory watching. Nearby were women who also came from the armory. Whatever their diverse cultures and races they were all blonde and part of a matched set to which the Players also belonged. These bombshells were equally dismissive of me. Some people would say they wore too much makeup. They were also shod in flip-flops, spoke the same tongues as the men, and smoked the identical brand. Giggling and chirping, the Blondes pretended no romantic concern for the guys at the net. Yet, I sensed the connection between these genders being more than a mating dance   it was a common desperation.

Suddenly, I heard the Blondes shriek, not a comely sound. A battalion of police came from the walkway next to the armory, flooding the promenade. Some uniforms entered the building, others descended on the volleyball court. Pushed and shoved, Players' hands were bound behind their backs with handcuffs. The Blondes scattered, but most were eventually nabbed by cops. Protesting, detainees cursed in a multitude of languages.

Bursting into the beach house I shouted, "The police are taking the Players." I was shocked by how quickly the usually sedate Brunch Bunch moved. Ellie grabbed my hand and we all hit the promenade. Following Alex's lead, we yelled, "You are violating their constitutional right to peaceful assembly." The Brunch Bunch had anticipated that the elite Jonathan Club up the beach might instigate this sort of move against the people living at the armory.

Knobby wore his priest clothes, having said Mass earlier that morning. He adjusted his white collar showing he had the power of God behind him. The head policemen looked increasingly uncomfortable the more Alex spoke, and the quieter Knobby became. "I am the attorney for these people," Alex said, waving a card pulled from his wallet. To the group being herded away the lawyer barked, "Say not one word. I'll meet you at the police station." Then they were all gone, Players, Blondes, the policemen, sticks, and guns. Walking back to the beach house, I looked behind me to see the volleyball court. The flip-flops, habitually organized by color, were now in chaos. The white ball sat alone, waiting for a game.

After that Labor Day of 1960, with John Kennedy's presidential nomination having been secured earlier in the summer, our Sundays changed. The relaxed brunches and Scrabble ceased. Dorothy was spending half her time in New York. Milton sold the house in the Hollywood Hills. He was going to a Buddhist monastery in Kyoto. Even for Milton this was odd since he didn't believe in Buddha. The rest of the Brunch Bunch met at supermarkets and church halls, registering voters.

Walter Cronkite reported daily on the TV News that Black people in the South were intimidated and killed while trying to vote in the presidential primaries. People had been illegally barred from the polls by random local requirements, like literacy. Grandmother Vanessa, an ever pragmatic social worker, organized a countywide carpool ready to take senior citizens to vote.

Ellie wore multiple 'Vote Kennedy' buttons on her nursing cap at the hospital. Nursing supervisors tried to stop her by threatening her termination, but they were too short-handed to follow through. No patients complained their nurse looked like a billboard. As a campaign organizing tool, my mother took more shifts.

When in Los Angeles, Dorothy joined us registering people to vote. I sat with her at a table in front of markets, handing out forms and pens. Dorothy checked the forms, making certain people signed their names or had her witness their 'X'. The Brunch Bunch never fully regrouped on Sundays after President Kennedy's election in November.

The next year, an unofficial poll of family and the Bunch determined that I should go to Catholic school. Separated from my cul-de-sac friends, I would miss Henry most. Catholic school was considered one of the few places a young Black girl might continue to develop excellent reading, writing, and maths skills. Knobby's assignment was to mitigate any negative effects of the religious environment by selecting the right school. He chose St. Paul's near Venice Beach. He thought embracing Catholicism would smooth my transition.

A nun of the Mary Knoll order prepared me for my First Communion—the next step since I had already been baptized as an infant. We met on Wednesday evening while my mother was at UCLA. 'Sister' was ancient with diamond twinkle eyes. "Catechism makes sure you know the difference between right and wrong. Before you make your first confession, it is important to know what you might need to confess," she said.

"I'm almost seven years old, I already know right from wrong," I said.

"Good, then this won't take long. What does civil rights mean?" Sister asked.

"I know that one." I explained all I had learned about voting rights and race, complete with the Brunch Bunch and family gesticulations and idioms.

"Excellent," Sister said. Boosted by the election of a Catholic president two years before, Sister was way off the ecclesiastical books, interpreting the scriptures to suit herself.

First Confessions happen on Saturday mornings, followed by First Communions on Sunday. St. Paul's in Venice, California, four miles south of Dorothy's old beach cottage, was the venue of mine. It was the Parish Church associated with the Catholic School that Knobby had chosen for me. Most of the sins I confessed involved knowingly harassing Lillie. Saying a bunch of Our Fathers and Hail Marys was my penance. The rest of the afternoon I learned the procession walk for the next day's communion ceremony. All the other participants were over age seven, most Spanish speaking.

Lourdes, who preferred to be called 'Lucy,' translated for me. Her hair was long, golden-hour dusk brown and would hang to her knees if not braided and tied with ribbons. Unlike me, Lucy was completely clued in to the details of her environment.

The evening following the confession, Ellie and I shopped for gloves, veil, and white dress. The next morning, it was back to church. I floated down the center aisle, peculiarly attired like a bride. With my stomach growling, having fasted overnight, I received my First Communion—a white wafer I wasn't allowed to chew placed on my tongue. Other than Knobby and Vanessa, not a one of the Brunch Bunch or other family in attendance actually believed in God.

We moved to Venice to be closer to my new school. Our house, on Sunset Avenue, was a few blocks from the beach and a healthy walking distance from St. Paul's Parish. Venice was a tri-racial ghetto of Black, Spanish, and poor White people, in direct proximity with Bohemian Beat culture and White liberals. The latter were often UCLA students or teachers. We were all in opposition to developers seeking to restore the beachfront to a former exclusive glory. Venice of the 1920s had been a playground of movie stars. The neighborhood suffered successive declines as Los Angeles grew. Now the Blue Goose was a dive bar on Washington Street. It was the venue of fights on

Friday nights, apologies on Sunday mornings, and shootings once a month.

Mine was the only bedroom in our house. Ellie slept on a pullout sofa in the living room. Everything we owned came from Tienda de Segunda Mano, second-hand stores. The best stores were in Hollywood, near Wanda's cafe on Melrose. It was worth a half hour drive from the beach to shop. Rich people always tossed out perfectly usable things. For my room Ellie painted old furniture white and trimmed it with antique gold.

At night Ellie read books to me, even when I could read them myself—Chaucer, Carroll, Dickens. Most important of all, she found a children's version of Virgil's Aeneid, where Ellie herself had first met the Founding Myths of Rome. The books were hard covered, the beautiful black words printed on thick white paper. I had problems with Alice in Wonderland. The illustrations on the inner cover had mutant dogs with turtle shells. These images caused me to itch nervously, a phobia for mutations and poisonings—even before I knew the Mad Hatter had mercury disease from making felt. Ellie found that photography books, like The Family of Man, soothed me. My seventh birthday she surprised me with my 1950, 35 mm Leica camera from the Segunda Mano. She expected I'd grow into it.

Without the cul-de-sac community, in Venice after homework I watched the channel 7 Big Afternoon Movie. Ours was a dilapidated television, requiring jiggling the tubes in the back to get the picture. Those films expanded my world. Even at seven years old I recognized they were among the most influential screenworks ever made. Excited, finding members of the Brunch Bunch in the credits, I kept a list.

Guy Endore had recommended a movie, Roman Holiday. He said it was about a princess who fell in love with a pauper. I knew that fairytale and was happy when the film showed up on TV. Guy's friend, Dalton Trumbo, wrote it. On the Blacklist, Dalton was one of the 'Hollywood Ten' who had gone to jail. Edie's full name was Edith Head, who created the clothes for that movie. Looking more closely at all film credits, Edie seemed to have designed the clothes for most good movies of her time, including my mother's favorite, September Affair. Edie's skills were essential to Hollywood's revenue. No one dared question her Blacklist relationships.

A Star is Born, the story of a couple ripped apart by alcoholism, was the first film ever to make me cry. When the credits rolled, Dorothy Parker was listed under 'script'. Written in 1937, it was one among her large body of work which had landed her on the Blacklist. We had not seen Dorothy much since she was spending most of her time in New York. One Sunday she paid a surprise visit to our house in Venice. I showed her my list of movies. There were lines drawn between the titles and different writers, actors, and directors related to our Brunch Bunch. Dorothy looked at my diagram carefully and said, "Glad you are on our side."

In 'my movies' the main characters lost the loves of their lives. Invariably, circumstances beyond the lovers' control caused the cracks in their hearts—war, disease, death, duty. "It's the god Mercury destroying Dido's and Aeneas' love, all over again," I explained to Dorothy. She turned her head to the side, looked at me, squinted, and nodded.

Dorothy was moving back to New York permanently and didn't imagine she would see us for a long while. The aging writer sat on one of the old mahogany dining chairs. She passed Ellie an envelope. I headed to the kitchen for snacks.

"What's this?" Ellie asked, pulling a check from its slip. When Dorothy hesitated to answer, my mother shot me a glance instructing me to mind my own business. Off I went down the hall, but I could still hear.

"Two year's tuition for Sicily's school. If by some quirk she tolerates religion longer than that, I'll send more."

"I'm not ungrateful—but why are you doing this?" Ellie asked.

"Darling, in this society, wealth comes by only a few ways— inheritance, marriage, or theft. The money from the first two is also stolen because it generally comes from someone else's labor. Hard work is insufficient to avoid or transcend poverty. Even Horatio Alger's characters depended on benefactors."

"I don't know what to say."

"Say nothing. Take the money and run," the aging writer suggested.

Things were always tight for us. Even when money flowed the timing never matched the immediate need. Once Ellie was broke and stole my Catholic school uniform from a Sears store. For years, my mother would not tell any one of this repugnant circumstance, but it compelled her to accept Dorothy's money.

"It's a gift for Sicily, and an advance payment for services you will supply in the future," Dorothy explained, fumbling an unlit cigarette.

"What services?" Ellie asked.

"Edie and Guy are going to teach you Yiddish. It will take up some of your time."

"Yiddish?" Ellie gasped. "Couldn't they teach me Spanish or French instead?"

"I'm leaving you with a list."

"For what?"

"That depends on who reads it—but for you, it's where to get money..."

"Money?"

"Darling girl, as long as people are trying to make a more fair world, they'll be killed and arrested. A defense fund will always be needed."

"What does that have to do with Yiddish?" Ellie asked.

"When most of the Brunch Bunch are gone, people with the money will know we sent you because you have 'the list' and you speak Yiddish." Dorothy fell into laughter, which sputtered into an uncontrolled cough. That was the last day I saw Dorothy.

Edie and Guy often came on Sundays for brunch at the house in Venice. When I arrived from mass with Knobby, lox and bagels were on the table. The room buzzed with Yiddish. One of those Sundays, Edie brought me a special hat. The designer placed the pink pill-shaped ornament on my head saying, "I made one of these for a lovely lady. But, bubeleh, she's not as gorgeous in it as you." I was the only little girl in town wearing a hat designed for Mrs. Jacqueline Kennedy.

14

VENICE BEACH CANALS

FALL 1963 TO 1964

PRACTICING HER YIDDISH DILIGENTLY, Ellie was fluent by the time of President Kennedy's assassination in November of 1963. A cascade of events causing her to use the new language broadened my understanding of 'injustice' beyond the Scrabble board. The Akira's move from the cul-de-sac coincided with Ellie's and mine to Venice. Japan Town was northeast of the Los Angeles Civic Center. Henry and Tony Akira lived near other American Japanese, a new experience. Linda had found them a two-room apartment in an older downtown building. It was barely affordable.

Mike had been unable to make the one-man landscaping business go. Linda became a 'shop girl'. Ends still would not meet. Mike took work as a 'picker' in the fields of the San Joaquin Valley, where both his and Linda's parents had worked. As a migrant farm worker, he was away from his family for a month at a time. Farmworkers' unions were already making the point that agriculture and mining left the water of the San Joaquin Valley, and the Sacramento River, dirty with pollutants. Ellie was visiting the Akira apartment when Linda confided her fears.

That evening, I wondered how our friends were doing in their new apartment. My mother was cautious but figured Henry would tell me, so she may as well. Both Linda and Ellie were afraid the environment where Mike worked was making him sick. It was a new word for me, and I asked Ellie to spell it—E-N-V-I-R-O-N-M-E-N-T. Ellie was trying to figure out a way to get Mike a new job. I said, "Too bad he can't work at the Hollywood Bowl. There are a lot of gardens there." Ellie hugged me and swung me around. She picked up the phone and called Joe.

Joe was the head of the grounds crew at the Los Angeles outdoor amphitheater affectionately known as 'The Bowl'. He liked my mother a lot. Even though she spurned his affections, they remained friendly. She had invited him to last year's winter holiday party on the cul-de-sac. Joe had commented on Mike's topiary adorning Bethune Street. Though the situation had been difficult to navigate, Joe found a way to show Ellie affection and she to accept it. He gave us all his complimentary performance tickets. That year alone we were treated to Leonard Bernstein conducting André Watts's debut piano concert in Los Angeles, and the Bolshoi Ballet. Confident Joe would help if he could, Ellie dialed the phone. I could hear his baritone voice through the receiver. My mother told him it wasn't tickets we needed but a different favor.

The next morning, Mike drove directly from the Valley to the job interview at the Bowl, without seeing Linda. Just before I left for school, Joe called Ellie, panicked. The interviewee had arrived sick, short of breath, in a cold sweat, and shaking. The gardener was confused and tongue tied, staggering as though he were drunk. When Joe could not prevent Mike from driving home, he called Ellie instead of the police.

Ellie was with Linda when Mike arrived from the Hollywood Bowl. He was only five and a half feet tall, but normally solidly built. Now he was gaunt. Each step he took seemed to cause him pain. Pupils shrunken, the light bothered his eyes. The Foster Grant sunglasses were not for style. When Mike was unable to recognize Ellie or his wife, the two loaded him into the back of his truck. Henry and his younger brother had already gone to the next door neighbor's. Linda climbed into the bed of the pick-up with her husband. She covered him with a blanket. Semi-conscious, his wife's voice singing a Japanese lullaby comforted the gardener. Ellie drove across the great divide between poor and rich to Cedars of Lebanon, now merged with Sinai Hospital, where she mostly worked.

Linda and Mike were left to register in the waiting area of the Emergency Room. An admitting clerk spoke loudly, ignorantly presuming Linda couldn't understand English—and was deaf.

Ellie waited in the corridor at the staff entrance of the ER. When an orderly left the door ajar she slipped through, grabbed a doctor and described Mike's symptoms along with her best guess at a diagnosis. This persuaded the physician to triage Mike, avoiding the long registration queue. Mike disappeared beyond the doors, into the center of the ER.

Hours later, the emergency room doctor came to the waiting room, where Ellie and Linda were exquisitely uncomfortable.

"Ellie, it is as you suspected, organophosphate pesticide poisoning. It's likely from a lifetime of exposure as a landscaper, peaking because of his recent farm work."

"Will he get better?" Ellie asked.

"We've stabilized his respiration and given him atropine and a benzodiazepine. He won't ever be able to function as he had in the past even if he survives. We lose a third of people who have blood levels as high as his," the doctor said, touching Linda's hand.

Linda stood mutely, terrified, frozen.

Mr. Akira got sick a week before Christmas 1963. Knobby took me to High Mass at St. Paul's. We sat close to the pulpit. The sermon was as dry as the mass, which was now in English. I didn't care, praying for Mr. Akira being my goal. Mike remained ill. No longer able to work, he spent most of his time in the one bedroom Japan Town apartment. Linda had three jobs.

A term from the pulpit interested me, 'liberation priests'. However, I quickly realized the phrase was used in the derogatory. The stubby finger of the blue faced parish priest pointed down at Knobby in our pew, saying, "These 'liberation priests' are not priests at all if they do not understand that they should not marry. Priests must have vows of celibacy. Nor is it the job of the priesthood to take on the civil rights battle. Excommunication is the fitting action for those who persist dragging the church in to the morass."

"What does 'excommunication' mean?" I whispered to Knobby.

"Thrown out of the priesthood," Knobby whispered back.

"I'm not staying in this church, or school, if they want to throw you out," I said, getting up, climbing over other parishioners. I made the sign of the cross and genuflected passing the Eucharist. Knobby jogged behind me as I bolted out of the church.

At home, I explained my period of being 'Catholic' was over. Ellie took this information without shock or reaction, only a simple, "Okay." Relieved I had abandoned this particular spiritual manifestation, Ellie struggled unsuccessfully to hide her smile. Not long after being excommunicated, Knobby married my teacher Rosa from St. Paul's. The couple moved to Delano, in the San Joaquin Valley, where Rosa grew up. I liked both Knobby and Rosa and was a flower girl at the wedding. It was years before I understood why the newlyweds would move to a place that poisoned Mike. They were plotting to change those circumstances.

Having rejected religion, I attended Westminster public elementary school in Venice. Venice was far from the Ritz it had been thirty years before. However, the school had not decreased in quality. While a Catholic, I had skipped parts of several grades. Barely nine, I was two years ahead of myself when starting grade six. The walk home from Westminster

School was shorter than from St. Paul's. Now I got home an hour earlier than Ellie. Lucy's grandmother, Abuela, was also angry at Knobby's treatment by the parish priest. She insisted her granddaughter had no place in such a 'reaccinonario' environment. When I left St Paul's, Lucy did too. Though in a different grade, living two blocks apart, we walked to and from Westminster together.

Lucy had a crush on a boy in my class, Michel from France, who looked like one of the Beatles. It was Lucy's brother Paco with whom I was enamored. He was almost five years older than me. While I would have years to catch Paco's attention, Lucy felt urgency as Michel would return to France the next year. They would never be pen pals if she didn't strike soon.

We walked toward the beach promenade, strolling behind Michel and his friend. Knowing we girls should go straight to one of our houses from school, on this particular day we chose to defy Ellie and Abuela, Lucy's grandmother. When the boys turned off, Lucy and I headed toward the beach alone. We giggled, as if we hadn't been stalking schoolmates. Before we knew it, the ocean was at our right, the town to the left, and Rose Avenue behind us. We were farther off course from home than intended.

The psychedelic age had started. Long hair was the counter-culture identifier, "Let It Be" the mantra of the times. Hippies were sleeping on the sand, blurring the lines between homeless vagabonds and Siddhartha. This was all in stark contrast to shop owners on the boardwalk and the Mr. Cleans of muscle beach, as we called the men who lifted weights. Wearing earrings and bulk laden, they looked like Black and Brown versions of the White bald genie on the bottle of the household cleaner, or vice versa. These guys were a remarkably integrated group for the times. Their code was not based on race but strength. The beach sang with the ringing of their weights set back on iron stands. Lucy and I called one of the weightlifters King Clean. He owned two dogs, and with them he controlled the tone of the boardwalk.

Though the promenade approached the ramshackle Venice pier, Lucy and I continued sauntering forward. Our noses squinched from smelly crude oil floating on the waters of the filthy Venice Canals. We had strayed into the 'No Man's Land'. Such a 'no man' approached us from behind, asking questions we knew better than to answer. Picking up our pace, he continued to harass us. We were both nine years old and scored high on the Tanner Puberty Development Scale, our menses a whisper away.

When the man reached out and touched us, we screeched profanities. Lucy was loudest, in rapid fire Spanish. Placing an arm around each of us, he shoved us to the ground, covering Lucy's mouth with his hand. My head hit the pavement, blood trickled from my left temple. His knee was on my upper back. Feeling my spine might break, I froze. Lucy bit his hand hard. He slapped her. Those combined actions gave me enough space to roll over. Never having hit anyone before, I shoved my knee into his groin, then weakly socked him in the stomach. He grabbed me at the neck with both hands, choking me until my vision grayed. Lucy jumped on his back, her arms yanking his long hair, overextending his neck.

Then I was free. Having heard our screams, like the gladiators they were, the Mr. Cleans arrived and yanked the assailant away. King Clean's two large dogs accompanied our heroes. They sank teeth into the attacker's belly. King Clean told us to run home as fast as we could, and not look back. Doing as told, we still heard the repeated cracking of bone on pavement, ferocious canines chomping, and a coward's whining.

"No, No God, No," Ellie said, seeing our faces battered, clothes dirty and ripped. I told my mother everything, ready to take whatever chastising was to come. There was plenty of it that day. Luckily, Ellie did not believe in hitting children. After cleaning us up, my mother would not let me join in escorting Lucy home. A neighbor came to watch me. We girls were fortunate. Abuela insisted our transgressions had already been well punished.

When Ellie returned from Lucy's, I was drowsy and confused. Concerned, my mother took me to the nearest emergency room, St. John's Hospital in Santa Monica. I had my first known seizure while we traveled. An electroencephalogram showed continuous abnormal brain activity. Given my history of being born breach and quiet, this hit on the head increased my risk for epilepsy. I was given medication intravenously, which stopped the altered brain activity. "What's happening, Mommy?" I asked when fully awake. Because Ellie was a nurse, she was allowed to take me home for observation while continuing to give me pills by mouth.

Though Lucy and I had to deal with Ellie and Abuela's wrath, Paco's opinion was harshest. Paco, Lucy's responsible older brother, was lean but strong. With shoulder length molasses-colored hair and loads of charisma, he had already organized demonstrations for students' rights. Paco steadfastly resisted street gang induction by being as tough as gang members, but smarter. His body flaunted training by the Mr. Cleans. Ellie was grateful he would now keep a closer eye on me. Paco was my first guardian angel.

The Venice 13 was a Latino gang. A war was brewing between them and the Westside Crips, a Black gang that was south, and inland, from the canals. In community meetings at our house, Ellie and Abuela called the situation "pobres de los pobres violencia, poor on poor violence."

The two dogs that helped save Lucy and me were named Venus and Dido, 'The Ladies Roman'. They were symbols of the 'balance' King Clean brought to the neighborhood. That's why Paco proposed Ellie might keep the canine heroes when their owner was 'going away'. Neither he nor Momma answered when I asked where King Clean was going. Ellie accepted the canine gifts with the saddest, most grateful heart.

With the Ladies Roman, Lucy and I were always noticed. We were the worthy children saved by the man who owned those dogs. Years later I understood King Clean's 'trip' was a prison sentence resulting from rescuing Lucy and me. During the trial a judge had asked the accused whether he felt remorse for his dogs mauling a man, near fatally. His answer was, "None at all. If I had it to do over, I would do it that way again."

⌒ ‿

Each weekday morning at 6AM Ellie's mantra was, "Let's hit the road." We raced out the door like soldiers headed toward peace. Project Action was a youth center in the neighborhood which operated out of a store front on Washington Street. Free breakfast was served to any child who presented. It had to happen fast, before school. The meal was always scrambled eggs, grits, milk, and orange juice. The kids never seemed to bore of this same meal over and over again. The morning food often replaced the absent dinner of the night before. Lucy arrived by 7AM. She and I helped clean up, then we walked together the block to Westminster School. Ellie left for the hospital in time for her shift.

Our house on Sunset Avenue became known as a training ground for civil and human rights, mostly focused on support for youth at Project Action. We hosted a regular Wednesday night community meeting. Lucy and I always sat on the floor because there were never enough seats. Afterward, Abuela usually needed to stay and chat with my mother. We girls always eavesdropped.

"I'm not sure I want to become the head of Project Action," Ellie said.

"Think of it as part of your psychology studies. It could be the topic of your master's thesis. You're already doing the work, you should have the title. We can't get grants if we don't have a structure. Someday we will have money to pay you," Abuela said with a rehearsed clarity.

"Keeping the doors open is good enough for me—keeping kids from hanging in the street."

"I agree," Abuela said. Tucking her long white braid under her coat, she buttoned it and walked to the door.

"Don't forget the lights," I said to Lucy as they left. Abuela's house was close but the street dark. We had a 'protocol' for their walks home. We watched them leave. When they arrived safe, Lucy flashed their lights three times.

Near our place on Sunset was a large warehouse. It turned out to belong to Synanon, a self-help organization for people with substance abuse problems. The headquarters of the organization was the red brick armory on the Santa Monica Beach. Over lunch its members returned to the main building for seminars. Someone at the Sunset warehouse, aware of Project Action, asked Ellie to be a speaker. I got to take a half day off school to go with her to that engagement.

The dining room of the armory took up most of the second floor of the building. The ceiling to floor windows looked west out to the ocean. Five years old when I had first entered the place, it was still familiar even though four years had passed. Volleyball players trickled in from the beach to attend Ellie's seminar. Seats were reserved at a table for Ellie and me. A member of the dining room staff, drawn from the ranks of the armory's residents, placed lunch in front of us.

The man from the warehouse stood near the podium. "We want to thank Ellie Marshall for speaking today. Ellie is a nurse, civil rights, peace, and child advocacy activist. She also studies psychology at UCLA," he said.

'Was that my mother?' I had never heard her described that way. A hundred-fifty people applauded for Ellie as if they had only recently been schooled in the art. Walking to the podium, instead of standing behind it, she grabbed an empty chair from a nearby table. Pulling the seat to the front of the crowd, she sat down facing the audience.

"Please raise your hand if you dreamt of being a dope fiend when you were a child," Ellie said. All hands stayed down. She continued, "What did you plan to be?" Hands raised. Ellie pointed to each of them, eliciting answers.

"A firemen," one man said.

"A mechanic," said a woman.

"An airline pilot..." said another.

"Timmy's mother on the television show Lassie," another guy said. Everyone laughed.

"Do you mean an actor?" Ellie asked.

"No, I mean a parent who looked after her kids and knew how to help them," the guy said.

"I see," Ellie said. "Why do you think you are not those things if you are not?" The room fell silent. Ellie herself did not fill the empty audio space.

"Me? Got into trouble—stole somethin' when I was ten, then again when I was twelve," said a Puerto Rican man with a thick New York accent, who looked in his thirties. He continued, "Then I went in and out of different joints until I came here last year. All that for a Coke and bag of chips."

"Why did you do it?" Ellie pumped him for more information.

"It was summer and 100 degrees, at night, in Black and Spanish Harlem." The audience shook their heads knowingly. "I didn't have fifty cent or anything to eat," the man said.

"What widens the gap between rich and poor?" Ellie asked the crowd.

That was my cue. I got up, passing three-by-five cards and pencils around the room. Ellie asked more questions. Who do you think is poorer, families headed by women or men?... Black people? Brown people?... White People?... Veterans of the Viet Nam War?... The audience answered the questions on the cards. Then they ranked each group with a number—10 being the poorest families and 1 being the least poor. Those answers led to an hour and a half conversation.   The people in the room, most without having finished junior high school, knew that those living in poverty were, as Ellie summarized, "... Part of families headed by women, disproportionately Black, Brown, or unemployed laborers, speakers of a first language other than English, old or very young, military veterans, living in the inner city or in rural areas, and former convicts."

"The list includes most people," one woman shouted out.

"It does. Few in the world have enough for health and growth." Ellie said.

"What good is it to know all this stuff is true?" Someone in the far back asked.

"Nothing if you don't commit to do what you can to help make change—but not stealing," Ellie said. The audience laughed, then stood clapping, this time with genuine enthusiasm.

The next week, an eighteen-wheeler truck pulled up in front of Project Action. Synanon had more things than they needed and were sharing. Movers unloaded tables—pool, ping-pong, dining. There were books, bookshelves, and a sofa. Boxes held paper goods—towels, napkins, plates, and cups. Pushed against a back wall was a new Hi-Fi stereo, with LPs and 45s. Even a piano was delivered. The truck driver sat down at it, crooning, "Sea of Love..." and expertly tapping the ivory and ebony keys. Others, including the kids, sang along. When the moving van drove off, it left a whole new world. Neighborhood teenagers, and their younger siblings, would have something to do over the long hot summer.

15

BLOOD RIVER

SUMMER 1965 TO 1968

HOT ENOUGH TO BLISTER the skin, the Santa Ana Winds ravaged Los Angeles. Sirens raced down Manchester to the hospital on the other side of the cul-de-sac. They were loud and frequent, stopping us from opening the windows to let even the hot breeze blow through. From the ranch house picture window we could see black clouds from fires burning eight miles south. Newscasters called it a riot. Later, the people who lived in that part of the city, and history, would call it The Watts Uprisings.

All the families on the cul-de-sac slept on floors and sofas at our house. Having just turned ten, my visit that weekend was to be a celebration with cul-de-sac friends. If not for the nauseating smell of ignited rubber, it might have seemed like a block party. Though I thought Ellie was at work when I asked my grandparents, "Where is my Mommy?" I was seeking confirmation. My spending a week of summer vacation on the cul-de-sac gave Ellie a holiday from parenting but not work. She made extra money by taking more shifts.

Fifteen miles west, at our house in Venice, Ellie was reading the book Games People Play, assigned for a psychology class. Having worked overnight, arriving home at dawn, she had fallen asleep on the sofa with the book open on her belly. Hearing the screen at the front door creak, she was awakened. Panicked kids' voices yelled, "Ellie, come quick. They are in front of Project Action, talkin' about breaking windows." Ellie opened the door. A gang of her favorite eight year olds from the breakfast program stood on the steps, their appropriate adults following quickly behind.

The phone rang. Ellie waived the surprise guests into the living room while diving to grab the receiver. A man's voice, which she did not recognize, was on the other end. Councilman Bradley explained that the city was under Marshall Law. The riots in Watts had spread to other parts of Los Angeles, including Venice. The National Guard would arrest those breaking the 6PM curfew, using what they would call 'necessary force' to control situations. "See what you can do," the Councilman said.

The curfew siren's preblasts drowned out Bradley's voice. Ellie pushed the button to hang up, then laid the receiver on the table, off the hook, avoiding other calls. "Quiet, I'm thinking," she told all in the room. The unexpected guests slammed their mouths shut. Then Ellie took refuge in the bathroom. Five minutes passed before she emerged in her white uniform, shoes, stockings, nursing hat, and neatly applied lipstick. She was going to the storefront which housed Project Action. The other mothers present wanted to accompany Ellie, but she forbade them.

When one of the children asked, Ellie explained I was safe at my grandparents' house in Morning Side Park, in South Central Los Angeles. Having called Franklin while still at work, she knew Bethune Street, with its dead end, remained an island of relative calm. A Venice update could only worry her parents. Heading out the door, Ellie grabbed her purse. If arrested, it would be good to have her address book and identification. Another of the mothers begged her to take the dogs with her. Taking the leashes from the porch hooks, Ellie whistled for the already agitated dogs. The Ladies Roman galloped to the gate.

Stomach churning, Ellie faked a relaxed saunter down Sunset Avenue, dogs in tow. A jeep turned a corner. Ellie made eye contact with two National Guardsmen. She must have looked a special kind of crazy strolling her dogs, in that get up and her best purse. The soldiers turned the jeep off her path. She imagined they shook their heads with pity. The curfew siren pre-alert gave three more quick blasts. Arriving at Project Action, more than a hundred school aged kids yelled and jumped around. Having the key, she opened the storefront door. Ellie herded all the younger children into the building. The teenagers were noncompliant and belligerent.

Jeeps appeared, boxing the children against the building. Ellie dragged a chair from inside Project Action's door. Hauling it to the pavement, she still held tight to the excited dogs leashes while she climbed on its seat. Her white uniform gleamed above the crowd. Venus and Dido stood alert, front paws stabilizing the sides of the nurse's pedestal, their leashes still wrapped around her wrists.

Understanding that it was hard for these kids to resist this way of getting attention when they were otherwise invisible, she made a decision. She would not abandon the children on the street. No sooner than she had thought it, the two National Guardsmen seen before jumped on their jeep's hood. They raised their rifles. Through a megaphone, another soldier gave orders to clear the street. The curfew siren rumbled, reaching its highest pitch. The dogs yapped. The soldier's words were inaudible. A child threw a baseball, hitting the man holding the megaphone. More rifles raised.

It occurred to Ellie that neither police nor soldiers came to Venice for gangs at war, drugs sales on the school grounds, or developers evicting people without notice. The fleeting thought was erased when the Ladies Roman sensed mounting tension and tugged at their leashes. Then they barked, as they always had, to the sound of the bells from St. Paul's striking six.

It took a beat before Ellie understood what was about to happen. Both Venus and Dido had cocked their heads toward a clicking sound in the opposite direction from the bells. Then Ellie's voice reverberated, "Get down, get down, get down!" The surrounding children dropped to the ground, butts in the air, hands curled over their heads, as trained by school drills pretending to prepare them for Atomic Bomb blasts. One dog broke away, then the other, lunging toward the soldiers. Two rifle pings killed each of the dogs in succession. Before the bells of St. Paul's stopped ringing, Ellie fell, also hit by gunfire.

Vanessa struggled to keep calm, knowing in her core something was wrong. Franklin determined they might need an attorney in case Ellie was arrested. Our family knew only one member of the court, Alex, from the Brunch Bunch. Franklin made the call. Alex agreed to help. Franklin sobbed, returning the receiver carefully to its cradle. Watts burning and Ellie in danger, Grandfather's submerged wartime damage, normally only apparent when dreaming, surfaced during daylight. His destabilization was manifest by yelling belligerently, which panicked the entire extended household.

Vanessa took over as she had during and immediately after WWII. She planted her husband and the children in the den to watch Gun Smoke on television. Grandmother then went on to organize a phone tree on the block.

Eight hours later the phone rang. Alex announced that my mother was at LA County hospital in surgery, a horrid place, but the best in the city for trauma. Vanessa breathed hard without any other response. In his excitement Alex had forgotten to mention that the bullet had missed the long bone in Ellie's right upper arm but clipped a vein which doctors thought easy to repair. He did so now. Vanessa exhaled. She wanted to know who attacked Ellie and was curiously relieved it had been the National Guard.

The next morning, arraigned in her absence, Alex appeared before a judge. He argued that Ellie was a community activist and registered nurse, mowed down in front of a crowd of children, "For God sakes, in her white uniform." He hoped that would hold off sentencing until he mounted a real defense. Surprisingly, the judge reduced the charges to a misdemeanor comparable to jaywalking. Recounting this minor victory, Alex said, "We got lucky."

I had been in the waiting areas and treatment rooms of hospitals before. It was different on a ward—no link to the outside. Holding my grandparents' hands, I walked between them. Our footsteps echoed against the linoleum floor. Snot-pink tiles lined the walls. Nurses and doctors raced around as if their uniforms protected them from the obligation of civility. When speaking to the clerk at the counter, Alex used his special lawyer voice to assert control.

"You can't bring a child in under the age of 12," the clerk said.

"Can't you see how tall she is?" Alex said.

"How old are you, dear?" the clerk asked.

"Twelve," I said. My grandparents nodded assent. This was the first lie I ever remember consciously telling. I knew it was well placed.

"I don't believe you," the clerk said.

"Sicily, spell the word 'Antidisestablishmentarianism,'" Alex said. He knew I could do it, Dorothy had taught me during a Scrabble game years before. The letters quickly spilled from my mouth. There was no way the clerk could keep up.

"Go ahead—bed 67B," the clerk said.

Alex leaned over and whispered to the woman at the desk, "Is she presentable?"

"Well, she is in custody."

"No, she is not. Here is the writ." He handed the clerk a piece of paper.

"Wait here," the clerk said.

I saw people on gurneys, writhing in pain and groaning. Doctors examined them in the halls. It didn't seem right to me. Most of those on the beds were Black, Spanish, or Asian.

The doctors were all White. Some of them were cursing, the physicians and the patients. The smell made me want to throw up. Two uniformed policemen followed the clerk back toward us. One was fastening handcuffs to his belt and the other held the piece of paper that Alex had given the clerk. The policemen passed, as though we were invisible. The clerk took her place behind the counter and gave a nod.

There were six beds in Ellie's room. Her back was to us. Moving around the bed, I was horrified when her eyes were closed. Was she dead? Then her lids fluttered and opened. One arm bandaged, she reached out her good one. Elation washed through me.

Conversion of the her civil disobedience indictment to a misdemeanor did not protect Ellie from losing her hospital job. When she was healed from the gunshot, she fell back on the uncertain income working at the Nurses' Registry. Project Action's funding was now nonexistent. Synanon had supplied all the furnishings. A local market had donated food for the breakfast program, barely before its expiry date. But the rent had always been pieced together by individual donations, including from my mother's own salary. That was no longer possible. Ellie was lauded by academics and nonprofit organizations for developing a youth program threatening enough to the status quo that no one would fund it. Praise didn't pay the rent. When Project Action had to close, something changed in Ellie. There were things she wanted to tell me urgently. What if she had been killed without completing my education?

Every night, Ellie told me more about the civil rights movement. She started with Harriet Tubman, a Union spy, who had personally directed hundreds of slaves to freedom in Canada through the Underground Railroad. This railroad did not run on tracks, Ellie explained, but ran on a network of good will and courage, with hiding places and protection by friends of all races. She focused on the details of how people were secretly moved from house to house, avoiding capture.

Finally, after many days, Ellie's history of struggle finished with the period of February 1965. A few months before she had been shot, Malcolm X had been murdered. I knew who Malcolm was, having heard talk of him around the house and seen a photo essay in Life Magazine. The author of the essay was photojournalist Gordon Parks—a concerned photographer and the only Black man I knew at the time with that job distinction.

Ellie said Malcolm was assassinated because he evolved beyond the narrow view that Black people had to be better than, instead of equal to, others. While at Mecca, the seat of the Islamic religion, his religion, he saw all races of people pray together. This equality flew in the face of less progressive religious and social interpretations. "With that approach," Ellie explained, "Malcolm was building ties to others committed to civil rights and a more universal worldview. His wisdom would make him the most important man in America, able to galvanize all kinds of people to work together."

As a result of her gunshot and recovery, Ellie's mood was often sad. She had difficulty keeping the house organized and clean. Luckily, I had always had chores, dishes, trash, laundry. I was able to do things when my mother could not. Ellie cried at night. Crawling into her bed, I tried to comfort her. At twenty-eight years old, my mother was exhausted by death, destruction, and struggle. If only she were dumb as a rock she could ignore the surrounding oppression, suppression, and depression.

About me, Ellie's instinct was still mostly correct. But her judgement was confused about other things. She had been dating a man. By her design, he wasn't much a part of my life—a good call. Unbeknownst to Ellie, her beau was married. The man's wife approached Momma and me in the grocery store, threatening aggression despite my presence. Ellie let loose, causing the woman to slither away while other patrons watched.

When we arrived home, the man was sitting on the front steps. He had come to pick up his free weights, which were in our yard. That was his bad luck. Ellie's anger had been brewing since being shot. She was tightly controlled when she said, "Sicily honey, please take the groceries in and start your homework." I followed my mother's instructions. Within seconds of my closing the door, the boyfriend howled,

"Are you crazy? That's my car..."

"I sure as shit am, and you sure as shit should stay away from me and mine," Ellie screamed.

Having heard glass crack, I peeked out the window. Ellie reeled the last of the boyfriend's disc-shaped iron weights through his front windshield. A crowd of neighbors gathered nearby. The boyfriend scrambled to his car filled with glass shards and pulled away. Neighbors clapped. Ellie came into the house.

"Darling Baby," she said, crying, "If you ever think I'm going to hit you, run out of the house yelling, 'Don't hit me.' Make sure everyone can hear."

"Mommy, you would never hit me."

"I never expected I would attack anyone's car with weights either—promise me."

Shortly after the 'free weight challenge,' while we were visiting my grandparents, Linda called asking Ellie to come to the hospital. Once there, Ellie sat on one side of Mike, Linda on the other, each holding his hand until he stepped away from life. Mike Akira's death flipped Ellie back into gear. Linda and the boys needed her, we all did. Community meetings resumed at the house as she and Abuela pulled together the shreds of Project Action, in honor of Mike.

Most days I came home from Westminster Elementary School excited. I learned to write articles for the Campus Crier, the school newspaper. 'Every Good Boy Does Fine' and 'FACE' made up the notes to the music I loved. There was a photography class with a darkroom. I learned to develop pictures from my Leica.

My seizure medicine was held in the school nurse's office. After lunch I would go there to get a pill. She asked me about my days, and not only because she was interested. If blank spots were reported they may have been seizures.

"Nothing ever happens," I said.

"Nothing is supposed to as long as you take your medicine," the nurse said.

Following the polio epidemic of the 1950s, public school nurses still had teeth and funding. At Westminster, the RN ran the immunization program and did routine annual physical exams. On one of those exams I was found to have scoliosis, a crooked spine. Despite my unlikely body type and height, the nurse chose to drop me into ballet and yoga classes. I welcomed the reprieve from the anguishing regular school physical education program. Sadly, I had to leave Lucy on the school yard.

The school dance teacher, Joanna, referred me to another special program run by a modeling agency. Meeting on Saturday mornings at the Oakwood playground in Venice, it was a charm school. The hallmarks of 'a lady' were passed to me—not that Ellie and Vanessa weren't ladies. This was a polishing. One must cross her legs with ankles always touching. Never wear more than four colors at one time—no matter how much influence London's Carnaby Street has on fashion—and don't mix checks with stripes or paisley. By the time I finished ten weeks of classes, I could walk with a stack of books on my head, sliding my rear end onto the seat of a car, without them falling. I learned to float gently over the earth because I attended a good public elementary school.

Twice a week I rounded out my physical routine with a class or performance with Joanna's real dance company. Alex from the Brunch Bunch met Joanna at one of my dance recitals. They grew closer, dated, and quickly married. Wanting to help Ellie, Joanna took me from Westminster and fed me dinner after dancing with her troop. This allowed Ellie to take more day shifts at the Registry.

Turning eleven years old in the summer of 1966, I would start high school in a month. Though my body was pretty much that of a woman, and my academic prowess at college level, I was still a kid in most other ways. With the Ladies Roman dead, the Mr. Cleans took it upon themselves to teach Lucy and me to lift weights and use basic Martial Arts for self-defense. Despite the best efforts of the guys at Muscle Beach, Ellie was uncomfortable with my being on a bus, alone for an hour, headed to Venice High. Paco having graduated increased her concerns. It had been nearly two years since the assault at the Venice Canals. I was a grade ahead of Lucy, who also was no intellectual slouch, but this year we were unable to travel together. Ellie missed some morning shifts because of driving me to school. Even with Joanna's pickup help our income went down.

Choices for Ellie's long term hospital employment remained slim. Having to use her old hospital as a reference when applying for jobs, 'Dismissed for being arrested during a riot' didn't help. After Ellie was shot in 1965, she had become obsessively protective of me. The assassinations of Bobby Kennedy and Dr. Martin Luther King Jr. the spring of 1968 multiplied her barely tolerable paranoia. No matter what, Ellie would not allow me to move about unescorted in, or outside, the neighborhood—though I was already twelve. Those murders also more fully radicalized Ellie's actions supporting human and constitutional rights.

On Friday afternoons, before 7PM, several carloads would be filled with people from Venice. We would head to the Federal Building on Wilshire. There we shouted "No More War!" while conscientious objectors refused army induction. They were arrested for not wanting to kill Vietnamese, nor anyone else. On Saturdays, with Abuela and Lucy, we often visited Knobby and Rosa on the United Farm Workers picket lines in Delano. Sometimes the Akira boys came with us while Linda worked. This is what we did while other kids, less burdened by reality, played miniature golf.

1 6

SAN FRANCISCO BAY

WINTER 1969 TO 1972

A FEW WEEKS BEFORE the incident occurred, Grandfather had mentioned the possibility to my mother. "Difficulty in funding Project Action, you being shot and blacklisted from hospitals, is not a coincidence. It's a reflection of the times and your role in them." It had never occurred to Ellie that she was emerging as a righteous force in the neighborhood. If the pesky poor people would disappear from Venice, with a bit of cleanup the acres were ripe for elite development. Increasing success with community organizing gave more power to existing residents. Property developers, corrupt politicians, and gangsters would not sit idle while some nurse blocked their fortunes.

The night 'it' happened, Ellie broke from her protocol of never leaving me without adult supervision. She needed to go out to buy white stockings for work. Lucy and I were in my room at the back of the house studying. Even in different schools, we were still best friends. Lucy's brother, Paco, was on his way to walk her home.

"Girls, ask Paco to stay until I get back. I won't be more than forty-five minutes," Ellie said.

"Ok, Momma—"

"Don't forget to keep the doors locked."

"We won't forget," Lucy said.

Paco often traveled through the back alleys of Venice, as he had that night, to reach our house. He tried the back door. Locked, as it should have been, he started to knock. That was when he heard the sound of our front windows shattering. Kicking the door open, he had a line of sight through the living room to the front yard. Two unfamiliar shadows held cigarette lighters. Whoosh, whoosh—Molotov cocktails, gasoline soaked cloth wicks in Coke bottles, flew through the already broken glass. The first hit the sofa, the second the coffee table. Both exploded into flames. Paco dropped to the floor, crawling past the fire and into my room.

"Lucy, Sicily," he yelled. "Where are you?" Water was running.

"Aquí en el cuarto de baño," Lucy whispered back.

We were lying in the bath tub with the shower on.

"Smart girls!" Paco said. He also soaked himself. Wrapped in wet blankets and sheets, we all leapt through the flames and out the back door.

"Get to Abeula—through the yards, not the street or alleys," Paco said, throwing the bedclothes on the ground, stamping out smoldering embers.

"Aren't you coming with us?" I asked, shaking from our narrow escape.

"I'll be there soon, after I keep the place from burning." There was a spigot with a garden hose. Paco turned the handle, water sprayed from the nozzle. Dragging the hose, he raced into the house. The men on the street were gone, but the flames were not. Under the sink was a plastic bottle of Ponds dish detergent. Squirting the soap ahead of him, he mixed it with the fan of water.

"What is he doing?" Lucy asked. She and I still stood outside the back door.

"I think he's using a science lesson. You know, the one where soap breaks down oil or gasoline. It'll help put out the fire," I said. We saw the flames transform to steam. Thinking Paco was safe, we ran.

Arriving home with her white nylons in a bag, Ellie found fire engines and police cars in front of the house. She pushed past them into the sloshing wet living room. Red bricks were on the floor and broken glass everywhere. The sickening smell of gasoline, burnt cloth, and soaked furniture was pervasive. Checking the bathroom, she turned off the shower. The damage to the house was not insurmountable. We three kids were not there. The firemen and police confirmed the house was empty when they had arrived. Though the carpet smoldered, the flames were doused by someone else, not them. Ellie's relief was brief. She called Abuela.

"Yes, both girls are here," Abuela said. "Can I talk to Paco?"

"Isn't he with you?" Ellie asked.

"No, but the girls said he saved them."

Ellie explained to the cops in the yard that Abuela's grandson was missing. Everyone knew Abuela. Everyone owed Abuela something, even the police and the gangs. If Paco had disappeared, this single fact made Ellie certain that whoever had burnt our house was not from the Venice community. Knowing Paco often traveled the back alleys, the neighbors spread out to find him. Ellie went through the kitchen to the backyard. Following the snaking water hose to the spigot she found Paco. He was on the ground wrapped in the rubber hose, his face bloody and his gas soaked shirt stuffed in his mouth. He writhed with pain, trying to break out of the rubber coil.

Paco did not recognize the two men who caught him putting out the fire. But he knew they were the ones he saw throwing Molotov cocktails. While his arms were in a cast for six weeks, Lucy and I took turns cutting Paco's food into cubes, feeding him with a spoon, holding his straw while he drank. Doing these methodical things, uncomfortable thoughts kept coming to me—King Clean, Venus and Dido, and now Paco were all hurt—because of me. Ellie had similar thoughts. Vanessa begged her daughter to abandon Venice and bring me to stay on the cul-de-sac.

"Why not?" Vanessa asked.

"Because... a boy nearly gave his life to keep our home from burning down. He did not run. We won't either," Ellie said.

"That's a hard answer to argue against." Vanessa was simultaneously frightened and proud of her daughter.

Franklin and the other men from the cul-de-sac arrived to make repairs on our place. They installed grates like prison bars over the windows. Grandmother Vanessa and the other women of Bethune Street brought curtains and other household things to replace those burned or soaked. When my grandparents and Lillie were the only visitors left, we two girls played Chinese Checkers in the refurbished living room. The adults sat on the steps in front of the house. Vanessa and Ellie drank iced tea, Franklin a Budweiser beer. I heard Grandfather lower his voice and say,

"I think we should set up some safety protocols for Sicily during this time."

"What did you have in mind?" Ellie asked.

"In the war we had code words. They alone were not always fail safe. The resistance folks produced objects, like a ring or egg shells. Things no one would expect," he said.

"How about this?" Ellie pulled the chain on the Maltese Cross, releasing it from her cleavage. That was the day the protocol was set up for my protection.

Ellie still took one class a semester, it was all she could afford. At that rate her master's degree in psychology would take another decade. Never again being left at home alone, I went to evening lectures with her, doing homework while she drove. We travelled the scenic route from Venice to Santa Monica, then up palm tree lined Wilshire Blvd, past the Veterans Hospital and the new Federal Building. Eventually, the Imperial floated up Westwood onto the UCLA campus.

Professor Angela Davis' philosophy class was three hours long. It was supposed to be a twelve student seminar but grew in popularity. The last class I attended on campus the venue was moved to Royce Hall, a romanesque, brick and tile building, whose auditorium seemed to hold a thousand people. Every seat was full, leaving some standing in the aisles. It was within days of the murders on campus of two UCLA students—members of the predominantly African American Black Panther Party.

The Black Panther Party members killed were John Huggins and Bunchy Carter. They were shot by Chuchessa Hubert of the US Organization. The murders happened in a room full of students at UCLA, following a meeting about the new African American Students program, its curriculum, and its location at the recently built Campbell hall. Plenty of post-meeting participants milled about, yet two members of the Black Panther Party leadership, John and Bunchy, were clearly targeted.

In Angela's class that last day I attended at Royce hall, she stood. She was tall—as I imagined I would be as an adult—had big hair, and she always wore earrings I liked. Pacing, she theorized local police, or FBI, involvement in the murders at Campbell Hall through paid agitators. History would show Angela was correct—not that she needed external confirmation. Sometime later an FBI interagency memo surfaced clarifying the plan to pit the Black Panther Party and the US Organization against one another by perpetuating fear of mutual murder conspiracies.

By then Ellie had me reading the Peloponnesian Wars. I understood what Angela was talking about. 'Divide and conquer' had long been the approach to power, a certain type of power. In 425 BC Greece, playing only to the differences between groups, insisting their goals were antithetical, made it true. Meanwhile, the gods danced above the fray while mortals massacred themselves.

On the drive home from UCLA I asked, "Why was Angela's class packed full?"

"She talks about things people are thinking," Ellie said.

"Why did you asks her about the prisons, instead of the murders on the campus?"

Ellie grabbed her bottom lip between her teeth, and pulling off the road to a curb on Westwood Blvd, she said, "I didn't know when I would get to speak with Angela again." Changing the subject she asked, "Darling Baby—do you know King Clean's given name?"

"I don't. After Lucy and I picked his nickname we never thought about his real name."

"His name was Ricky, Ricky Jones. His prison sentence was supposed to be one year to life."

"But it's much more than a year already."

"Baby, the dogs were considered to be deadly weapons. He got the worst sentence."

"He didn't tell the dogs to do anything. They wanted to help. So when will he get out?

"Ricky was sent to a prison near Monterey California. It's called Soledad. There was trouble with the guards, who are exceptionally cruel at that prison. His sentence was extended," Ellie said.

"What do you mean 'trouble'?"

"He was in fights, trying to protect himself and probably others. That was the way he was."

"This happened because Lucy and I were stupid."

"No darling, this happened because, more than anything, prisons are a business designed to keep people in them, one way or another, for profit," Ellie said.

"Will King—I mean Ricky—be okay?"

"No, Darling Baby, he won't."

"Why? Can we visit him? In the movies, people always visit their family in prison."

"No, we can't."

"Is it because we are not his real family?"

"Sicily... Ricky was killed," Ellie said.

The reality of 'killed' banged the walls of my skull, echoing, twice in one day. The man who saved me from rape had been murdered. I couldn't catch my breath. When I did, it was to sob. With each inhalation there was terrible pain. Ellie engulfed me with her arms. We both cried, there in the Chrysler Imperial. Staring at the crowns on the upholstery, I now hated those symbols of wealth.

Feeling no other news could be worse than that which she had already delivered, Ellie said, "I don't want it to be a surprise because I know you like Angela, but the University of California is going to fire her."

I looked up, my eyes still blurred by tears, and asked, "Why?"

"Because she wants those like Ricky to stop being murdered—and she is a communist."

"Why did she tell them? Doesn't she know about the Blacklist?" I gurgled.

"She told them because she is not a coward, and the United States Constitution protects our right to join any political party we choose, and to believe in any philosophy or religion we choose—as long as we don't commit a crime while doing it. They knew she was a communist when she was hired. The university only expected her to sit around in an armchair, writing but not actually trying to change anything." I shuttered a few times. Ellie checked to be sure I was not seizing. My head against the window, eyes closed, feeling the Chrysler Imperial rumble away from the curb, I slept.

Shortly after the Royce Hall class, Angela Davis was fired from the University of California for her political beliefs. Later that year, in October, a legal challenge of Angela's dismissal based on the right of American's to believe as they choose, forced the University to rehire her. She would be fired again.

⌒ ⌣

The Soledad Brothers were three men, George Lester Jackson, Fleeta Drumgo, and John Wesley Clutchette. While inmates they were accused of killing a guard at Soledad Prison, before Ricky Jones, aka King Clean, had died. The evidence against the three was bogus, and all of them were politically active in the prison. George in particular was a Field Marshall of the Black Panther Party and wrote eloquently about the oppression of Black and poor people. Ellie spent every free moment organizing a defense committee for the Soledad Brothers. The committee included people from all facets of Los Angeles—Watts to Hollywood, Congressmen to Sanitation Workers. My mother made phone calls from our living room to lawyers, places for demonstrations, meetings, and the press. Then she had to go all those places.

Never being left home alone, I was always by Ellie's side or with someone she trusted. It became my habit to act older than I was. I learned to type and run a mimeograph machine. Blue ink constantly smudged my finger tips. There were only a few other kids around. One of them was Jonathan, Soledad Brother George Jackson's younger sibling. He, like me, was bigger and smarter than his age. I was fourteen when we had first met, and he sixteen. Having Jonathan stand next to me while passing out leaflets was protective against my being harassed. People rudely said, "No" to me at the Mall. With Jonathan at my side, they said, "No, thank you."

Angela was the chair of the Soledad Brothers' Defense Committee. By June 20, 1970, she had been fired from UCLA again. Not only did the Board of Regents of the University of California dislike what she was saying, but also the way she said it. I remember the date because we celebrated Jonathan's seventeenth birthday three days later, June 23. Jonathan was smart but generally more lighthearted than on that day. He had no recollection of ever spending a birthday with his brother George, who had been imprisoned most of Jonathan's life. I asked if this birthday made him feel worse than others. He said, "You can beat the 'human' out of anyone if you try hard enough." I assumed he was talking about his brother.

Ellie and I drove to a downtown deli one Sunday shortly after Jonathan's birthday. We bought a large bag of bagels and a smaller one with lox and cream cheese. From there we went to a house in midtown Los Angeles with a carefully manicured lawn. The sign on the door said, 'Sunset Hall'. It was a large place, maybe twenty rooms.

"Who lives here?" I asked.

"It's a home for old Reds, radical Unitarians, and other folks who made the world a lot better than they found it," Ellie said, "You might know a few people here." Ellie smiled, then knocked.

Edie opened the door. She was as I remembered her from years before. Guy popped out, hugging me, much harder than expected for his advanced age. In the old days the two were frequent visitors at Sunset House, and they had come now to see a friend from New York who was staying there. Ellie handed Guy the bags with the food.

"Es s tsayt tsu bakumen di gelt," Ellie said.

"What does that mean?" I asked.

"It is time to get the money, in Yiddish," Edie answered.

Guy ushered us into the communal dining room where he had laid out plates and cutlery for everyone around. The room smelt of the paprika chicken being prepared for dinner in the kitchen. Already at the table was a pleasant looking Black lady, with close cut hair, like Ellie used to wear.

"Sicily and Ellie, this is Charlene, from New York," Edie said.

Charlene stood and hugged Ellie. They had first met eating cream puffs at the Grant home in Springfield, Illinois, over twenty years before. "Sicily, this is the person who makes Angela Davises," Ellie said. This special person kissed me on both cheeks, then gave me a bone crushing hug.

"Ir visn, zey veln nit haltn in firing ir," Guy said, passing lox around on plates.

"And what does that mean?" I asked.

"They won't stop at firing Angela," Ellie said.

"They'll try to arrest her on a trumped up charge, or kill her—maybe both," Charlene looked ashamed for her bluntness in my presence. She placed a sympathetic hand over mine.

"It's okay," I said, "—better to be prepared for bad things, before they happen."

"How old are you?"

"I'm fourteen, soon I'll be fifteen..."

"Then you are right on time." Pen in hand, an accountant by profession, Charlene opened a large ledger and scribbled. Ellie pulled an envelope from her purse. It contained 'the list'. Money would be needed for the long legal battle against the University of California for dismissing Angela. Funds would also be needed for other storms which might make landfall near the professor's feet.

'The Golden Gate' is a geographical designation for the point where the San Francisco Bay opens its mouth to the Pacific Ocean. The bridge, named for that geography, spans the distance across the water from San Francisco on the South to Marin County on the North. The Marin landscape is deceptively placid, especially since it houses San Quinton Prison.

August 7, 1970, was a Friday. My dance teacher, Joanna, picked me up from Abuela's. That surprised me. I was expecting Ellie, who was oddly at Alex's office, near the Palisades in Santa Monica. When I asked Joanna if I might play the car radio, she preferred that I not. Ellie waited at the door to the office for us. She hugged me and would not let me go. Joanna went inside. When I was finally released, my mother and I sat on the stone steps looking over the manicured flowers on the boulevard running down the middle of the road. Then she told me. A revolt by Black prisoners in the Marin County courthouse was independently initiated by my seventeen year old friend Jonathan—at gun point.

Jonathan's stated intention was to force the release of the Soledad Brothers, particularly his own sibling, George. He had tossed guns to the San Quinton prisoners on trial in the courthouse. They took hostages. The ensuing chaos left four dead, including Marin County Judge the Honorable Harold J. Haley, both of the prisoners, and Jonathan. At that moment neither why nor how mattered to me. In the days and years that followed, people suggested Jonathan believed his plan would work. I knew he was smarter than that. This was the legacy of his brother's years in prison for having stolen $70. Persistent proximity to oppression, and fearing his brother's being framed for murder, beat the human out of Jonathan.

Quickly as a teletype could run, Professor Angela Davis, activist, scholar, vigorous campaigner for prisoners' rights—and communist—was wrongfully accused of conspiracy to commit murder in the Marin County courthouse. The gun that killed Judge Haley was reported as registered in Angela's name. Jonathan had complete ingress and egress to her home. It was as Charlene predicted. Angela would have to live long enough to mount a legal defense. That wasn't easy when the FBI had orders to deliver her 'Dead or Alive'. An underground railroad conveyed the professor to another jurisdiction— one where the governor was not the head of the University board of regents that had fired her. By the time she was arrested in New York and extradited back to the Bay Area, the whole world chanted, "Free Angela Davis and All Political Prisoners."

On August 21, 1971, having been slammed as far to the opposite side of 'good' as possible while still holding corporal form, George Jackson was murdered in San Quinton—though 'assassinated' is a more accurate description. Just after the spring equinox of 1972, the surviving Soledad Brothers were acquitted. That summer on July 5, in Santa Clara County, Professor Angela Davis was also acquitted of conspiracy to commit murder at the Marin County courthouse, where Jonathan had died. During this period, Ellie learnt her craft of protecting and defending imprisoned activists, while my lesson was that grief and guilt are often intertwined.

1 7

CASPIAN SEA

DECEMBER 1973

BRIGHT BLUE LIGHT STREAMS from a window above the staircase, warming the hard marble floor of the Rotunda. Collegiate students litter the sunny surface, lounging while eating their lunches.

Sicily sits cross-legged, back leaning on the wall. She sips tea. A school mate, a guy, is next to her.

He looks up at the landing and whispers, "See the 'man-magnet' going up to the landing?"

"Um huh," Sicily says, blowing over the hot tea.

"She's the smartest person in the building. That's who you should get to tutor the kids on Wednesday nights."

"I've noticed her before." Sicily passes her cup to the mate, then slips the Leica out of her book bag. The 'man-magnet' climbs the stairs, hips rocking in rhythm with her curly auburn hair. Sicily fires off a sequence of shots, capturing the motion. CLICK, CLICK, CLICK.

"All that and great at maths, too..." The mate is wistful.

"Good—I'd hate to think all this talk is only because you have a crush on her."

Even from a distance, they hear a deep guttural, sexy language, laden with hard fast 'G's. Vowels from the enigma's mouth are so soft as to barely exist. She talks with her hands, silver bracelets chiming from her wrists, linguistically as important as her spoken words. "Ok—sold," Sicily says, stuffing the camera back into her bag then heading up the stairs. Once at the landing, the girl, more of a woman, turns her large almond eyes to look directly at Sicily.

"You are a photographer," the stranger says.

"I'm sorry—I should have asked you first... Are you Palestinian?" Sicily hopes the question justifies her photo-voyeurism.

"Persian..."

"I'm afraid I don't know where Persia is," Sicily says.

"Her name was changed to 'Iran' in the 1950s."

"I don't know where that is either."

"That's surprising—"

"I'm from the USA. You can't be more surprised than me at my poor knowledge of the rest of the world."

"For now, know Iran is bordered by the Persian Gulf on the West and the Caspian Sea to the North."

"Okay. Are you going to class?" Sicily asks.

"Does this staircase go somewhere else, somewhere better, that I don't know about?"

"My name is Sicily, what's yours?"

"I'm Monirae. They call me Moni."

"'Money—?'"

"'Money' is close enough. Persian vowels do not translate well to English."

"Or perhaps it is the other way around." Sicily says.

"Language is the opposite of maths, where you cannot change the steps. You'll see, when I teach you calculus and chemistry. I see in class that you are not very good at them. You can help with my English."

"Your English is better than mine, and I can't find a functional place for science in my life."

"You study quite a bit. I've seen you in the library, taking notes from reference books."

"I'm not studying, well not chemistry anyway. I'm searching for someone."

The class bell rings. Sicily's eyes panic. "We're late. I can barely follow when I'm on time."

Running up the stairs Sicily asks, "How did you get so good at chemistry and math anyway?"

"It's my birthright, though I prefer Dostoyevsky, Impressionism, and ballet," Moni murmurs.

"Hey, what do you do on Wednesday nights?" Sicily asks, as they slip through the door.

⌒ ⌣

Moni, who agrees to tutor the kids, can draw the genius out of a stone. The fourth week of the man-magnet mathematician's participation, she is under the weather. Sending her new friend off to bed in her dorm room, Sicily finishes the work of cleaning the Rotunda alone. She turns on the radio. The CBC news is horrid. Switching to the classical music station, a medley of contemporary show tunes and ballets play.

Brass from West Side Story's Mambo echoes off the Rotunda marble. Sicily finds herself dancing, with Forest as her imaginary partner, again. She moves, hips swaying, high kicking, as if she were wearing Latina Red. Racing up the stairs to the landing, she runs her hands over the light switches, illuminating the Rotunda's dome. Striking the frozen pose of the last chord of the mambo, she breathes.

Stravinsky's Firebird pours from the radio. She relinquishes control of her body to her dance from the Festival. The large heavy wooden door, separating the Rotunda from the foyer, opens. Sophie and her grandmother sneak in. Swallowed by her memories, Sicily does not notice. Dancing herself to the line of the longest diagonal distance of the room, she prepares for the climax, the running leap. Her three flying steps should end in Forest's arms. Instead of Forest, she looks up and finds her audience of two.

A remarkable thing happens. Sophie with her limping gait, arms outstretched, runs to Sicily. Sicily grabs the child, twirling. The girl's laugh is one only children can have as they move in faster and faster circles. Sophie dances Sicily's role and Sicily Forest's. Lowering Sophie to the floor, the ballerina sticks out her hand, greeting Mum. The older woman takes the hand.

"I'm surprised you are here this late," Sicily says.

When Mum does not comment, Sophie chirps, "Mum wants you."

Checking the wall clock, Sicily realizes it is nearly time to meet Rainy for the regular Wednesday night bar rescue rendezvous.

"Thank you for your help with Sophie, and for helping Rainy," Mum says. Her English is crystal clear.

"You are welcome," Sicily says, adding, "I could do more."

"How?" Mum asks.

"I could maybe get Sophie into dance classes at the ballet school."

"How would that help her?"

"She would be able to walk better. Her muscles and brain are young. They can be trained."

"Then you should do it," Mum says.

Sophie hugs Sicily around the legs.

"We would have to get Rainy's permission."

"I'll take care of Rainy. You tell her the particulars."

"I'll get my coat and leave with you." Sicily runs around, turning off the lights. Grabbing her belongings, she heads toward the heavy wooden door. Mum and Sophie are gone. She looks outside, a light snow falls. Not even their footsteps are left. Sicily locks up and walks to the pub on Portage to meet Rainy for rescue work.

When Sicily explains Mum and Sophie's visit and disappearance. Rainy is not surprised.

"They needed to catch a bus," Rainy says.

"Is it okay with you if I try to get Sophie into ballet classes?" Sicily tests the waters.

"It doesn't interest me. Why?"

"I think it will help her limp."

"She doesn't look like or move like the kids I see marching into that dance school."

"Neither did I, and I was a lot older than she."

"Well, okay, if you think it will help," Rainy says.

⁀ ‿

The School of the Queen's Ballet is on the corner of Hargrave and Portage Avenues, across the street from Eaton's department store and up from the Hudson Bay Company. The Ballet, is on the second floor of a retail building which is at risk for collapse because of the resonant thump of dancers. In the hall, Victor catches and releases Sicily in a bear hug, as he often does seeing her. Pinching the extra fat on her butt he says, "On you it looks good." His actions show favoritism. Both of them are past caring.

"Vic, Mack is not responding to the letter I sent her asking that an unknown child be given a first year ballet scholarship."

"The kid with the limp?" he asks.

"Um huh."

"What are you gonna do for me?" He teases."

"I'm sure you will find something," she says.

Behind Victor is Rudy, a friend with whom Victor danced in the Soviet Union. Rudy visits from time to time. He smiles broadly as if he has a great idea.

"No Rudy, I can't do that this week. Find something else. I'm sorry, but I can't go out boogieing with you two. I have to study for exams."

"Don't take it personally," Victor says to Rudy, "Sicily is my big fish that is always trying to get away." He goes on to explain, "When she puts her heart into it, she is among the best on the floor. But though she arrives at the studio on time, rarely is she fully present." Victor doesn't understand how correct he is. Dancing reminds Sicily of moving with Forest. When the music stops, she misses him all the more. The less she brings to the dance, the less lonely she is afterward. Victor does not pry, instead searching for ways to keep Sicily close.

As an illicit treat, Sicily often slips pieces of hard candy to her ballet colleagues. Girls who dance consider water a snack. They are always hungry. A peppermint is a meal. She tells her dance mates about the offer to go out with Victor and Rudy.

"You're going, aren't you?" one of the other dancers asks.

"I have midterm exams. I don't have time for extra dance," Sicily says.

"You're crazy," the other dancer says.

"Nobody dances forever, unless you're Margot Fonteyn. Got to keep my options open."

The Queen's Ballet dance director is irreverently and appropriately nicknamed Mack. Tiny and chiseled, as if by a feather, she is as powerful as a Mack truck. Appointed principal shortly after Queen Elizabeth II made the ballet 'Royal,' the director's eye for talent is uncanny. She often takes chances, Sicily among them. Yet, Sicily and Mack's relationship remains unchanged since meeting at the audition months ago. They never acknowledge contact, not even if they collide while turning a corner in the corridor.

While Sicily hands out candy in the hallway, she hears Mack's legendary leather pumps. The heel clicking is louder than ever. The school's director walks straight toward Sicily, locked in a gaggle of gossiping girls, unable to get out of the circle inconspicuously. Wonder of wonders, the elder dancer walks past, not a word, not a glance. As Sicily exhales, she feels the sharp fingers of an open palm jabbing into her diaphragm. It is the pose Mack uses when confiscating gum out of the mouths of dancers before they enter her studio, as if forcing the student to vomit. That hand wants the bag of contraband which Sicily drops into it. "A single piece is sufficient," Mack says, tossing the bag back. Sicily fishes out a butterscotch, passing it to the director who unwraps the candy and pops it into her mouth. Mack turns, as if en pointe, then clicks her way back down the hall. A breath before rounding the corner, the principal looks back at Sicily and winks.

Still dazed by the events in the corridor as well as a grueling two hour class, Sicily goes to the changing room. She finds an envelope stuck in the air shutter of her locker. It says, "'Dear Miss Marshall: Your request to have young Sophie begin first year dance on scholarship is granted. The condition is that you agree to understudy the role of 'Odette' in the spring production of Swan Lake.
Sincerely, Sincerely, Victor Benson.'"Victor Benson.'"

'He has stepped off the deep end. I'm not the kind who does Odette,' Sicily thinks. 'Maybe I could pull off the shorter role, Odette's evil black twin Odile.' Victor, and Mack, are pushing the envelope. It might be the first time in a major North American Ballet company that a Black ballerina performed this role. Bizarre as the terms are, Sicily accepts. She wants Sophie to dance. Besides, an understudy is rarely called to duty.

⌒ ‿

Moni's illness evolves to high fever while she studies for winter exams. Ellie is a substitute parent, snatching the desperately ill young woman out of the dorms to #1 Creighton. Steeped in safe nursing care for ethnic peoples of color, Ellie suspects it is Mediterranean Fever because of the arthritis and rash. Dragging Moni to the Health Science Center, Ellie manages to have her seen by one of the doctors supporting the Defense and Aid Fund. The visit is not to a clinic but a research laboratory.

"Right you are again Ellie—Mediterranean Fever," Doctor Calabria says, looking at Moni. "I'm sorry. It could take months to fully recover."

"I've known worse circumstances," Moni says.

"Thanks for the praise, Phillip. I wish I had been wrong. Moni, Dr. Calabria is an internist, a pathologist who does research, and a comrade in arms," Ellie says.

Moni acknowledges with a smile and nod.

"How's your daughter doing? Any more seizures?" Calabria asks. Not knowing of Sicily's seizures before, Moni tilts her head curiously.

"Stable since you changed her prescription... busy with dance and the Collegiate," Ellie says.

"Please give her my best. I hope to meet her sometime soon," Calabria says.

Moni realizes she is accidentally privy to private information which is not her own. She decides to watch over Sicily more closely but otherwise mind her own business.

Back home in the breakfast room, having tea, Ellie lays out a plan with Moni and Sicily. Moni's father is a professor of chemistry and a prominent Iranian progressive voice. A socialist, he is anti-monarchist and anti-political Islam. Sicily doesn't even want to know how Ellie comes by all of this. "We have to stay vigilant to avoid a relapse. Moni, I think you should stay with us until you finish your studies," Ellie says.

"Why is that?" Sicily asks, curious, not objecting.

"What's the best way I can put it...?" Ellie pauses to think.

"My father is a prominent leftist in a country that suppresses all of his beliefs," Moni says. "My being here on Creighton puts up what I think they call 'a red flag'. I might need protection for more reasons than my health," Moni laughs.

"Then it's settled," Ellie says, "I suspect your dorm rent is already paid for the semester. No reason to slog all your belongings over until the snow banks clear in the spring. In the meantime, you should sleep and eat here."

"We can keep using my room at the university for a study hall," Moni says, kissing Ellie on both cheeks as the nurse leaves for work.

Still drinking tea, the two young women look out at the frozen river. Since they are living in close quarters, Sicily broaches the subject of Forest.

"Let me be sure I have this right. You are having an affair with a man you met traveling, and your parents sent him to protect you?" Moni asks.

"Um huh," Sicily says.

"Somehow you managed to keep that from me for all these months?"

"Um huh."

"You are good at keeping secrets while seeming open and innocent," Moni says.

"That is Forest's influence on me, or maybe my mother's. I'll consider your comment a compliment—since after all these months, I'm learning how you got good at chemistry. Mine is not a hard secret to keep—my lover has disappeared off the face of the earth."

Scrutinizing Sicily's face, Moni says, "I notice you wear lipstick, as if he may surprise you any minute. It seems you are still hopeful he will come back."

1 8

NELSON RIVER

JANUARY 1974

LEANING AGAINST A WALL outside the usual res-
cue work bar on Portage Avenue, Rainy smokes a cigarette. Sicily arrives two hours earlier than their normal Wednesday midnight rendezvous, at Rainy's request. Rainy shifts her position
on the wall. Sicily notices her friend's uncommon elegance is
the stuff of highend fashion models' dreams. The effect is only
slightly marred by Rainy pulling a small piece of tobacco from
the tip of her tongue.

"You shouldn't smoke, it's bad for you and bad for Sophie,"
Sicily says.

"Some things are worse."

"Maybe not..." Sicily is criticizing Rainy for the first time
ever.

"Okay. I'm done." She stubs out the cigarette with her cowboy boot.

"Like that?"

"You meant it 'like that' didn't you?"

"Well, yes I did."

"Then I'm done with smoking."

"I'm curious, you had to know it was bad for you already.
Why stop now?" Sicily asks.

"Jeez—do you want me to stop or not?"

"I do. But I'm curious."

"Nobody ever told me it was bad for Sophie. I try not to do anything bad for her. I don't want to make the hell she was born into more unpleasant."

"All right then, you're a good mother."

Rainy neither acknowledges nor denigrates Sicily's compliment. Instead she says, "Let's go over to May Lee's and get tomorrow's dinner off the buffet." This is one of those times when Rainy's tone changes fast enough to give a listener whiplash.

The waiter provides illicit to-go bags from the four half-eaten plates in front of them, for which Rainy tips him her partially full pack of Rothmans cigarettes and a smile.

"Shame on you," Sicily glares cooly at her supper companion.

"You should have told him not to smoke too, but you didn't." Rainy snaps back. "Give me a pen." Sicily rummages in her book bag and emerges with several writing implements displayed in a fan. Rainy takes one, then grabs Sicily's hand, writing on the palm. Casual touching is not in their lexicon of contact. Sicily tries hiding her discomfort saying,

"Seriously, you shouldn't have given the waiter your cigarettes."

"I know," Rainy says. She is faintly compassionate while finishing the treatise she is scribbling.

"He might have children, too."

"I see why Forest likes you."

"What?" Sicily thinks she must have misunderstood. Often seeing Forest where he isn't, she possibly is fantasizing his name being used. Rainy does not repeat herself.

"What did you say?" Sicily asks.

"Yes, indeed, he wants to see you," Rainy says.

"How did you...?"

"Smoke signal, moccasin telegraph, grapevine, by the by, whatever you want to call it."

"How do you know Forest wants to see me?"

"Why wouldn't he?"

"Stop quizzing me. How the fuck do you know him?" Sicily is feeling a unique anger, or perhaps resentment, toward Rainy.

"That's something you should talk about with him. And Sicily, don't you ever fuckin' curse at me again."

Sicily stands up. Having lost reason, she pushes the table, banging it against Rainy's belly. The look in Rainy's eyes conveys the probability that this Metis woman could hurl the stainless steel furnishing at Sicily's head without breaking a sweat. Sicily bolts for the door, leaving her book bag behind. Looking over her shoulder, she sees Rainy calmly dangling the heavy case from the handle, using only one hooked index finger. Cautiously, Sicily walks back to grasp the bag. Rainy does not relinquish. It is a tug of war for that which Sicily thinks rightfully hers.

"If you didn't want my help, why did you tell me about him?" Rainy asks, loosening her grip on the bag. Sicily, caught off guard, stumbles backward a few steps, not answering the question. Rainy continues, "Make time to go up to Churchill, and stay a couple of days. He's got a way for you to get there." Sicily holds the briefcase in the hand on which Rainy has written. "That, on your palm is the date and time of your flight. The route will take you straight north. You'll get a good look at Lake Winnipeg and all the construction on the Nelson River Hydro-electric Diversion project," Rainy says.

"I am not interested in the Nelson River." Sicily is coldly defiant.

"Too bad for you, since Forest is. Be pissed at me all you want, but the only thing keeping you from him is that book bag."

Sicily looks down and realizes she can't see what Rainy has written. She opens her hand. The brief case drops to the floor.

"'6AM, February 12, cargo, Stevenson Field...' I don't understand. Who is Stevenson Field?"

"'Stevenson Field' is the airport. And don't be talkin' to a bunch of people 'bout it."

"Why?"

"That's something else you have to work out between the two of you."

Dazed, Sicily turns to leave.

"Aren't you forgetting something?" Rainy asks.

"I forgot about going to the bars."

"No, you won't be much use tonight. You're excused from rescue work."

"Okay," Sicily continues walking away then stops. She looks back at her mentor, friend or whatever Rainy is to her, saying, "I forgot—thank you."

"You are welcome," Rainy says, "and, in case you're wondering, Forest is Sophie's uncle."

19

CHURCHILL RIVER

FEBRUARY 1974

LAM AIR IS AMONG the oldest airlines in Canada and one of only a few flying as far as the Arctic Circle. The DH6 Twin Otter's rear seats are full of boxes. The pilot tells Sicily to sit in the cockpit. He is only vaguely familiar until she recognizes his bomber jacket.

"Haven't we met before?" she asks.

"Nope," the pilot says.

"Are you sure?"

"You saw me once... the elevator at the CBC."

"Right..."

Sicily knows pushing for explanations marks her as being from the States. He's not asking her any questions, likely because he knows the answers. The aerial view of Lake Winnipeg segues her out of silence.

"What are those dots below?"

"Ice fisher huts... That's the lake."

"What Lake?"

"Winnipeg... It's the eleventh largest freshwater lake in the world. The drainage region covers everything north of the Mississippi and west of Lake Superior."

"I had no idea. Is it frozen solid?"

"Nope, but the ice is a meter thick most places."

"I'm not good with the whole metric conversion thing..."

"Three feet of ice, 39 feet of frigid water below. Some places the water is deep as 120 feet... One of the most important fisheries in North America. We'll be flying over it for about 300 miles."

Sicily is mesmerized by the geography... and by the enormity of Forest's waterway quest.

"Forest likes you," the pilot says, jolting her from internal chatter.

"How do you mean?" Sicily asks.

"I mean all the ways you're thinking."

"Why do you say that?"

"We were at Indian School together until Forest got moved to Ontario cause he was smart. I know him real good. Also, the fact he's flying you to Churchill is a good indicator."

Sicily is surprised, among other things, that this dirty blonde haired, blue-eyed guy had been to Indian School. The pilot's stepfather, a Native Canadian man, legally adopted him and his sister, the children of a non-Native Canadian woman.

"If my mother were native and had married a non-Indian man, she would have lost her treaty rights. That's what happened to Rainy. You know Rainy, right?"

"Does anyone truly know Rainy?"

The two laugh.

"What's your name anyway?" Sicily asks.

"People call me 'Pilot'".

"Pilot?"

"Yeah, I always wanted to be one from the moment I saw my first plane."

"How did you learn to fly?"

"In the Royal Canadian Air Force..."

Sicily finds that fact embarrassingly comforting. "Here?" she asks.

"Everywhere..."

"You wouldn't be related to a man called Roxley, would you?"

"He's my sister's husband."

"Does she still have treaty rights?"

"Not anymore, her man is as English Canadian as they come. He's a New Democrat, and has been a Liberal and a Conservative too. He's what you call 'versatile' that way."

"Is your sister as different from him as you?"

"You have to know how to handle Roxley. She does. When I left the commercial airline, he helped me get this job flying cargo. To do it as a private contractor, it was Forest bought me this plane," Pilot says.

Flying in a tiny plane over frozen air is not exactly like ice skating, unless you count the falls. They plummet downward. The idle chatter ends. Pilot focuses. Heading north, the plane buzzes low over the unfinished Churchill-Nelson River Hydro-electric Water Diversion project. Sicily admits to herself that, 'Rainy was right.' The visual complexity of the diversion project fascinates her. The nerve of humans to manipulate nature like this. Without warning the plane flies into shimmering air.

"What's going on with the sky?" Sicily asks.

"It's a peculiar mix between light and dark. We get about six hours of daylight this time of year up here. That includes twilight, when the Northern Lights show good, like they are doing right now."

Sicily takes out her camera. She can barely click the shutter with her fingers freezing. Then she sees them, great white mounds moving, polar bears walking on ice flows.

"It's called walking hibernation. Easier for bears to fish from the ice," Pilot says.

"This is the Arctic?"

"More Subarctic, we are only at the 58th parallel, north latitude" Pilot says.

She's out of her depth again—and loves it.

⌒ ⌣

The inside of the Churchill airport terminal is nearly as cold as its outside. Wearing a parka, hood up, and sun glasses, Forest appears as suddenly as he disappeared in Berlin. The bulky coats prevent them getting their arms around one another. She shivers. He takes off her mitts. Surprisingly, he does not wear any. Pulling her closer to him, he sticks her hands inside his parka squeezing them in his arm pits. 'This is the single kindest thing anyone has ever done for me,' she thinks.

Still warming Sicily's hands, Forest pulls a tightly wrapped box from his pocket. He palms the package to Pilot.

"I'll be back for her early Wednesday morning," Pilot says.

"I might even try to get her here."

Pilot gives Forest a mock salute.

"Hey, thanks brother."

The flyboy dashes out the door.

"You're here," Forest says. He whoops his joy. The terminal door flaps open. The wind chauffeurs his voice into the wilds.

"You knew I would come."

"You might not have wanted to."

She doesn't dignify the comment with a response.

"Any trouble flying?" he asks.

"After suppressing the need to upchuck on takeoff in that egg crate, I loved it."

"Don't you be knockin' that Twin Otter. Up here, we have pigs that fly."

Forest's vehicle is a free born red 1973 Toyota Land Cruiser. Sicily gets in. Forest closes the door behind her. Still outside, he turns the wheel hubs manually, clicking them into 4-wheel drive. Large eagle feathers are fastened to the rear view mirror with beaded ties. Sicily looks around the ornament to see Forest. An electrical cord runs from an outlet on a post in the parking lot to the block heater under the truck's hood. Forest rolls up the extension cord, dumping it in the back of the truck. Climbing into the driver's seat he says,

"It keeps the battery warm enough for the engine to start in the bitter cold."

"I know. I live in Winnipeg now."

The sarcasm in her tone is not wasted on Forest. He asks, "How are you?"

"I'm warmer here than in the terminal."

"That temperature is a damned low standard of comfort to meet—I mean in general, how are you?"

"Which part of me?" she asks.

"I'm interested in all of 'em," he says.

"My hands are still looking for a warm place."

"It's warm under my parka. You can put them in there anywhere you want."

"I meant it as a metaphor. To tell you the truth, I'm pissed at you," she says.

"Funny, I think about you pissing plenty, the airport men's room, and during rehearsal..."

He turns over the ignition and the truck crunches the ice beneath its tires. Sicily keeps her hands to herself. Resist as she may, the shared remembrance of that mirrored room in Berlin steams the windows. Churchill's one and two story buildings jut up from the tundra. Thick billows of steam rise out of sheet metal chimneys. Avalanches of snow, fallen from angled roofs, make piles of ice. No one is on the streets, and there is not a tree in sight.

"Where are we going?" Sicily asks.

"I'm hoping, to bed..." Forest flirts, reaching around her hips, sliding her across the seat closer to him.

"I'm distracted by the circumstances of our reunion, and the environment itself," she says coolly, scooting away from him.

"I'm happy you're here," Forest says. Realizing he is moving too fast, he retreats, "How are Ellie and Vern?"

"Busy, trying to end apartheid, preventing the Canadian government from deporting 24,000 Haitians back to Papa Doc, and supporting the bus drivers' strike... the usual," Sicily says.

Forest is grateful that she laughs a bit. "—How angry is El-lie?" he asks.

"Not as angry at you as with me, nor as angry with me as I am with you." Noticing the moisture in the air is frozen like sheets of mica, she asks, "How cold is it here anyway?"

"About minus twenty-two, Celsius, without wind chill."

"How can human beings be living here?"

"We crossed to Alaska from Siberia fifteen thousand years ago."

"This place looks like the deepest level of hell to me—not another world, the Underworld, with all those billows of white steam, ice, and the lightless day," she says.

"You know who that makes me?"

"Who?"

"Mercury, escorting the nymph to the Underworld..."

"I'm the nymph Larunda? He sexually assaulted her and never got her there."

"I prefer to think the sex was, and is gonna be, consensual."

"More like coercion... A nymph would do most anything to stay out of Hades' hands." Sicily looks out the window. Once again, he has seduced her with his mind. A hundred stanzas away from exploring his disappearance in Berlin, she relinquishes herself to his strange world.

"People below the 58th parallel think here in the Arctic it's all daylight in the summer, then perpetual darkness all winter," Forest says.

"—Though it's more about seeing the sunlight, even when the sky is darkest" she finishes his thought.

He smiles, remembering how bright a young woman she is.

"I've been studying science and geography," she says.

"I've heard. I like to think I've influenced you."

"Who told you?"

Forest does not answer what should be a simple question. Seeing a train in the distance, still a half mile away, he stops instead of crossing the tracks. Black, red, and yellow boxcars snake through the snow, holding a power over him. Sicily recognizes his sudden mood shift.

"Do you like trains?" she asks.

"No—as with all deadly things, I respect them. I was a trainspotter when I was a kid."

"What's that?"

"It can be a dangerous thing... Pilot, our friend Ben Wolf, and I identified and recorded train cars, competitively—the types and numbers, the locations, dates, and who saw them first. A permanent record was kept by writing on our jeans. We had to use the proper names of the cars, locomotives, boxcars, temperature controlled, livestock, flat-cars, center-beam flat, gondolas, coil steel, open hoppers, covered hoppers..."

"You paid them a lot of attention for something you didn't like," Sicily says.

"I used to like them. At the end of the week, one of us would be named Chief Engineer until the next week. Ben was never as fast as Pilot or me, partly because he was clumsy. He badly wanted to be chief. We watched Ben disappear behind a Canadian National Railway train. He was trying to log on his jeans from two trains at once. Then we heard his scream. He fell on the track, at the tail end of one of the trains. They said his hand was crushed and the pressure caused his forearm to pop open. The rest of that train seared the muscle to the bone. He managed to crawl off that track, climbing over a different one. He almost made it, until his leg was crushed by a second engine. There was no way we could reach him."

"How old were you then?"

"We were all eleven."

As Forest explains this tragedy, Sicily realizes he is inside a secret part of his head, where he is defeated, guilty, and afraid. That space makes her uncomfortable. Being the queen of the awkward segue, she asks him, "How do people stay warm up here?" Her ploy works.

"Lots of babies are conceived in the winter." He winks.

"Is this the tundra?" She continues to divert his pain. He never could resist adding detail.

"Not tundra, a packed snow and ice road, built on a frozen tributary off the shore of Hudson Bay. It will disappear in the spring, leaving crossing only possible by boat."

"That body of water, that looks like an ocean, is Hudson Bay?" she asks.

"A half million cubic miles of salt water, feeding the Arctic Ocean."

"Can you tell me what the hell you're doing up here?"

"This is my mother's land—twenty acres."

"The land you sold?"

"No, my mother's land, the land surrounded by my father's. It was his I sold."

"And why are you here?"

"Why is it I'm anywhere?"

"Mercury? How much mercury could be way out here in this pristine landscape?"

"I'm figuring that out..."

The destination is a snow covered cabin, discerned only by the path cleared to the door and smoke coming from a tin chimney. Forest sends her ahead while he removes the battery from the Land Cruiser.

She asks, "What are you doing?"

"We bring it in to stop the cold from draining it at night. You don't know everything yet."

Laura Stone introduces herself as Forest's sister. She puts a cup of hot black tea on the table. "You have to put milk and sugar in it, or it will eat away at the lining of your stomach." Sicily does as instructed. Laura drops a set of fur-lined elbow high mitts and a pair of knee high beaded mukluks on the table. Sicily picks up a mukluk, fingering the crafting.

"These are incredible," Sicily says.

"They're yours."

"I can't..."

"You're going out on the ice, you watch. Better wear this gear while you are here. The lining is real warm. You dance too?" Laura asks.

"Right," Sicily says. She has learned to no longer make a distinction between powwow and ballet. It's all about letting music move you.

"Forest asked me to make you these earrings. He designed the pattern and chose the colors. Even though they are for fancy dance, you can wear 'em whenever you want."

The earrings have hundreds of clear cut crystal beads, interspersed with others that are the bright Firebird colors. The strands would rest on Sicily's clavicles when worn. The floral pattern is a fleur-de-lis, a stylized iris.

"They are exquisite. They remind me of the lilies on the Bohemian Crown Jewels at the Prague Castle," Sicily says. Forced to recall her last moments with Jorge, she gulps for air as if drowning in rough seas. Laura gets up, wrapping her arms around the now weeping woman, who is still seated. Sicily's head leans against Laura's belly.

Forest comes in from the mud porch, shaking his long black hair out of his cap. Wearing it unbraided holds more warmth. The intimacy of his lover and sister tugs at his soul. The earrings are on the table. The flower pattern homage to Lidice, to Jorge, and to her time in Prague, has unleashed a torrent of emotion. Laura perceives Forest is best equipped to restore Sicily's comfort. She signals her brother to take his rightful place.

"I know," Forest says. He touches a finger to Sicily's lips, closing her mouth, forcing the tears to continue streaming from her eyes.

"I had lost both of you," she says.

"I'm sorry." His voice quivers.

When her uncontrollable sobbing subsides, with the back of her hand she feigns shooing Forest, an annoying gnat. She fingers the earrings. Attention returning to Laura, despite having disintegrated into a bowl of jelly, Sicily says, "They are too beautiful. I can't accept them."

"I've never seen Forest happier than when he knew you were coming. They were made for you. Nothin' else I can do with them," Laura says.

Sicily realizes she simply should say, "Thank you."

"Forest, you go back out and bring in more firewood for the stove. I'll get Sicily settled," Laura says. Back out into the cold he goes.

"How did I get here?" Sicily asks.

"Didn't you come by plane?" Laura giggles. Pushing the chair from the table she announces, "Time for bed."

"How do you know when to go to bed when you can't tell day from night?" Sicily asks.

"When you get tired, that's when you sleep," Laura says. She grabs Sicily's bag, walking ahead, wide and oval, navigating the narrow rectangular hall. Her body type has a definite appeal—like warming your hands over the perfect round surface of a just-baked cake.

The walls of Laura's room are covered with photos of contemporary First Nation actors and dancers. There are also historical posters. One of them is the Lakota chief Sitting Bull, captioned, 'Resisting Terrorism for hundreds of years'. Laura places Sicily's bag on a table. Hanging from the ceiling, above the full sized bed, Sicily sees a dream catcher. It is a net of spiderweb thin thread, interspersed with random glass beads, stretching over a tree branch bent into a circle. "It holds good dreams close to you, if you let it," Laura says. Sicily smiles.

"I was kidding about how you got here. Forest can't explain. He didn't do it—I did."

Sicily looks surprised.

"Rainy sent me a letter months ago. She told me about this Black sister who was new in town helping her at the bars. I recognized it was you right away. Forest has a picture. It's one with you and him on a stage in Berlin."

"I don't even have a picture of us. Happens lots when you are a photographer," Sicily says.

"He talks about you a lot, 'Sicily did this, and Sicily did that...'"

"Why didn't he get in touch with me?"

"I didn't tell him. I asked Pilot for advice."

"Ahh, he told you he saw me looking for Forest at the CBC."

"Right. I didn't want to ask Rainy more about it."

"Why?"

"Rainy is strange about some things, like talking about people..."

"Especially when they are not around." Both laugh.

"Pilot said he could get your number from Ben 'cause you left it with the CBC receptionist. Ben wanted us to deal with Rainy. I didn't agree. The guys outvoted me."

"Why Rainy?" Sicily asks.

"Ben met you once, with her."

"He did?" By this time Sicily has encountered some 40 people with Rainy, most of whom were drunk. She doesn't recall a 'Ben'.

"You would remember him, he's real cute, walks with a limp and is missing an arm."

'Ben Wolf, the injured trainspotter, aka Son of aBitch...' Sicily thinks, then says, "I was close. But Forest wasn't looking for me."

"He didn't have to. He wasn't worried. You were with your parents."

"Good point... I never thought of it that way. How does Rainy fit in?" Sicily asks.

"Forest is Sophie's uncle and I'm her aunt. Rainy is our sister, not by blood, but that's how we call our connection."

"Mum?"

"Mum is Forest's and my Mother, and Rainy's adopted mother."

"And not Sophie's grandmother?"

"Mum is everyone's grandmother."

Forest taps on the door of Laura's room.

"Okay women, are ya done yet?"

"We are." As she leaves, Laura opens the door wider for Forest to enter.

"I'm feeling guilty about putting my hostess out of her bed," Sicily says.

"It's okay." Laura waves her chin toward Forest, saying, "I'm gonna bunk in his room. He can sleep on the sofa... Or maybe he'll get lucky."

2 0

HUDSON BAY

FEBRUARY 1974

NERVOUSLY, FOREST AND SICILY face one another. She is wrapped in layers, a bulky sweater with Long Johns beneath. 'Maybe not a bra,' he thinks, knowing she finds them uncomfortable. Cautiously, he rubs her belly as though the gesture would bring him luck. She doesn't recoil. His rolling up the bottom edge of her dark blue woolen jumper reveals the beige thermal undergarments. On her, this getup looks sexy. Her nipples peek through the waffle holes of the fabric. He has missed her intimacy, the familiarity of her body.

She neither pulls away nor approaches, fully intending to make him 'work for it.' Her plan is that he should suffer as she had those months alone in bed, longing for him. But not a word of protest comes from her mouth as he cups her bosom in his warm hands. Instead she mews. Brushing his thumbs back and forth over her nipples makes them hard. "You can get frost bite on these," he says, "Let's see if they still work."

He licks the tip of one cloth-clad breast then swallows it whole. He is a master of hot, wet, pressure. "That one works fine," he says. Looking past him, she still doesn't move. He repeats 'the test' on the opposite hardened tip. Feigning mortification he says, "It's as I was afraid, this one has been damaged.

Don't worry. I can fix it," he whispers into the nape of her neck. Filling one hand with fictitiously injured mammary, he licks the fingers of the other, slipping them down the front of her Long Johns to her flimsy underwear. Recognizing the silk from Berlin, he says, "You wore these for me." Considering denying his accusation, she finally looks into his eyes. Tugging at the lace waistband, he makes his way to stroke her satin box. Her denial is derailed.

Holding his shoulders, she stabilizes herself, trying not to collapse under his spell. But she's destined for the fall. "Now you can have me however you want," she says, more to herself than to him. Raising both arms over her head, he is invited to pull off the half drenched T-shirt. He slides the panties slowly over her hips down to her ankles. She steps out of them. "Ahh—" He is stunned by his own pleasure as she is left completely exposed.

Her resolve crumbles. She unfastens the silver buttons on the front of his jeans. They drop to the floor... no underwear. He throws back the stack of thick woolen blankets on the bed, wanting to delicately lower her to the sheets. She is no longer interested in gentility. Sitting on the mattress's edge, she grabs him at the back of his thighs, forcing his shaft into her warm wet mouth. He has forgotten how strong she is. The motion of her tongue magnifies the heat. He leans his palms against the wall behind her, maximizing his rhythm. She freezes abruptly. Her eyes dare him to take control.

He scoops her up. Her legs wrap around his waist. Hard between her thighs, he pushes, forcing her hips closer. She releases into a back bend, legs still holding him, palms braced by the floor. He enters her with hard, sharp shocks. Grabbing her flank, he uses all his power to generate a kiln in which they meld. Cradling her buttocks, pulling her closer, he dives deeper than ever before. Here they are, finally, back where they had begun.

When close to consciousness, Sicily is papoosed by Forest's torso. Perhaps naïve, she trusts he hasn't had time to catch a venereal disease elsewhere. Did he even notice the intrauterine device she had had placed at Planned Parenthood when she was sixteen? —Water under the bridge. Lazily absorbing details of the room, she sees a handcarved cradle in a corner on the Waterfloor, gorgeously adorned with painted flowers. Her heavy eyelids close, like Dorothy's in the poppy field of Oz.

The dark morning is painful for the threat of their bodies separating.

"Each night before bed, I died," Sicily says.

"What do you mean?" Forest is perplexed.

"First, I removed my jewelry, adding it to the pile of rings which no longer fit."

"Darling ..." Forest starts, then thinks better of it. He notices she is even thinner than before, gaunt even for a dancer.

"The crucible of my being deteriorated to bone and pits."

He sucks in his breath, understanding this is about him.

"On and off stage, I wore my lips ruby red, painted on with a thin camel hair brush, wanting you to think I was beautiful if you found me. Every night it disappeared in a soap paste rinse, it looked like blood in the water."

"Do you hate me?" he asks.

"No, you denied me even that," she says.

"Do you forgive me?"

"Can you convince me my abandonment was your only option?"

"That last part will take time. But now, we have to get out of this bed."

Sicily lingers, watching him dress. The cradle in the corner is more realistic than before.

"Whose is that?" she asks.

"It belonged to Sophie," Forest hesitates, a beat longer than he should have.

"Your niece?"

"Yeah..."

"Did she live here?"

"Until she was two."

"Two years ago?"

"Yes," he says.

"What happened?"

"Rainy didn't want to stay here anymore."

"Because you sold the land?"

"That too... Rainy and Laura are friends since they were kids learning to play Jacks. But, this is a story for another time. I have to work while it's warmest outside. Will you come with me?"

"Anywhere," she reminds them both.

The empty fragile glass tubes, with red rubber corks, are in one of Sicily's coat pockets. She wishes they weren't, needing those pockets to protect her hands from the whistling wind blowing across the ice.

"Minus what?" Her frozen mouth has trouble sounding the 'M'.

"Minus thirty... the wind chill makes it lower," Forest yells over an ice gust. He carries large syringes, half-foot long needles, and thin plastic tubes wrapped like hoses. Using a gloved hand, not as warm as a mitten, he clears the top layer of snow from the water's frozen cover. A drill bores a fine-gauge hole into the ice. The needle, syringe, and plastic tube are assembled into a device much like a phlebotomist uses in a hospital.

"What are you doing?" Sicily asks.

"It's called the Seldinger Technique, for cannulation of any round corridor. It's named for a Swedish radiologist who developed it. It's old as sex itself. I've only repurposed it, instead of depositing, I'm extracting."

"You're drawing blood from the planet," Sicily says.

They huddle, protecting the apparatus. Sometimes ice clogs a tube. Then, there is no sample. Forest starts again with another clean setup. After each success, he says something barely audible.

"What are you saying?" Sicily asks.

"It's a prayer..."

"Why?"

"Gratitude..."

"For the sample?"

"That too..." He smiles under the scarf covering his mouth.

Sicily decants the water into prenumbered tubes by puncturing the rubber corks with the needle, then pushing the syringe plunger. The precious cylinders are placed in her other pocket. Alone, Forest has performed this ritual in different locations, returning to compare mercury concentrations one season, and one place, to another.

"Like where?" Sicily asks.

"Berlin..."

"You returned to the River Spree?"

"I had to."

"I would have helped you," she says.

"To do this work, I need to be invisible. You, my darling, don't do invisible. Even the leaves of trees turn to watch when you pass."

Sicily does not think of herself in the context of external beauty. Often seeing men and women who others would call homely as attractive, and certainly never 'ugly,' her perspective is the privilege of one truly gorgeous. She hopes Forest's compliment is not a ploy to dismiss her curiosity.

They gather the equipment, get in the Land Cruiser and drive toward another location. Forest knows where the land stops and the water begins because he has tagged areas with long poles. The truck is warmer than the air outside. Forest leaves the engine running while he is collecting. That insures the car's battery is not drained by the cold. When her mouth thaws Sicily says,

"Ellie said she didn't know where to find you."

"She knew when I would be at Kumamoto. Other than that, your mother had no idea."

"Kumamoto?" Sicily is aware she is inescapably lured to the low hanging fruit of the conversation.

"Japan, the university..."

"I know where it is. When?"

"A couple of months after the festival," he says.

"For how long?"

"Two months..."

"That long? What did you do?" Sicily is determined to account for every minute they had been separated.

"I saw Henry. He's well. Of course I didn't think it was my place to tell him about us. Also, I confirmed that everything I suspected is mercury poisoning, here, meets the criteria. I met families and children who were affected."

"What did you actually see?" The steam of her breath freezes against the car window.

"Typical symptoms of Minamata disease—sensory disturbances, numbness spreading over the hands like gloves and the legs like stockings. It causes difficulty grasping, poor balance and gait. Sometimes the signs are subtle and mistaken for other illness."

"That's not too horrible, is it?"

"In more severe cases people have strange vocalizations and narrowing of the visual field, affecting blindness or disattention to things on the periphery of sight. There is also violent shaking, escalating to seizures." Forest reaches to better cover Sicily's nose with her scarf.

"Thanks," she says.

"Shall I go on?" Forest asks. She nods, 'yes.' The Land Cruiser jumps and lurches through a snow bank. Forest handles it like a fish does water. Sicily holds onto the roll bar and the dash.

"The polluters don't want the symptoms of mercury poisoning correlated with the water concentrations of either methyl or elemental mercury," he says.

"Forest, I get that the work is important. But how could you never think to contact me?"

"I did think, and decided not to."

"Why?"

"The effect of the mercury is dose dependent. The higher the blood levels, the greater the symptoms." He does not acknowledge her personal question.

"And this is related to you not contacting me how?" Sicily asks.

"We've been over this. It's not safe."

"Yet, here I am."

"This moment, this is our time together," he says, jumping out of the truck, setting up work at a new station. The rhythm of the procedure has a cadence like a drum. Her job as Forest's assistant becomes automatic. She doesn't want to make a mistake, causing them to spend one moment longer than needed in the shocking cold. Forest hums a tune. She realizes it is what has set the work pace all the while.

"What are you humming?" she asks.

"It's an aria, Dido's Lament, Henry Purcell, from the opera Dido and Aeneas," Forest says. He looks up at her. "You seem amazed."

"Me—? Why? Here near the top of the world, a Dene-Ojibwa man is humming opera. Not just any opera, Dido and Aeneas, from Virgil's Roman founding myths," she says.

Forest sings,

"When I am laid, Am laid in earth, May my
wrongs create no trouble, no trouble in thy breast;
Remember me, remember me, but ah! Forget my fate."

"What's amazing is you can actually sing," she says. They huddle together walking to another part of the tundra from which samples are needed.

"I was an Altar Boy and sang in the choir at Indian school for a whole year," Forest says.

"We all have our secrets. I'll still be your Dido, I was briefly Catholic myself."

"Funny, I think it is I who is your Dido." His twinkling eyes are surrounded by the frost on his lashes.

"Nope, your heroic Aeneas credentials are as solid as Don Quixote's for dreaming impossible dreams. Though Aeneas' mother, Venus, had to help him out of tight spots."

"You can bet my mum's not gonna be doing that."

"I hate the part of that story where Dido's death is necessary for Aeneas to fulfill his destiny," Sicily says.

"If her love had held him in North Africa, there would be no Rome. But if you have to be mad at someone it should be Mercury. He carried the message that ripped them apart. Do you believe in fate?" Forest asks. His eyebrows are too caked with ice for them to raise.

"Of course, and I'm sure you do. Come on, what's your fate?" she asks.

"Honestly?"

"No, I want you to lie to me," she says.

"Mine is to let you go, so you meet your destiny," he says.

"You've got it wrong way around."

"You were born a bird to fly a mission. My mission was created by my own stupidity."

"I'm a dancer. I want a simple life. You confuse me with someone else," Sicily says.

"You forget, I know you, every portal of your body and your mind. That girl you described doesn't exist. I doubt she ever did."

The data collecting ritual goes an hour more, until fantasies of tea and warm bannock draw them back to the cabin. Laura comes out as they return.

"I'll see you later, I have a gig. Bread's on the stove," Laura says.

"When will you be back?" Sicily asks.

"Depends on how long it takes me to run the guy down."

"Where do you work?"

"Everywhere... It's not fancy. I'm a skipchaser. 'I catch deadbeats and thieves, cheaters and wife beaters,'" Laura sings her slogan.

Sicily looks confused.

"I find guys that don't pay car notes or child support, and bail jumpers, stuff like that."

"She's a licensed P. I. and far too modest. If it can be lost, she can find it," Forest says.

"Hope you'll be back before I leave in the morning," Sicily says.

"Can't promise... Better give me a good hug now." Laura holds out her arms.

Forest and Sicily sit at the kitchen table, packing the samples tightly into a box, waiting for the tea water to boil. Only twenty of them were collected after all those hours of work.

"These are for Pilot," Forest says.

"Where does he take them?" Sicily asks.

"To the lab... He gives them to Roxley, since he goes to the same building everyday."

"How can you trust Roxley?"

"Roxley is an ass but a known quantity. Pilot's got enough on him to put him in jail and definitely get him divorced. Besides that, he's mercenary and I pay well."

"Creepy..." Sicily shakes off the willies.

"He thinks I'm building a Quickie Convenience Store on my mum's land," Forest says.

Forest goes into his bedroom, returning with a brown leather bound notebook which is zipped closed. "Hold this for me," he says, handing her the book. She unzips the case, flipping pages full of unintelligible diagrams and equations. Forest explains, "This is the record of the earliest samples, and the guide for what I think I'm doing. Sometime I might need this back. If something happens to me, Rainy or Laura will know what to do with it."

"Then why don't you leave it with Laura or Rainy?" Sicily is miffed.

"There is safety in the anonymity of your and my relationship."

"It's anonymous except for the thousands of people at the World Youth Festival."

"That's problematic—lucky most of them are on our side," he says.

"Wait—like what might happen?" she asks.

"I love you as much today as I did the day we met in Montreal. No, that's not true, I love you more. Things happen sometimes. People get separated in crowds on train platforms."

"Did you leave me on purpose?"

"I don't like goodbyes."

"Is that a 'yes'?"

"We don't have enough time to say all that needs to be said."

"We could start."

"Sicily, before you my future has been a blind spot. Now, I find myself focusing harder on staying alive. Still, finishing this work is the most important thing I will ever do."

Sicily looks at Forest closely. He is pale from the Arctic winter. A strand of his hair has fallen over his face. She reaches across the table, tucking the smooth black ribbon behind his ear. "Rainy says what I choose to withhold is more important than what I tell," Sicily says.

"That goes ditto in spades for Rainy." Forest winces with a tinge of pain.

"Well?"

"Well, what?" he asks. Sicily's got his number. "Things I don't even know how to express," he says.

"I shouldn't have stuck out my tongue at you, on the German farm—when you told me about the Indian School. I didn't understand the torture those places could be."

"I cried myself to sleep every night at those schools, away from Laura and Mum—I couldn't speak my own languages, being beaten, and unable to fight back for myself or others. Somehow, I couldn't stop myself from being a good student."

"What do you think was the result of all that pain?" Sicily asks.

"They took us to the schools to make us abandon our culture, resistance, and land."

"Did it work?"

"Damned near. Luckily, I was brought back from the brink."

"How?"

"Mum's unwavering commitment to our intact identity," he says.

Without the sun to track the time, the end of the two days sneaks up on the lovers.

"I have to go straight to school in the morning when I arrive. I'm gonna need to shower," Sicily says.

"We don't do that here, not in winter anyway."

"I smell like sweat, other biological fluids, and wood smoke."

"Is that bad?"

"Seriously, how do I get cleaned up?"

"Undress and stand by the stove."

"Are you trying to get me naked?"

"Always..." He adds a log to the fire saying, "I'll be right back." Throwing on his parka, he disappears into the wind baffle.

Forest returns with two milk buckets filled with snow. Stepping into the kitchen he is breathless on seeing her bare body shimmer in the fire's golden glow. "I'm freezing, could we hurry up," she says, teasing. He jerks back to task, setting the buckets on the cast iron plates of the potbellied stove. The snow melts quickly.

Reaching for the Ivory dish soap on the counter, Forest pours some in one of the buckets. Opening a kitchen cabinet, he pulls dried sage, peppermint, and lavender out of paper bags, adding them to the buckets, saying, "One is for washing, the other for rinsing." When the redolent steam rises, Sicily recognizes the fragrance. It smells like Forest.

Dragging a chair to the deep kitchen sink, holding Sicily's hand, he guides her to step up and into the bright white porcelain. Under the sink he finds a large clean sea sponge, and soaking it in the scented soapy water, he carefully washes her. The feel of her firm skin under the slippery suds inches him toward ecstasy. With the soapless concoction, he rinses her body and hair. Cupping her buttocks with his hands steadies her as she leans her shoulders and arms against the wall at the back of the sink. He feels her tilt her pelvis toward him, and reads the gesture as an invitation. His tongue slips into the warm wet channel, swimming toward the gateway of her womb. Holding the base of his head, she pushes him deeper. His lips tight against her, tongue playing with her magic button, she explodes into his mouth.

Both their thirsts satisfied, wrapping her in a red blanket, he carries her to bed.

"When will I see you again?" Sicily hopes he will try to answer, even if with a lie.

"Soon as I can," he says. There's a dry towel in his hand, "May I?"

She nods 'yes,' her eyes glistening. He dries her, head to toe, then covers her with lotion and oils found on Laura's end table. This is becoming his ritual of adoration. Then he does the most intimate of things. Braiding her hair into a hundred branches, he binds them together with one of Laura's beaded ties. After kissing her, he murmurs, "Happy Valentine's Day."

"I forgot," she says.

"I'll let you make it up to me."

He takes her one last time before she leaves in the morning.

2 1

THE SOUNDS

MAY 1974

THE ST. LAWRENCE SEAWAY is still frozen, locking Canada's international shipping economy. The extreme cold has also paralyzed the river in front of #1 Creighton. Usually by May the ice cracks, a thunderous sound unleashing the water's flow. This first Sunday of May 1974, dogs still play on the waterway, a promise it will be solid weeks more. Worse, Winnipeg's universe is at a halt. Six feet of additional snow accumulated overnight and is still falling. Moni's plan to move her belongings from the Collegiate dorm is thwarted. Never having visited before, Rainy oddly chooses this morning to navigate the blizzard racked river between her home and Sicily's.

Arriving at the door of #1 Creighton, Rainy is wet up to her waist. Ellie answers the bell. The two women, knowing one another only by reputation, greet like old friends. Going upstairs, Ellie returns with a change of clothes that includes a warm sweater, warmer than anything Rainy normally wears. Shyness not being in her DNA, Rainy strips naked at the doorway, changing into the dry goods. Ellie takes the wet clothes to the washer in the basement.

Moni and Sicily are in the breakfast room off the kitchen having second cups of black coffee. Glaring snow magnifies the morning backlight streaming through the window. Ellie pours Rainy tea, then excuses herself to prepare for the arduous task of getting to work in a storm.

Before sitting down, Rainy begins,

"Forest is on The Sounds."

"What does 'Sounds' mean in this context?" Moni asks.

Sicily introduces the two new acquaintances, who exchange respectful nods. Since the Hudson Bay reunion, Sicily and Rainy still meet on Wednesday nights. They do the bar rescue work despite their personal interactions being notably strained. They never speak about Forest. Sicily considers jealousy a form of slavery. Yet, she knows the irritation has something to do with an intimacy Rainy and Forest share, to which she herself is not a party. Moni takes control of the friction.

"Again, what is the meaning of 'Sounds' in this context?"

"A 'sound' is a geographical designation, referring to a stretch of water connecting two larger aquatic bodies. Synonyms are channel or narrow." Rainy flaunts her capacity for academic affect.

"He is doing something with the water?" Moni asks.

"And the people, mostly Indian, who live near it," Rainy says.

"You mean 'First Nation,'" Sicily says.

Hearing Sicily's new found insolence, Rainy shakes her head. While reaching into her jeans pocket, she remembers that she is not wearing her own clothes. Distantly, the washing machine agitates. Rainy hears it. "Shit. Where's the washer?" Sicily points to the door between the kitchen and the basement stairs. Rainy bolts through it. Clattering back up the steps, she emerges holding a pile of wet powder blue confetti, the remains of Forest's message. "This was supposed to go into that brown leather book Forest gave you," Rainy says, looking at Sicily.

With the macerated paper pile in the middle of the table, the three sit quietly. Rainy, despondent, knows she has screwed up royally. Sicily thinks how strange it is that Rainy had a note from Forest in her possession at all. Moni, who loves art, fortunately still thinks like a scientist.

"Did you see the paper when it was intact?" Moni asks.

"Yes," Rainy says.

"Can you remember what was on it?"

"Not much..."

"It is in your brain somewhere. Try harder," Moni says.

"Well, all right then," Rainy capitulates to the Persian's clarity.

"Sicily, get a pen and white paper," Moni says, fingering the colored pulp on the table, "... Better make the pen blue."

Positioning the writing tools in front of Rainy, Moni asks, "What was the nature of things on the paper?"

"Mostly a diagram with some words. Not words, letters of the alphabet, plus and minus signs..." Rainy says.

"Draw what you saw."

"How can I do that, when I can't remember?"

"Try harder," Moni says.

Moni finishes her coffee while Rainy completes the diagram. The Persian woman holds the paper up to study it.

"And...?" Sicily asks impatiently.

"I'm thinking," Moni says, eyes on the paper.

Rainy fills the silence saying, "The Ontario government report came out yesterday. Indians living on reserves near the Sounds are bein' forced onto public assistance."

"Why?" Moni asks, looking up from the diagram.

"People up there live off fish, selling, canning, guiding fishing tours, and eating it. There is mercury in the water. The government knows mercury is dangerous there. They have banned fishing. For the reserves, that's starving them out. The paper company doing the polluting only got a slap on the hands after promising to stop dumping mercury into the water," Rainy says.

"What's the income on public assistance?" Sicily asks.

"Thirty-five bucks per person a month. It won't cover the cost of bottled water in rural areas," Rainy says. "The people up there are between a rock and a boulder. Most of 'em keep eating contaminated fish and drinking the water from the lakes."

"Well, Rainy, either you have a photographic memory or a chemistry degree," Moni says.

"Do you understand it?" Rainy asks.

"What I understand is how smart a scientific reporter Forest is." Moni points to equations using symbols for sodium, chloride and mercury. "There is a factory that dumps mercury not directly into the water anymore. See the Xs over the equation by the water? They show mercury, Hg, leaves a smoke stack, lands on the ground and gets to the water anyway."

"Makes sense... Paper factories use mercury in the chloralkali industrial process for electrolysis of sodium chloride. It produces chlorine and sodium hydroxide. Mercury is the catalyst that drives the reaction. It happens in water," Sicily says.

Moni and Rainy both stare at Sicily.

"It makes paper white. You can evaporate the water. Mercury can aerosolize at temperatures as low as our bodies. Boiling water containing the mercury practically makes fog," Sicily says, "and what are you two looking at?"

"I'm surprised how facile you are with this chemistry. It seems like you have finally found a functional place for science in your life," Moni says.

"I've spent some time with Forest, and not always in bed. Besides, Moni, you've been tutoring me," Sicily says. "What's your excuse, Rainy?"

"I didn't say a word," Rainy says.

"Well, your face did... At least this explains why this diagram goes into the book—but not why you, Rainy, walked through frozen agony to get here this particular morning," Sicily says.

"That's the second part of Forest's message. The people of the Sounds, the Ojibwa Warriors Society and others, are gonna take over a park in Southwest Ontario this summer. It's not too far from this factory."

"But why did you choose this morning?" Sicily asks, again.

"To ask Ellie for her help, and you too. Forest said Ellie goes to work later on Sundays."

"You talked to Forest?" Sicily asks, irritated.

"I got this diagram from Pilot. Then, yeah, I spoke with Forest by phone."

"You don't even have a telephone."

"He called one of the pubs where he knows Ben and I frequent. What's your point?"

"Forest never calls me," Sicily says, sulking.

"Give it a fuckin' rest. This isn't about you," Rainy says.

"I also don't get messages from Pilot," Sicily says. She sucks in her cheeks.

"That's between you and Forest, I am only here to talk about what is between all of us."

"This is how it is going to be? I don't hear from Forest for ten weeks, except from someone else?" Sicily can't shut off her resentment.

"Worse than that, you'll only hear from him when he wants something," Rainy says.

"What the hell does he want?" Sicily asks.

Rainy squints at Sicily. It is an intentionally foreboding expression.

"I'm not cursing at you, I'm cursing at him."

Rainy flicks her eyebrows up and gives a nod.

The three younger women notice Ellie leaning against the door molding, taking a last gulp of coffee before heading to work. She says, "Daughter, there are some things you need to understand."

"All right," Sicily is cautious, recognizing a rarely used admonishment in her mother's voice.

"There is no dental care or health facilities in any of the Native communities of Northwestern Ontario, and it's 1974, in a country with legislated universal health care," Ellie says. She takes a gulp from her cup.

Moni says, "Shit."

"More than a thousand Native Canadians were arrested in Ontario and Manitoba last year alone. Human rights organizations documented the brutalization of those people while in custody."

"Momma, I understand," Sicily says.

"I don't think you do. Native women disappear. The authorities don't look for them. Folks also turn up dead. It keeps happening. There is impunity for crimes against indigenous people."

"What do you mean by 'impunity'?" Moni asks.

"The assailants and murders are not often sought and are rarely brought to justice by the authorities." Ellie continues, "This is a campaign of systematic degradation of a people— slow motion genocide. Our job is to raise consciousness about it. History suggests some people will give a damn if we do. Darling Baby, Sicily, Forest has a lot more than you to worry about."

Her mother's affectionate nickname adds a gentle touch. Though the truth according to Ellie is that Sicily is not, and should never expect to be, Forest's top priority. Washing her cup in the sink, Ellie says, "Rainy, tell Forest we're on it. We will put together a coalition to help with material support while they are in the park. Everything—food, drinking water, diapers, firewood, trash hauling—whatever needs to get in and out." She blows kisses to the three young women, then adds, "Also let him know we will start putting together the defense team."

Ellie is headed to work in a nursing home. As a health care provider, she walks up unplowed streets to a main artery where a transport picks her up in this unprecedented blizzard. Sicily imagines, as she always has, her mother's invisible superhero cape catching the breeze. This time the breeze is augmented by her being chauffeured on a snowmobile.

22

LAKE OF THE WOODS

JULY 1974

SITTING IN FRONT OF #1 Creighton, a twenty year old chartreuse school bus's bumper blocks the driveway of #3, the house next to Vern and Ellie's. Those neighbors, likely chased away by situations such as this, have recently listed their place for sale. Ellie stands in front of the sign on their lawn. She reads from a clipboard,

"Diapers?"

"Check," Rainy says, counting then tossing the items to Sicily and Moni, who stack them on the bus.

"Blankets?"

"... 49, 50, check."

"That's it, we're ready for the first run," Ellie says. Looking down at her clipboard she sighs, "Damn it. I have a rider for the weekdays next week but nobody this weekend."

"What will the rider do?" Moni asks.

"Load and unload in the park, and keep the driver awake by babbling," Ellie says.

"I might be able to do it," Rainy offers.

"You shouldn't be making runs because of Sophie and Mum, and you are the contact for getting all the supplies here in town. Moni, you might get deported. Besides, the first run is Friday, tomorrow, and don't you have school?"

"I don't have to go to class, Moni can get my notes tomorrow," Sicily says.

"Who's driving anyway?" Rainy asks.

"We have a few of them," Ellie says, skimming her clipboard. "This weekend it will be a volunteer from one of the churches. Apparently, he knows the area well and is a vetted driver for demonstrations."

"I can go. I don't have any performances this weekend either," Sicily says.

Ellie is visibly uncomfortable. Her 'tell' is twisting the chain on the Maltese Cross she wears on her neck. "Sicily, this is not a time for you to be chasing Forest."

"Do you think I can't separate an assignment from a date?" Sicily asks.

"I think it is better if someone from the Anti-apartheid Coalition rides along."

"Good luck with that on no notice. Besides, Momma, you are being duplicitous."

"Why do you believe that?"

"It's okay for others but not your daughter to be endangered."

"I was worried about Rainy's and Moni's safety too. You have no idea what may happen in that park. Think Wounded Knee, and I mean the one in 1890," Ellie says.

"I get that there are some who would rather see people in the movement for indigenous rights dead than to see it succeed."

"Honey, I don't want you in danger. I also don't want you putting anyone else at risk."

"Mother, I can handle myself and my emotions"

"Ooh, you're in deep shit now Ellie, she called you 'Mother,' not 'Momma'." Rainy says.

"Shut up, Rainy," Sicily says.

"Lucky for you, your Momma is here," Rainy says.

"Mother, you guaranteed I can take virtually anyone in a physical fight, even one stacked unfairly against me," Sicily says. Rainy rolls her eyes, knowing she herself is the exception.

"It's not your body or your emotions I'm worried about. It's your heart. I don't want you to shut down... Not yet. I don't want you to have to," Ellie says.

Rainy watches this encounter unfold. She is taking parenting lessons from Ellie. Moni and she sit on the curb, watching as if at the cinema.

"When apartheid is killing children in South Africa with tanks, are you going to abandon Vern to handle it alone?" Sicily asks.

"It's not a fair comparison because your relationship with Forest is..."

"'Trivial' is the word for which you are mistakenly looking."

"It is trivial, in the context of the Indigenous People's movement afoot on this continent."

"It doesn't have to be! I'm available until Monday when school starts. You need to decide," Sicily says, turning her back to her mother, marching toward the house.

Ellie hesitates, knowing it is best not to push her daughter into a corner of resistance, since someone's leg might be broken in the kicking. "Ok, I think volunteers from the YWCA have the other days covered for the next three weekends after this. You do this one."

"Will the occupation be longer than a week?" Sicily asks.

Rainy says, "You talk a good game, but you aren't cooked yet. You'll get there."

"Where's 'there'?" Sicily asks.

"Enlightenment—Yeah, the occupation will be longer than a week, if they don't send in Mounties to break it up sooner," Rainy says.

"Mounties?" Moni asks, standing up from the curb to stretch. Rainy explains,

"The Royal Canadian Mounted Police are the FBI, Coast Guard, and town Sheriff in one."

⌒ ⌣

The bus driver from the Council of Churches arrives at dawn on Friday. Under that organization's humanitarian auspices the bus is allowed to enter the park. It's a good time to get on the road. Ellie, Moni, and Rainy at the curb wish the bus a bon voyage. Delivering milk, Vern is absent. Ellie grabs her daughter, hugging her tight. Sicily rightfully translates her mother's gesture as, 'I love you and be vigilant.' Sicily settles into the empty seat nearest the driver, an ordinary White guy—save his carrot colored hair. "Be sure to give Forest our love!" Rainy says, chasing the bus. Sicily waves.

Arriving in the park hours later, Sicily wanders between powwow dancers, drums, fire pits, and children running. Someone behind her covers her eyes, a gesture reminiscent of Jorge. Struggling, she turns around to see Pilot, who is like a playful bear cub.

"The press conference is about to start," Pilot says.

"That's good," Sicily says with considerable lackluster.

"Mercury is getting a lot of traction too."

"Um huh," she murmurs, peering around Pilot, searching for Forest.

"Laura is around somewhere, flying to the moon on a Galloping Ghost," Pilot adds.

"That's good," Sicily says.

"There's Forest," Pilot shouts.

Sicily reels around, alert and wide-eyed. Pilot laughs.

"I'm teasing. Laura's not here either, she's handling some security issues outside of the park. I'll take you to him even though I'm not supposed to."

"What do you mean?" Sicily asks.

"Promise me you'll tread lightly. Maybe hover on your angel wings."

"Pilot, you are the one with the wings."

"Don't be upset. He's different when he's 'on the job,'"

Grabbing her from the back at both shoulders, guiding her through the crowd, he holds her like a shield from Forest's anticipated wrath. Standing in a clearing are more than twenty reporters and photographers. The press encircles Forest, questioning, shoving cameras and microphones at his face.

"How far over the limit do you think the mercury levels are around here?" one reporter shouts.

"Evidence is that mercury is eight to ten times the acceptable maximum water levels—accumulated human blood levels have not been calculated yet," Forest says. Flash, Flash, Flash.

"Forest, what's the normal blood level for mercury?" another barks.

"Human blood has no normal mercury level. Lethality depends on blood concentration, the weight and the age of the person or animal when exposed, and if exposure is chronic or acute. There is more of it around now because it's been used industrially for two centuries." Flash, Flash, Click.

"Whose fault is that? Weren't you fired from the Broadcast Service for making unconfirmed allegations?" shouts another reporter.

"The real problem is failing to admit and change dangerous industrial practices. I was let go from the Broadcast Service because, with some rigor, my suspicions are easy to confirm, and I'm doing it," Forest says.

Sicily whispers to Pilot. "He's 'outed' himself on national TV." Acutely aware of her presence in the crowd, Forest looks straight at and past her, not offering a smile or a wink of acknowledgment. She's devastated.

"Sicily, a lot of people around here think he's too much in the limelight. He's one of them. He barely talks to me and he wouldn't even let Laura come. He's doing what he planned. He's validating the struggle and protecting the leadership—Louie Cameron, Vern Harper, and other folks up here on the line."

"As if genocide alone isn't enough to trigger this occupation," Sicily says.

"In the crowd of reporters, you can be mistaken for one of them. If you show up intimate with Forest, it's a risk to you. A risk to you is a risk to him," Pilot says.

"You're here. They could hit you as easily as they could me."

"I'm a damned fighter pilot. I can take down anyone in this park, and would, to protect Forest, or for that matter you. He gave me specific instructions to control your contact with him if you somehow showed up. He expected Ellie to stop you."

"Why does everyone doubt that I can take care of myself?"

"Please sit tight," Pilot whimpers.

She can't rest. Her voice joins those of the reporters calling out, "Forest, Forest." She yells louder than the others. He recognizes her with the briefest pause in his statement, then continues. Sicily sobs into Pilot's chest saying, "I feel like there's someone else."

"There is. His name is Mercury," Pilot says, then walks her back to the bus.

Having gone back to Winnipeg overnight for more supplies, Sicily returns to the park reluctantly on the second day, Saturday. She wishes she had not committed to do this given the emotional rift forming with Forest. Instead of leaving Creighton near dawn, mechanical problems precluded the bus being loaded and roadworthy until noon. Supplies are allowed to enter the park on humanitarian grounds, compliments of the churches, anti-apartheid movement, some labor unions, and leftist political parties. The RCMP stops the bus at the entrance of the park, searching for weapons and incendiary devices. This had not happened the day before. Sicily and the driver stand outside, in the rain.

"They say they have a tip from an unnamed source about weapons," the driver says.

"Who would say that?" Sicily asks.

"Paid police informants."

"Bad things happen when they get involved," she says.

"It would give the Mounties a reason to break up the occupation."

"Why would they bother with an excuse?"

"That's the way it's done, all legal."

At this vulnerable moment, she considers the lengths gone to by liars. Sicily realizes she is being bamboozled. To what end? Rainy had already known the maimed trainspotter, Ben, when Sicily met him on Portage Avenue. She had to have. Long before the bar rescue worker admitted it, she knew Forest was the man for whom Sicily searched. Now every aspect of Sicily's relationship with Forest is tainted with doubt.

Between the rain and the search of every vehicle at the entrance to the park, it is 5PM before the supplies are unloaded and the refuse bags tied to the rack on the top of the bus. Because most of the drive back to Winnipeg would be in the dark, if not also in the rain, the driver decides to stay overnight and leave with a full load in the morning. He reaches Ellie by two way radio. Reluctantly she agrees that the dark rainy road, in a rickety bus, is more dangerous than being surrounded by police at an occupation. Sicily promises Ellie she will stay on the bus. When the rain stops, the Powwow planned for that night proceeds. The driver goes to watch.

Having locked the bus's accordion doors she organizes empty cans and bottles. In reality she is hiding from, instead of searching for, her lover. Fires in the distance flicker a gold light. Opening a window brings relief from the muggy summer air. She hears the powwow drums and singers in the background, sounds which have become a part of her life's comfort zone. Flopping on the long rear seat, she falls asleep.

When Sicily wakes, Forest sits near her on the floor of the bus. His arms are wrapped around his bent knees. Fires reflect in his eyes. "It doesn't help to lock the door if you leave the window open," he says. Leaning toward her, he stops abruptly to untie the medicine bag from his neck. He lifts her kinky hair, sliding the bag's rawhide tie under it. While securing the leather satchel, Forest answers the question in her mind from the day before, "There is only you."

"Good to know your ability to read my thoughts traverses time and distance..." Sicily says, all doubt of his affection drifts away.

"I'm not hiding from you. I'm hiding you from..." He doesn't finish, apparently overcome by lust for her clavicles. Dropping the straps on her summer dress, he runs his lips over the bones. It was a dress she had worn in Berlin. Forest liked it best because he found it easy to take off of her. Gently, his arms around her hips, using his weight to rock her off the bus seat perch, he pulls her onto him. As she bends to kiss him, she notices the twinkle of the glass beads of his choker. Without the Maltese Cross and medicine bag, his neck is relatively bare.

Curled on the floor, to the rhythm of the powwow drums, they make love as the dancers they are. Covered with sweat, she smells his sweet spice filling her. Whenever the last day of Sicily's life comes, it will be with the knowledge that she had been well loved in Forest's arms, on this crazy bus.

Near dawn, they lay talking like old married people whose children are grown, as they assess lives spent together. She tells him about living with Moni at #1 Creighton, maybe because the idea smacks of normalcy, not struggle. "The neighbors next door, at #3, are selling. My fantasy is that Moni and I could live over there. We have a lot of guests and meetings at Vern and Ellie's making it hard to study. There's an old boat in the yard next door. It was there when the neighbors bought the place twenty years ago. Whoever takes the house also gets the boat. Imagine, a boat. Something only for fun," she says.

"Would you have room for me?" he asks.

"Of course." She thinks he is joking.

"I could buy you that house."

"You could, but Mum would decimate me if I took your money."

"I could buy it and you live there."

"That wouldn't fool anyone. Moni and I will make do."

"Isn't your room the size of a matchbox?"

"Yes…"

"Do you think you could forgive me anything?"

"Even everything," she says.

"What's the worst you could imagine?"

"That you killed your father."

"Only mother."

"That you hate me."

"Not a chance in this universe…"

"That you love me and we could not be together."

"I do, and eventually, we will. You know, your mind tends toward the logical. You're wired for science."

"No, I don't know, because I don't have a good mind for science," she says. "I'm barely holding a 'B' in my exams."

"That's against some of the brightest of your peers on the planet. Let's get a third opinion. I'll ask Pilot to introduce you to Dr. Calabria, the researcher I'm working with at the University, unless you've met already."

"How would I have done that?"

"It's an expression. He needs another lab assistant. The more help he has the quicker I'll be done."

"Even if I found the time between dancing and studying to work, how is working for someone you pay different from you paying me?" Sicily asks.

"This guy is not going to hire you unless you are qualified. He's not the type who can be bought or sold."

"Ok," she says.

"Connection with Calabria allows me to support his research and he mine. Only a few know about that relationship. It has to stay that way," Forest says.

Sicily nods. "Does Ellie know?"

"Only a few know…"

In the distance, the driver's path to the bus is lit by his torch. Forest scrambles, unburying his jeans on the floor from beneath Sicily's dress. "I don't want the driver to see us together," he says.

"Why? He's been vetted by the Churches."

"Only I can vet the people who know about you and me," Forest says, unburying their clothes from beneath them.

"Will it always be like this?" she asks.

"Damn, I hope not! Do you have your camera?"

"Is there a sky above us?"

"Bring it."

They manage to get into their clothes despite the difficulty of sweat and humidity. "Meet me in that stand of white barked trees to the right of the bus," Forest says. Then he slips quietly out the bus window from which he had entered.

Being out all night at the Powwow and conferences, the exhausted driver is disinclined to head straight back to Winnipeg this morning. He could not have cared less about Forest and Sicily's affair, even if he'd caught them naked on the floor. "Hey, I need some sleep," the driver says climbing on the bus. "Aye, wake me up in a few hours, in time to drive back before sunset," he tells Sicily. Drifting to the long seat at the back, he is snoring before Sicily steps off the bus. She notices clouds are forming again, then sees Forest tucked between the trees.

"It's not going to be easy for us to get out of this park," he whispers into her neck.

"Are we leaving the park?" she asks.

"Are you up for it?"

"I would do anything to get out of here with you."

"Sorry, I'll be coming back. This occupation is not a garden party. Like everyone else, we are not always united in our approach. By the way, that also is not for general distribution."

"Have you forgotten I am Ellie's daughter?"

"Ellie can't be happy with me that you are here."

"She couldn't have stopped me."

"She would have been correct to do it. People are willing to die here. Promise me you will not come back."

"I'll think about your request," Sicily says, raising her voice. Forest covers her lips with his index finger.

"Shhh—I want you to be able to give witness if others can't."

"You're trying to frighten me for no reason. I get that people take risks when they feel nothing is left to lose. Nothing from nothing leaves nothing."

"Can you run fast in those sandals?" he asks.

"Better than you in your cowboy boots." She adjusts the camera strap to cross between her breasts, like a resistance fighter shouldering a rifle.

Before the day is fully lit, clouds extending the shadows of dawn provide cover for their escape. The camp is quiet except for snoring watchmen and rustling fires. Sicily follows Forest, stepping in his footprints, slipping into the woods, avoiding roads that enter or leave the park.

At first they walk. When they no longer see the camp fires, Forest breaks into a run and Sicily hurries after him. Twenty minutes later, they come to a thick stand of Aspen trees. Old leaf-laden branches bend the willowy white trunks into hairpins whose tips touch the ground. Forest stoops, leading Sicily into the thick of them. There, he pulls a hidden motorcycle from behind a pile of branches.

"Ever ride on one of these?" he asks.

"A Kawasaki Ninja H2?... More often than horses on the ranch."

Forest presses his lips together and raises an eyebrow thinking, 'She is my ideal woman at precisely the wrong time in my life.'

"How did you get this bike here?" Sicily asks.

"Pilot stashed it."

"He looks out for you."

"We're brothers."

"Is he single?"

"Are you shopping?"

"Should I be?"

"Laura, she is his heart. She won't give him the time of day."

"Why?" Sicily asks.

"He is one of the few people who have my back that can actually protect me. She's afraid of losing either of us. He doesn't know that, and neither does she," Forest says.

They push the bike for a mile until reaching the far side of the woods from the park. Coming to a narrow dirt road, Forest climbs astride the bike, Sicily hopping on behind him. They travel along the banks of narrows and sounds nearly an hour more. Forest stops the bike. Sicily finds herself face to face with fifty miles of lakes filled with hundreds of miniature islands. This is clearly a wonder of the world. Her awe is interrupted. She sees in the distance flickers of the Firebird colors. "What is that?" she asks.

"Wild fires, even with that late snowstorm this year, precipitation is down."

"But it rained earlier..."

"Not enough to snuff out all the fires burning in Ontario this summer."

"Where exactly are we?" she asks.

"This is Lake of the Woods." He dismounts the Kawasaki, then helps her off. "We're about eighty kilometers north of the park." He points to a wide expanse of water asking, "See that river?"

"I use reading glasses, I'm not blind."

"It's the Winnipeg River, and it eventually feeds..."

"... Into Lake Winnipeg, then into the Nelson," she says.

"Right," he smiles, "It used to be a main fur trading route. Six hydroelectric power plants are planned along it."

"... Acidifying the water and enhancing methyl mercury in the fish," she says.

"You're a fast learner."

"Be sure you mention that to Rainy the next time you speak with her."

Stashing the Kawasaki in the bushes, they walk along a shore until Forest finds a hidden canoe. This is apparently one of his frequent trips to this region. "It will be easier if you take off your sandals," Forest says. She does. He pulls off his boots.

Floating the boat to the shore's edge, he steadies it while Sicily boards. His paddle stroke is a whisper. The route is lined with high walls of dazzling green reeds reflecting on mirror blue water.

"It's wild rice, one of the most lucrative exports of Canada. A lot of the fields are on treaty land, helping those communities' solvency."

"I've never seen rice growing."

"In truth, wild rice is more grass than grain. The view is deceptive. The water as far as you can see is mercury contaminated. It may hinder crop yields and sales because the seeds accumulate toxins, as do those who eat them." Beaching the canoe on the shore of one of the tiny islands, they walk to the rhythm of the lapping lake. Sicily swats mosquitoes. Forest helps her put on his jean shirt and, protecting the camera, he smooths a thin layer of mud over any of her skin left exposed, then on himself. Laughing, she slings mud at him.

Soon they hear another laugh join theirs. It belongs to a young girl, slightly older than Sophie by her looks, maybe age five. She skips stones on the water. Seeing Forest, the girl flies into his arms. Other than the German kinder, Sicily has never seen Forest with a kid. He tosses the delighted child into the drink and runs toward Sicily, grabbing her. She holds her hands up making him stop, pulls off the shirt and the camera, gently resting them on beach stones. In a flash, Forest throws her in the water. Both 'females' turn on him to attack. He out-swims them.

"Sicily, this is Anna," Forest yells from a distance, when finally surfacing for air.

"Good to meet you, Anna," Sicily says, drifting close enough to Forest to push his head back under the water.

Anna dog paddles to reach and shake Sicily's hand.

A woman's voice calls out, "Anna, time to eat."

"Run ahead and tell your mum we are coming," Forest says.

Anna splashes out of the water and toward the trees that line the mud and sand beach.

· 231 ·

Forest and Sicily are met at the door by Anna's mother, who is ready with towels. They dry their hair. They wring out their clothes and put them back on. It is hot but muggy. Their clothes will still be wet even if hung to dry. Forest checks a plastic bag in his jeans pocket. It contains microtubes and butterfly needles for drawing blood. Assured the contents are safe he shoves the package back into his pocket. Sicily delicately dusts and blows sand from the seams of her camera. Anna crosses the yard. Sicily is distracted by the girl, unable to pinpoint why. Then she realizes—the child's gait is slightly off.

In the kitchen, Anna's mother offers Sicily a cup of tea, then pulls a bannock from the oven. A broom straw pokes the crust, finding it unfinished. Back into the oven the bread goes.

From another room, a howl crescendoes. The mother excuses herself to handle the situation.

"Let me go, we don't want that bannock ruined," Forest says, standing. Anna hops into his arms. He shifts the burden, carrying her piggy back. "Sicily, come and bring the camera," he raises his voice over the wailing.

"Is it okay with you if I take pictures in your house and of you and your daughter?" Sicily asks Anna's gentle, quiet, and fatigued mother. The woman smiles, almost grateful, nodding 'yes.' Sicily raises the camera to her eye, CLICK.

In a bright room, a mattress is on the floor. A screeching, abnormally small girl lays on it, Sarah. Sicily notices the perfection in the littler girl's two braids. Anna, the larger but younger sister, has hair as messy as a child's ought to be in the summer. Sarah's eyes are sightless. Her contracted hands, absent of coordination, splay about randomly. She is shaking, somewhere between a convulsion and a resting tremor. CLICK, CLICK.

Anna climbs on the bed, soothing the wild beast screams of her sister, stroking her arm. A cup with water sits nearby with a spoon. CLICK. Anna props Sarah against her own chest. Forest spoons liquid into Sarah's mouth. Sarah immediately quiets. Her rubbery spinal cord does not prevent her flopping to the side. Anna sets her sister upright, kissing her cheek. The smaller girl's blind eyes light up. CLICK, CLICK, CLICK. Sicily watches through the lens, then says, "She's seizing." Calmly, Sicily lowers the camera to the floor. She rolls the shaking child on her right side, building a cocoon of pillows around her.

"Anna, run get dilantin from your mum. Her level must be low." He looks at Sicily admiring, "You are good to have around in an emergency."

"This type anyway. I've awakened multiple times similarly cradled in padding. Has she got cerebral palsy?" Sicily asks.

"Worse, she was poisoned in utero," Forest says.

"Poisoned?"

"This house is downstream from the paper mill in the town of Dryden. They used to live even closer to it."

"That's the diagram you sent with Rainy," Sicily says, placing two fingers over her lips as she begins to comprehend.

Forest takes a deep breath, as if being unburdened from a secret.

Anna comes back in the room with a bottle of dilantin capsules. She sits and strokes her sister's legs. Forest empties half the capsule into a spoon, dissolving it in water. He places the slurry under the afflicted girl's now flickering tongue.

"That should do it. I'll get a level and let your mum know about any other changes," Forest says. Anna nods her head. She knows this routine.

"How do you know how to do that?"

"Doc Calabria taught me. We check dilantin when we do her mercury levels. A few granules in water is enough to work."

"Sarah has Minamata Disease?" Sicily meets Forest's glance.

"Yes," he says. He brings a fervent sadness to the simple word.

The tubes he pulls from the plastic envelop in his pocket are miniatures of those used for water samples at Hudson Bay. Next come two tiny butterfly needles. From his wrist he takes a thick rubber band, a tourniquet.

"Can you two hold Sarah while I get her blood?" Forest asks.

Anna sits on the mattress, Sarah on her lap. Sicily positions herself behind Anna, engulfing both girls with her arms and legs, as if she were about to birth them. "I'm going to sing about a bird whose song can only be understood by little girls," Sicily says, then sings "Au chant de l'alouette..." The singing allows Forest to extract Sarah's blood delicately while the child slips into slumber. This gives Anna confidence when it is her turn for a phlebotomy.

"You're testing Anna too?" Sicily asks.

"Sarah's levels have remained higher than her younger sister's. When their mother found out she was pregnant with Anna, she moved further from the factory. I'm tracking them both," Forest says.

"Anna doesn't seem damaged at all."

"Doesn't she?"

"... The limp?" she asks. Forest nods. Sicily feels a vague nausea which she refuses to explore, dismissing it as hunger. She is grateful the bannock is ready.

⌒ ⌣

Pilot meets Forest and Sicily at the edge of the Aspen woods. "Things are hot. The bus got out before the raid. The driver will pick Sicily up at the Manitoba border," he says.

"What's going on?" Forest asks.

"They sent water bombers, flying over the park on the way to the wild fires. They buzzed low, straight-up provocation. Of course everybody in the park decided we were being attacked."

"Were we?" Forest asks.

"Hell no, those planes are giant squirt guns. I wish they had showered us, it's damned hot."

"Ah shit, don't tell me," Forest says.

"You got it. Somebody started firing at the planes with rifles."

"Weapons?" Sicily asks, shocked. The guys ignore her.

"Shots are being fired on all sides, pigs, private contractors, agents, and crazy assed brothers with nothing better to do than die for the cause."

"The Mounties got their excuse to raid?" Forest asked.

"At the moment they are 'negotiating'. We can't put down the guns even if we wanted to."

"Wait, how did the driver get out?"

"He's clean. I got him out. I had to argue with people who wanted to use the kids as shields."

"Shields?" Sicily asks.

"Some idiots thought the violence would be less with the kids around. I put them and their momma's on the bus too. When Canada evoked the War Measures Act against the Quebecois in 1970, I was military. I know what they'll do to us."

"I don't understand..." Sicily whines.

"It's a long story, for another time," Forest says.

Multiple rounds of gunfire are heard in the distance. Sicily jerks, as if each crack hits her. Forest dismounts, leaving Sicily on the back of the bike. He passes the handlebars to Pilot, who slips onto the driver's seat. It is a swift, planned choreography.

"Take her and keep her squeaky clean," Forest says to Pilot.

"What does that mean?" Sicily asks.

"That you should be kept untouched by this mess," Pilot says.

"And you?" Sicily asks Forest.

"Is Ben in the park with a crew?" Forest ignores her question.

"He got here when I was coming to find you," Pilot says.

"If he interviews me live, the camera's might intimidate the RCMP. Maybe it'll protect the occupation for a while."

"They're gonna arrest you," Sicily yells at Forest.

"Only if I'm lucky," he says. "Let Ellie and Vern know what's going on."

"That will be damned hard since I don't know myself," she says.

Forest gives her a full mouthed kiss, squeezes Pilot's shoulder, and turns heading into the woods, faster than Sicily wipes the first tear from her eye.

"Wait," Sicily shouts after Forest, jumping off the bike.

"I can't," Forest says, not turning around.

"The tubes!" she yells. Forest reaches into his pocket. Taking three long strides back to the bike, he tries to pass the samples to Pilot's waiting hand. Sicily intercepts the cylinders, slipping them into the bodice of her sundress, patting them tight against her breast, then she climbs back onto the bike. Forest kisses her at the back of the neck, where the rawhide of the medicine bag sits. Lightning cracks, thunder rumbles. Multiple rounds of gunfire ping in the distance. A sheet of rain falls.

"Be safe my love," Sicily speaks into Pilot's shoulder as the Kawasaki shoots away. She can't bear to look back, knowing Forest is already gone.

2 3

IONIAN SEA

AUGUST 1974

ELLIE COOKS. SICILY STANDS in the doorway between the kitchen and the little dining room, worried. After 39 days, the park occupation has ended in a siege by the RCMP.

"Still no word from Forest?" Sicily asks.

"He hasn't been arrested, hospitalized, or found dead," Ellie says.

'That's a low standard to meet,' Sicily thinks.

"We need more lawyers if we are going to get any of those folks acquitted. That's the support their movement has asked for, 'defense and aid'. That is my only job for now. If Forest wanted us to know where he is, we would," Ellie says. Before she stirs the pot of curry, she scratches her palm, a habit when lying.

"Does it ever end?" Sicily asks.

"What?"

"All of this suffering and worrying?"

"Darling Baby, 'freedom is a constant struggle,' driven by our own good cheer."

⌢ ⌣

Separated from the laboratory by a wooden sliding door, Dr. Calabria's office is a six by ten foot rectangular closet. His desk is covered to the ceiling by a mountain of scientific articles, each with gorgeous black fonts, printed on thick white paper. With a fountain pen he has scribbled black India ink notes in the margins, anticipating his posthumous archival collection. Trying to cross her legs in the cramped chaos, Sicily thinks, 'This man is either a genius or crazy.'

In his thick New York Italian accent, Calabria summarizes his research. Masking her utter confusion will not, in the long run, go well for Sicily if she is hired. Using what she has learned from her First Nation friends, her face goes blank. The doctor is forced to continue explaining. Then she gets it, saying, "Using electron microscope photographs of sections of pig heart nervous tissue, you can figure out how much radioactive mercury it absorbs..."

"Exactly," Calabria says. Leaning forward in his rolling desk chair, looking over the tops of his horn-rimmed glasses, he adds, "I would like to offer you the job."

Sicily knows the money from this work, combined with Moni and another renter, would allow her to buy the house at #3 Creighton, in partnership with her parents. Thinking the better part of valor is protecting Forest's research, she asks, "Aren't their others more qualified than me?"

"I can teach a monkey the protocols. Scientific integrity requires a certain type of intelligence. Besides, you are a photographer and I need one."

"Sir, I have something to tell you."

"Please," Calabria says.

"I am a friend of Forest Odjig. He suggested I apply."

"I know."

"You do? I asked him not to tell you."

"He knows he would be unlikely to influence my hiring. If it makes you more comfortable, he didn't break your confidence."

"Then how...?"

Calabria repositions himself, showing Sicily his profile. Something is familiar about him to her, "You are related to Pascal... His father?" she asks.

"In Berlin, Pascal heard you make an argument for the integration of art and science. He was impressed."

"It's surprising you would remember such an insignificant point," she says.

"As an Italian, I admit immediate interest in a story about a woman named 'Sicily,'"

"Are you Sicilian?" she asks.

"Reggio Calabria, but I saw the island across the Ionian Sea every day."

"Tip of the boot..."

"You know the geography," he says.

"Roman Mythology—I read a lot of it growing up."

"My people fished. They spoke no English and were buried in their New York graves illiterate. You know, there is also plenty of heavy metal pollution in the Mediterranean."

Horn-rimmed glasses and tie fail to mask Calabria's appearing more like a longshoreman than an MD-PhD pathologist. Graduating from City College of New York, that little school that generated a bevy of Nobel laureates, the doctor had worked on the loading docks at the harbor until weeks before defending his PhD thesis. He then went on to medicine. Having moved to Winnipeg two years ago with his Quebecois wife, after twenty years in research, he finally has his own lab. Pascal remains at the University of Montreal as a medical student, with his lover, Camille.

"You need to know that I have a seizure disorder."

"I know that too."

"How?"

"Check your prescription bottle. I've been a supporter of the DAF for years."

"Should I be surprised my mother didn't tell me?" She is facetious.

"Probably not... You also need to know I do autopsies regularly—some here at the General Hospital, others at Deer Lodge."

"What is Deer Lodge?"

"It's a rehabilitation facility and nursing home. It also has a decent acute care unit, serving military veterans, young and old. There's a morgue. I do posts for deaths occurring in that facility there, rather than transporting the remains to the General. I also have a three month annual teaching tour for pathology residents. There will be extended periods where you will run the lab alone."

'This explains why Forest wanted me in this lab,' Sicily thinks.

"Also, it would be perfectly acceptable for you to use the lab darkroom for your personal photography." The darkroom offer seals the deal. Struggling to sound nonchalant she asks,

"Have you seen Forest recently?"

"Never met him, and haven't heard from him by phone in six weeks," Calabria says.

"You haven't?" Sicily asks, feeling less marginalized but terrified.

"However, he's been sending samples all week, both water and blood."

Sicily breathes a sigh of relief.

⌒ ⌣

Sicily works eighteen hours per week, mostly at night or on weekends, accommodating her studies and dance. Calabria's radio perpetually plays Italian operas, maintaining her cadence, reminding her of Forest. When the timer dings, her mouth puckers as if giving a kiss. A delicate glass straw, a pipette, slips between her lips. It contains a bubble with a filter protecting her while she sucks up a red translucent liquid, laden with a microcurrie of radioactive mercury. She blows the red into a test tube. The fluid turns green. A tweezer, whose tips attenuate to invisibility, drops a sliver of pig nerve into the tube. The pickled porcine is spun in a centrifuge, the nerve sliced with a microblade, fixed on a slide, and photographed—all before Maria Callas finishes singing Ave Maria.

Though trying to stay focused on her assays, Sicily is stalked by bioethical issues, the most paramount, the pig. She supervises the harvest of the porcine nervous tissue for the lab studies. Inept technicians chase the animals while slipping in manure, terrifying the creatures half to death. This introduces inconsistency, never mind immorality, into the experiments.

"What do you propose?" Calabria asks.

"A more humane sacrifice," says Sicily.

"How?"

"A Chilean refugee cowboy from the pampas pushes a broom in the animal quarters. He's a fan of Charlotte's Web and can complete an animal sacrifice, humanely, in under a minute."

"If he's not a research animal technician, that supercilious manager of the research animal quarters has to agree," Calabria says.

"Roxley? He already has."

"How'd you get him to do that?"

"I appealed to his moral conscience."

"He doesn't seem the type who's got one."

"We've become... friends."

"Likely facilitated by the money he makes delivering Forest's packages from Pilot by Pony Express," Calabria says. Rummaging the mountain of papers on his desk, the doctor adds, "I've been told today that at the end of the month I leave to spend three months in Japan, until January. Schedule your work as you choose. Catch up on your studies for exams."

"Three months is a long time. October to January?" she asks.

"Yes," Calabria says. He unearths a manuscript from the pile on the desk, passing it to Sicily. "I'll be presenting there. I'd appreciate you reading this paper and giving me comments."

Sicily reads the title aloud, "Declaration of Helsinki-Ethical Principles for Medical Research Involving Human Subjects; amendments for Tokyo Conference, 1974."

While she scans the pages, Calabria adds, "Forest will be joining me there."

2 4

LAKE WINNIPEG LOCKS

SEPTEMBER 1974

SPREADING PEANUT BUTTER OVER a slice of bannock, Sicily says, "I don't understand what the Caravan is all about." Rainy and she stand at Ellie's kitchen counter. Sicily packs a bag of food for Rainy to take on the road, where she and Laura will meet Forest. The rendezvous is at an undisclosed location on the route of the Native People's Caravan.

"Starting in three days, on September 14, Native people are walkin' across the country to Ottawa. Some leave from British Columbia in the West, others from Nova Scotia in the East. On September 30, we'll be on the front steps of the Canadian Parliament when it opens," Rainy says, diving into the jar of peanut butter with a spoon.

"Lots can happen during that long a walk," Sicily says.

"We hope." Rainy rinses down the dry peanut butter with a spoonful of honey. "Canada is a self-governing colony. The constitution is still in the United Kingdom with the Queen of England. Soon it's coming across the ocean."

"Colony? How could I not know that?" Sicily asks.

"Well, you know now. An amendment process is built into the arrival of the constitution in North America."

"Does that mean the constitution can be changed?"

"Yep indeed, rights can be lost and added, including the rights of Native peoples. The Caravan will present demands for amendments, in manifesto form," Rainy says.

"Demands?" Sicily asks.

"Making sure the treaties made with the Queen of England for land rights are not abandoned but honored. Closing the Indian Schools is high on the list too. Even one step further, we want to teach our languages, and our religion. We need to try 'n' reverse the effects of the physical, mental, and sexual abuse almost everyone suffered. If I didn't have Forest, Pilot, and Ben around, who knows..."

"Who knows what?"

"It was a long time ago..."

Sicily senses Rainy is shutting down. Time to change subjects. "How did you get to Indian School since your mother was no longer treaty?"

"Mum... She knew I would die without Laura, Forest, and our friends. It was weird. I was seven. Mum lied and said I was hers. I fought to get into the school, once there I tried to burn it down."

"Well, all right then. How do you think it's going to go?"

"In Ottawa? We're gonna get the shit kicked out of us. That's me talkin'... You might have noticed, I'm not an optimist."

"You're kidding, right? If you get hurt, what about Sophie?"

"I'm sure Mum will take care of her." Rainy looks into Sicily's eyes and says, "This is the most important year in a century for our people. I don't wanna tell Sophie I sat on the side lines. The cameras need to see sisters in the front row of that march. I'll fare better than most."

"What do you mean?"

"Who's the strongest woman you know?"

"Hands down, you, stronger than any man too. Why are you meeting Forest before the Caravan? And...can I go with you?" Sicily asks.

"Laura and me wanna talk him out of walking, and 'no,' you can't."

"Why?"

"Because if he wanted you to come he would have asked you."

"I know that—not why I can't go—why are you trying to stop him from marching?"

"He's doing work no one else of us can. If he goes down, his work does too."

"Besides, he is supposed to be in Japan next month," Sicily says.

"Yeah... well that's another reason he can't go back to jail again."

"Back up... what do you mean 'again'?" Sicily says.

"Like the park occupation... Whoops," Rainy says miming zipping her mouth shut.

"Hell, good luck stopping him, or Ellie, or any of you from doing whatever you want," Sicily says, suppressing her rage... or is it hurt?

"You outta be more pissed at him, at all of us, than that weak ass comment," Rainy says.

"I'm learning not to be."

"Why?"

"I remind myself, as long as I feel Forest's presence, he's communicating with me and I know he is okay."

"How 'Indian' of you..."

"More like 'how Indian' of him... Besides, I sign up for this 'need to know basis' thing. Though I didn't believe him, and it's taken more than a year to not have my feelings hurt each time he disappears." Sicily hands Rainy the backpack filled with food.

"Forest disappears, but he always comes back. I'm never sure which is worse, the coming or the going," Rainy says. When Rainy gives Sicily the first hug in their history, it surprises both of them.

Sicily realizes it's improbable Rainy 'accidentally' leaked Forest's jail time. Rainy doesn't accidentally say or do anything. More likely, she decided Sicily should know. Now feeling she has an ally, Sicily doesn't resent Rainy, Laura, and Forest meeting as much. It's been two months since the park occupation, in which time she hasn't spoken with her lover, though she has processed his water and blood samples.

Rainy descends the front porch stairs. Turning back she says,

"Look after Sophie and Mum for me."

"You look after Forest, Laura, and yourself."

As Rainy turns away, Sicily says, "Hold on..." She races back into the house. Returning instantly, she raises the Leica to her eye. Surrounded by the bright orange tiger lilies lining the walkway, Rainy has a look Sicily has never before seen in her, a vulnerable innocence. CLICK.

⌒ ‿

Franklin, Sicily's grandfather, knows how to do most anything practical. Arriving from Los Angeles, carrying his tools which cost overweight baggage fees, he surveys the new house at #3 Creighton. Dragging Sicily and Moni to the hardware store, the implementation of the layered rehab plan begins. Between classes, performances, and work, Franklin teaches the young women to strip, sand, and stain the walnut floors, among other things.

"Did I ever tell you about being on Miss Josephine Baker's security detail?"

"No, we would remember that," Sicily and Moni say in unison.

"It was in North Africa." Franklin clears his throat. "She dressed in white, like a lady going to church. Walking to the edge of the stage, all those soldiers of different races and nations stood and saluted and wouldn't sit until she said, 'At ease...'"

Sicily and Moni miss Franklin's stories when the remodeling finishes. But his light remains indelible, a yellow kitchen and three bedrooms, blue, green, and purple. Franklin's physical strength at sixty-four years old matches Vern's, who is half that age. They hoist railway ties, building stairs down the yard's slope to the river. 'The Bear' is the registered name of the 24-foot cabin cruiser that came with the #3 house. A U-shaped dock, on the river in front of #1, berths the boat. Franklin's fishing line now dangles daily from the back of the vessel as he finishes his vacation from the shipyard in California.

The others of the two house Creighton complex are at work and school. Franklin lounges on the cushioned bench of the stern, smoking the single Camel cigarette he allows himself daily. He reads the Winnipeg Free Press as the boat sways with the rhythm of the Red River. The thick maple leaf canopy of late summer casts a green hue, the light shifts with the breeze. Emerging from the placidity comes an elderly woman in a long brown skirt and white shirt. She and a young girl navigate the railway ties, heading toward Franklin.

"I am looking for Sicily, can you help me?" Mum asks.

"She's not back from work yet. Her parents are not here either. I am her grandfather, Franklin."

"We can wait." Mum says.

"Please, make yourself at home. If you like, we can go inside," Franklin offers.

"Better for us to stay outdoors," Mum says.

"We have sandwiches, soda, and beer in the cooler. Are you hungry?"

"Do you want to eat?" Mum asks Sophie.

Sophie nods her head 'yes,' avoiding the use of her voice with a stranger, as is her habit.

"We could take a ride up to see the locks at Lockport while we wait," Franklin says.

Ignoring the suggestion Mum asks, "Do you have a radio?"

"I do," he says.

"Better if we stay here. I need to hear the news, then I need to see Sicily," Mum explains.

Franklin holds out his hand, helping Mum balance while climbing from the dock to the boat. He lifts Sophie like she is a flower petal. She too lands on the deck.

Turning on the radio, Ben Wolf's strong clear voice reports, "Live from the Native People's Caravan outside the Canadian Parliament building in Ottawa for CBC News..."

"Is this the station?" Franklin asks.

Mum nods her head, staring at the radio with the respect she would give a person speaking. Ben Wolf continues, "Over 1000 unarmed native people, women, children, and men who made the journey across the country were met by the Royal Mounted Canadian Police Armed Riot Squad..."

In the background is the sound of combat, with cries and yelling. Yet, the beating pow-wow drum and singing is relentless, overriding the mayhem. Franklin looks at Mum, who hugs Sophie close to her. He recognizes that pain. "Do you have someone there?" he asks.

"Everyone..." Mum says.

Vern and Ellie arrive home within the hour, both aware of the attack on the Caravan. They are ready to mobilize support for those on the line in Ottawa. Soon after, others arrive, packing the living room at #1 Creighton. Mum wants to join those in the house saying,

"Better if Sophie stays on the dock with you."

"If we get bored maybe we will take that ride down to the locks at Lake Winnipeg. Would that be okay?" Franklin asks Mum.

"How long will that take?" Mum asks.

"Less than twenty minutes, the fishing is good up that way."

"I trust you. It would be okay," Mum says.

Sicily and Moni meet at the bus stop and walk home together. They turn the corner onto Creighton. Moni notices two people in a car dressed blandly enough to be remarkable. Picking up the pace, Moni says, "Walk faster. No matter who tells us to stop, do not stop until you get inside of #1."

"Why?" Sicily asks.

"Those extra cars on the street—three of them are un-marked police cars."

"How do you know that?"

"When people looking as 'plain' as that were in front of our house in Tehran, my father was about to be arrested," Moni says.

A man and woman, excessively plain-clothed, jump out of the car. Moni grabs Sicily's hand, running toward the house. "This is private property," Vern says, voice booming as the girls dart into the gate. Arms crossed, Vern stands in the doorway, silently daring the officers to breech the threshold. They do not.

It was inevitable that Sicily eventually finds Forest's mother next to her own, in an armchair, near the living room window at #1 Creighton. Mum explains to the group, "The problem is now that the story is about the police instead of the Caravan's demands."

"She's used more words in that statement than I've heard her speak in a whole year," Sicily whispers to Moni. Looking out the window, she sees Franklin and Sophie hang off the boat netting a fish, a sweet calming scene in a perilous time. A few moment's later, wake from the boat washes onto the dock as it motors downriver toward Lake Winnipeg. Ellie lays out the plan. "The church groups and some of the unions will get observers on the site immediately and letters to the Prime Minister. The letters should demand unconditional release of members of the Caravan." Vern passes out blue-inked mimeo-graphed sheets with suggested language to be included in the letters.

"We need more money for legal support. Our DAF is de-pleted because of other recent events. Let's hear some ideas, folks," Ellie says.

That evening, at #3 Creighton, Sicily puts a sleeping Sophie in the trundlebed of the spare room, next to the bathroom. It's the space secretly planned for Forest. The child is exhausted but happy from her day on the water. After placing clean towels on the desk, Sicily turns down the other part of the bed for Mum.

"Forest should use some of that money for the Caravan defense," Sicily says.

"The money is not his," Mum says, unsurprised that Sicily knows about the cash.

"Then whose is it?"

"It belongs to the land."

"Then he should use more of it to protect the people trying to take care of the land."

"You are right, Sicily. Also, I too hope they are all okay." Mum surprises Sicily by calling her name, and identifying with her anxiety.

Canadian Thanksgiving, the second Monday of October, is only a week a way. No one has heard from Laura, Forest, or Rainy since the attack on the Caravan over a week ago. RCMP still camp at the head of the street in unmarked vehicles. They wait for something to happen that won't. The place for best avoiding the eyes of unwanted observers is the path between the combined back yards of the two houses, near the vegetable garden and grove of black-eyed susan. Looking over the fecund garden, Ellie, always attentive to the potential for waste, says, "We have to harvest the garden before the frost hits." She mentions nothing about our going to work or school. The residents of the Creighton complex are held hostage by Ellie's good sense.

2 5

TADOULE LAKE

OCTOBER 1974

CREAKING HARDWOOD FLOORBOARDS IN the downstairs hall wake Sicily. It might have been the wind. The clock says 3AM. Pitch dark, a moonless night, her eyes close. Holding her breath, she listens... Nothing. Having drifted back to sleep for a moment, she jerks awake sick with fright, a reminiscence of previous impending assaults. A hand is over her mouth. 'They always do that,' she thinks fleetingly. This assailant is smart, restraining her in a way that prevents her from being able to bite. Another hand holds her chest against the mattress. 'I'm in deep shit,' Sicily thinks, thrashing her body wildly, she starts her closed mouth roar.

"Shhh, it's me."

Sicily stops fighting. Rainy removes her hand from Sicily's mouth, then the surprise guest collapses on the bed. Sicily reaches for the lamp. Rainy springs up saying, "Don't touch that damned light," then collapses again.

Rainy's face is badly cut, bruised, and swollen. Her clothes are covered with mud and blood. Slipping downstairs to the kitchen, Sicily returns with soap, bandaids, warm water in a pot, aspirin, ice, tea towels, and the antiseptic mercurochrome. Sicily begins washing Rainy's wounds.

"What?... Need to sleep," Rainy says, her diction garbled by swollen lips.

"You also need to clean up," Sicily says.

"Not a beauty contestant..."

"Sophie and Mum can't see you like this."

"Have time before going to them..." Rainy says, this side of comatose.

"They're in the next room. When Sophie wakes up, I'll take her downstairs to eat. You can slip into the shower. In case she comes here first, we need to get some of the blood off your face. How the hell did you get here without the Mounties seeing you?" Sicily asks quietly.

"You assume they didn't..." Rainy says.

"Don't tell me if you don't want to," Sicily says.

"Waded along the shore, climbed up... on that sweet dock in yard," giggling hurts her swollen lips and she winces, "Back porch... wasn't locked."

"Shit. You're damned lucky Vern didn't shoot you."

"... Watching from window... waved me here."

"Did you see him?"

"No..."

"I mean Forest."

"I know who you mean... No, not even in Ottawa."

"Not 'even'? He wasn't supposed to be there at all."

"Didn't agree... he's okay."

"How can you be sure?"

Rainy reaches in her back jean pocket, moaning, withdrawing a mangled wet postcard, handing it to Sicily. The card shows a bull moose standing in a stream, drinking. Scrawled in weeping ballpoint ink it says, "S, Thinking of you, F." Sicily brings the card to her lips, weeping relief.

"I should cry," Rainy laughs. "Ouch, shit," she says feeling pain in her shoulder. "... Close enough to get that card in my pocket... I didn't notice... Could'a killed me."

"Did you break your arm?" Sicily asks, realizing Rainy guards the limb.

"Someone broke it for me," Rainy winces.

Sicily grabs her winter scarf off the nearby chair, using it as a sling for the arm.

Two aspirins and a sip of water later, Rainy falls asleep. Taking a scissors, cutting the bloody muddy clothes off her friend, Sicily washes the bruised face carefully with soap and water, then as much of Rainy's skin as she can access without being disturbing. Using bandaids she closes the facial cuts with butterflies, as learnt in basic mountaineering training. 'The patient' never moves during the procedure. Sicily leans her ear toward Rainy's face, relieved to feel breath.

At dawn, Sophie flushes the toilet. Sicily catches the child before she comes back into the hallway, leading her downstairs to the kitchen. Fresh produce for the Thanksgiving meal is all over the counters and tabletop. Sicily clears space for Sophie. A bowl of warm cornmeal porridge with butter is placed in front of the girl, who quickly laps it up. Sicily makes hot chocolate. It's already a day that Sophie deserves a special treat.

"Thank you, Auntie," Sophie says.

"You are very welcome." Sicily is grateful that the Sophie is comfortable to speak with her and consider her family.

Ellie arrives at #3 Creighton a few hours later, finding Sophie and Sicily curled sleeping on the living room sofa.

"Baby..." Ellie coos quietly.

Sicily's eyes opened slowly.

"Baby, Vern said you had a visitor last night."

Sicily points upstairs, whispering, "Her arm is broken."

"It's not broken, it's dislocated," Mum says from a chair in a dark corner of the living room, scaring the other two women. They all laugh.

"Go back to sleep. Mum and I will deal with it," Ellie says.

Rainy showers to cleanse as well as relax her muscles. Ellie has the wounded warrior lay face-down on the kitchen table, her dislocated arm hanging over the side. A ten pound sack of potatoes is tied to Rainy's left wrist using duct tape. Fifteen minutes later, Rainy lets out a quick scream while Ellie yanks the arm back into socket. "It's fixed," Rainy says, blowing out.

Ellie cuts the potatoes and the duct tape from the arm. "Touch the hand on the injured side to the opposite shoulder," she says. Rainy is able to comply. "Good, you should keep it in the sling until the swelling goes down. You might have some muscle tearing."

Moni is awakened by the commotion under her room in the kitchen. Coming downstairs, she prepares breakfast. Unsurprised and without comment on the Metis's injuries, Moni puts a straw in a tea cup, setting it in front of Rainy. Sophie diligently writes the alphabet on every scrap of paper she can find. The houseful of women sit yammering as if it were a normal day. There is a loud rap at the front door. Ellie goes to deal with it, holding a hand up, stopping the others from moving. "It's Vern," she sighs, seeing his shadow on the sun porch. She opens the door. He looks over both of his shoulders saying,

"Our Mountie guest have cleared out. This is addressed to Sicily." He carries a box. Sicily arrives in the front hall, holding out an open palm. Ellie stops Vern from passing the package to her daughter, having known South African comrades who were killed by letter bomb.

"How did it get here?" Ellie asks.

"It was on the steps at #1."

"It came by 'Pony Express,'" Sicily says, grabbing the package.

'Pony Express' is, of course, how Calabria refers to the deliveries received via the relay between Roxley, Pilot, and Forest. Sicily recognizes the writing on the box and the wrapping as Forest's. This box is far too large for test tubes. Sitting on the living room couch, assisted by Sophie, Sicily unwraps the package. It contains a portable high fidelity audio cassette tape player. Vern lets out a whistle commenting, "Japanese, 'state of the art.'"

Looking through the audio tapes, Sicily sees he has recorded the background music of their affair. The #3 house now has Cat Stevens, all nine Beethoven symphonies, the Firebird, Swan Lake, and Purcell's Dido and Aeneas. The selections are rounded out with plenty of Motown and recorded Powwow music. Sicily reads the note aloud, "This should help you with your work, especially understudying Swan Lake."

"Japan was on his schedule before the Caravan. But where's Laura?" Sicily asks.

"Forest talked her out of going all the way to Ottawa," Rainy says.

"Not you?" Sicily asks.

"She's good at advance work—she registered everyone's name and address to know who was missing in case what happened, happened."

"Laura has been feeding us information on who didn't arrive home, is in the hospital or jail, and documenting injuries for the lawyers," Ellie says.

⁀ ‿

When Sicily returns from the airport with her parents, having dropped off her grandfather, the others have gone to bed. Heading to the back porch she checks the bolt on the door. Returning to the kitchen, Rainy startles her, appearing in the darkness.

"Christ, you could give a girl some warning..." Sicily says.

"That bad?"

"What?"

"My face..." Rainy's expression shows a tinge of uncharacteristic sadness. The swelling has subsided, the bandaids are gone, but the lacerations are not fully healed.

"Stop whining. Be happy your cheeks don't match your eye color anymore. The black and blue bruises are more yellow and orange now, an autumn motif." Sicily is glad, as always, that she can make Rainy laugh.

"Laura sent word by Pilot that she's busy trackin' members of the Caravan who haven't reported home. She won't make it to Winnipeg for Thanksgiving," Rainy says.

"A year ago, I couldn't have imagined my friends' nomadic lives would seem common place."

"I hope you don't mind—Ellie invited Mum, Sophie and me to stay here until after Thanksgiving."

"Why would I mind?"

"Guess I'm picking up some useless expressions of courtesy."

"I'm not sure you wear them well."

"I also asked if Ben Wolf could join us. It'll keep me from havin' to drag him out of the bars the night before Thanksgiving." They both laugh. Rainy is in no shape to haul anyone anywhere.

"Another advantage of Ben coming is that he'll bring wild rice from the Co-op outside of Lockport, where the Winnipeg River dumps into the lake," Rainy says.

"I imagine this would be a tough holiday for him. A lot has happened over the past few months. Hey... I noticed something is going on between us, way before the Caravan," Sicily says, putting the kettle on to boil.

"You and Ben?" Rainy says.

"You don't wear obtuse well either," Sicily says. The kettle's angry belly rumbles, begging to be emptied. Sicily pours two cups of tea. Adding milk, she carries the cups to the back door, one in each hand. Rainy still says nothing. Sicily hands one cup to Rainy, then uses her free hand to slide the bolt. Taking the cup back, she heads down the stairs to the garden. Rainy moves slowly, one arm still encumbered with a sling. When they reach the dead leaf covered ground Sicily asks Rainy,

"Are you hurting?"

"In every way," Rainy is humorously vague.

"I'm not going to ask if you are not going to bother to answer," Sicily says.

"I always answer you."

"Like when I asked, that first night, if you knew Ben Wolf?"

"I'm sure I answered."

"Do you recall what you said?"

"Not exactly..."

"You said, 'Somethin' like that...'"

"That was, and is, the truth. I kinda know him and I kinda don't."

"Rainy, I'm a dancer, I don't need to go all that deep. I would have been happy with, 'Yeah, I met him at the curling rink.'"

Rainy laughs, knowing none of them were likely to be found in such a place. "It might have been obfuscation. I didn't know you then."

"What about when I asked about Forest being Sophie's uncle?"

"You didn't ask me that. I told you Forest was Sophie's uncle."

"And when I tried to sort it out you said...?"

"'Something like that...' Because you need things to be more concrete doesn't mean I have to pretend they are."

"I don't care what you said. Tell me why you said it."

"I don't talk about people who are not present."

"Make an exception." Sicily's ire is bitter in her throat.

Rainy neither makes eye contact nor speaks. By remaining quiet herself, Sicily sends the message she would 'wait until hell freezes over' for an answer. Neither of them are wearing coats. The temperature is dropping.

"Why are you asking about this?" Rainy pushes.

"Because I want to know."

With the frost between them, Sicily takes the empty cup from Rainy's still swollen hand and walks toward the porch. Rainy properly reads the action as it was intended, a gesture of disgust.

"I know some things about Ben. He has lots of reasons to drink. He also has lots of reasons not to. I've been there. I kinda know what makes him tick."

"Want to know what I think?" Sicily asks.

"Like I could stop you from telling me…" Rainy says.

"I think you didn't tell me about Ben because then you would have to tell me about Forest and Sophie. Whatever that thing is you won't tell me, it puts a block between me and you. I might be able to live without you, but it also places a wedge between Forest and me," Sicily says, starting up the stairs to the back door. Looking over her shoulder at Rainy she adds, "What you have to decide is whether or not that is what you intend to do."

"Forest sold his father's land and is causing Mum's to be flooded because of me and Sophie. He made me his fuckin' accomplice," Rainy blurts out.

Sicily stops on the third step. "He's got his ways of doing that," she says, smirking sympathetically. Her back is still to Rainy.

"He wants Sophie to have everything, whatever she needs and whatever she wants."

Sicily's heart sinks. She feels the truth coming and isn't sure how she will bear it. Rainy swallows, trying to find moisture in her mouth.

"Forest is Sophie's uncle because I would not let him be her father," Rainy says.

"Why?" Sicily asks, reflexly hiding her resolute despair at having opened this door.

"They told me that she had fetal alcohol syndrome."

"You drink?" Sicily struggles to decide which mystery she wants to solve most.

"Drank, like a fish. I stopped a year before I was pregnant with Sophie. Laura and I had been close friends when we were younger. We kept in touch. I moved to the cabin at Hudson Bay so that Laura and Mum could rescue me. They did it by teaching me Native traditions. Forest was only rarely home my first year at the cabin. He finished his degree and worked as a freelance journalist. After his father died, Forest came home to Hudson Bay every couple of months, checkin' on things."

"I need to hear you say it, if it's true—a simple declarative sentence," Sicily insists.

"Yes, Forest is Sophie's father. But it's not what you think. It happened while I was living at the cabin. I was already dried out. Forest helped save my life. People fall in love with people who save them, but it's not romance," Rainy says.

"Apparently people also fall in love with those who capture and then torture them."

"I stayed in Forest's room when he was away, in Laura's when he was home."

Sicily places the tea cups on the steps and turns around to face Rainy.

"I'm the one who crawled into bed with him," Rainy says, "Laura was away on a job. Mum was down south visiting people at Tadoule Lake, near the caribou hunting grounds. Forest showed up unexpectedly. When his dad worked in the cannery, in the far north, he also kept a place down in Churchill. Forest avoided cleaning out his father's room for a whole year after the death. When the lease was up, he was forced to deal with it. Laura wanted nothing to do with the task. The riff between the parents was wide enough to contaminate both kids.

"In his dad's Churchill room, there was a map. It showed land his father owned, surrounding Mum's twenty acres and the cabin. In the envelope with the map was a will and a business card. The card held the contacts of an agent who was buying land for the hydroelectric river diversion project. Mum had forbidden the selling of any of it, saying, 'They will have to drown me to get this land.' Mum's husband didn't have the nerve to call his wife's bluff, but hoped his son would. It was the chance for the family to be wealthy. That's why his father's land was left only to Forest.

"All was quiet when Forest got to the cabin, his father's last testament, map, and the business card in his pocket. He found me on his bed, beading. He sat on the edge of the bed, I guess you would say, 'sharing the stress,' dealing with his father's last wishes. The day Forest went through his father's belongings was the day Sophie was conceived. I kissed him. One thing led to another. I'd never been with a man, not when I was stone cold sober. Turns out, it's not for me."

"Forest rejected you?" Sicily asks.

"He saved me by letting me go. You may have noticed, Forest knows a lot about women. He could tell, he wasn't what I wanted."

"With Sophie and married, you would have treaty rights again."

"It would have been a price too high for me to pay. Sicily, I'm a two-spirit," Rainy says.

"What the hell does that mean?"

"Someone who walks between man and woman, not one or the other."

"Are you telling me you prefer to have sex with women. The concept is not foreign to me. What part of 'I'm a dancer from San Francisco' are you not getting?"

"If that's the only way your pea brain can understand, okay."

"Rainy, use your damned words. Try to explain. If you can't make me understand, no one can," Sicily says.

"It's more like I prefer sex with nobody," Rainy chuckles.

"Go on," Sicily says.

"I don't have to define my attractions to men or women, or which part of myself I like best. I don't need to be one or the other to be me. When Sophie was coming, I tried to pretend. Forest had a different notion. He wanted a ballerina. Hell, I don't even powwow dance."

"'Ballerina'?" Sicily is surprised.

"Years before he laid eyes on you, he had the idea of you. He even joked with me that I should hold out for a ballerina too. It became our catch word for someone who could dance anywhere, in his world or mine."

"He used you," Sicily says, walking toward Rainy, who still stands at the garden's edge with pumpkins reflecting the moon's yellow light onto her battered body.

"How do you mean?" Rainy asks.

"He knew that he was thinking about going against his mother's wishes by selling his father's land, making hers an island, or worse, flooding it."

"Well, if she was going to move to Tadoule Lake, it wouldn't matter," Rainy says.

"She still would not want to hurt the land even if she wasn't gonna be living on it. He needed something, or someone, to help get his mind off his betrayal, and you were available."

"Remind me to stop pissin' you off. On a dime, you flipped on a man I know you love."

"It's the facts as I see them," Sicily says.

"When I told Forest about Sophie coming, he decided to sell, for Sophie. He figured out the dams on rivers increased mercury levels in the living things around them, but it was after he had sold it. I wasn't gonna mess with Mum's wishes. Without her, I'd be dead," Rainy says.

"That's why you left the cabin and Mum decided to go with you?"

"No, I left because Forest tested Sophie for mercury, when she was two. Her mercury levels were higher than any of the rest of us at the cabin. She had balance problems when she started walking and a weird voice."

"Forest's investigations showed selling the land was going to make a bad mercury situation worse?" Sicily asks.

"Cerebral palsy, they called it—instead of Fetal Alcohol or what it is—mercury poisoning. No drinking, but I ate fish every day I was pregnant."

Sicily shakes her head at the shame of it.

"I figured he would have told you all of it, eventually. It wasn't my place." Rainy shivers.

Sicily thinks back to the night on the balcony at the Humboldt dorms, where Forest first described the mercury work to her, she says,

"I think he tried, in Berlin. I wouldn't let him."

"The last power plant in the diversion project won't go on line until 1976. He is trying to torpedo that launch with his research findings, at least long enough for an impact investigation," Rainy says.

"He's counting on Calabria to finish in time?" Sicily asks.

"No, you still don't quite have it yet. Forest is counting on you," Rainy says. "You are redeeming him, the lab is only part of it. Don't you see, you are the only bridge between all the parts of his life. They said, 'This is a message for your boyfriend' while they kicked me. It wasn't the RCMP. It was thugs, with baseball bats and caps. Sicily, they thought I was you. Their informants are close to us, but not close enough."

"You think they were trying to get to Forest through you?" Sicily asks.

"You're not hearing—not through me—but you."

"Where is Forest?" Sicily says.

"Wherever he was supposed to be," Rainy assures Sicily.

"That would be Japan. But how do you know he's okay?"

"The postcard was in my pocket before I was attacked. If he knew I was beaten, he would have died avenging me—and that would have hit the news by now." Rainy speaks with the certainty of Forest's child's mother.

"We have to tell him," Sicily says.

"No I don't, and you are not going to either."

"Rainy, if they catch him, they'll kill him," Sicily says.

"They'd have to catch him first. He's always known the stakes, even if you haven't. Let them think they sent a message to him through the right woman. He's close to finishing. Watch your step and stay anonymous."

The two women look at one another. Tears roll down their cheeks, freezing as the temperature drops. "Fuck," Rainy says, "My cuts are stingin' from the salt."

2 6

CLEAR LAKE

JANUARY 1975

AT #1 CREIGHTON, ELLIE looks through her bedroom window at the bare trees. Their bark is gray, sap receding to the trunk's core for the winter. Frozen air gives the morning light a peculiar clarity. Vern comes in, finding his wife pensive, standing over the half-packed suitcase on their bed.

"Doc Calabria called. Forest will be leaving Japan in the next couple of days," she says.

"Without knowledge of Rainy being attacked at the Caravan?"

"Doc doesn't think he knows. The Tokyo trip is the one bit of luck in this disaster. Rainy's injuries are almost healed," Ellie says.

"That should diminish the impact when Forest sees her."

Ellie holds up a light weight sweater, asking, "How cold do you think it will be?"

"Warmer than here by ten degrees... If we can't erase the effects of Rainy's beating on Forest, I wish there was some way of postponing them until we get back," he says.

"Sicily is honest to a fault. If she's in his proximity, even if she tries not, she will tell him."

"But if Forest sticks to his rule of minimal contact with her, they may not see one another for a month more," Vern says.

"True. Rainy can keep a secret, and she'll make sure her crew does too," Ellie says.

There is reason for concern. When brothers like Forest seek retribution, they invariably end up in jail, dead, or both. Ellie closes the worn leather bag, snapping shut the dull brass latches. She and Vern are ready to leave for the airport. They will be attending a large Anti-apartheid conference in Amsterdam. This is how Vern, Ellie, and Forest all come to be absent from North America the morning Moni answers the call from Sicily's Aunt Lillie in Los Angeles.

The Los Angeles Veterans Administration Hospital, badly damaged in the 1973 Sylmar Earthquake, is nearly fully rebuilt. Directed to ward 4 East, at the nurses' station Sicily announces herself. Moments later, a well dressed woman wearing a white clinical jacket joins her at the desk. Blonde with curly hair and hazel eyes, the young doctor must also be 5'9" and wearing three inch platform shoes since she and Sicily stand eye to eye.

"I am Lisa Cook, an intern in the UCLA program. I've been involved in your grandfather's care. I recognize you from the photo at his bedside." The young doctor extends her hand and they shake.

"I'm Sicily Marshall. Good to meet you. Well, maybe good under other circumstances."

"What would you like me to call you?"

"Sicily is fine, and you?"

"Lisa is good. Would you like to talk about his illness now, or see Mr. Grant first?"

"I'd like to see him."

Franklin is sleeping. He is smaller. Always slim, he has lost forty pounds since he was in Winnipeg.

"He doesn't seem to do well when awakened by others," Lisa says.

"It's a side effect of the war."

"We see too much of that around here—a secret war crime. I'll see you later," Lisa says, slipping out of the room.

"Bonjour, mademoiselle, je suis Gaston Poulet," says a man in the other bed. He has a massive head tumor leaving only a single lavender eye unobstructed. Sicily's incapacity to see 'ugly' serves her well in a hospital. He reminds her only of a field of iris. His is name is another story.

"C'est vrai? M. Chicken?" Sicily laughs.

"Oui..." He laughs too. "Vous habitez au Canada?"

"Oui, à Winnipeg," Sicily says.

M. Poulet explains that between stints in the allied forces of WWI and WWII, he was a left-handed fencing partner for swashbuckling movie actor Douglas Fairbanks, Jr. It is a profession enhancing the older gentleman's current panache. Franklin wakes to his 95 year old roommate charming his granddaughter.

"How are you feeling Grandfather?"

"Like a man who has lived a full life," Franklin says.

"I'm pinch hitting. Ellie and Vern are in Amsterdam for a couple of weeks at a conference. What's going on?"

"I have a battle or two left, but not the ones everyone thinks," he says.

"What are the ones everyone thinks, Grandfather?"

"Sici, I have cancer, made worse by an occupational lung disease called asbestosis. It's from smoking, being a mechanic, and working in refrigeration and air-conditioning."

"Will it get better?"

"No..."

"What do you mean?"

"'No,' the lung cancer has metastasized to my brain. Let's keep this between we three for now," he winks at M. Poulet. "I'll let them mess around with radiation a bit. It will buy time for your grandmother and Lillie, for everyone, to get used to the idea."

"Nobody is going to get used to this idea, Grandfather."

"Humor me..."

"Are you in pain?"

"Not much... Granddaughter, promise me, when I'm ready, you will get me back to the cul-de-sac. I don't want to die here."

"Grandfather, I—okay, I promise."

Lillie walks into the room saying, "I'm sure your mother taught you not to make promises you can't keep."

"Well, she keeps trying, but it doesn't take," Sicily says, falling into Lillie's arms.

Lillie has delivered a son and been divorced since Sicily last saw her. Her almond eyes and high cheek bones are stunning. She has light brown skin like Vanessa's, and Ellie's hourglass body. A union heavy equipment operator, she shatters all stereotypes.

"Okay you two, we have work to do," Franklin says.

"Work?" Sicily asks.

"I wish your mother were here. She can always handle a campaign," Lillie says.

"Move it along girls. Some of us have less time to waste than others," Franklin says.

Lisa Cook knocks at the door. Behind her is a troop of men in white coats of varying lengths. "May we interrupt you?" Lisa asks.

"You may, but I'm not sure about the rest of them," Franklin says.

Lisa has the grace to laugh and attempts to introduce Sicily to the group. The man who is the attending physician checks his Rolex watch. Two young men in blue jeans climb over Sicily to get to the bed, without excusing themselves. Another says, "You may want to step out."

"My kids don't need to step out," Franklin says.

"Oh? I do. Sici, Daddy, Mr. P, I'll see you later." Lillie bolts for the door. Her dangerous occupation does not confer immunity from fear of white coats. A medical student begins,

"Franklin is a—"

"Mr. Grant..." Sicily says. All the white coats in the room turn to glare at her, silently. The student falls mute. Sicily continues, "Mr. Grant, a decorated veteran of World War II, purple heart, father of two, grandfather of two, husband, 20 years a supervising engineer in refrigeration and air conditioning at Todd Shipyard, crane follower, mechanic, former assistant page of the Illinois State Legislature—"

"Mr. Grant," the student begins again. There was hope for him.

Rounds continued another fifteen minutes, identifying the major clinical issues of lung tumors generally, mesothelioma and adenocarcinoma specifically. He would be getting two more weeks of radiation therapy, 'palliatively'.

"What does 'palliatively' mean?" Sicily asks.

"To shrink the tumor. We can't cure it but maybe we will make things more comfortable for a while," the Rolex wearing attending answers.

"How long?" Sicily asks.

"Weeks to months... I'm sorry, we have to move on," the attending says quite sincerely, shaking Franklin's hand.

The flock flows out of the room, Sicily surfaces from the depths of despair realizing Franklin is having an exchange with M. Poulet. They are laughing. The specter of death, whether in battle or cancer, makes fast friends.

"What'd I tell you?" Grandfather says.

"I agree. She can do it, if anyone can," M. Poulet said.

"Do what?" Sicily asks.

⌢ ‿

At the stoplight outside of the hospital front door the smog makes Sicily cough. The Westwood neighborhood is familiar from her childhood. Palm trees stream past the National Cemetery, up Wilshire Boulevard toward UCLA. She decides to walk, though Los Angeles is not typically walkable. Franklin and M. Poulet made two requests. The first is that she read the new biography of Josephine Baker aloud to them while they wait for radiation therapy. She thinks she will find the book at a shop on Westwood Blvd, eight blocks away. The second request is likely impossible but she hopes to appease the gentlemen by achieving the first.

"Hi," Dr. Lisa Cook says, arriving at the corner.

"Hi back," Sicily says.

"You gave them 'what for' today," Lisa says.

"That happens when I'm pissed off."

"Well, I thought it was great. Maybe medicine should piss off more people."

"Where are you from?" Sicily asks.

"Saint Paul, Minnesota... Why?"

"The term 'what for'... A Californian would say that I had 'kicked ass and called names.'"

Lisa smiles, knowing those words would never come out of her own Minnesotan mouth.

"I know, I'm lame," she says.

"Saint Paul isn't. The Mississippi runs through it. That river has the largest drainage in North America. The basin covers parts of Canada, catches the Minnesota River not far from the Laurentian Divide, then goes all the way to the Gulf of Mexico." Sicily's encyclopedic waterway praise astounds Lisa.

"Talk about lame... and how do you know all that?" Lisa asks.

"I'm a second year zoology and ecology major." Sicily omits reference to Forest.

"Where are you headed now?" Lisa asks.

"To get some air and find a bookstore."

"Tower Records on Westwood is next to a bookstore. Would you want to have dinner with me? Tower is also across the street from a restaurant called Yesterdays."

"I could eat," Sicily says, realizing Lisa is the best bet for the second project assigned by Franklin and M. Poulet.

Waiting for supper at Yesterdays, the two young women look at the Josephine Baker book. Sicily rarely drinks, but it would be to her advantage if Lisa were a bit tipsy when asked the favor for Franklin and M. Poulet. The young doctor doesn't seem the type to drink alone. The waiter fills Sicily's wine glass and refills Lisa's.

"M. Poulet has had a glass of wine every day, twice a day, since he was 10 years old. He wants some now, at 95, while he is in the hospital dying," Sicily says.

"It's too bad, isn't it?" Lisa says, then sips.

"You should write an order for eight ounces at lunch and dinner."

"Am I allowed to do that? It's a hospital."

"Does it make sense to you that you can write for narcotics and not for wine?"

"It's a hospital full of Vets. As a policy, where would it end?"

"In that room with Franklin Grant and Gaston Poulet."

"I could try," Lisa says, "provided you meet my condition."

Lisa is shaping up to be the adventurous type Sicily likes. "Umm, what condition?"

"I want to know when you are going to medical school."

"Around the time you check yourself into an insane asylum..."

"How much do you care about that old man's wine?"

"I'm a ballet dancer."

"One who studies science... After internship, I'm going into psychiatry. Physical medicine bores me. After all, the mind drags the body around. You see, I'll soon be in an asylum."

Sicily laughs, "Not soon enough..."

⌒‿

The next morning, a nurse wakes Sicily from the formica lounge chair in Franklin and Gaston's room where she has spent the night. Moni is calling. Sicily apologizes for not having checked in when she arrived in LA. "It's a tale of two drunken giantesses, one black, the other white, on the streets of Westwood, plotting to change the face of medicine," Sicily says. "I needed a favor from the blonde. She's not dumb and made me trade for it. I might have promised to take the Medical College Admission Test."

"You don't know for sure?" Moni asks.

"Alcohol was involved."

"That's a sizable trade."

"You're my science tutor, thought you'd need to know first."

"You've had all the prerequisites for that exam already."

"I have?"

"Yeah you only need five specific courses to register for the MCAT—Biology, Theoretical Chemistry, Organic Chemistry, Physics, and English. You are good at all of them, thanks to me." Moni laughs. "We'll register you for the spring examine when you get back."

"I hope Ellie can live with it. Being a nurse has decreased her opinion of most doctors, even though she started out premed."

"What stopped her?" Moni asked.

"The times and other things, including me..."

"You'll be good at it," Moni says. "Back to business, Lillie told me you are sleeping at the hospital. Ellie will call you at the nurses' station, this afternoon around three o'clock your time."

"Good, I need her."

"I let them know at the ballet school why you won't be in class. Turns out Victor is guest performing in Los Angeles," Moni says.

"Seriously, here?"

"I got his number from Mack."

"Whoa, you charmed Mack," Sicily says.

"I suppose. Victor is at 213-555-5200. Call him," Moni says.

When Ellie calls at 3PM, Sicily assures her that Franklin's death is not imminent. Victor's premiere is at the end of the week, and Ellie will arrive two days after.

The Shrine Auditorium seat Victor arranges for Sicily is close enough that she will feel the spray of dancers' sweat. Snuggling into the velvet chair, she worries that her 'old men' at the hospital are without her for the evening. As the lights go down, a short, well-built man in a leather cap and anklelength matching trench coat slips into the seat on Sicily's right. He grabs her hand. When she turns to curse him, he kisses her on the cheek. It's Rudy, Victor's friend.

The ballet is nearly flawless, the series of standing ovations long. Rudy and Sicily climb the front of the stage, slip behind the red velvet curtain, and join the cast. "One down, seven performances to go," Victor says then insists 'his' dancers eat and get some rest. As usual, Vic himself still intends to go out and boogie before breakfast. He beckons Rudy and Sicily to join him in the dressing room while he peels off his makeup.

Rudy flings the door open, bowing deeply, allowing the star to enter first. Sicily walks through the door next. A hand, as if from nowhere, extends a clean white towel to Victor. The star uses it to dab sweat from his face. Seeing two enormous bouquets of white peonies on the dressing table, Victor fawns over the blossoms. "Gorgeous," he says.

"They are not both for you. One is for mademoiselle," a familiar voice says.

Victor gazes past Sicily. Slowly, she turns around.

"I'll be damned. Victor, who would have guessed you could keep a secret," Sicily says, falling into Forest's arms.

Victor explains, "I didn't have time to tell you. He showed up at the back door right before curtain. Then there was that Persian girl who intimidated me over the phone..."

"How did you get here?" Sicily asks Forest.

"Calabria said you wouldn't be in the lab to receive my samples because your grandfather was sick in LA," Forest says. "There was no reason for me to work."

Tony Basil and the Lockers are finishing a run at the Roxy Theater, and that cast party is the only boogie venue of Victor and Rudy's interest. The four stand at the curb outside of the Shrine. Sicily is carrying one of the huge bouquets of white flowers still in the vase, reminiscent of a bride. Rudy asks, "Where are you two sleeping tonight?"

"I've been sleeping in the formica chair in my grandfather's hospital room," Sicily says.

"I'll be sleeping where she sleeps," says Forest.

"Take my suite at the Beverly Wilshire. I'll bunk with Victor and leave a key for you at the desk. It's not far from the VA hospital," Rudy says, hailing his driver and car with a loud whistle.

"Wait, I don't want to go to the hotel yet," Sicily says, as she and Forest get into the car.

"Take them wherever they want to go," Rudy tells the driver and taps the limousine's roof.

"Where Sunset ends," Sicily says.

"The rides going to be slower than usual tonight," the driver says.

"Why?"

"Grunion running..."

"Tonight? Isn't it too early in the year?"

"The state fish and wild life department announced an off-season run because of oceanic conditions. But no flash lights."

"How lucky can we get?" Sicily is excited.

"What's running?" Forest asks.

"Grunion... and you claim to have a biology degree?" Sicily teases.

"I do," Forest says.

"Darn, we don't have a bucket," she says.

"I have two," says the driver. "Parking at the beach will be impossible. I'll circle back to where I drop you off, every half hour until you are ready... I'll take my tip in grunion."

"It's a deal," Sicily says.

The car descends from the palisade, down the hill to where Sunset Blvd meets the Pacific Coast Highway.

"This is where I first fell in love with the ocean," Sicily says.

The full moon reflects off the water and a wide shifting band of silver tracing the shore.

"What the hell is that?" Forest asks.

"Grunion," Sicily squeals.

Between the Santa Monica Pier and the Jonathan Club, hundreds of people with buckets run toward the water, sweeping the lovers into the flow. Moonlight reflects multitudes of silver, half foot-long, smelt-like fish, spawning in the sand then leaping back into the water. People scoop the long narrow fish into buckets, by hand.

"Wow, how long does this go on?" Forest asks.

"Two to three hours..."

"They don't have a chance, do they?" he says.

"Nets are not allowed, and you can't dig holes to trap them. Grunion hunters are vicious if you break the rules. It's not as easy as it sounds," she says.

The two wade into the slippery schools of fish. Forest tries to pick one up. It wiggles free, leaping back into the water. He dives after it, emerging soaked. "Still feeling sorry for the poor grunion?" she asks him. Resentful of her dryness, Forest tosses a bucket of water at her. Now the game is on.

⌒⌣

At two o'clock in the morning, Forest and Sicily approach the night manager at the Beverly Wilshire reception desk. They are barefoot, sandy, and wet. Forest carries a bucket of sea water with leaping fish in one hand and sandy cowboy boots in the other. Sicily carries her flower bouquet and sandals.

"I'm Sicily Marshall. I think you have a key for us," she says, trying to hold a straight face.

"Welcome, Ms. Marshall. Have you any other... luggage?" the polite manager asks, waving the bellman to take the bucket from Forest. Forest travels lightly—the clothes he is wearing and a wallet. This hotel has seen stranger sights, but it is hard to imagine what they might have been.

"Any chance that our clothes could be laundered?" Sicily asks.

"Of course. Ring when you are ready." Seeing Forest carrying his cowboy boots, the manager adds, "I can also have those polished if you leave them outside the door, sir."

The word 'opulent' cannot begin to describe Rudy's suite. The shower is a clear quartz prism. When Forest steps into it, his refraction scatters through the mirrored walls. Sicily dumps the fish and sea water into one of the double sinks. She adds a bottle of Canada Dry to the vase of peonies, then climbs into the flow behind Forest. His unbraided mane stretches past his mid back. She slides his hair over one shoulder. French milled soap makes whipped cream thick suds in Sicily's hands. The foam smooths her massage of his shoulders, back, and buttocks.

"I think water is our aphrodisiac," Forest says.

"There is an awful lot of it on the planet. Maybe that explains why I'm always hot for you."

When she reaches her hand between his legs, she feels him firm under her palm. Turning, he pushes her into the corner. The water pours from their crowns. Kissing her mouth wide, he is a man emerging from the desert, drinking. Sliding the soap down her belly between her legs, they move rhythmically. Water shines over both hairless bodies, making them seem as delicate as blown glass. The soap slips from his hand to the floor, freeing his fingers to open the flower between her legs, his stem seeking reunion with the bud. He wants to take his lips from hers to hear her voice but can't bring himself to abandon the satin linings of either of her mouths. Their rhythm resonates until they shatter like the Tacoma Narrows Bridge. Their remains drain to the open sea. Long hard belly laughs express their joy.

In the suite's bedroom, Sicily turns on the radio which plays Marvin Gaye's song, "Ecology".

Sicily leans against the molding of the bathroom door. "Can you believe they changed the name of this song to 'Mercy, Mercy Me —from Ecology'?"

"God help the brother whose got his own," Forest does a parody of Billy Holiday singing God Bless the Child. He uses the acoustics of the bathroom for all they are worth.

Wrapping a towel around his waist, he comes through the door. Sicily is bare as the moment she was born. Defiantly leaning against the door jam, daring him to make her move so he can pass. He grabs her hands making her dance, something between a waltz and swing. They sing the name of the song "Oh Mercy, Mercy Me!"— In the soft decrescendo he pulls her close so he feels ever inch of her body then grabs her satin skinned waist and twirls her. At first it's imperceptible because they are so comfortable doing it, their pas de deux— from the festival. Feeling unequally exposed, Sicily rips his towel off of him. They dance and sing until finally collapsing on the bed. Forest sprawls across her, drawn as the moon by earth's gravity. He blindly reaches the night table, shutting off the radio.

"Twenty-one..." Sicily says.

"Twenty-one what?" he asks.

"Twenty-one days in our lives. That's the number of days we have actually seen one another."

"You counted them?"

"Like diamonds in a safe deposit box."

He looks at her body against the white sheets, wishing he were a painter or sculptor, anything to freeze this moment. "We're a long way from making love over war debris on a polluted farm outside of Berlin," he says, eyes drifting over the embossed wall paper and embroidered bedspread.

"What are your plans for the day?" Forest asks.

"Ellie arrives tomorrow. I have to book a flight back to school. The whole medical college thing—can't be missing classes."

Forest of all people, other than Moni, is not surprised by the ballerina's direction toward medical school. "I still need an office in Winnipeg, and I hear you have a room for rent," he says.

Sicily turns around to face him, screaming at the top of her lungs repeatedly, "Yes, yes, yes!" From the hallway, anyone passing would swear more than conversation yielded that. Forest stops the yelling by covering her mouth with his. They curl into the double tear drop, their hearts aligned, and fall asleep.

Sicily wakes with a start at 6AM.

"What's wrong? Honey—you need more sleep. Did you take your seizure medicine?" Forest asks, groggy.

"I have to tell you something," she says.

"Okay." He forces himself up on one elbow.

"It's about Rainy."

"Ah, I've been meaning to talk to you about her... and about Sophie."

"She told me. This is more important."

He has been confident Rainy would not divulge the depths of their intimacy beyond adoptive kinship. Being wrong surprises him.

"They beat the hell out of her in Ottawa," Sicily blurts out.

"What are you talking about?" Forest snaps.

"They did a number on her face, her arm. It was horrible. Ellie wanted me to wait to tell you. But I can't lie to you, or much to anyone, even by omission."

"I was there when the Riot Squad moved on the Caravan. Afterward, when I knew she was safe, asleep in a park with others a mile away, I slipped a card into her pocket."

"It was after that," Sicily says.

"Oh no, is she..." He trembles with pain.

"It'll take more than baseball bats to drop Rainy," she says.

"Laura and Rainy told me it was better if I didn't go. I didn't listen but decided to wear my hair up in a baseball cap, took off my jewelry, put on a shirt with a collar, and wore runners... keeping my distance from everyone who might recognize me," he says, "... until the attack, but I didn't think anyone would notice me after that."

"Rainy didn't realize you had been near until she found the postcard in her pocket."

"She was safe," he says again, shaking his head.

"I think it's about mercury. Otherwise, the leadership of the Caravan would be the target, not you, not Rainy," Sicily says.

Prepared for Forest's anger, Sicily had not considered him suffering. It makes her hesitant to tell the rest, but she has to do so. "They were sending you a message. Rainy says they mistook her for me, for your woman. They were thugs—not cops, not soldiers."

"Fucking mercenaries..." Forest's body stiffens with anger.

"You know them?" she asks. He won't answer. Wrapping his arms around her, laying her against his chest he says, "Get some more sleep." His brain doesn't dare shut his eyes knowing his universe has shifted.

At 9AM the alarm clock radio, set by the previous guest, plays Leonard Cohen's "Suzanne". Forest sings along. It hardly qualifies as singing but more a soft murmurer.

Inching toward consciousness, Sicily feels the sun streaming from the window, muted by translucent apricot sheers. Then she panics realizing Forest is not in bed beside her.

Hearing his whisper she relaxes. The voice now drops only to a hum, the melody. He sits in one of the stuffed armchairs next to a round table. His clothes clean, hair braided and bound, he watches her. Naked, she crawls from the bed to his lap, finishing the verse of "Suzanne" with him.

When she lets him up to breathe from her kiss, Forest whispers,

"You know, Johnny Trudell is one of the craziest brothers on the earth." He is tying up the loose end of a past conversation.

"Grandfather says, 'You gotta be crazy to think you can change the world, that's how oppression also takes its toll.'"

"—Time for me to meet your grandfather," Forest says.

Instead of waiting for the elevator at the hospital, they climb the four floors to the ward, avoiding comment on the bucket of fish or the beauty of the peonies. The charge nurse intercepts Sicily as she approaches Franklin's room. "Miss Marshall," the nurse touches Sicily's arm, forebodingly, "I am sorry to tell you..." Sicily shoves the vase of flowers into the nurse's hands and pushes the door open, stepping into the room. Franklin sleeps in his bed, breathing gurgling oxygen. Setting the bucket down, Forest holds Sicily close, preventing her collapse with relief. Finally exhaling, unburying her face from Forest's neck, she looks over his shoulder. Gaston Poulet's bed is carefully made, waiting for a new occupant.

Franklin says, "That young pharmacy intern filled Dr. Cook's orders. He had it yesterday. Pinot Grigio at lunch, Merlot with dinner. Gaston said the kid had good taste."

Sicily cries as her grandfather holds out his arms to her. "Sici, come," Franklin says. He envelops her before asking, "Is this your young man?"

"Yes, Grandfather, it is."

"One friend goes and another comes," Franklin says as he reaches out his hand. Forest holds it firmly, helping the older man by lifting the head of the hospital bed.

"It's a pleasure to meet you, grandson. How is your mother?"

Forest avoids explaining that he has no first hand knowledge of his mother's state.

"Sici, ask them to call Dr. Cook and let her know that I'm ready to go home."

She also calls her grandmother. Vanessa's relative absence during the past week reflects not denial but a social worker on autopilot. She has been working, banking sick and vacation time. Members of Vanessa's profession define themselves by the ability to help people function in an imperfect world. Knowing this moment would come, Franklin's wife had made plans. She will not be working but home with her husband until he dies.

Arriving the next morning, Vanessa pins gardenias from the bush at the cul-de-sac on each of the ward staffs' lapels. As Dr. Cook receives her flower, she and Sicily agree to stay in touch during the medical school application process. The charge nurse quicksteps to catch up as Forest pushes Franklin's wheelchair. She carries a large bottle of Taittinger Champagne and hands it to Franklin. It has a note attached, written in M. Poulet's wobbly script. Forest sees it is written in French. He translates, "It says, 'I will see you on the other side, my friend.'"

Flying back from Amsterdam, Ellie does not stop in Winnipeg but comes directly to Los Angeles. Lillie having fetched her from the airport, Sicily's mother is already at the cul-de-sac when Franklin and his entourage arrive. It's late January. The Christmas tree is still up in the living room, waiting. Franklin settles into his bed, drifting to sleep amid the chatter of familiar voices. Dinner preparation begins, the grunion. Assigned to pick lemons, Forest goes to the back yard. The juice will be the fish marinade. Ellie joins him. They need the time and space alone. After exchanging pleasantries about Vern and their mutual travels, Forest says, "I know about Rainy."

"As I expected," Ellie says, hugging her friend now son. A hallmark of oppression, poverty, and struggle is that people who should be in contact are often separated, refugees, exiles, prisoners. This is the first time Ellie and Forest share a table in two years. Picking fruit in the California sunshine, they hardly feel entitled to sympathy but have felt the absence.

"I can't let it go," he says.

"Neither can I. But what are your plans?" she asks.

"I'm not sure, I have to find the bastards first."

"You know I can't let you put Sicily in more danger."

He sucks his bottom lip, suppressing a tidal wave of emotion.

"Are you open to suggestions?" she asks.

"From you? Always..." His eyes plead for help.

"The safest would be if you were off the map."

"Hard to get further off than I am already. Are you joining the legions of those wishing to help my permanent absence? They're growing daily." The two share a much needed laugh.

"You may believe your calling is finishing this one research paper but I don't see that in you. You won't stop fighting for environmental justice, hell for all justice, until the day you die—maybe not even then. We will find a way," she says.

Ellie and Forest spend an hour at the patio table, slicing and squeezing lemons while talking. Before heading back to the kitchen they look at one another with resolve, a decision made. The concept they sell to Sicily is simple. They will follow Rainy's plan. The lovers' connection remains invisible until something changes. However, Forest is as aware as was Einstein, 'Nothing changes until something moves.'

⌢ ⌣

The next morning Forest accompanies Sicily to LAX. Los Angeles allows the two of them anonymity in plain sight. The route less traveled will take her back to Canada. He scheduled it himself.

"Tell me again, why are you going to Clear Lake?" she asks.

"I think I told you," he says.

"Perhaps I don't believe you. You may have some floozy mermaid on the side."

"Clear Lake, California, close to the Pomo lands, is near the old Socrates Quicksilver Mine. I suspect the lake has some of the highest levels of mercury in North America."

"Do people have Minamata disease?" Sicily asks.

"Nobody has looked. I'll get water and blood samples, do some interviews, then come home."

"The work is the excuse for abandoning me against which I can never argue. I'm about to shoot my foot," Sicily says, "but here goes—fish ingestion is the primary transmission of human mercury poisoning. Shouldn't you also be matching fish fat mercury concentrations wherever you are getting water and blood?"

Forest reaches into his jean jacket breast pocket, pulling out a folded cheque and passing it to her. "The first three months rent on my office. It's gonna take a while to get there. Apparently, I have to make extra time for fishing." He forces a smile.

"This is more than three months rent." She looks at the cheque.

"How do you know? You didn't give me a price."

"Hope you like green, that's the color of the walls in the room next to the bathroom."

Pulling her close he murmurs, "Do you think you will get to see Franklin again?"

"Unlikely," she says, "but at least we've had our time together. Please tell me what you are going to do about the attack on Rainy."

"Watching, waiting... as we agreed with Ellie." He does not look her in the eye.

Their passionate last kiss leaves passersby applauding. "Travel safe, my love. I'll see you on the other side," Forest whispers to himself as he watches her heading down the gang plank. Sicily turns back, flashing him one last unbearably bright smile.

2 7

WINNIPEG RIVER

FEBRUARY TO APRIL 1975

SICILY IS ABLE TO study for the Medical College Admissions Test during most of the Swan Lake rehearsals. However, the principal dancer takes a fall, pressing Sicily, the understudy, into service a week before the opening. Victor, as the principal male dancer of the Ballet company, is the Prince. During the prima's absence, Sicily's scenes are well executed, not lackluster. Studying science has made her an even better technical dancer. In a crucial rehearsal of Swan Lake's last act, Sicily dances the good nobleman's true love, Odette. Victor sees a clarity in the ballerina's eyes as she takes the floor. He realizes the release of her full dance potential is imminent.

In the ballet Swan Lake, the Evil Knight's spell forces Odette to spend half her days as a swan. Odette's lover Prince mistakenly kills her while aiming at the Knight. It is the Prince's love which causes Odette's demise. Upon her death the swan becomes her human corporal self. The Prince carries her body into the lake, drowning himself, allowing them to share the hereafter. Sicily is not acting, but lives, and breathes, these moments. A star is born, not a performer but a celestial body.

Stunned, the other cast members watch spent Sicily crumble to the floor. A full minute passes before Victor stretches his hand down, pulling her to stand, cradling her head against his chest. Her colleagues' applause is as loud as that of an opening night full house. Still, Sicily hopes the universe protects her from ever having to dance that role again. The rendition is one she would be unlikely to repeat or survive. Hearing of Sicily's glory, the injured prima ballerina makes sure to present herself good as new at the next rehearsal.

⌢ ⌣

Unlike the previous year, this spring arrives early and is unseasonably warm. Vern is already on the dock servicing the boat though it is only April. An advantage of #3 Creighton is a sunporch with double panes for fall and winter, screens for spring and summer. Dozing intermittently on the porch's wicker chaise, Sicily waits for Moni to arrive from classes before preparing dinner.

Forest's postcard depicting the glorious rice fields of California's Yolo Valley rests on Sicily's chest, over her heart. The abandoned Socrates Mercury Mine is only twenty-five miles upstream from the crops. From his familiar shorthand, she gleans his cryptic suspicion—Clear Lake's mercury contaminated waters irrigate that grain. He is right. Sicily knows, already having tested samples delivered by Pony Express a week ago. Forest heads 'to fish' at Lake of the Woods. Then finally, home.

Next to the chaise on the floor sits a stack of old mail, including the results of Sicily's Medical College Admissions Test. Her rank is high enough that if accepted, she would be eligible to complete her first two years of medical school along with a bachelor of performing arts. Admission would likely be a year away, a bridge to cross when she comes to it.

Calabria's confidence in Sicily's capacity coincides with his annual three months' teaching at the hospital morgue. Sicily is increasingly at the helm of the lab through summer. Slipping in and out of slumber she remembers the doctor's exuberance when telling her, "The abstract for the mercury research paper has been well received. August is the anticipated date of the full paper's publication." Since the announcement, the ballerina wakes most mornings hopeful. She sees a normal life ahead— one with Forest.

Footsteps climbing the porch rouse Sicily. She always wishes the feet are Forest's, but in reality they should be Moni's. Despite paying rent, he has yet to visit his office. However, it is Rainy who creaks through the screen door. "How did you get here?" Sicily asks. Walking on river water isn't possible, buses are slow, and Rainy's house is a long stroll by street.

"Hitched," Rainy says, leaning against the wall of the porch, sliding down to sit on the painted yellow floor.

"What's up?" Sicily asks.

Sicily sees her friend's blue irises float against bright red sclera. Rainy is crying. The idea of such a reality is unfathomable for Sicily. Knowing she will disintegrate if she gives an inch, Sicily's control is chilling. As she stares, Rainy begins,

"Forest was on the Winnipeg River today, near where it flows into the lake..." But the two spirit is unable to finish. Her mouth slams shut, forbidding words to escape. Recognizing her friend's paused speech as a warning, Sicily's throat closes, leaving her hoarse.

"Where is he now?" Sicily asks.

"It's a crime scene..." Rainy says.

"How do you know about it?"

"Ben... but he's not sure. It came over the police radio at the studio. He heard a description, then called my neighbor."

"How long ago?"

"Half hour..." Rainy says, her palms now a reservoir for her tears. "Ben's headed up there with a cameraman."

"I'm going." Sicily says.

"They'll finish before you get there, and they are not gonna let you see him anyway," Rainy mutters.

Standing abruptly, flinging the screen door open, barefoot Sicily steps onto the pavement. In her periphery there is motion on the dock—Vern. Cold mud squishes between her toes while navigating the railroad ties. Vern fills the boat's tank from a bright red gas can. Sicily surprises him by untying the mooring. He wants an explanation, which she is loathe to articulate.

Moni comes home from class at her usual time. Glancing over the hedge of budding pink peonies, she sees the drama unfolding at the water's edge. Rainy comes from the porch, struggling to tell the Persian what is happening. They see Vern's difficulty preventing Sicily from boarding the boat. Reaching the dock, man-magnet mathematician Moni's voice, generally reminiscent of a chocolate truffle, now bellows, "Damn it, stop." The others freeze.

Riding the bus daily, passing road signs stipulating distances to different destinations, Moni retains the information as easily as she breathes. "It's 80 kilometers by the highway, an hour drive. It is only 15 kilometers by water, with The Bear doing 45 per hour it's under 20 minutes. Take the boat," Moni says. Vern checks the math in his head and assents with a nod to Moni, who continues, "Rainy, you go with Vern and Sicily. I will find Ellie and come with her by car."

⌒ ‿

The Royal Canadian Mounted Police, who patrol Canada's internal waterways along with the land, spot the fast moving craft by radar. Kicking wake, Vern speeds past the locks between the Red River and Lake Winnipeg. The police boat approaches. The Bear accelerates. The RCMP bullhorn orders the pilot to stop. Vern, however, wants to get closer to the confluence of the lake with the Winnipeg River. There is emergency activity on the far bank of the river's mouth. The Bear's motor drones.

"What's worse, the boat dying, or dying too far from the shore?" Vern yells over to Rainy.

"You know best." Rainy stares at him implying he need not ask.

Vern dares pushing the throttle further than he should. He hopes a mile can be gained before the boat's last gasp.

"Sicily, get off before they get here," Vern shouts, bringing the bow around to face the pursuing police. Sicily does not respond. Instead she stands, not holding the rails, swaying to keep her balance. Remarkably, her mind is elsewhere. 'They already tried to shoot me...' she remembers Forest saying. The boat bumps against its own wake. Cold water splashes her face. Sicily closes her eyes. Rainy and Sicily both struggle to balance on the water drenched deck.

"Now!" Vern says, hoping Rainy can enforce his command.

"Sicily, you gotta get off the boat," Rainy says.

"You are always telling me what I gotta, or ought to do, or feel," Sicily says, "What I feel is Forest's presence and that he is okay."

"If you believe that, go prove it. You sometimes swim 5000 meters, right?"

"Huh? Yes—" Sicily says.

"Good, then you can easily swim this. Sicily, jump off the back of the fuckin' boat. Get to shore. That's where the answers are—" Perhaps the only moment of weakness in Rainy's life has just passed. Shaking her head with disgust, or maybe pity, Rainy shoves Sicily over the rail at the stern and into the blue-black water.

Stunned, slipping silently beneath the circular wake, Sicily dives deep. Not yet warmed by summer, the water temperature is barely above freezing. Turbulence is worse for the lake wind clashing against the river's current. She manages ten strokes before her breath demands she surface. Forcing her lungs to drain, she inhales deep, as she would for a series of dance leaps, then dives again, and again. Fingertips finally touching grass growing from the bed of the river, she crawls to the part of the bank where she sees police lights. The sun drops low. Golden hour wanes toward darkness, cloaking her approach.

Emerging at the shore, muddy dress, drenched, Sicily drags herself to a stand. She walks toward long orange tarps on the ground. Now the Mounties on the land see her. Astonishment at the sight of a Black mermaid stymies intervention as the police first response. "Halt, or be shot," one of them finally yells. Barefoot on a jagged rock beach, she continues. Her cut feet bleed. Shivering, teeth rattling, oblivious to the RCMP, she keeps walking. Intentionally out of range, warning shots are fired. No doubt the marksmen are protective of the orange plastic sheets, four of them, twenty feet square seamed together at the edges. Someone, immobile, is supine at the center of the array. She is confident beyond reason that Forest is not laying on that ground.

Reaching the corner of one of the tarps she hears the RCMP commander bellow into a bullhorn, "Apprehend that woman." Uniforms rush toward her. Her path does not deviate.

Ben Wolf and his cameraman arrive, pulling next to a single St. John's ambulance. The reporters follow the medics. They are all stopped at the police line. Ben flashes his press credentials at the junior officer who blocks their passage. The young cop recognizes Ben, "Hey aren't you on the CBC..." Ben limps past, ignoring his fan.

Ellie and Moni arrive moments after the news truck. Ben sees them. The guard holds up his hand, blocking Ellie. Ben has heard about the defiance he sees in Ellie's eyes. "They are with my crew," the reporter says.

"Stay behind the police line," the cop says.

Reflected orange light from the sunset above, and the plastic beneath, bounces off Sicily. She moves toward the center of the tarps, approaching the immobile person on the ground. Trepidation sneaks into her gait. "Now would be a good time to talk, Forest, talk to me," Sicily says, her words floating away on the silence. Her feet crunch the tarp, leaving bloody footprints. Stopping over the man on the ground, looking at his cowboy boots, anguish crawls from her belly into her mouth. Bending from the waist, she vomits. The approaching officers spontaneously jump back for a moment. They plan to physically extract her.

Ellie dips under the police tape, anticipating the mayhem that might follow.

"Ma'am, this is an active crime area," the RCMP commander barks at Ellie.

"Can you get her off that tarp and not hurt her more? I can. I'm her mother—and a nurse."

The Commander knows no routine response to this peculiar situation. He decides to avoid a blood bath. "Stand down, Stand down and pull back. Her mother is going in."

Walking towards Sicily, Ellie stops abruptly. Yes, she is sure. She sees a slight movement of Forest's hand. Two steps more and she stops again. An officer holds Sicily's shoulders. Sicily head butts him in the chest. Another uniform approaches. He is surprised by the young woman's enormous strength. She holds him by the neck and kicks. Then Ellie hears the sound, seared deep in her memory—rifles cocking. The embattled officers wrench away from Sicily's reach, out of the line of gun sight. Ellie's voice thunders, "SICILY, GET DOWN, GET DOWN!" Her daughter's body drops, layering over Forest.

The volley of bullets fired chase the birds from the thickets. The deafening wing movements cast a shadow, blackening the dusk. Nurse Ellie rolls Sicily onto her back. No blood, but she flops with a global seizure. "Stay with me Sicily—Darling Baby, stay with me," Ellie whispers. She rolls her child to the side in the safety position, assisting the St. John's Ambulance attendants getting her on the litter.

Having diverted the RCMP vessel with verbal finesse, Vern had been directed by the officers toward a cove where the best fish might be found. The information was ignored upon the police launch speeding off. Now Vern and Rainy arrive at the riverbank, where the crime scene has fallen into chaos. Seeing medics whisk Sicily away on a stretcher with Ellie running along side, Vern catches up to them.

Forest is alone. Rainy goes to him. He waits only for a licensed physician's declaration that he is dead. The rules of emergency triage say that in situations of scarcity, the obligation is to use the available resources for the most good. Sicily has won the ride in the only ambulance now on scene. Sliding behind him, Rainy cradles Forest in her strong limbs. Rocking him she offers prayers on his behalf to Gitche Manitou, the creative force.

The RCMP commander barks orders, "Stop that woman." Ellie turns back to see Rainy with Forest. She remembers the brief flash of movement. Climbing into the ambulance rig, Vern now at her side she says, "Make sure Rainy doesn't let anyone take Forest from her, not even at the hospital." Vern scratches his head, confused. Squinting, he tries to understand his wife's meaning.

'When all else fails, follow instructions,' he thinks. Hell, turning back he sees Rainy is already fighting. Arms holding Forest tight, she kicks and bites the knuckles of a cop.

"This man is dead and she is the mother of his child!" Vern says. His voice booms. "In her religion, she must stay with him until his immortal soul has fully left this domain." Even Rainy looks askance at Vern speaking spiritual mumble-jumble. Then she 'prays' more loudly.

With all the foot traffic, there is no chance this crime scene is intact, which may explain the uncharacteristic gentility of the RCMP senior officer about the death of a Native person. The chief cop shakes his head saying, "Why should the mother of his child be an exception in this mess? When the wagon comes let her ride with him."

Moni stands next to Ben Wolf. "You can do it," she says, helping him muster the stamina to interview everyone else milling about, especially the ricers who had found Forest. Both Moni and Ben know it is important to record the witness statements, in case faulty memories or coercion force them to be changed. Besides, it is what Forest would want from his dear friend. Ben shouts, "Roll." The cameraman's bright light shrinks the reporter's pupils.

2 8

SWAN LAKE

MAY 1975

ONE OF DR. CALABRIA'S hands nervously slides the wooden door of his cubicle. His other holds the phone receiver. "The seizures finally responded to intravenous benzodiazepines. She isn't conscious yet," Ellie says. Retreating to clinical brevity helps keep both their emotions in check.

"She'll be okay," Calabria says, relieved the doubt on his face is invisible through the phone.

"The convulsions saved her. She fell to the ground in time to avoid being riddled with bullets. But I have another problem."

"I can't imagine anything else counts," he says.

"Vern is here doing the paperwork. I need Moni with me for strength when Sicily wakes up. Rainy is in the ambulance bay at the Emergency Room with Forest's body. I'm confident she hasn't let anyone touch him. At first I thought maybe Forest—well, if you can get to her, tell her I sent you and she can let him go." Ellie's voice gurgles.

"I'll handle it. Pilot ought to be arriving at the airport. He'll help."

At the ER, the pathologist exchanges greetings with the attending doctor on duty.

"We're far too busy to have a girl and a corpse wasting an emergency vehicle. But she is too strong to fight. Apparently she carried the corpse to the ambulance herself, refusing to let the medics touch him," says the ER doc.

"How long has he been dead?" Calabria asks as the two walk toward the ambulance bay.

"Who knows? Ricers found him face down in near freezing river water, bashed in the head. It may be long as an hour and a half ago—the girl wouldn't let me touch him."

"I'll take care of this for you. He'll end up on my slab anyway."

"Thanks, I owe you one." The ER doctor quickly heads back to his post.

The medics have abandoned the scene, taking a different ambulance to another emergency. It will be a few minutes before the police arrive. The doors to the ambulance rig are open. Rainy, on the floor in the back, still cradles Forest. Michelangelo's sculpture the Pieta comes to the Italian doctor's mind. The work depicts Mary holding her recently crucified son. The Metis woman's lips are blue from sharing her body heat with a human icicle. She curses Forest, in Michif, as if making his spirit angry might bring him back. Grabbing one of the bright red blankets on the ambulance's shelf, Calabria drapes it around the young woman while conveying Ellie's message.

Trying to reposition Forest, the doctor notices something odd. There is no pulse or breath, as expected. But the supposedly dead man also has no lividity, the bluish skin blotches accompanying the stiffness of rigor mortise. Neither sign of death is present. An orderly passes. Calabria barks, "Get me a gurney and a body bag." The worker hops to it.

"Rainy, did anyone try to resuscitate him with mouth to mouth, oxygen, or electric paddles?" Calabria asks.

"I don't know. When I got to the beach he was already dead." Rainy's teeth chatter.

Lifting Forest eyelids, Calabria thinks, 'Neither of his pupils are fixed nor dilated... One is a little larger than the other but not by much. It's likely from the pressure of the head bang,' he thinks, running a gloved hand through blood-matted hair above a deep slit in Forest's scalp. He mutters, "Bleeding is from soft tissue—the skull has only a hairline crack. Thank you, God, for mercies."

When the gurney arrives, the attendant 'bags' Forest. Calabria dismisses the orderly, then proceeds to loot the ambulance. He pulls a portable defibrillator from a nook. "It's bulky and heavy, but we need to sneak it into the morgue. Damn," he says, setting the thing on the ambulance floor. He takes off his horn-rimmed glasses, cleaning them with the inside of his white clinical coat, and resets them on his face. It occurs to him that what he is about to do is completely illegal. But his litmus test is whether or not it is immoral. He thinks not. Still having the heart of a dock worker, his body is that of an older academic, forcing him to lift the defibrillator with both hands.

"You can't hide it that way. Give it here," Rainy says. Taking the defibrillator from his two hands, with her one, she slides it beneath the blanket she now wears as a shawl. From the ambulances stock, Calabria quickly pilfers several bags of normal saline, intravenous infusion tubing, and some catheters. He hides all of it in the body bag with Forest.

"Why are we doing this?" Rainy asks.

"We don't ever need this stuff in the morgue, but we might today. There is research being done, right her in Winnipeg, suggesting Forest is not dead until he is 'warm and dead.'"

⌒ ‿

Pilot leans against the morgue door. He sees the doctor and the two spirit running the gurney down the basement hall. A soldier, Pilot is good at taking orders, while Dr. Calabria is proficient at giving them. "Get Roxley over here with a van from the animal quarters," the doctor tells Pilot. Out of her character, Rainy looks confused. Pilot is already at the wall-phone negotiating with his in-law.

"Rewarming successful or not, I will be signing Forest Odjig's death certificate today," Calabria explains. "The causes of death will be drowning, hypothermia, and traumatic head injury. The stated opinion will be that these diagnoses derive from intent to murder. If the heavens are with us, the man on this gurney will need admitting to hospital, one with an acute unit and rehab capacity. He also needs protection from whomever is trying to kill him. Ambulances leave paper trails, other vans don't. He's got to have a new name as well—one he can remember."

"That would be Jorge, Jorge Neruda," Pilot says, helping to free Forest's body from the black bag.

Calabria places a tube down Forest's throat, into his windpipe, while explaining,"Drowning in freezing water may put a person in a type of suspended animation, like a drained car battery in the cold. Sometimes it's not permanently dead, and gentle rewarming helps when you try to jump-start it. I know the researchers who are working on this."

The doctor attaches a clear rubber Ambu Bag to the tube in Forest's trachea. Ambu, is short for ambulance. The bag has and oxygen reservoir filled from a nearby tank. Pilot knows the drill from his military training. He squeezes and releases the Bag, rhythmically forcing air in and out of Forest's lungs. Calabria inserts three separate large intravenous tubes into Forest's neck, arm, and groin using the Seldinger Technique. Rainy learns how to open sterile saline. As one bag empties into Forest's veins, she hangs another.

Calabria explains to Pilot, "Give him four or five chest compressions between those breaths." Pilot responds, like the combat soldier he is, well trained in what will become the state of the art in trauma care. Calabria continues, "They called it the Winnipeg Protocol for Resuscitation of Cold Water Drowning Victims. It's not mainstream yet, but it will be soon." Charging the defibrillator, Calabria orders, "Step away and don't touch anything."

Rainy and Pilot jump back. The pathologist pushes buttons on the tops of two rubber knobs attached to metal paddles, delivering 280 joules of electricity into Forest's chest. Forest's body bounces against the gurney. "This is like a Frankenstein movie," Rainy says, her own skin tone now green. Pressing his fingers into Forest's neck below the jaw, the pathologist is disappointed. He turns the knob on the machine, cranking up the voltage, repeating the electric shock, once, twice, and a third time. After the last jolt, Forest's carotid arteries pulse.

"Got him." Calabria smiles.

Pilot grabs Rainy in a bear vice hug saying, "Now we have to keep him. Where the hell is Roxley with that van?" The beeping of the monitor assures Forest's heart still beats, though he remains unconscious. Calabria continues forcing air into his patient's trachea with the bag.

"It's okay," Calabria says, "I need a minute to fill out the death certificate and call over to get 'Jorge' admitted to Deer Lodge. Roxley is always telling me he has the best animal furnace in the country—we also need pig ashes—they are almost the right density."

"Why?" Rainy asks, looking confused.

"I get it," Pilot says, glowing with enlightenment. "If we don't have a body—"

"—We have to intern Forest's ashes." Calabria's hand salutes Pilot.

Upstairs from the morgue, Sicily's seizures mercifully obliterate her memory. Her eyes open. Attached to a machine which forces air into her lungs, the tube down her throat hurts. Monitors flash green and red, without noise. People talking fill the room. She cannot hear them. Sicily sees but is unable to move her body. She panics. Ellie leans into her eye line and kisses her cheek.

A man in a blaring white clinical jacket approaches with a hypodermic needle. "We paralyzed you with a curare type muscle relaxant to give your body a rest. That's why only your eyelids are working. The drug is wearing off. I'll help it along," he mouths. Sicily cannot hear a word. He injects the antidote into her intravenous line. With a rush, Sicily's body shoots upright. The stranger doctor disconnects the respirator, then threads the tube out of her trachea. She coughs and gags spontaneously, settling down as nasal prong oxygen drifts into her nostrils. Still, she hears nothing. The whoosh of the bullets on the beach try to surface from her subconscious.

Ellie writes on a hand chalk board then mouths the words while holding the writing up to show Sicily, "... Hearing will come back... you had seizures, cold, + shock." Ellie says. Slowly, Sicily racks her mind trying to remember how to read. Comprehending, her eyes widen, searching the crowded room. Moni and Vern are at the end of her bed, touching her blanketed feet as if they were the Magi and she Zarathustra. Whispering to one another they seem locked between obligations to the truth and lies. "Where is he, Momma?" Sicily asks, her voice only audible in her head.

Another white coat's back faces Sicily... but no Forest. Ellie twists the chain of her Maltese Cross, then she writes furiously once more on the chalk board, holding the board up for Sicily to see. Sicily reads aloud, "'Darling Baby... he didn't make it.'" Squinting at the words fails to aid her understanding. Her mother's anguished face is more comprehensible.

Dr. Calabria, the other white coat, moves into Sicily's view. Making eye contact, his expression is between sadness and devastation. He shakes his head 'no.' Sicily wonders, 'What the hell does that mean?' Looking around the room, she searches for the person whose honesty is unimpeachable. Rainy is absent, as is Pilot.

Forest's eyes flutter open for the first time since the attempt on his life three weeks before. The ceiling of his Deer Lodge Hospital room is forty feet high and puke green. His lids close again. He feels himself run—along a lake. It's a familiar body of water—the Swan Lake construction site. For Forest this is real, not a recollection. He pants and struggles to catch his breath—one, two, three men chase him. His pursuers carry baseball bats, and one has a gun. For a while Forest outruns them, until a fourth man blocks his path by standing in front of him. "You!" Forest says, then Swack! All goes black. Sweating, Forest's consciousness returns to the bile colored hospital room.

"Hello brother, we have missed you man," Pilot says, pulling his chair closer to the bed, touching Forest's hand as if it is fine china.

"Where...?" Forest asks, struggling to speak.

"You are in Deer Lodge Hospital. I'm going to get someone and let them know you are awake. I'll be right back." Pilot dashes out.

Waiting, Forest feels he is rocking, swaying, drifting on water. No, it's more than a feeling. He must be in the water. The cold prevents him breathing or even shivering. People are talking. He doesn't understand what they are saying yet knows their language. They lift him out of the wet—

Pilot comes back into the hospital room. He brings a man clad in a color that matches the ceiling. Deterred from ruminating on his horrifying inner voice, Forest is relieved. "Welcome back," says the other man, a physician in training. "You are at Deer Lodge Hospital. Let's see if we can help you sit up." The intern and Pilot swing Forest's legs over the side of the bed. Finally in sitting position, Forest slumps backward to the mattress. Propping the patient up, the intern says, "Your work with the physical and occupational therapist will start right away, this afternoon. It will help you recover the fastest."

Pilot grins. 'I know that man's teeth,' Forest thinks.

Pilot is relieved that Forest recognizes him. Over the next days they piece together a chronology of events covering the several preceding weeks. It explains Forest's remembrance of someone warm against his cold, wet body. Now he knows it was soft Sicily, though he can't easily recall her name, he remembers her. He learns Rainy had rocked him like a baby and protected him per Ellie's instructions. Calabria had resuscitated him, using new science, then declared him dead.

"They keep calling me George," Forest says, mixing up the Spanish version of the name with the English.

"It's a 'trauma name'—and it is actually 'Jorge,'" Pilot says.

"'Trauma name...'?" Forest asks.

"When patients are in danger, in the emergency room, the staff change their names." Pilot winces at his own half truth, then says, "Whoever hurt them is less likely to find 'em in the hospital and finish the job."

"Am I in danger?" Forest asks, his eyebrows arching.

Pilot nods slowly 'yes'. "Please remember, your name is Jorge, not George—Jorge Neruda."

"Isn't he dead?"

"It was two summers ago—but he lives on in you, man," Pilot says.

A bore hole with a drain runs from Forest's skull to a ping-pong ball sized rubber reservoir taped to his back. It had removed fluid compressing his brain. The job finished, the tube comes out. He feels lopsided when looking in the mirror, hair shorn only on the injured left side. "Can I shave it all off?" he asks. The Certified Nurse Assistant does it. The sutured head scar is more visible. Hair will grow over it, the CNA assures him. The crew cut is Forest's optimal disguise.

With his traumatic brain injury, Forest goes daily to the physical therapy gym filled with its equipment and mirrors. Learning he is a dancer, the therapists plays Powwow music while he practices walking. The music helps wake his muscle memory.

Gripping parallel bars at first, he relearns to balance, abandoning his cane by day three. An occupational therapist plays cards with him, has him draw, ask questions, and put together puzzles. A speech therapist helps him articulate, first in English, then realizing he is multilingual, works on his French and tests his Spanish. Exhausted after the sessions, he is irritable. Frustrated by his inept body and mind, he becomes easily belligerent. He is distressed by his frequent incivility. The occupational therapist explains, "Getting enough rest is essential for impulse control." Forest doesn't like to sleep because that's when the images of his attack surface.

No one other than Pilot has come to see Forest's miraculous recovery, not even Calabria. After weeks of Pilot's probing, Forest realizes the Swan Lake construction site was where he found the person who had attacked Rainy. Sadly, he is unable to recall that precise information, other than a flash of orange, like the Firebird feathers. Pilot agrees. Samples from Swan Lake were among those never arriving in Churchill for the Pony Express. Someone put Forest in a boat knowing it would float downstream, assuring he would be far from the location of 'the murder' when found.

"Did you bring me a newspaper?" Forest, now Jorge, asks. Pilot slaps the Winnipeg Free Press into his friend's hand. Reading it front to back, getting to the last page, Forest pauses. He looks up at Pilot and then back down at the words. "This is surreal as hell," he says. "My memorial is the last Saturday in May. Am I dead?"

"For now—your safety, your family, and your ongoing research depend on Forest Odjig staying dead," Pilot says.

"Do they know I'm okay?... Mum, Sicily?"

Pilot shakes his head, "Best if they don't." Forest isn't asking about Rainy. Pilot decides it is better not to volunteer the involvement of anyone else.

"I'm confused," Forest says, closing his eyes.

"Trust me," Pilot says, tiptoeing out of the room.

⌢ ‿

The last Friday of May, Sicily staggers down the stairs at #1 Creighton, now stable enough to abandon the banister. The jungle of house plants merges with late spring foliage outside the living room window. Headquartered in the dining room off the kitchen, her mother passes out mimeographed press releases and barks assignments to her crew, Moni, Rainy, and Vern. Sicily is not quite ready for all this yet.

In contrast to her daughter, Ellie's modus operandi is consistent with the adage 'Ain't gonna be no crying until the struggle is over.' Others jump up to greet and kiss Sicily. Ellie is writing. She pauses, looking up at her daughter lovingly, then resumes her scribbling. There is no time to waste. Forest's memorial is set for tomorrow.

"Sicily, I need you with me. Please be dressed, waiting on your front steps, at 4PM," Vern says. His modulated South African English, with vestiges of secondary education in England, particularly annoys Sicily today. But she is soothed by his hug, combined with his shoving a cup of coffee into her hand, as he whisks out the door.

"Um huh," Sicily answers, long after Vern is gone, wishing he had written down his instructions. Feeling like a filleted fish whose skeleton is tossed away, she wonders, 'How are the others able to function?'

Removing the medicine bag returned to her neck on leaving the hospital, Sicily steps into the shower at #3 Creighton. She finds the faucet knobs unfamiliar. Left completely alone with her grief and confusion, drying herself is daunting. A white towel wrapped around her, she goes into Forest's office. Covering the walls are black and white mounted photos of Forest in Switzerland, Berlin, Los Angeles. There are also those of the world's waterways—not all of them, only those waters competing with Sicily for Forest's attentions. Each is 11 by 14 inches, painstakingly printed in Calabria's lab darkroom.

The first photograph to go is of Swan Lake. Her lover had shown her an advertisement of that nasty decorative mining pit, filled with water and mercury. Later she had photographed it from a real estate magazine, blew it up, and voila, here it is, being ripped off the wall. She tears it into confetti. All the other photos have similar fates. The ceramic pencil holder shatters when she throws it against the wall. Crashing the Underwood typewriter to the floor, she is forced to jump out of its way. The towel slips from her waist, leaving her naked, cold, sliding on wet footprints. The impotent dream catcher, hanging over Forest's unused day bed, falls as she slams the door, escaping. In the hall she sprawls over the hard wood floor, weeping, wishing it were her casket.

Sicily finds herself waiting on the wooden steps at #3, wearing a sundress that is, or was, among Forest's favorites, though she had intended to burn it. The humid evening is illuminated by flashes of lightning emanating from distant clouds. A red umbrella rests across her knees. When the rain starts, she is hesitant to take cover. Water is the closest she can get to Forest in this life. Soaked, she opens the red canopy. It amplifies the shower's sound. With that volume, her heart sweeps back to Berlin. Losing Forest this time is different from that storm. Lurking in her mind is the truth. It is she who forced him out of the shadows, heightening the danger associated with his quest.

'Don't be ridiculous,' she hears Forest say in her head, clear as the day is not.

"This isn't the time for you to talk to me. Can't you see?" She says aloud. Catching a glimpse of a tree branch blowing in the wind she thinks, 'Maybe it is Forest's hair, bound tight with black leather tassels, come back to life.'

Distracting her despair, Vern's car pulls in front of #1 Creighton. A Lincoln limousine follows, stopping near Sicily at the curb. The driver pops out, opening the door for the passengers. With a wave, Vern coaxes Sicily to greet the guests and share her umbrella. She neither considers the identities of the visitors nor cares about them. Robotic, she follows Vern's hand signals. The first of the two Japanese scientists emerge. Sicily releases herself from the correctness of acknowledging these men as separate human beings.

Vern bows a greeting, introducing himself to the Japanese guests. He apologizes that Ellie is late and will join them for dinner. The translator emerges last. As he pushes out of the limo, head first, Sicily sees his square-topped, spiky, short hair. As Vern begins to introduce his daughter, the translator tosses the umbrella from her hand, throws her into a dip, and kisses her neck. Despite the wetness, her old friend wraps himself around her.

"Henry? Henry!" Sicily says, as he sets her upright.

"There is always a point where the present meets the past," Henry whispers in her ear, the one Forest always used. Over Henry's shoulder, the eyes of the Japanese gentlemen widen. By the looks on their face, this display of unexplained intimacy is embarrassing to them. "We were childhood friends who started school together," Henry says in Japanese, then translates his statements for Sicily and Vern. He finishes in a voice soft enough to barely meet the threshold for hearing. "When my father died of pesticide poisoning, Sicily's mother was with him." Tears roll down Sicily's and Henry's cheeks, mixing with the rain.

⌢ ⌣

Two hundred invited guests stream in. Ellie is relieved by the volume of members of the press who responded to her media release. The eight foot long square block timber railway ties forming the stairs to the dock make good benches for sitting in the natural amphitheater of the yard. Vern and kids from the Native Youth set up a stage and tables for serving food. The place looks prepared for a wedding, peonies and black-eyed susan run garlands around the scene.

Wearing the fancy dance earrings, Sicily nervously fondles them as they tickle her clavicles. Intermittently, they bang against the medicine bag on her neck. Leaning against the wood siding of the house under the picture window, both her mind and heart race. Even though she saw Forest dead, she is a millennium from accepting it. These two years have been simultaneously the happiest and most painful of her life. After the Anti-apartheid Movement folks, Mack and Victor arrive with several of Sicily's dance classmates, kissing and hugging her before finding seats. In her head Sicily hears the last movement of Tchaikovsky's Swan Lake. "Lying on that beach, Forest and I were lying on the edge of life next one another but our timing was so lousy we couldn't even do death together," she says. Rainy hears her and has to comment,

"Don't be gettin' all magical. This is Winnipeg, with or without your presence, it's where people would come to murder a First Nation whistleblower and journalist and hide it."

"Somehow, I'm going to change that, even if it takes me the rest of my life."

"I know," Rainy says.

Vern welcomes the guests. He introduces Ben Wolf, "A devoted journalist and documentarian of Native Canadian and other aboriginal peoples."

Sophie situates herself between Sicily and Rainy. She holds Sicily's skirt and her mother's belt loop. Moni stands on Sicily's other side, their shoulders touching. Laura leans against Rainy. Pilot arrives, sliding behind Laura, providing his chest for her head to rest. Roxley and his wife will join them after finding parking.

Ben Wolf's limp bestows an odd dignity to the makeshift podium. Under his amputated arm is a typed sheet containing his remarks. Rainy whispers to Sicily, "That son of a bitch cleans up damned good." The wall of Forest's friends and family laugh, seeming inappropriate to other mourners. Ben starts his remarks, in Ojibwa. He is laudatory of Ellie and Vern, the hosts of the memorial service. Sicily's attention flickers away with the movement of the maple leaves in the breeze. Her mind goes nowhere, transiently relieved from this reality. The applause for Ben brings her back.

Next, the Japanese scientists push Henry toward the podium, like a chick dumped from the nest. Henry stands for a beat, allowing the guests a mental pause before forcing them to reach the conclusion he next iterates. No longer translating, authorized to speak for the Minamata team, Henry wades into the core of the mercury dialog gradually leading to the crescendo,

"The criteria for Minamata Disease is being met, not only in Japan but here in Canada, the United States, Southern and Eastern Africa, Indonesia, India, in the European Western and Eastern Blocks. Have no doubt, mercury poisoning's sometimes subtle features are the tip of the iceberg of disease and suffering by these environmental toxins." Henry pauses for the flurry of flash bulbs and shutter clicks threatening to drown him out. "Those with the most problems are obliged to find the most solutions. Forest Odjig honored that obligation." Amid applause, the Japanese research team bows respectfully.

The cultural program of First Nation music and dance follows. Then Ellie takes the podium. "I ask that during this 'minute of silence' called to honor our fallen comrade, brother, and son, Forest Odjig, please commit to his life and work." Standing on the stage with Ellie are Mum, Vern, Ben, Henry, and the Japanese scientists. Mum takes the microphone. She is to conclude the moment of silence. Speaking in clear English she says, "Doc Calabria, come from the back, and bring the others with you." Unnoticed until then, Calabria has collected Pascal and Camille from the airport, and they stand near him. All those leaning on the house's wall, including Sophie, hold hands, snaking a conga line between the seated mourners to reach the stage.

Mum says a Dené prayer for her son, and for all mothers' children, to "travel safe." Then she passes the mic to Sicily. Sicily tries to give it to anyone instead. The others reject the device, leaving it with her by default. She is silent as stone. She has volumes to say which at the moment clog the corridor of her throat. Moni sends a scrap of paper, pulled from her bosom, along the line of friends and family. Sicily unfolds it, reading the words to herself—they are the turnkey to her emotions. The look she gives Moni expresses boundless affection.

"My sister has reminded me of a quote by W. H. Auden. It gives words to my feelings. It reads, 'Murder is unique in that it abolishes the party it injures, so that society has to take the place of the victim and on his behalf demand atonement or grant forgiveness; it is the one crime in which society, as a whole, has a direct interest.'"

Sicily tucks the paper in her own bosom then reaches for Sophie's hand, and Sophie for Rainy's, until all those on the stage are linked. In the tradition of dance, her last performance with Forest, and respect for those gathered, Sicily leads the bow from the waist. The powwow drum initiates the applause. Together, they face the river, their eyes navigating Bear Bay. Vern idles the boat's motor while Pilot helps Mum, Laura, Sophie, Rainy, Ellie, and Sicily climb aboard. The Bear chugs into the river's middle and stops. The crowd watches. The press snaps shots.

A sweetgrass and sisal basket is filled with flowers and stones. Sicily is hesitant to receive the packet from Mum, who insists. The ashes are swaddled in two layers of cheese cloth. Laura's beaded ties attach an array of feathers adorning the woven casket's sides. Sicily lowers the basket into the water. The lighterweight flowers drift into the current. The cloth releases the ashes in milky puffs snaking north toward the locks at Lake Winnipeg. The basket floats longer than physics would have expected for the remains of a man of Forest's stature and muscle. As it fully submerges, Dido's Lament plays on the cassette recorder at the boats stern, "Remember me, remember me, but ah! Forget my fate..." Sicily lingers, hanging over the rail of the boat. Pilot holds her at her waist, assuring she does not try to follow Forest into the deep.

29

LAURENTIAN DIVIDE

AUGUST 1975

STANDING ON THE STEPS of #3 Creighton, Sicily waits for the postal carrier. Skipping over envelopes from medical schools, she goes straight for the August volume of the North American Health Sciences Research Journal. The table of contents lists the article on page five, Confirming methyl mercury poisoning beyond Japan: Canadian Minamata disease. Sicily flips to it. Under the title there is a dedication to Dr. Masazumi Harada's team at Kumamoto University, and especially Haruki Akira. It is exactly as Forest had wanted.

After seeing the published article, it is a week more before Sicily tackles the mountain of mail accumulated over the past months. She sits on the sunporch separating the junk from the condolences. To her surprise, two months ago, she was waitlisted for admission to the combined medical school performing arts program—for this year, not next. In a second letter, dated four weeks after the first, the program granted her early entry. This was based on the recommendation of both Mack and Dr. Calabria. However, the offer is contingent on her presence at the midwestern US medical college by the first Tuesday in September, only six weeks away. She has no physical reason for not accepting. But, oh her heart, her wounded heart.

⌒‿

The morning Sicily leaves for medical school, tea cups and half-eaten bannock are on the table in the dining room, where Sicily, Laura, Rainy, Ben Wolf, and Moni all cram into the space. Always an early riser, Sophie is now an industrious six year old, busy stacking branches in a pile near the shore. 'Her adults' watch from the window. This fall she will 'go to real school.' All wait for Vern to return home from the milk run, and Ellie from her shift. Shortly after, Sicily's parents will drive her to the bus. Though everyone at the Creighton complex has urged her to take the acceptance to the Chicago program, the group in the dining room is uncommonly quiet. They resemble a family of orphans knowing one sibling will be torn away.

Laura breaks the silence, "I'm sorry we didn't deal with this before. It was only last night I found out what we needed to know about using Forest's money to finish the work. It's the only way to deal with his murder."

"It won't be dealing with it, but it might make us feel his absence less," says Rainy.

"I always wanted the money to fix what it destroyed. Maybe a foundation..." Sicily says.

"Glad you agree, since you are the only person who can get to that money," Laura says.

"It's in the bank in Switzerland. You're his heir," Sicily says.

"I'm not—you are," Laura says.

"Nonsense..." Sicily looks around, realizing Pilot is absent. Her eyes beg Ben for help.

"Forest wouldn't chance Laura ending up like him, cut off from Mum," says Ben.

"Where is Pilot anyway?" Sicily asks.

"He had a last minute emergency cargo delivery down in the States. He couldn't cancel because there were customs issues," Ben says.

"The point is you have to get the money," Laura says.

"'Dead men can't write cheques.' Forest knows that," Rainy comments, her eyes still focused outside on Sophie.

"He knew that..." Sicily corrects Rainy.

Without looking at Sicily, Rainy says, "Either way, face it girl, the baton is yours. You gotta run with it."

"That's right, you're the only person on that Swiss account. Forest and Jorge were the others," Laura says.

"Clearly the anonymity of the Swiss banks is no match for your detective skills. Still, I can't go to Zürich. In a few days I have to be at medical school, where Forest wanted me to be. This money thing has to be worked out later."

"All we need is the account number and a routing number. The funds can be moved by wire transfer," Laura says.

"Do you have those numbers?" Sicily asks.

"Nope, I called the bank with Forest's name. I told them he was dead. They said to check with you. Some guy, name's Baise, thinks you might remember him," Laura says.

"Seriously?" Sicily asks, looking at Rainy.

"Forest always could think ahead like that," Rainy says.

"He recited those numbers by heart at the bank. I don't have them," Sicily says.

"Even if he had survived the hit on the head, he would'a had trouble remembering the numbers now," says Ben Wolf.

"Be that as it may, I still don't have them," Sicily says.

"I am sure you do," Rainy says.

"I am sure I don't."

Rainy looks to Moni saying, "Time for a pro... You take it from here."

Having decided to study Romance Languages, the Persian is peculiarly quiet, pondering her own impending departure to Paris. "Sicily, try accepting that you have the numbers, then ask your mind, 'Where?'—nothing is ever lost in the universe."

Everyone in the room jerks around at the nearly religious tone atheist Moni strikes.

"That's what I hate about religion. They try to take credit for everything. Because the Buddha said it too, doesn't mean it's not science," Moni says.

"Do you mean where it is in my brain," Sicily asks, cutting herself a piece of bannock.

"That's a good start," Moni says, then blows on her tea.

Everyone watches Sicily squint. Biting the bannock, she chews. Drawing her eyebrows together, she looks enlightened, followed quickly by discouragement. Sophie comes in from the back porch. "Look what I made." The girl has built a habitable house on the shore. Sophie wears Forest's bone, leather, and beaded Ojibwa choker. Its glass beads, like tiny stars, match the child's gleeful eyes. The twinkles also compliment the fancy dance earrings which Sicily wears.

"Can I see one of them earrings?" Laura asks Sicily. Separating the strands of dangling beads, Laura spreads them on the table. Drawing lines on a brown paper bag transforms it into graph paper. Each bead color is assigned a number, red is zero, orange is one, yellow two, making a pattern with the Firebird shades. "Forest designed these for you," Laura says, while working out a repeating number. She counts the digits, saying, "It's only one of them, probably just for routing. We also need the account number."

"Hey, that's my birthday," Sophie says, pointing to the repetitious digits on the bag. Rainy pulls Sophie onto her lap and hugs her. Laura looks up at her niece and smiles.

Sicily's eyes are as bright as headlight beams. "It's okay... you're right. I have the other one too." Every day she wears Forest's medicine bag next to her heart. He had made sure he would no longer wear it himself in case of his demise, forever linking his lover and his family. Untying the pouch's leather string cinching, Sicily reverently removes the herbs, placing them to the side, revealing a slip of paper bearing tiny writing.

Sicily is aboard a Canadian Gray Goose bus. She blows kisses to her parents through the tinted window glass, heart aching. Though armed with her fancy dance earrings and medicine bag, she is certain it will not be enough. All else which ties her to Forest is being left in Canada. She notices her mother twists the chain on the Maltese Cross, distraught. Sicily wonders 'When will I see them again.' The dance scholarship and loans for medical school will barely cover her diet of nuts and berries, never mind airplane flights. The bus crawls away from the curb. Sicily jumps up, climbing over her seat mate yelling, "Wait, please!" No stranger to this syndrome, the driver stops, having already noticed the two pained Black people standing on the sidewalk.

Sicily is on the curb with her parents. Using her own finger as a windshield wiper, Ellie squeegees away her daughter's tears. Then Vern hugs Sicily, burying her face in his chest, her heart safe in his tight arms. Ellie opens her purse, sighing resolutely. She extracts a birthday card sized envelope, bearing Sicily's name, and surreptitiously slips it into a pocket of the jean jacket her daughter wears. Ellie gives Vern a nod. He releases the dear girl from his arms. Kissing her daughter on both cheeks, the mother turns her around, marching her off to the medical battlefield where she is doomed to fight. "Don't worry, Darling Baby, soon you won't remember this suffering," Ellie says. Sicily hopes her mother is right. Climbing back onto the bus, and over the passenger with whom she shares a seat, parents out of sight, nothing else to do, she sleeps.

Hours later, at the International Peace Garden in Grand Forks, North Dakota, a uniformed United States sailor boards the bus. Squealing bus brakes rouse Sicily. They are at Virginia, a town sitting on the Laurentian Continental Divide—above which waters run toward Hudson Bay, in route to the Arctic Ocean. Below the Laurentian, the flow has two options. It either enters the Mississippi, eventually dropping into the Gulf of Mexico, or it traverses the Great Lakes to the Saint Lawrence Seaway, reaching the Atlantic. The commingling push and pull of gravity and water controls these massive flows. This day, at this place, a greater force is at play.

A young woman boards. Sicily notices the only available seat on the bus is next to the sailor. He gets up, placing his gear on the rack above, signaling that she deserves comfort. With red curly hair and pale translucent skin, she is the type of woman bullied constantly during primary school. The sailor scans his newspaper then shares a section of it with her. At first their chat is that superficial word-dance of strangers, mostly logistics. Then it grows. Sicily knows they are falling in love, as people sometimes do under the influence of Mercury. He is, after all, the god of commerce, messages, and also travelers.

The next stop is Hibbing, where Bob Dylan grew up, complete with its open pit iron mine. Her seat mate, built like a miner gathers his gear. Nodding his goodbye he sees Sicily has eyes only for the sailor and the redhead. "Will they get off the bus together?" She wonders aloud, pulling her legs up on the adjacent empty seat. Arms around her knees. 'I think they will,' she hears the memory of Forest in her mind, as is often the case. Indeed, the sailor and the redhead do exit together, near Lake Superior.

Sicily stretches. Folding her jean jacket into a pillow for her head, she is surprised by stiffness in one of its pockets. She fishes out the envelope. It is addressed to her, while the return address is Pilot's. Not hearing from her angel-winged friend had upset Sicily. Now things are in order. Slowly the postcard is pulled from its sheath. She recognizes the image, Lake of the Woods. The message on the back is only one word—'Soon,' unmistakably penned by Forest's hand. Sicily's confusion is eclipsed by her joy.

The End

EPILOGUE

In the world's wealthiest communities, people stand over fish counters at markets sorting through 'Pacific wild caught' versus 'Atlantic farmed' salmon. Often those shoppers don't know exactly why, cannot recognize the term Minamata disease, nor identify a single symptom of severe human mercury poisoning. Minamata disease is named for a Japanese fishing and industrial town where over 12,000 people are still living with confirmed diagnoses. Ingested fish, contaminated with high levels of mercury, causes neurotoxicity ranging from forgetfulness and unsteadiness of gait, to seizures, coma, and death.

During the 1970s, private citizens in Canada reached out to the Japanese Minamata disease-afflicted community, medical researchers, and activists. This coalition, Sicily and Forest among them, identified the early clusters of North American severe human mercury poisoning.

There was a need for the world to respond to industrial pollution. The Minamata Convention on Mercury was drafted and ratified, with the collaboration of more than 140 nations and set to go into force on August 16, 2017, more than forty years after a ballerina and a powwow dancer met in the Montreal airport. The convention is designed to protect the environment, and all those who live in it, from mercury contamination. It also outlines a model for dealing with other disease causing industrial wastes.

But this is only the beginning of the story, what about the middle and the end? Wait and watch for the next book in the *Chasing Mercury* Toxic Trilogy, *Weighing Lead.*

ABOUT THE AUTHOR

September Williams is an American physician-writer, bioethicist and filmmaker. Her work focuses on promoting resilience for people who are ill, aging, dying, or stressed by environmental and humanitarian violation. Her first novel, and the first of a series of three books, is *Chasing Mercury*, a romantic suspense memoir about families committed to human rights and environmental justice. Dr. Williams is a member of the National Writers Union (AFLCIO/UAW 1981), and an affiliate of the International Federation of Journalists. September's nonfiction writing is about bioethics and film.

A graduate of the University of Winnipeg Collegiate Division, September has a BSc. in Zoology from the University of Manitoba, attended Creighton University School of Medicine, and completed internal medicine residency at Cook County Hospital. Among other clinical fellowships Dr. Williams is a former Lowell T. Coggleshall Fellow at the University of Chicago MacLean Center for Clinical Medical Ethics. She studied film and screenwriting in the MFA program at Columbia College, Chicago and Boston University, and was a National Endowment for the Humanities Institute fellow in film.

September Williams has two millennial adult children and lives in Marin County, California, where she writes, dances, and open water rows.

SEE: HTTP://WWW.SEPTEMBERWILLIAMS.COM

AUTHOR'S ACKNOWLEDGEMENTS

Chasing Mercury spans three continents, and nearly forty years from 1937 to 1975. My world view is dense with people and places and so is *Chasing Mercury*. Some of those most important to this project are living while others have passed—but they live on in me through what I have learned from them. In no particular order these are some of the people who inspired and supported *Chasing Mercury*—

Journalist Lloyd Henderson, Cameraman Gary Grayeyes, Wan Bli Otawi (Vanessa) Brown, Artists Johnny Cheekie, and Daphanie Odjig, Leslie Curry, Lyle Ironstand, The Peoples of Minamata Japan, Dr. Masazumi Harada,White Dog First Nation, Grassy Narrows First Nation, Aileen Mioko Smith, W. Eugene Smith, Lorraine Johansen, Mercedeh Ghandaharian, Abdi Darai, Pascal Zamprelli, Claudine Zamperelli, Berthe Derrin, James Zamprelli, Philip Polimeni, Victor Pierre, William Dubay, Charlene Mitchell, Marie Branch, Angela Davis, Fanya Davis, Jonathan Jackson, Paul Hettle, Laurie Miller Pepper, Anthony Minghella, Dorothy Parker, Guy Endore, Edith Head, Bing Muller, Gea Mulder, James Foley, Dorothy K. Watson, Curd F. Watson, Sylvester Campbell, Jean Mackenzie, Trevor Fowler, and my mother Shyrlee Williams.

This book would not exist were it not for Susan Dalsimer's developmental editorial guidance. Her concise but gentle direction helped me to figure out the story I wanted and needed to

tell without telling me how to do so. I will be forever grateful to
Eric Stern for introducing me to Susan. My amazing copy editor cum friend Eric P. Carlson and Therese Francis for so many
thing it's hard to count from fiscal to holistic health guidance.
My long time collaborator and film editor Sharon Karp of Media Monster who allowed me to read to her while we edited
film. My dear friend William Ullman who has always supported me and my adventures, keeping me afloat well beyond my
expiration date.

Composer, Musician cum brother Micheal Friedman, who
stood on a stage with me 40 years ago in Berlin, then found me
thirty years later and reminded me how important those moments on that stage were to the woman I would become.

I have had three years of conversations with my aunt Joy Grant
(who I also owe a big thank you for creating clothing for my
personal appearances), Dianne Houston, Lighiah Villalobos,
Victoria Sweet, Asya Abraham, Monice Mitchell Simms, Silver Wainhouse, Henri Colt and Katie Small (for early concept
visualization through her art), Monique Anawis who suffered
through the reading of the first two drafts, Sumaya Evans, and
to all the beta readers, and especially Abagail Hansen for being
Beta Reader #1 and Liz Kantor for being close behind Abby.

Artist, designer Marta Johansen has provided me a means
to recognize my brand through photography, websites, blog,
book cover design and fashion choice. If I dream it, Marta can
provide a physical form — and if I can't dream it she will. My
son Curd Williams-Hertz supports my need to lighten up and
watch superheroes and also gave me an ensemble of electronic
capacity which outstripped my abilities as a writer and forced

me to grow into it. My daughter Autumn Williams-Hertz who endured listening to early audio recordings while driving through rush hour traffic, and always points out things that don't ring true but more importantly those that do. And my little brother Torianno Trevor Fowler who has a magical way of keeping me grounded.

My sisters and brothers in the National Writers Union and the International Federation of Journalists, and a special thanks to Ismael Parra for recruiting me to join NWU, Michael Larson of the San Francisco Writers Conference, LitQuake/LitCrawl San Francisco Wikipedia, Zyzzyva Magazine for hooking me up with Vanessa Hau, and Elissa Bernstein of Pronoun.

Writing can be very isolating. My alternate venues have been important and have included the Chileno Valley Ranch, Marin County, CA where I have been hosted by friends Mike and Sally Gale. Micheal and Marilyn Friedman's beautiful Grandview Heights guest suite in Gibsons, British Columbia, Asya Abdrahman's studio filled with her amazing progressive multi-media art. In Southern California: the Cooper-Houston home and the Watson-Grant family home which is the heart of the cul-de-sac in *Chasing Mercury*. In New England, The Mason County School House in West Bethel Maine, the Nissenbaum-Celletti home in Boxford Massachusetts, The Mechanics Institute Library, San Francisco, and the Mill Valley Public Library, Marin County.

Some working spaces are not at a desk but well beyond. The 5 Rhythms and Open Floor Dance Community of the Northern San Francisco Bay and the Sylvie Minot's Syzygy Dance Project are where I visualized the dances in *Chasing Mercury*. To Sandra Lebuhn who made sure I was dancing when I was least inclined and improves the quality of my life beyond measure. My best writing in my head has been when I am on the open water rowing in Sausalito. Thanks to Alex Mazur for the use of his boat and kindness. Dear friend Ola Bonds for respecting my absence, and always being supportive.

The authors, composers and filmmakers of referenced ballets, operas, compositions, and screen works, including Virgil's Founding Myths of Rome. They are essential to this story and left breadcrumbs for readers to follow. Finally, this novel was meant to be an homage to those who developed and brought the world the Minamata Convention on Mercury and continue to struggle for environmental justice (mercuryconvention. org).

A portion of the proceeds from *Chasing Mercury* go to: free-grassy.net and to greenaction.org

CPSIA information can be obtained
at www.ICGtesting.com
Printed in the USA
LVHW091915050421
683482LV00003B/565